It's Love

In the past few years millions of Americans have become devoted readers of a new phenomenon in women's fiction. First discovered when Rosemary Rogers' novel, *Sweet Savage Love,* became a national bestseller, the bold, tempestuous—and sensual—historical romance is now an established genre. Rosemary soon repeated her success with *Dark Fires* and *Wicked, Loving Lies.* Last year a new author, Jennifer Wilde, wrote *Love's Tender Fury,* and that exciting novel also became an instant success. During this period dozens of novels attempting to imitate the style of Rosemary and Jennifer were published. But none could compare in terms of reader reaction, until Patricia Matthews' novel, *Love's Avenging Heart,* was published in early 1977. Within weeks it had sold more than a million copies and, as we go to press with this book, *Love's Avenging Heart* is climbing up the bestseller lists all across the country. It may well be that Patricia Matthews will have two bestsellers published within months of each other! And there'll be more, for Patricia is a born storyteller. To begin one of her novels is to become caught in the grip of her story, the passions of her people, and the magic of her compelling style. As Patricia so simply put it, "It's all a matter of Love . . . I just love to write what I'd love to read!"

D1322669

please turn page)

He was the first . . .

He froze in the doorway, his breath leaving him with a soft grunt at the sight of Sarah standing in the tub, naked as Eve. He feasted his eyes on beauty such as he had never before seen. Without her filthy, torn clothing, Sarah was a vision of pink and white loveliness, her lustrous black hair a dark cloud down below her shoulders. Her skin glowed with the translucence of a pearl.

She glanced up, startled at the sight of him, and made a futile effort to cover herself. He strode toward her. "Do not play the role of coy maiden with me any longer, madam!"

Sarah sank down into the tub, still trying to cover herself. "I'll scream!"

"Scream all you like. No one will come to your aid. A ship's captain has to answer to no one for his actions on board his ship." He reached down, seized Sarah by the arm, and hauled her up, splashing and wriggling.

Later, Sarah was to wonder why she hadn't screamed. Was it because of the shocking suddenness? Or was it because she had wanted it to happen all along?

Jeb half-carried, half-dragged her to the bed. . . . She had never seen a man naked before and had only a vague idea of what one looked like. Jeb was solid as a tree trunk, not an ounce of excess flesh on his body, and as he stepped out of his breeches, she made a move to flee from the assault on her virtue she knew was coming. With the speed of a jungle cat, he pinned her to the bed, his big hands on her shoulders, his mouth open, his breath hot, and his green eyes flashing.

In a short time the pain receded. His kisses nearly smothered her and Sarah felt a strange warmth spread throughout her lower body. Not exactly pleasurable, yet not unpleasant either, it puzzled her. And even more strange, her body seemed to have a will of its own, wanting to move, wanting to be a part of him.

Then, all at once, it was all over. Sarah could scarcely breathe. She said coldly, "Are you finished, sir? Having taken me by brute force, sir, I was wondering if I now might return to my cabin? There, at least, I will be safe from being further violated."

"I'm sorry, Sarah. I don't know what made me act in such a manner." Jeb turned his head, and his gaze was riveted by the spots of blood on the bed clothing. "By the Lord Jehovah, you were a virgin! But it's not possible!"

"Is not the evidence enough for you, Captain? A woman's maidenhood is her most prized possession, the ultimate gift she brings to her husband on her wedding night. Now you have taken that from me . . ."

"Believe me, Sarah, I am indeed . . . " and he scowled, "I *am* sorry."

Angered, Sarah sat up in bed. "And I have no intention of this happening again."

Jeb's stare turned curious. "Just how do you intend to avoid that?"

"I don't know, but I'll find a way," she said spiritedly. "You can be certain of that."

. . . *and she'd be the last.*

Also by Patricia Matthews:

LOVE'S AVENGING HEART

And published by Corgi Books

Patricia Matthews

Love's Wildest Promise

CORGI BOOKS
A DIVISION OF TRANSWORLD PUBLISHERS LTD

LOVE'S WILDEST PROMISE
A Corgi Book 0552 10651 8

First Publication in Great Britain

PRINTING HISTORY
Corgi Edition published 1978

Copyright © 1977 by Patricia Matthews

This Book is set in 10/12 Baskerville

Corgi Books are published by Transworld Publishers Ltd.,
Century House, 61–63 Uxbridge Road,
Ealing, London, W.5.
Made and printed in Great Britain by
Hunt Barnard Printing Ltd., Aylesbury, Bucks.

To Jay Garon and Andrew Ettinger, without whom it would not have happened.

PART ONE

The New Land

Chapter One

Sarah Moody paused for a moment on her hurried journey down the dark, twisting street that was called Chick Lane. She had thought that she heard the sound of footsteps behind her, but now, as she stood feeling the dampness seep through her slippers, she heard nothing but the sound of water gurgling in the filthy gutters and a far-off cry from some luckless soul, who, like herself, had the bad sense, or the bad luck, to be out after dark.

In London in 1782, of the decent folk, only the very foolish or the very brave ventured out at night, particularly in this district, known as Jack Ketch's Warren. As a woman, Sarah was doubly vulnerable; the only unescorted women on the street at this hour were whores, thieves, and beggars.

She hurried on, trying not to think of the stories she had heard about what happened to those hapless girls who, for one reason or another, were so foolish as to venture out after the sun had set.

She hadn't intended to be so late. She had begged a half-day off from her duties as lady's maid to Mistress Allgood with a promise to be back by five. She had gone across town to visit her sister, who was big with child. But just before Sarah was about to depart, Nan had started having labor pains, and Sarah had to hurry out for the midwife and then help with the birthing of the child. Everything else had gone right out of her mind. The first thing she knew it was full dark.

Now she was very late. She didn't have the money for a hackney, and the shortest way to Mistress Allgood's was through the Warren.

The darkness was almost Stygian. The only light came from cracks in shuttered windows and an occasional guttering candle-lantern on a street corner. Fog, like patches of smoke, drifted along the ground and collected in alleyways. The rough cobblestones bruised her feet, and the stench of garbage and waste was overwhelming. She thought of getting her handkerchief from her reticule to cover her mouth and nose, but she was afraid to take the time to remove it. She thought of the tales of mad dogs roaming the streets of London at night.

Clutching her reticule in both hands, she hurried faster. There were only a few small coins in the reticule, nothing worth a cutpurse's time, but a cutpurse would act first and discover that fact later.

As she started past a dark, noxious alleyway, she heard a rustling sound. Sarah started to run, but a hand shot out of the dark and seized her arm. In the instant, she was yanked brutally into the alleyway.

Hot breath, stinking of rotting teeth and sour wine, was foul in her nostrils. The hands on her arms bruised her flesh, and she was dragged farther back into the darkness. Sarah screamed and began to struggle, hitting out with her elbows, clawing with her free hand at the face near hers.

A man yelped in pain, and a strong arm hooked under her chin, forcing her head back at a cruel angle. As she attempted to scream again, a hand was clamped over her mouth. She experienced the complete panic of the trapped.

"Blimey, but the bitch is a wild one," a rough voice said. "Help me hold her, Corky."

Other hands were on her body now. She was pulled back against a man's body. Hands roamed freely over her, squeezing, fondling. A lewd chuckle sounded. "She's also a prize packet, Bart. Tits like melons and a prime arse."

Sarah was clutched tighter against the male figure, and she felt a growing hardness against her buttocks. She increased her struggles and finally managed to get her mouth free to scream again.

"We've no time for that, Corky," the first voice snarled. "Her screeches are gonna bring the constables down on us. Help me bind her."

The arm tightened around Sarah's neck, forcing her head back. Her breath was cut off, and spots danced before her eyes. She felt her arms twisted behind her, ropes cutting into her flesh. She wondered if she was dying, and then, as consciousness faded, she thought she was.

When she regained consciousness, Sarah realized that she was being carried. A vile, smelly rag was tied over her mouth, and her arms were fastened cruelly with bonds. She struggled weakly.

"She's still got some fight in her." A fist clubbed Sarah on the side of her head, and she passed out again.

When she struggled painfully to consciousness a second time, Sarah found herself lying on a hard surface. She was aware of movement. She heard the creaking of wheels and the clip-clop of a horse's hooves. She realized then that she was in some sort of cart. It was without a top; she could see the glitter of stars in the night sky.

She also discovered that she wasn't alone. There were other figures, one close to her on either side, and both female by the feel of them. Touching them with her bound hands, Sarah discovered that they were also bound and gagged.

No, not all of them. She heard a voice singing drunkenly. She raised her head with an effort. There was enough light to reveal three figures, all female, seated on the open end of the cart, their legs dangling off. They were passing a jug of liquor back and forth between them and singing in raucous voices.

The words of the song were shameful! Sarah tried not to listen.

But then another of her senses was assaulted. The odors around her were mixed and awful: vomit, urine, sour wine, strong body odors, and some essences of perfume, musky and cloying. What sort of women were these? But more important, what was this all about? Where were they being taken? And for what purpose?

Sarah's nostrils flared as she detected a new odor. The salt tang of the sea, along with other odors of a port. They were approaching the sea, probably the London docks along the Thames where as many as 14,000 vessels of all sizes often rode at anchor. She could smell the rotting fruit and vegetables, spices of every sort, and could hear the rough voices of men. Sailors.

She had often strolled along the docks, her mind afire with wonder. Sailing vessels from all over the world were moored here. The ships from different countries were all together in a line, with open water lanes between them as a sort of street for the passage of smaller boats.

Sarah had been fascinated. Although the ships themselves looked alike, those from each country had a different odor and flew their own colors. But the voices, the different languages one heard! A Tower of Babel indeed! Even the garb of the seafaring men varied from country to country.

But right now Sarah was concerned about why she had been seized, bound, and brought here. Because now there was no doubt that this was their destination.

She again heard the rough voice she'd heard in the alleyway. "Hop it, ducks! This here's the ship!"

With squeals of laughter, the three women who had been dangling their feet off the end of the cart jumped down. Rough hands seized Sarah's ankles and began to drag her. Her long skirt, and then her petticoats, caught on the splintered planking, and her naked loins were revealed. Coarse laughter greeted this display. Shame burned Sarah's cheeks.

Then she was out and trying to stand upright on numb legs. The two men made no move to help her; they were dragging two other bound and gagged women from the cart.

Sarah leaned against the cart for a moment. She was gagged, her hands bound behind her back, but her feet were unfettered. She thought of attempting to flee, but her legs were still numb, and her head ached abominably from the blow she had received.

She looked about her. The dock area was dark, except for a few lanterns on the ships creaking at anchor. Up the street were two taverns; sounds of drunken laughter and boisterous voices drifted to her ears. On some of the ships, men leaned over the railings, now and then calling down bawdy comments to the women.

If she could run a goodly distance before her captors noticed, she might escape into the darkness. She took a tentative step away from the cart, but one leg buckled and she almost fell.

"Haw, wench! Thinking of legging it, were ye? Well, think again!"

The man called Bart seized her shoulder in a brutal grip and gave her a hard shove toward the gangplank leading up to the nearest ship. Sarah stumbled a few steps and fell to her knees.

She looked up, tossing the long black hair out of her eyes. She saw the three unbound women, arms around each other's waists, starting up the gangplank, singing lustily.

"Put a bung in it, ye silly bitches!" hissed Bart in a venomous whisper. "Mum's the word. The ship's master is a terror. He's likely in his bunk. Wake him, and he'll flog the lot of you." He shoved the other three up alongside Sarah. "On your feet, Your Ladyship, or I'll clout ye alongside the head so hard, ye'll hear ringing for a fortnight." He sank his fingers into her hair and hauled her upright. "Up the gangway now, all of ye, and be quiet about it!"

The four women made their way clumsily up the gangplank. At the top they were greeted by a powerful, swarthy man in a first mate's uniform. "This the last of the lot, Bart?"

"This is the last, Giles Brock."

The two men drew apart and conversed in whispers, while the man called Corky kept a close watch on the seven women.

Sarah was wretchedly tired, sick at heart with despair, and weak with terror, yet she strained her ears to listen and heard a few snatches of conversation.

". . . sail with the morning tide."

". . . me money."

"You'll get your money before you leave the ship, Bart. My promise on it." The mate's voice had risen. "Now let's get this lot below and stowed away. And be damned quiet about it, for God's sake! If the captain hears and comes to see some of 'em tied up, he'll have our heads!"

Sarah tried frantically to think of some way she could make a noise, some way to attract the attention of the ship's captain. Perhaps he would free her, if he saw the way she was bound and gagged.

Then they were being hurried below, down a narrow ladderway. It was close down there and hot. The odor was foul. Like an animal's lair, Sarah thought. And it was dark, only a dim lantern burning at each end of the passageway. She could hear singing and shouting and screaming from behind the cabin doors they passed.

"Here, there's room for one in here," the man called Brock said.

A heavy door was swung open, and Sarah was propelled from behind and sent sprawling on her face and knees into the cabin. The door thudded shut, and she heard the clanking of an iron bolt shot home.

The cabin was tiny, not much larger than a cubicle. It was illuminated by the stub of a candle. The only furnishings were two canvas hammocks hung from the walls opposite each other.

Sarah started to struggle to her feet. She heard the

2

rustle of clothing and glanced up to see a woman standing before her.

"Let me help you up, dearie," the woman said in a husky voice.

She helped Sarah to her feet, then clucked as she saw the gag and the bonds. "Those whoresons! Hold still whilst I untie you."

She untied the gag, then worked on the bonds. Sarah's mouth was dry and cottony. She swallowed convulsively several times before she managed to make some kind of sound.

"I'm Meg Fields, ducks. What's yours?"

"Sarah. Sarah Moody."

The woman stepped back, and Sarah saw that she was about thirty, with a full figure, reddish hair, and a plump face. There was a blowsy look about her.

"Did they bind and gag you, too?"

A hoarse chuckle sounded. "Nah. I came along 'thout that. Glad to come. Anything's better than what I been used to."

"But why—why are we here, all these women?"

"You mean you don't *know*?"

"No. I was grabbed off the street, pulled into an alley. . . ."

"Lord love us! Wait, let's have a look at you." Meg Fields turned about and found another candle, which she lit from the burning stub. She held it up before Sarah's face. "How old be you, dearie?"

"Nineteen."

"You look younger. And cleaner than most of the doxies they have rounded up."

"Doxies?" Sarah whispered. "All doxies? You, too?"

The hoarse chuckle again. "What else? Look here, girl, you're not trying to tell me you're not?"

"No, of course not!" Sarah said in horror. "I'm a lady's maid for Mistress Allgood."

"Oh, you poor child. Damn their black souls to perdition! That Corky and Bart must be just grabbing anything female that comes along." Struck by a sudden thought, Meg cocked her head. "Don't tell me you be virgin?"

Sarah threw back her head. "Yes!"

"Lord save us! Don't be letting any of these rowdies on board know that or you're in for it. They'd like nothing better than to be cocking a virginhead!"

Sarah shrank away in loathing. "I've got to get off this ship!"

Meg shook her head. "Nothing you can do, dearie. Them cabin doors won't be unbolted until we sail in the morning."

"But I heard them say that the captain. . . . Maybe if I screamed?"

"Over that?" Meg gestured, and Sarah knew that she was right. The sounds of other screams and drunken shouting would drown out any scream she might make.

"The captain wouldn't believe you anyways. He has orders to sail with a load of whores, and I'm sure that pair have convinced him, or Giles Brock, that we're all whores."

Sarah sank down onto the nearest hammock, her heart filled with despair. Aften a moment she looked up at Meg. "Where is this ship bound for?"

"Why, to the Colonies, ducks," Meg said cheerfully. "King George is shipping a load of whores to service his Redcoats on New York Island."

Chapter Two

Captain Jebadiah Hawkins was in a foul mood as he paced the quarterdeck, overseeing the departure of the *North Star*.

Thanks be to Jehovah, the sounds of the sailors at their work drowned out much of the caterwauling of those double-damned wenches below decks!

At thirty-two, Captain Jeb Hawkins was a fine figure of a man—tall, with broad shoulders, and a lithe, graceful stride. He had a full, flaming red beard and piercing green eyes, always set in a slight squint from almost a lifetime spent at sea. He drew many admiring glances from women, and many had used all their wiles in an attempt to wed him. But he wasn't having any, thank you. He enjoyed a romp and tickle with a woman as much as any man, but none was going to put the yoke of matrimony around his neck. A seafaring man had no business with a family anyway.

And now here he was setting sail across the Atlantic with some fifty females, all whores, no more morals than alley cats, probably half of them with the French disease. It went against the grain of a boyhood spent in the strict Calvinist household of his aunt and uncle.

Yet he'd had little choice in the matter. The *North Star* belonged to the Cartwright Shipping Company, and Horace Cartwright himself had made it an ultimatum.

Cartwright was a prosperous man of fifty, with mutton-chop whiskers, a powdered wig, probably hiding a bald pate, a pursy mouth, gimlet eyes like two pieces of coal, and a paunch like that of a woman near her birthing time. Across the paunch dangled a gold watch chain. In moments of anger, Jeb had often been tempted to ask if the chain was to be a teething ring for the baby. But Cartwright had no sense of humor.

"We are under orders from King George himself," Cartwright had said in his grating voice. "It seems the rebel women don't take overmuch to his Redcoats over there, and they are badly in need of some female companionship. It is deemed an unseemly chore for one of His Majesty's own ships of the line. For which we can be thankful, since we are being paid handsomely to transport this cargo of strumpets to the Colonies."

"It's not a cargo for a respectable vessel, sir," Jeb said harshly. "It's little better than slave trading. And from what I hear the rebels are winning. They may have won ere the *North Star* reaches New York Harbor."

"That statement, sir, smacks of treason!" Horace Cartwright stared hard. Jeb returned the stare without flinching, but he said nothing.

After a moment Horace Cartwright continued, "You have little choice in the matter, Captain. The *North Star* is our best ship, sir. And you are her master. If you refuse to accept my orders, you know what will happen, I am sure?"

Jeb merely stared at him without expression.

"You are the youngest captain of the line. Probably the youngest captain of any vessel sailing out of London or Liverpool. An able ship's master, I grant you. Otherwise, I would not have promoted you. But if you balk me, I will beach you. And I will let other shipping lines know of your rebellious nature." Horace Cartwright leaned forward, black eyes icy. "In other words, Captain Hawkins, you will never again be master of any ship sailing out of any port in the British Isles."

So there it was—captain of the *North Star* with its cargo of strumpets or else. Jeb knew nothing but the sea. It was his life, his reason for being. And he knew that Cartwright had the power to beach him permanently.

Confined to land, for the rest of his life, he would be like Prometheus on his rock. Once clear of land, he was master of all that he surveyed. He knew how to train a crew to snap to and sail a trim ship, without resorting overmuch to the cat-o'-nine-tails. He saw to it that they were always well provisioned and, while master beyond dispute, he wasn't the tyrant so many ship captains were. For that reason he had not only their respect but their liking as well.

There was a side benefit to this relationship with his crew. It gave him much leisure time to spend in his cabin, instead of prowling the ship looking for slackers. Before each voyage he spent a small fortune on books, books of every sort, and pored over them for hours on end. Having gone to sea as a cabin boy at twelve, Jeb had little formal education, yet he allowed that he was better read than most schoolmasters.

They were coming out into the open sea now, leav-

15

ing the Thames behind. The wind to the west freshened, snapping the sails, and the ship began to dip and sway. Jeb stood with his feet braced, hands locked together behind his back, savoring the familiar smell of the sea. The sea gulls that had convoyed them on either side, like winged pilots, began to break off and turn back toward the land.

Captain Jeb Hawkins was proud of his ship. While not a Dutch East Indiaman, she was of the pattern. A three-masted, square-rigged frigate, the *North Star* was 130 feet long, with a 200-ton-cargo-carrying capacity, and boasted twenty-two cannon. Jeb had sailed her a number of times around the Horn, to China and India.

A typical outward-bound cargo would be household goods, bolts of cloth, watches, liquors, etcetera. She would return laden with spices, sugar, opium, and ivory.

It had been a good life. A ship's captain was the elite of the maritime world, entitled to a thirteen-gun salute and a guard of honor on arrival in distant ports, and while a captain's pay was a nominal 10 pounds a month, there were advantageous side benefits. The most profitable was the privilege of shipping out fifty tons of his own trade goods and returning with twenty. Aye, a few more such profitable years, and he would be a wealthy man.

Then had come the uprising in the Colonies, disrupting a way of life. Certainly he could not claim, nor would he want to, any share of the proceeds from the cargo presently below decks! They had ripped his ship apart, building temporary quarters below to house the females, taking up what had been valuable cargo space.

He snorted softly in disgust and paced, taking three steps one way, three steps back.

Secretly, he held much sympathy for the revolutionary Americans. King George was a detestable tyrant, no gainsaying that. Jeb had been a seaman on board a ship anchored in Boston Harbor that December night nine years ago when the Colonists, disguised as Mohawk Indians, boarded three tea ships and dumped their cargoes into the bay. Fortunately Jeb's ship had not been carrying tea and was not boarded.

In his present mood, Jeb was about ready to join the rebels.

To Horace Cartwright, he had said, "Sir, how on Jehovah's broad ocean am I to keep those women separated from seamen made goatish by a month or more at sea? I shall have a mutiny on my hands. I certainly will not allow them to fornicate on my ship!"

"Ah! That has been taken into consideration, Captain Hawkins." Horace Cartwright leaned back, pursy mouth shaping one of its rare smiles. "First, liberal doses of saltpeter in the men's rations should dampen their carnal natures considerably. But second, and more important, your crew will be increased by ten extra men, whose sole duty it will be to see to the women. They will see to it that the strumpets and your seamen do not mingle."

"And how shall I keep *their* carnal appetites curbed?" Jeb asked, his voice edged with sarcasm.

"By the threat of the lash or whatever measures are necessary, sir. It is a ship master's duty to keep the men of his command under control."

So now, not only did he have the problem of keeping his regular crew from the women, he had ten extra thrown in. So the question—was he still master of this vessel? Yes, by the Lord Jehovah he was! Jeb slammed a fist into his open hand.

There was a bright side to it. The sailors, the old hands who had sailed with him before, were well disciplined. If any problem occurred, it would likely come from the additional men.

It was close to nooning now; the *North Star* was spanking along merrily under the thrust of a stiff breeze. Jeb turned slowly, surveying every inch of the ship within his sight. Everything seemed to be in order, all hands at their assigned tasks. Only the extra ten men were standing about with idle hands. Jeb scowled at them, then looked away with a shrug. England was nothing more than a smudge on the horizon.

"I am going to my cabin, helmsman," Jeb said crisply. "You know the course. Keep her steady on."

"Aye, aye, sir!"

Timothy, the fourteen-year-old cabin boy, had been keeping a sharp eye out, as Jeb knew he would, and he came hurrying with the noon meal almost before Jeb was inside his cabin.

Tim was a willing lad, as bright as a newly minted coin, and Jeb was fond of him. It would never do to show it, of course.

"All right, boy, snap to it! You know how famished I am after I shake the stink of land from my nostrils."

"Aye, aye, sir." Tim ducked his head to hide a grin and put the food on the table: a tankard of ale, cold mutton, bread, and cheese. Then he left the cabin with another duck of his head.

The cabin was larger than the usual captain's quarters. One unusual aspect of it was the large bunk bed held by draw chains to one wall. The *North Star*'s

18

former captain had been a married man and had taken his wife along on all voyages. Jeb had left the large bed intact. It was a luxury he had come to enjoy.

The rest of the cabin was taken up by the fixed table, his desk bolted to one wall, and bookshelves along two walls, with wooden slats to keep the books from tumbling out during heavy seas. His clothes hung from hooks on the fourth wall, and there was a washstand and mirror in that corner.

After finishing his meal, Jeb fired a cheroot from a candle stub and smoked peacefully for a few minutes. Such moments of content would be scarce on this voyage, he was certain.

Then he crossed to his desk and opened the ship's log and made an entry: "Sailed on the morning tide from London docks on this day of Our Lord, 7 Sept., 1782. *North Star* on course and nothing untoward."

He felt like adding—nothing untoward *at this time*. But such comments had no place in a ship's log. He closed the log and paced back and forth before his bookshelves, surveying his new treasures. He finally selected a novel, *Amelia,* by Henry Fielding. It had been published several years back, but Jeb had yet to read it. He was not in the mood for anything heavier.

He had scarcely settled down at his desk to read before there was a heavy knock on the door. He closed the book with a snap and said irritably, "Yes, yes! Enter!"

The door swung inward, and Giles Brock, the new first mate, marched in. He stood at attention and saluted smartly. "Captain Hawkins, sir!"

"Yes, yes, what is it, Mister Brock?" Jeb said, scowling.

His new mate was an additional irritation on this damnable voyage. Two days before they were to sail, Caleb Martin, the first mate who had sailed with him for two years, had still not put in an appearance, and there had been no word from him. Jeb had thought it damned odd, since Caleb was so dependable, but he'd had no choice but to send an urgent request to Horace Cartwright for a replacement. There had been no time to look for a substitute himself.

Giles Brock was the man Cartwright had sent. Jeb hadn't liked him on sight. His papers were all in order, and the two days spent preparing the ship to sail had proven that he was an able seaman, if perhaps a trifle harsh with the men. Yet there was a shiftiness about him. He showed the proper respect for a master's rank, but somehow he managed to appear subservient and insolent at the same time. Jeb had to accept him or sail without a first mate, but he had determined to keep a watchful eye on him.

Jeb said, "Well, Mister Brock, what is it?"

"It's the wenches—the women, sir. They're setting up a howl to be let up on deck. You recollect telling me, sir, to promise them that soon as we were out to sea . . ."

"I did, didn't I?" Jeb sighed. "Well, I suppose there's no help for it."

"Captain Hawkins, sir, if I may make a suggestion?"

"I am never adverse to a suggestion from my first mate, Mister Brock. Out with it!"

"They could be kept below, Captain, in their quarters. Less likely to be trouble with the men that way."

Jeb stared. "Kept in their quarters all the way

across the Atlantic? Great God, man, they're not cattle, no matter what else they may be!"

"Just a suggestion, sir," said Brock, those pale gray eyes staring at some point slightly to Jeb's right.

"A damned poor one, sir!" Jeb snorted. "Let them out for an hour, but not all at once. Ten at a time. We'll do that morning and afternoon, unless we run into foul weather. But hear this now: They're to be kept well apart from the men. You tell that to those guards Cartwright sent along. If they don't see to it, they'll answer to me!"

"Aye, aye, sir." Brock touched his forelock with a snappy salute.

Jeb waved his hand in dismissal and turned back to his book. In a moment he realized that the man was still there. He glanced up. "Yes, Mister Brock?"

"Well, there is something else, Captain. One of the women is making a cackle about talking to the captain of the ship."

"Out of the question!"

"That was my thought, but she keeps on about it. Name's Sarah Moody, so she claims. Says she has to talk to someone."

Jeb hesitated. "What does the blasted woman want?"

"Won't say, sir. Says she'll talk only to the captain. She is a comely wench, Captain, more choice than the others." A sly and somewhat lewd look crept over Brock's face.

"What does that have to do with it?"

"Well, I was thinking, Captain—" Brock's gaze darted to the double bunk against the wall and away again. "It *is* a long voyage and she is right comely. Mayhap she wants to share the captain's bunk. The

21

men would think nothing untoward if the captain decided to—"

Jeb shot to his feet in outrage. "Mister Brock! That is an impertinent and vile suggestion! If you ever so much as hint at such a thing again . . . I cannot have my first mate flogged before the men, but by God, sir, *I* will thrash you with my bare hands!"

Although nothing changed in his face, Brock seemed not in the least repentant. "Just thinking of the captain's welfare, sir."

"Were you indeed? I'll manage my own welfare without advice from you, Mister Brock. And my welfare does not include sharing my bunk with one of these strumpets on board!" He gestured. "Send the damned woman to me. I'll talk to her."

"Aye, Captain. Right away, sir!"

The man's face now carried a secretive smile as he saluted again, wheeled smartly about, and left the cabin.

Jeb sank down into his chair, the book forgotten. He was appalled at what he had consented to do. What on earth had possessed him? He knew that a part of it had to do with the first mate's barely concealed insolence. The man had so much as intimated that he, Jeb, was fearful of being alone in his cabin with this woman.

But Jeb knew it could well be a regrettable error on his part. The news that the ship's captain was seeing one of the women alone would be all over the vessel within minutes.

He snorted softly. Well, damn their eyes, he was still master of the *North Star,* and if one of the seamen so much as looked at him slantwise, he'd have the man flogged!

Chapter Three

Sarah had spent a miserable night, sleeping very little. Aside from her personal predicament, the unyielding hammock had only a pair of thin blankets, not at all like her soft bed at the Allgood residence. In the hammock across from her, Meg Fields snored contentedly.

Only extreme fatigue finally drove Sarah into a fitful slumber shortly before dawn. It seemed she'd only been asleep for a minute or so when she awoke with a start at the sound of men shouting overhead and banging noises.

"Ever been to sea, ducks?" asked the hoarse voice from across the cabin.

"No," Sarah said. "I've never been in any kind of a boat."

"Well, you're about to, dearie. We're underway, heading across the sea to provide comfort for King George's Redcoats."

By now Sarah could feel the ship moving. She had a hollow, queasy feeling in the pit of her stomach and hoped she wasn't going to be sick. The only thing in the cubicle to service the body functions was a yellowed chamberpot in one corner.

By the time they reached the open sea, Sarah was miserable and vomiting into the pot. When she was positive she was empty as could be, there was a rattle of a bolt. The door opened, and a cheery voice said, "Here 'tis, ladies! Eat hearty!"

Two steaming bowls and a pail of water were placed on the floor, and the door slammed and bolted.

"Like feeding pigs in a trough," Meg grumbled.

The food odors sent Sarah into convulsions again. With gentle hands Meg helped her up and laved her face with a wet cloth, then led her to the hammock.

"Maybe a bit of porridge might perk you up?"

"God in Heaven, no!" Sarah shuddered at the thought of food. "The stench in here is foul, and I fear I've only added to it. I'm sorry, Meg."

Meg hunkered down by one of the bowls, busily spooning the porridge into her mouth. She stopped long enough to say, "They did promise—that ship's mate, Brock, did promise that the captain would let us out on deck for some fresh air soon as we're well out to sea."

Sarah sat up. "The captain! I must speak to him!"

Meg shrugged. "Not much chance of that, I be thinking, dearie. And what good? Even if you could convince him you're a virginhead. . . ." Her laughter was raucous. "You think he'd be turning back for you?"

"Nonetheless, I must try."

Sarah took stock of herself in dismay. Her hair was tangled and damp with perspiration, her dress was dirty and torn, and her hands were grimy, as she knew her face must be. And all she had was what was on her person.

Suddenly, she glanced around frantically. Her reticule! For the first time she realized that even her reticule was missing. Her captors must have taken it. Her glance lit on a small chest in the corner.

"Meg, is that your chest?"

"That it is, dearie. Everything I have in this world. Ain't much, is it?"

"Do you have a mirror, maybe a comb I could use?"

"I might," Meg said craftily. "I'll make you a trade, ducks. If you'll let me have your bowl of porridge, since you ain't eating it, I'll see what I can find for you."

Sarah agreed with a simple nod. So she wouldn't have to watch Meg gobble up the second bowl of porridge, she lay back on the hammock.

Within a short time, there was a clang of metal, and the door swung open. Meg stood up with an empty bowl in each hand, then retreated a step or two into the cabin. Sarah raised her head as a man came in. It was the mate, Giles Brock, the one she had seen on the deck last night.

His nose elevated at the smell. "Damnation, it stinks in here!"

Meg whined, "You promised we'd get some deck air today."

"The captain promised. I made no such promise. Left to me, you'd all rot down here in your own stink all the way across the Atlantic."

Sarah pushed herself up off the hammock and called out to him, "Sir, I have to talk to the captain! Please, sir, I must!"

Giles Brock stood with hands on hips, looking Sarah over from head to toe. A lascivious grin lit his face. "Well now, you're a comely one, you be! Want

3

to see the captain, do you? Why don't you come up to my cabin first, lovey, and we'll talk on it?"

Sarah's head went back, and she said in a firm voice, "No! Just take me to the captain!"

"Now why should I do that, pray? Can you give me one good reason?"

"What I have to say is for his ears alone."

"Is it now? Wouldn't be that you're thinking of sharing his bunk, now would it? So's to get out of this hole?" He stroked his chin, studying her closely.

Sarah returned his gaze steadily. Let him think what he wished, so long as he took her to the captain.

"Might not be a bad thing at that," Giles Brock said thoughtfully. "Keep him busy. I hear tell he's a demanding ship's master." He wheeled away abruptly, flinging his final words back over his shoulder. "I'll tell him you wish words with him, woman. The rest is up to you—and him."

Two hours later, Sarah trailed after Giles Brock on the way to the captain's cabin on the afterdeck. She had repaired what damage she could with Meg's comb and mirror, yet she knew that she was still a sorry sight.

There were ten women, all ages, shapes, and sizes, taking the air on deck. Sarah tried to ignore their remarks as she followed Giles Brock.

"Seeing the captain, be ye? Good luck now!"

"Let him cock ye good and ye'll have it nice and cushy all the way across, girlie."

"Give as good as you get, ducks. That's what I always say in such times as this."

"He may give ye a hard go, but ye look strong enough to bear up."

26

Head high, Sarah strode on. Her stomach heaved with every sickening dip of the ship. Once on deck, her first look around had been dismaying. There wasn't a speck of land in sight, only green heaving swells of foam-tipped water.

At the captain's cabin, Brock knocked sharply. A deep voice growled from inside. The first mate pushed the door open and went in, motioning behind his back for Sarah to follow him. Once inside, Brock snapped smartly to attention and said, "The woman, Sarah Moody, Captain Hawkins."

"All right, Mister Brock, you may leave us alone. But remain within earshot. I may have need of you."

"Aye, sir." Giles Brock saluted, wheeled about, and marched past Sarah, lowering one eyelid in a wink.

The cabin was dim enough with the door open, but after Brock had closed it, Sarah had difficulty seeing. The only light came from two open portholes and one candle stub.

Sarah could see only a towering, red-bearded figure of a man, standing with his hands behind his back, his booted feet planted wide apart. Already intimidated, she was frightened all the more by his shadowy figure.

And then came that deep growl of a voice, causing her to start. "Well, woman? You wanted an audience with the captain. Now what is it you wish of me?"

Sarah could make out his features now, as he scowled down at her from his great height, green eyes glittering with contempt.

"I—I—" she stuttered. Then she rallied herself. Why should she be intimidated by this man? He was in the wrong, he and his minions who had captured

27

Sarah and the others, not her. Sarah drew herself up. "I do not belong on this ship!"

"Do not belong here?" His scowl darkened. "Why not, pray? You came along of your own volition. Nobody forced you."

"That is not true, Captain! I was dragged off the street into an alleyway, subdued, then bound and gagged and brought here against my will!"

"Madam, what do you take me for? Some flop-doodle of a dunderhead? It was sworn to me that all the strump—all the *women* aboard my vessel would be here of their own free will!"

"Not so, sir. Not only not so with me, but I saw at least three others bound and gagged as well." Her head went back, her eyes sparking spirit. "I swear on all that I deem holy that I speak the truth!"

She spoke with such intense sincerity that the captain seemed taken aback. He squinted at her, snorted softly, then began to pace, hands locked behind his back, three steps one way, three steps the other.

Finally he stopped, glaring at her. "Damnation, madam, this is too big a bite to swallow! At any rate, you *are* a—uh, your, uh, profession— What does it matter, the streets of London or New York Island?"

Sarah straightened her back and raised her chin. "I am not a whore, Captain. I am a lady's maid to Mistress Allgood. I was foolish enough to be on the streets at night when I was seized." She drew a steadying breath, feeling a blush pink her cheeks. "I have never lain with a man, sir."

"What!" he thundered. "You are telling me that you are a virgin?"

"I am, Captain."

Again he paced, back and forth, mumbling under

his breath. Sarah noticed that he cut a fine figure, as graceful in his stride as a great cat.

He rounded on her. "Can you offer proof of what you say? I mean— Oh, damnation! I don't mean the state of your virginity, but the rest?"

"Mistress Allgood will tell you. . . ."

He was shaking his head. "My ship is underway, madam, and she will not be turned back, not for any reason whatsoever."

"Your man then, the man outside. He can tell you. He was there when we were dragged on board."

"Giles Brock?" Captain Hawkins' expression indicated skepticism. "He was present and knows of this?"

"He does, Captain," Sarah said firmly.

He scowled at her for a moment longer, blunt fingers combing his beard. Then he bellowed, "Mister Brock! In here at once, sir!"

Immediately the door opened, and Giles Brock hurried in. "Yes, Captain?"

"This young woman—" The captain cleared his throat. "This young woman claims that she was brought on board bound and gagged, along with others, and that you, Mister Mate, witnessed this. What say you, sir?"

"Why, the woman lies, Captain," Brock said blandly. "I was there, true. 'Twas my duty, sir. But all came on board of their own free will."

Captain Hawkins glared at him from under lowering brows for a long moment, then swung his gaze to Sarah. "Well, madam?"

"It is—" Sarah hesitated, then threw her head high. "He was there and saw, Captain. What I say is true, I swear!"

"The word of a doxie, Captain?" Brock said smoothly.

"You are apt at swearing, aren't you, madam?" the Captain said. He paced for a little, his head sunk in thought.

"Captain, the woman sharing my cabin, Meg Fields, her name is. She was there when they threw me in. She unbound me. Have her come; she will tell you!"

"Very well!" Captain Hawkins threw his arms wide and heaved a prodigious sigh. "Bring the other woman, this Meg Fields, Mister Brock, and we shall see what she has to say."

"Right away, Captain!" Brock left quickly.

The captain turned his back on Sarah. From his desk he took a cheroot and fired it, then stepped to an open port, where he stood smoking furiously, ignoring her.

Sarah, not knowing what to do with herself, stood sick, miserable, and humiliated, her stomach heaving with every pitch of the ship. Despair such as she had never known filled her. She knew now that, no matter what Meg said, no matter what the captain thought, she was doomed. First, to spend days on end on board this ship, and then to a fate that she did not dare think about.

"I knew this voyage was ill-fated from the beginning."

His growling voice startled her. Looking up, she saw him facing her again, smoke spiraling up from his cigar.

"And now you, you and this mare's-nest tale you bring to me!"

Her temper sparked. "Do not lay blame on me, sir!

It is not my fault that I was brought aboard your vessel by villainous force!"

"So you say," he grumbled. "So you say. But I must remark one thing." He seemed to be looking at her with new eyes. "Underneath all that filth and disarray, I sense a freshness, a beauty, I would not expect to find in a—" He was interrupted by a rap on the door. "Enter!"

Giles Brock came in with Meg right behind him. She had also made an effort to pretty herself up, without a great deal of success. She looked worried. She quickly glanced at Sarah and just as quickly looked away again.

The first mate came to attention. "The woman who calls herself Meg Fields, Captain."

"Very well, Mister Brock." He gestured as Brock made a move to leave. "Stay, Mister Mate. This should not take overlong." He pinned Meg with his glare. "This woman who shares your quarters . . . It is my understanding that you were there when she arrived. In what condition was she?"

"Why, somewhat like she is now, Your Lordship. Oh, mayhap a little tarred by the street. You see, I tried as best I could to pretty her up when I learned she was to see Your Lordship, but—"

"Meg!" Sarah took a step toward her. "Tell the truth! For the love of God, tell the truth!"

"Silence, madam!" Captain Hawkins roared. "And you, Meg Fields, I am *not* Your Lordship! Please address me as Captain."

"Yes, Your—Yes, Captain, sir," Meg said, cringing.

Captain Hawkins paced back and forth, then stomped to a stop before Meg. "She was not bound and gagged then? The truth now, woman!"

"Bound and gagged? Not to my knowing, Captain, sir. She came aboard like the rest. Oh, she may—" Meg took a step forward, lowering her voice. "She may have been a little the worse for drink. From her wild tale, I suspicioned as much, you see."

"Drinking? She had been *drinking?*"

Meg dropped her gaze demurely. "I fear so, Captain, sir."

"Damnation!" His scowl aimed at Sarah was cold and forbidding. "Not only are you a liar and a doxie, but a sot as well."

Sarah felt helpless before his wrath. "I told you the truth, sir," she said simply. "That is all I can do."

"They, then, are the liars, eh? Is that your contention? Why, pray? What purpose would their lying serve?"

"I know not, Captain," she said steadily. "I know only that they lie."

"Paugh!" He snorted, turned, and strode off to stand at the port with his back to them.

Sarah looked around and caught Giles Brock staring at her. His face wore a sly look of triumph. But why? Why had he lied? And Meg as well.

The captain came storming back. "Take them below, Mister Brock. Out of my sight. I do not know why the woman set about this bit of tomfoolry. But I want to hear no more of it, do you understand?"

"Aye, Captain. I understand. The captain will not be bothered again." Brock made a shooing motion. "Out, both of you!"

The spirit had drained out of Sarah, and she went along without resistance.

Just before she reached the door, the captain's voice, oddly different, halted her. "Madam?"

Sarah turned back.

His wrath seemed to have dissipated. As he brooded upon her, his eyes had a bold, questioning look. " 'Tis too bad we cannot also prove or disprove your virginity as easily, eh?"

Chapter Four

Back in the cubicle below decks, the door slammed and bolted behind her, Sarah found Meg abject with apologies.

"I'm sorry, ducks. I'm a wretched bitch, I know, for not standing up for you."

"The captain was near to believing my story," Sarah said angrily. "A few words from you, and he would have."

"But what was I to do?" Meg cried. "That villainous mate swore to me he'd toss my arse overboard some dark night if'n I didn't lie to cover him! *After* he beat me black and blue!"

But despite Meg's protestations, Sarah glimpsed a gleam of something wicked in her eyes, and Sarah was sure Meg wasn't so fearful of Giles Brock as she claimed.

But suddenly Sarah didn't really care. She was heavy with despair, her heart leaden.

Meg came to take her hand. "Will you be forgiving me, love? I'm ever so sorry, but naught else could I do. I'll give you my share of porridge this eve in penance."

"I don't want your porridge, Meg. I have no stomach for it." Sarah shuddered and snatched away her hand. "Anyway, I suppose it really doesn't matter what you said. The captain told me that he wouldn't turn the ship back to England under any circumstances. So, no matter what he believed of me, I'd still have no choice but to finish out the voyage."

"That's the spirit, dearie." Meg's gaze turned calculating. "If you don't want your porridge then, mayhap I could have it?"

"You may have it," Sarah said dispiritedly.

"Course, you're gonna have to start eating somethun, else you'll waste away. My guess is 'tis true you be a lady's maid, you being so finicky. You've not known hunger such as me. Times I've seen I'd be willing to eat sewer rats, could I catch one. To have regular victuals of any kind be somethun I'm not accustomed to." An edge of resentment sharpened Meg's voice now. "But you'll come around to eating, my word on that!"

Sarah turned away without responding. She stretched out on the uncomfortable hammock, back to Meg, and didn't stir when the cabin door clanged open for their evening's ration of food to be delivered.

Meg was right, of course. Sarah knew that she had two choices. She could starve until she wasted away into the arms of death. Or she could eat what food was served her, no matter how distasteful, and survive.

Yet there was an irony about Meg's accusation. For Sarah *had* known hunger. Perhaps not the desperate hunger that Meg had known, but there had been almost a year after the death of her mother, three years back now, when Sarah had gone for days on end with a belly growling and clamoring for sustenance.

Sarah's father, a bootmaker with a shop in London, had been fairly prosperous. A kind and generous man, he had seen to it that Sarah had a good education. He was unlike most fathers of the day who thought a daughter fit only for marriage and therefore taught her only what she needed to know to become a wife. Tutors came dear, and it was only after her father's sudden death of apoplexy that Sarah realized what her education had cost him.

He was no sooner in the ground than his creditors came clamoring, dividing up what little was left, like carrion picking the bones of a dead beast. The shop and their living quarters above it were rented, and Sarah and her mother were forced to move. They found poor lodgings a few streets away, and Sarah's mother earned what she could as a seamstress.

Unfortunately, Sarah's education was no help in earning money. The only jobs available for women were menial; no shopkeeper would hire a woman clerk; no tradesman would countenance a woman bookkeeper; and Sarah had never learned to sew well.

For a few short months, the two women managed to eke out a meager existence, and then Sarah's mother died—from a broken heart, Sarah believed—and Sarah was completely alone.

Being of a sensible turn of mind, even at that early age, Sarah took stock of her prospects. It seemed to her that she had only two alternatives: to sell her body on the streets or to seek out a position as a lady's maid or nursemaid.

The idea of selling her body was not only unthinkable on moral grounds, but, she realized, impractical, because she lacked any knowledge of how to go about such a transaction.

Given her present situation, it was ironic. At that time, she could not have walked the streets as a common doxie, being too genteel of bearing and manner of dress. The other doxies would have driven her off the streets or out of the taverns with cawing laughter, likely doing her physical harm.

And so it seemed she had but one chance to make any kind of life for herself. She would seek employment with a wealthy family for whom her education and manners would be an asset.

After a few weeks of near starvation, with the good fortune that sometimes favors the innocent and the foolish, she obtained such a position. An old friend of her father, just returned to the city, had found her in dire circumstances and had immediately taken her in. Learning of her plans, he had tapped the local information sources and found that a good family was indeed in need of such services as Sarah could offer. Within a few days, she found herself in the employ of Robert Allgood and his family. Robert Allgood was a well-to-do merchant with a wife and two children, both girls. One was little more than a baby, the other eight.

Actually, Sarah was employed because she could do more than serve as a lady's maid. With her education she could instruct the older girl in her early learning and act as a nursemaid to the baby.

With all these duties on her shoulders, her hours were long, yet Mistress Allgood was not a vain woman and did not demand too much attention. Sarah had her own room, tiny though it was, plenty to eat, and she adored the two girls, sweet, innocent, creatures who returned her affection.

All in all, she had been reasonably content during the more than two years she spent with the Allgoods. Only occasionally was she chafed by the subservience of her station in life and the two equally poor alternatives before her: remain a lady's maid until she withered and died, or wed some loutish servant lad and bear his children.

Still, at nineteen, her thoughts were not often occupied with speculations on her future. And she often chided herself for her rebellious thoughts and infrequent spells of discontent.

The other girls she met when she took the baby in the carriage for an hour or so in the park all seemed content with their lot in life. Their talk consisted of giggling comments about possible marriage prospects, or whispered gossip about their employers.

Now, lying on the hammock, belly roiled by the swaying of the ship, Sarah realized how fortunate she had been. How quickly things changed! If by some witch's magic, she could be instantly transported back to her room in the Allgood household, she would never again entertain a rebellious thought! She felt tears start in her eyes.

All of a sudden, Sarah was angry at herself. She had never been one for tears, for self-pity. She resolved to face whatever came with as much strength and courage as she could summon.

And somehow, in the days and weeks that followed, Sarah did find the strength to face up to her predicament. Perhaps part of it had to do with the fact that she slowly became accustomed to the roll of the ship. Within three days she was even eating with a good appetite. The food served them wasn't the best, but it was ample and nourishing.

And Sarah looked forward to the times each day she was allowed on deck. She hated the cell-like confinement of the cabin, the heat and the stench of it. Being cooped up with Meg in the cubicle grated on her nerves. Meg was a good soul, so long as something didn't conflict with her own comfort, but she was foul of mouth and almost never washed. Sarah washed as best she could in the small bucket of water they were allowed once a day.

So, she lived for the two hours each day on deck. She would isolate herself as much as possible from the other women, reveling in the fresh, salt tang of the air and the cooling spray on her face. This didn't make her popular with the other women, but Sarah closed her ears to their taunts and shouted insults, and remained to herself as much as possible.

A few times she saw Captain Hawkins pacing the afterdeck, seldom looking in their direction. But once, standing at the railing, Sarah had the feeling she was being watched. She turned about quickly, looking up.

Captain Hawkins stood at the railing of the afterdeck, staring directly at her. They locked stares for a long moment. Sarah felt something like a shiver pass over her. Then the captain nodded, almost imperceptibly, and turned away.

The women were kept contained amidships when on deck. The ten men assigned to guard them, wearing clothing closer to military than sailor garb and carrying pistols in their belts, kept the seamen away. Many of the women would fling ribald invitations at sailors passing nearby, receiving an answer in kind, but the sailors were always barred by one of the guards if they came too close.

The only one of the ship's crew who was allowed to pass freely back and forth was Giles Brock. Every

40

time his glance encountered Sarah's he would scowl blackly, but he never spoke to her. Often, she saw him in a whispered conference with Rhys Pommet, the man in charge of the guards, a tall individual with a melancholy face, as thin and spare as a cadaver, and it struck Sarah that there was something conspiratorial about the pair. In fact, she got the impression that Giles Brock was really in command of the guards, not Captain Hawkins.

But since she knew little about the line of authority on board a sailing vessel—except that a ship's captain seemed something like a distant god, once removed from mere mortals—Sarah didn't give it much thought. It could well be that Giles Brock was simply a link in the chain of command from the captain to the man in charge of the guards.

Sarah had one occasion to talk to Giles Brock. Into their second week at sea, two women in the cabin directly across from the one occupied by Sarah and Meg Fields died of the fever. When Sarah learned of this she experienced a flare of hope. Once the burial at sea ceremony was finished, she sought out Giles Brock. Sarah felt some qualms about the request she was about to make, for in essence she was taking advantage of the misfortune of others. But by now her instinct for survival had been fully aroused, and she was willing to do anything not too degrading to get quarters of her own.

Brock stared at her, those gray eyes so pale they gave him a strangely corpselike look. "You're asking me to give you a *whole* cabin to yourself?"

"Why not? There is an extra cabin now. It should matter not to you if I use it. I—" She faltered, then

4

hurried on. "I am not accustomed to sharing sleeping quarters with another person."

"How so?" His smile was cruel, mocking. "How did you accommodate your customers then? In alleyways? Against a lamppost?"

Sarah felt her face burn. "I'm not a tart, I swear I'm not!"

"Swear? Why should I believe the word of a whore?" He dismissed her cry of protest with a contemptuous shrug. "But mayhap we could strike a bargain, Your Highness. I might consent to your using the empty cabin, for a night now and again, should you in turn consent to allow me to share it with you."

"No!" Sarah backed a step.

"So be it." He shrugged again. "I'm sure I will be able to find someone less finicky who *will* agree to my terms."

And this, Sarah was soon to learn, he did indeed do.

One evening, a few days later, Meg seemed unduly tense, moving restlessly about their small quarters. Then the bolt sounded, and Meg's face lit up. She hurried to the door, which opened just enough for her to slip out, then closed again, but not before Sarah had caught a glimpse of Giles Brock's leering face.

She placed her ear to the door and heard the one across the way open and shut. She knew then that Brock had chosen Meg purposely to taunt her. He could undoubtedly have had any woman on board the ship, with a promise of extra rations or a like inducement, and some of them were far comelier than Meg Fields.

Sarah blew out the candle and lay waiting tensely

for Meg's return. It was well over two hours before the door opened and Meg stepped in.

She leaned over Sarah's hammock, and it was immediately apparent what Brock's inducement had been—Meg's breath reeked with the odor of rum.

"You awake, lovie?" Meg asked in slurred tones. When Sarah didn't answer, she continued, "I know you be, but play-act asleep if you like. I know that Giles Brock made his proposal to you first. 'Tis all right, Meg don't mind that. But I just thought you'd like to know that Brock is much man. If you have a drop of red blood in your veins, you can feel sorry that you didn't let him bed you. He can have me any time, rum or no."

When Sarah still didn't respond, Meg chuckled. "Well, sweet dreams, ducks. Mine will be, you can be sure."

Still chuckling, Meg dropped down onto her hammock and was snoring within seconds.

Chapter Five

Giles Brock detested the sea and everything about it. Yet, this was a man who had a first mate's rank, a man who had spent twenty of his thirty-four years at sea.

He had not chosen his career willingly. At the age of fourteen, he had been shanghaied off the London docks and taken on board a ship bound for the Orient. It was four years before he set eyes on England again, and by that time it was too late, or at least too hard, to start over again at another trade.

Giles Brock was a man who liked the easy path, and since he had a quick, if uneducated, mind, he decided that the easiest way to take advantage of the trade that had been forced upon him was to become a ship's officer.

It wasn't difficult to do. Most seamen were content to sail out their voyages, womanize and drink on shore until their pay was spent, then ship out again. So all a man had to do was apply himself, currying favor with shipowners and shipmasters alike.

This course had one drawback: it meant spending money on better clothes and maritime instruction, instead of on women and drink. Brock wasn't a great one for drink, but he liked his women as well as the next man. However, he was handsome enough and possessed a brutal vitality that appealed to many women, so he rarely had to pay for a bed tumble.

So, Mister Giles Brock became a first mate at thirty-two. He found that he liked the position. Most ship captains delegated authority and seldom questioned methods used so long as their ships operated smoothly. This gave Brock an authority usually unquestioned, an authority he could, ordinarily, abuse with impunity.

Early on, Brock had learned what a brutal world it was. He had been abused, both as a boy and as a seaman, in the early years. Now it was his turn, and he took great delight in ladling out cruel punishment to recalcitrant or malingering sailors.

This voyage, however, was different. Brock had yet to take the full measure of this new captain, and he didn't know how much he was going to get away with. Already, he had experienced the salty edge of Captain Hawkins' tongue for the rough treatment Brock had dealt out to the sailors. Most shipmasters looked upon their crews as little more than cattle. In that respect, Captain Hawkins was different.

Yet, if the plans Brock had for the end of this voyage reached fruition, it mattered not a whit what Captain Hawkins thought. For it was possible that Captain Hawkins would lose his master's status and might even become a fugitive. The thought of the high and mighty Captain Jeb Hawkins being named a criminal filled Brock with great pleasure.

His feelings toward Captain Hawkins were not the result of envy, for Brock had never harbored any desire to be elevated to a captain's rank. The responsibility of a ship's captain was awesome, frightening in its scope. True, a shipmaster was a monarch at sea, reigning supreme, but should anything go amiss, the blame was always the captain's, be it his fault or not. Brock wanted no part of it.

However, he did court wealth. For years he had schemed to get his hands on a large sum of money. Now he was sure he had finally found a means. It had taken much sly maneuvering on his part to put himself into a position to bring it off. First, he had had to convince Horace Cartwright that a cargo of whores shipped to New York would be profitable. That hadn't been particularly difficult to do, taking into consideration Cartwright's greed. But the man knew nothing of doxies and how they operated.

At least one thing Brock had told Cartwright was true—King George's Redcoats were yearning for female companionship, and His Royal Highness was willing to pay generously any shipping company eager to undertake the unsavory task. Brock was also able to convince Horace Cartwright that the women themselves would be anxious to pay a handsome fee, due at the end of the voyage, for the privilege of plying their trade in such a lucrative location. That had been the final seal on the transaction.

Brock chuckled to himself each time he thought of how easily he had gulled Cartwright into swallowing that. A man with any knowledge whatsoever of a whore's trade knew that they rarely had an extra shilling.

Since Brock's intended destination was not New York, he had little concern for the women. He would decide their fate when the time came.

But there was one chore he definitely had to do. He had to see to it that Sarah Moody did not live to see the end of the voyage. She knew too much about him, and if she got another chance to talk to the captain, she just might succeed in convincing him that she had been brought on board bound and gagged. Brock knew that Captain Hawkins half-believed her as it was. Aside from that, she had both defied and spurned him. No damned sassy wench did that to Giles Brock without paying dearly.

A push over the railing some dark and preferably stormy night, and a tumble into the sea, would mean an end to the wench and to any threat she might pose to him. That was the payment he meant to exact from the high and mighty Miss Sarah Moody.

Captain Jeb Hawkins had taken notice of Sarah many more times than she knew. He had made it a point to be on the afterdeck during those two times each day she took the air. His glance followed her every movement, watching the provocative sway of her figure, observing the fact that she always managed to isolate herself from the other women. Surreptitiously, Jeb studied her features as he would a maritime chart, until he could close his eyes and see her face clearly in his mind's eye—the full, yet heart-shaped face, the sensual shape of her mouth, her even teeth flashing with the whiteness of ivory, her blue, no, violet eyes, the fullness of her breasts. . . . Every time Jeb reached this point in summoning up Sarah's image in his mind, he shook his head sharply, swearing at himself and his carnal nature.

The one time she had caught him studying her, Jeb swore to himself that he would cease watching her, yet, the next morning, he was on the afterdeck when Sarah and her nine companions were escorted above decks. This time, Jeb stood well back, where it was more difficult for her to see him, and silently cursed himself for a sneak and a dolt.

Often, lying awake in his bunk at night, he puzzled over the question of why he was drawn to her. On other voyages he had learned to keep his carnal urges under control. Once out of sight of land, he seldom thought of women, devoting all his energies to seeing to his ship. Of course, her proximity had something to do with it, but it was more than that. For one thing, he admired her spirit. He liked spirit and fire in anyone, man or woman. Even during those times he was forced to discipline a rebellious seaman, Jeb secretly admired the spirit he felt it his duty to subdue by the lash. He had rarely found it necessary to dally with doxies and knew little of their nature. Yet he had always thought them pale shadows of real women, their will broken by their trade, craven creatures willing to do anything demanded of them by men for a few coins.

Sarah Moody certainly had spirit and fire, and even as she despaired of her plight, this spirit remained undaunted. And he had glimpsed the lovely woman that she could be, washed, coiffed, and gowned as a proper lady should be. She spoke well, as well as any woman of quality he had ever met. This indicated an education he knew had to be uncommon in whores.

These two factors caused him to doubt his own judgment of her. The doubts gnawed at him in the dark hours of the night. Suppose what she had sworn to him to be true *was* true? Suppose she was a woman of quality, impressed into this cargo of strumpets? If such were her circumstances, he had done her a terrible injustice. And he could well imagine her suffering, if her story was indeed true.

Such speculations, of course, were fruitless. Hellfire and damnation, why did concern for the damned woman continue to plague him?

Jeb even went so far as to talk to Giles Brock of it again in the privacy of the captain's cabin. "Mister Mate, harking back to the time we sailed and the matter of the woman, Sarah Moody . . . Could it be possible that she was stating the truth?"

Brock's thin lips tightened, and he came as close as he ever had to showing anger in Jeb's presence. "The captain is questioning my word?"

Jeb squirmed inwardly, knowing that he had made a mistake broaching the matter again. He blurted, "No, no, Mister Brock. I merely meant could she have been brought on board bound and gagged without your knowledge?"

"Not very well, Captain." Now a light of cold amusement danced in those pale gray eyes. "I myself was at the gangplank when every female with us was brought on board. I assure the captain that Sarah Moody boarded of her own free will." His gaze grew bolder, becoming downright insolent. "Might I inquire as to the captain's interest in this particular wench?"

"No, you may not! I do not have to explain myself to you, Mister Brock!" Jeb retorted heatedly. "And this had better be the truth you're telling. Should I ever learn that you have lied to me, you will sorely rue the day!"

Brock stiffened. The pale eyes became the color of flint. He said softly, "I don't take kindly to threats, Captain."

Jeb was momentarily taken aback. He was accustomed to thinly veiled insolence from this man, but this sudden revelation of a violent inner self was something new.

In an equally soft voice, Jeb said, "Not threatening, Mister Brock. A promise, sir. If I discover you have been deceiving me, you will not only be punished and humiliated before the men, but I will see to it that you are returned to an ordinary seaman's status!"

As suddenly as the inner core of the man had been revealed, it vanished, and the first mate became subservient again. He seemed to cringe away without moving a muscle. "My apologies, sir. I forgot my station for a moment. It will not happen again."

"Good!" Jeb snapped. "See that it does not."

"It's just that—" Brock hesitated. "I am not accustomed to having my honor questioned."

"That will be all, Mister Brock. Dismissed!"

"Aye, aye, Captain." Brock snapped off a salute. "By the captain's leave!" He wheeled and marched out of the cabin.

As the door closed, Jeb sank down at his desk. Absently he took a cigar from the box and fired it, his thoughts roaming back over the conversation. This new insight into the character of his first mate had shaken him slightly. And he still was not sure of the truth about Sarah Moody.

Yet, why would Giles Brock work a deception with the women? What could it possibly gain him? It could gain him nothing, of course, absolutely nothing.

Still, there remained the enigma of Sarah Moody. Jeb sat for a long time, smoking and brooding on it.

As the days and weeks passed, Sarah found herself adjusting to her surroundings and her predicament.

The predicament she faced at the end of the voyage remained unchanged, but since there was nothing she could do about that at the moment, she refused to brood about it. She would confront it when the time came.

Her adjustment to life at sea helped immeasurably. Not only had she adjusted, but she had come to love the sea itself. She found it constantly fascinating and was now as seaworthy as a hardened seaman.

Even stormy weather exhilarated her. Twice, during the time she had been on the *North Star,* sudden storms had come up while she was on deck. The other women squalled and shrieked in terror, but Sarah stood at the railing, the wind howling around her, plucking at her hair and clothing, rain drenching her. She gloried in it, and each time had to be forcibly returned below decks.

But the second occasion had differed from the first, and she was on deck longer, because the guards, as frightened as the women, cowered back out of harm's way, as a strange light flickered high on the masts. Like cold flame, it danced along the spars, outlining them with an eerie light. Sarah stood with her head arched back, watching as the air filled with the smell of ozone. It was an awesome sight, the most beautiful thing she had ever seen.

A deep voice behind her said, "You should retire below, madam."

Sarah whipped around. Captain Jeb Hawkins stood behind her, smiling slightly. "But it's beautiful!" she cried. "What is it, Captain?"

"Seamen call it Saint Elmo's fire. It's a phenomenon often seen at sea during rough weather."

"Is it lightning? Is it dangerous?"

"Not lightning, no. It has never been defined for me. At least, I've never received a logical explanation for it. And no, it is not dangerous. Many superstitious sailors refer to it as witches' fire. But you should retire below decks," he said gravely. "We are in for a bout of rough weather." He glanced back over his shoulder. "The others are being hurried below. You had better join them."

Yet Sarah lingered a moment longer, watching the dazzling dance of light above. Then she saw Rhys Pommet approaching, his cadaverous face forbidding.

"Oh, all right, I'm coming!" she said crossly. She flashed a smile at Captain Hawkins, her animosity toward him forgotten at the moment in her awe at the display she had just seen. "Thank you, Captain, for taking the bother to explain it to me."

The slight smile still on his bearded face, he made a leg and murmured, " 'Twas my pleasure, madam."

Sarah felt his eyes on her as she made her way toward the hatchway. Just before she started down, she glanced back and saw that he hadn't moved; his hooded gaze was still fastened on her.

The following week something happened that made things even easier for Sarah on board the *North Star*.

By now, she had grown accustomed to Meg's sneaking across to the empty cabin to be with Giles Brock. It happened two or three times a week.

On this particular evening, after Meg had left their cabin, Sarah idly tried the door and found it unbolted. Astonished, she cautiously poked her head out. The dim passageway was empty.

After a moment she took a deep breath and ventured boldly out, closing the cabin door without bolting it. She hurried along the passageway and climbed up through the open hatch. Sarah knew that she need not fear the guards. She had learned from Meg that once their afternoon stint was done, the guards went to have their supper and get quietly drunk on rum supplied by Giles Brock, secure in the thought that their charges were safe behind bolted and padlocked doors, to which only Brock and Rhys Pommet had keys.

It was cool on deck, but the night was cloudless. There was no moon. Stars glinted in the night sky like sparks of fire. Sarah found a place along the rail in deep shadow, partially hidden by a cannon stationed at a gun port, and leaned there, the salt air like perfume in her nostrils.

The breeze was stiff, and the ship was under full sail, taking full advantage of the wind. Sarah knew that they were overdue in New York. She had learned from Meg that they were expected to reach New York Harbor in about a week. She forced all thought of what awaited her at the end of the voyage from her mind.

The vessel was quiet, except for an occasional shout from a sailor somewhere on the ship, the gunfire snapping of a sail, the creaking of the rigging, the sound of water breaking on either side of the bow.

Content for the moment, Sarah leaned on the rail, letting the peace and quiet of the ocean flow through her. By now, she could pretty much estimate how long Meg would be in the cabin across the way, so she had returned below decks and was on the hammock, feigning sleep, when the other woman slipped in.

It had been Sarah's thought that Brock had mistakenly left the cabin door unbolted. Yet, two nights later, when Meg and the first mate were across the passageway in the other cabin, Sarah found the door unbolted once more. Again, she sneaked above decks, wondering if Giles Brock had softened toward her and was granting her this boon to partially make up for what had happened to her. She didn't dwell on it overmuch, but accepted her good fortune.

This time, when she got above decks, Sarah found that the night was cloudy, misting rain, and the ship was pitching heavily. It was black as the inside of a cave. Uncaring, she sought out her dark spot by the cannon and leaned there. She turned her face into the mist, letting it wash across her face, reveling in it.

Suddenly, she heard a footfall along the deck. She shrank back against the cannon, holding her breath. She sensed rather than saw the approach of another person. Sarah felt her heart begin to pound with fear. There was something menacing about the very stealth with which the other person advanced.

Abruptly, a hand brushed her arm. Realizing that she was caught, Sarah decided to brazen it through. "Who are you?" she said boldly. "What are you doing here?"

She heard a hiss of indrawn breath, followed by a sibilant, evil laugh. Then a hand clamped around her arm, bruising her flesh. It was so dark Sarah could make out no distinguishing features. She knew only that the figure was certainly male and cruelly strong.

Belatedly, she realized her peril and cried out, "What do you want of me? Let me go!"

With her free hand she struck out blindly in the direction of the man's face. Her hand struck flesh, and then was seized. Now her assailant had her by both arms and was forcing her along the cannon to the ship's rail. His intent was clear. She was going to be thrown overboard!

Knowing it was much too late, Sarah opened her mouth and screamed.

Chapter Six

Captain Jeb Hawkins paced back and forth on the afterdeck, peering ahead into the murk, wondering about the wisdom of running before the wind on such a dark night. He had lookouts posted to watch for the running lights of other ships. Still, the danger of a collision was always a risk at night.

How he yearned to get the damned voyage over with! He wanted to rid himself of the cargo of doxies —and Sarah Moody.

Never had he been so plagued with thoughts of a woman. His personal torment had increased twofold since his meeting her on deck during the display of Saint Elmo's fire several days before. For the first time he had seen her face alight with happiness, her own predicament momentarily forgotten, and he had seen the promise of her beauty fulfilled. He was certain in his own heart now that at least a part of the story she had told him was true.

This, of course, only increased his agony. For there was nothing he could do about it. Once Sarah was taken ashore with the other women, whatever authority over her life Jeb had was gone. He had even considered letting the others be taken ashore and keeping Sarah on board, allowing her to return to London with him. But it would be some time before that happened. He was under orders to sail down the coast to

5

the Carolinas and take on a cargo of tobacco before returning to England. And before that could be done, the cubicles below had to be torn out and the hold of the *North Star* returned to its normal function. All of that would require time.

Aside from the certain fact that his keeping a lone female on board to sail with them to England would set the crew to buzzing with gossip and lessen their respect for their captain, Jeb knew that he would never get away with it. When Horace Cartwright learned of it, he would be outraged and do what he had already threatened to do—beach Captain Jebadiah Hawkins permanently.

Jeb suspected his own motives as well. Did he anticipate that Sarah Moody, out of gratitude for his saving her, would agree to share his bunk and slake the lust that raged through his blood like a fever? This thought only weighed more heavily on his already burdened conscience.

Jeb drew on his cheroot. His mouth filled with a bitter taste, and with a muttered oath, he flung the cigar into the sea. His gaze followed the red eye of fire until it was snuffed out by the mist.

Then he froze as a woman's shrill scream from amidships ripped apart the quiet of the ship.

He was already scrambling down the afterdeck ladder when the second scream came. Jeb loped toward the direction of the scream. Up ahead, he saw two figures struggling against a cannon. Jeb shouted and ran toward them.

While he was still too far away to recognize anyone, he saw them separate, and one figure hurried off into the darkness. Jeb started after the vanishing figure, then changed his mind and turned toward the woman leaning against the cannon.

"Are you all right?" She started to slump, and Jeb caught her around the waist.

"I—I think so," she said in a faint voice.

Jeb recognized Sarah's voice. He wasn't surprised; he had somehow thought it would be she. She leaned against him, and Jeb imagined that he could feel the throb of her heart against his waistcoat. Touched by her vulnerability and stirred by her nearness, he said again. "Are you all right?"

Sarah nodded weakly, and then, suddenly realizing her position, she drew back and tried to hold herself erect. She had been badly shaken by her brush with death, and the nearness of this man confused her strangely. She fought a sudden urge to fall into his arms and weep on his waistcoat, which smelled pleasantly of tobacco and wet wool. She had been alone so long.

Jeb, struggling with the desire to pull her back into the shelter of his arms, also drew back.

"What happened?" he asked, more sternly than he intended.

Sarah clung to the cannon for a moment, reliving the fear she had experienced as she had looked down at the dark water rushing past the side of the ship.

"Someone tried to push me overboard," she said.

"Who was it? Do you know?"

"It was too dark to see, Captain."

He said gruffly, "Then you have no thoughts on who the villain was?"

"Thoughts?" She was silent for a moment. "Thoughts, yes. But you wouldn't believe me." Bitterness edged her voice. "You did not believe me before. Why should you now?"

Stung, Jeb stepped back. Then he scowled at her. "Why are you above decks at this hour, madam? I gave no orders for such!"

"My cabin door was left open. Not for the first time." There was more of her old spirit in her voice now. "I think it was left open on purpose, so I would be lured on deck and made vulnerable to attack in the dark."

"That is Mister Brock's responsibility," he said grimly. "I shall have words with my mate about that."

"No, please, Captain. Don't do that. You see—" Sarah hesitated briefly, considering how much she should tell him of her suspicions, then plunged ahead. "I think he is the one who tried to push me overboard."

Jeb stiffened. "Hell and damnation, madam! Do you know what you are saying? Can you offer proof of your charge?"

"No, I told you I didn't recognize my attacker. And it is not a charge, Captain Hawkins, merely my suspicions."

"You must have grounds for such suspicions," he growled. "I demand that you tell me at once!"

"Always making demands, aren't you, Captain? Such a fierce, unyielding man—"

Sarah swayed and began to fall. Jeb caught her again, knowing not if she was feigning faintness. Supporting her, he helped her along to his cabin. He ushered her inside and to his dining table.

"A tot of brandy is what you need."

Sarah murmured a protest. "No, no, I do not drink."

"You will on this occasion, madam. Purely medicinal, I assure you." In a moment he was back with a bottle of French brandy and two tankards. "I feel in need of one myself." He splashed brandy into the tankards and gave her one. "Now drink, madam. Drink hearty."

Sarah stared doubtfully at the liquor. Then she tilted the tankard up and drank, too much and too quickly, being unaccustomed to drinking. She began to cough and splutter. With a slight smile, Jeb pounded her on the back.

Sarah sat up and glared at him. "That is not necessary, sir!"

"That is considered the proper treatment for a strangling fit, madam." Jeb laughed aloud at the look of indignation on her face, which was now rosy with color from the brandy.

Sobering, Jeb began to pace. "To return to your suspicions about Mister Brock. What earthly reason could he have to wish you dead?"

"Perhaps he fears that you will come to believe my story of how I was brought on board."

"Paugh! There would be no reason for him to fear that. Unless he was somehow involved." He scowled over at her. "As I recall, you told me there were others brought aboard like you?"

"That is correct, sir. Two with me. At least those two."

"Then why have they not come forward?"

"Because he has put fear in them, as he did Meg Fields to get her to lie for him!"

Jeb muttered almost inaudibly, "Could it be possible he was somehow engaged in a conspiracy with these other men you speak of to impress dox—women on board my ship? But what possible reason could he have?"

He began to pace, and Sarah watched him, reflecting once again on what a handsome figure he cut. She spoke almost without thinking. "It could also be that he wishes to kill me because I know that he is bedding Meg Fields in the cabin across the way."

Jeb wheeled on her. "What? What is this?"

Sorry that she had spoken, Sarah shrank back, feeling her face turn fiery red. Reluctantly, she repeated what she knew of Giles Brock and Meg.

"But this is scandalous, if true!" he thundered. "By the Lord Jehovah, is there no end to the goings-on aboard my ship?" He flung his hands in the air.

Jeb brooded on Sarah, trying once again to decide if she was telling the truth or if she was simply a mischief maker by nature.

For the first time, Sarah noticed a wooden tub by the captain's washstand along one wall. She stared at it wistfully. What she wouldn't give for a good, hot bath!

Dimly, she heard his voice thundering at her. She blinked around at him. "I'm sorry, Captain. What?"

"Madam, have you heard a word I've said?"

"Captain, the tub," she said. "Is it for bathing?"

He stared at her as if she had suddenly gone mad. "Of course it is, madam! What else could it be? My cabin boy, Tim, heats a tub of water for me when I wish to bathe."

"Captain Hawkins," Sarah said in sudden daring, "do you know what I desire more than anything in the world right now? A bath!"

"Dear Lord!" Jeb gave a shout of laughter. "The woman is indeed demented. You have just escaped with your life, if what you claim is true, and you want a bath!"

"Do you know what it is like below, sir?" she said steadily. "A filthy existence, washing from a basin of cold sea water, no way to wash your clothes and body. And the heat, the heat is terrible. God only knows what vermin crawl down there!"

Jeb stared at her with a sober countenance. Then he sighed and, shaking his head, strode to the cabin door and threw it open. "Tim!" he bellowed. "On the double!"

As always, Tim popped up as though he'd been waiting for the summons. His long blond hair flopped over his forehead as he slid to a breathless stop before Jeb. He pushed the hair out of his blue eyes, and said, "Yes, Captain?"

"Fetch hot water for the tub, boy."

"Right away, sir!"

Leaving the cabin door open, Jeb strode to his desk and rummaged for a cigar. He fired it from the candle and moved over to stand with his back to Sarah, blowing smoke out the open porthole. His mood was black. He swung from wanting to believe her accusations against Giles Brock, to cursing her for being a tart and a liar. One reason he resisted belief in her story, Jeb knew, was his own dislike of his first mate. He tended to be scrupulously fair to someone he did not like, and he had disliked Brock on sight.

He heard a strangled sound from the cabin door and turned. Tim, carrying two full pails of water, stood in the doorway gaping at Sarah.

"Well?" Jeb snarled. "Don't stand there gaping like a fool, lad. Get on with it! Fill the tub."

"Yes-s, Captain." With his face averted from Sarah, Tim hurried over to dump water into the tub, then hastened out for more.

Looking at Sarah, Jeb found her hiding laughter behind her hand. "The situation is not one for laughter, madam!"

Sarah dropped her hand and struggled to stop, but her violet eyes still bubbled with amusement. "I am aware of that, sir. But the lad's face! Has he not seen a woman in your cabin before?"

Jeb snorted. "Indeed he has not! It is not my custom to have females accompany me on my voyages."

"Some ship captains do, I understand. Some take their wives along."

"I am not wed."

"But—" Her gaze strayed toward the bunk bed.

Jeb took an involuntary step to put himself between her and the bed, as though to hide it from her eyes. Then he gave a soft snort of laughter and halted. "The bed was installed by the *North Star*'s former captain, and I did not go to the bother of having it removed."

"I see. Tell me, Captain—" She looked at him in speculation. "I have heard that sailors believe that a woman on board a ship brings bad fortune. Is that true, Captain Hawkins?"

"Some harbor that superstition, yes." The direct gaze of those violet eyes was disconcerting. To escape it, Jeb began to pace. "I have never believed it. But from the unfortunate circumstances of this ill-fated voyage, I may come to place some faith in the superstition myself."

"But surely you cannot hold me responsible, Captain," she said artlessly, "since I did not come on board of my own free will."

"So you say, madam, so you say."

Glancing at her, Jeb saw her eyes began to smoke, and he braced himself for the lash of her tongue. Just then Tim hurried in with two more pails of water. The lad hastened over to dump the steaming water into the tub, and left quickly without looking at Sarah. One more trip, and the tub was full. This time, Jeb followed Tim out.

He halted in the doorway. "You may take your bath now, madam. I will wait outside. When you are finished, rap on the cabin door."

The sails had been trimmed now, as the night had grown darker, and the vessel was moving only fast enough to maintain headway. Jeb paced the deck outside his cabin, mulling over the problem of Sarah Moody and Giles Brock. He had already decided that, come morning, he would call Brock in for an accounting of his actions. He knew this was foredoomed to failure. If Giles Brock were the villain Sarah claimed him to be, he was such a smooth and convincing liar that Jeb knew he would never catch him out.

As he paced, Jeb could occasionally hear the splashing of water within and snatches of song from Sarah. He smiled to himself, pleased that she was happy in her bath.

And then his thoughts took another turn. Despite all that he could do, images of Sarah, naked and rosy in her bath, invaded his mind. Soon, he was afire with lust. He was positive that she was well formed and alluring once stripped of her clothing. He had

had glimpses of the fullness of her breasts straining against the bodice of her dress, and he could easily imagine them filling his cupped hands, the nipples stiffening. Her limbs would be long and the color of ivory, her belly flat yet softly rounded. He thought of her on the large bed, opening her embrace to receive him.

Jeb groaned softly to himself.

Then he stopped short, scowling. Why was he castigating himself for such lustful thoughts? He was a normal male, and Sarah Moody had lain with men before. Despite her protestations to the contrary, Jeb was certain that she was far from the innocent she claimed to be. Even if part of her story was true and she wasn't a doxie by profession, why had she been about the streets of London, alone, and after dark? There could only be one explanation for that. She had been late returning from a rendezvous with a lover.

Jeb well knew that any other man in his position would not hesitate an instant. So why should he? The thought that finally goaded him beyond the bonds of self-restraint was the fact that within a short period of two days, no more, Sarah would be ashore on New York Island and beyond his reach forever.

That was his last reasonable thought for some time. He wheeled about, took the necessary few steps, and opened the cabin door, which he had left unlocked behind him.

He froze in the doorway, his breath leaving him with a soft grunt at the sight of Sarah standing in the tub, naked as Eve, drying herself with the muslin towel Tim had left. Jeb feasted his eyes on beauty such as he had never before seen. Without her filthy, torn clothing, she was a vision of pink and white loveliness. The lustrous black hair was a dark cloud down below her shoulders. Her skin glowed with the translucence of a pearl.

Jeb made an elemental sound deep in his throat, and Sarah glanced up, startled. At the sight of him, she cried out and made a futile effort to cover herself with the towel.

"Sir! I did not knock for you to enter!"

Jeb closed the door, in his haste forgetting to lock it, and strode toward her.

"What do you want of me, sir?"

"You know what I want. Do not play the role of coy maiden with me any longer, madam!"

Sarah sank down into the tub, still trying to cover herself. "I'll scream!"

"Scream all you like. No one will come to your aid. A ship's captain has to answer to no one for his actions on board his ship." A small part of Jeb's mind was amazed at his behavior. It was totally unlike him to act in such a manner.

He reached down, seized Sarah by the arm, and hauled her up. She stood, dripping water.

Later, Sarah was to wonder why she hadn't screamed. Was it because of the shocking suddenness? Or was it because she had wanted it to happen all along?

Jeb half-carried, half-dragged her to the bed and dumped her there. Standing back, but not so far that he couldn't intercept her should she make a move toward the door, he hastily stripped away his clothing.

Sarah, still cowering and trying to cover as much of herself as she could with the towel, watched out of the corner of her eyes as he undressed. She had never seen a man naked before and had only a vague idea of what one looked like: Jeb was solid as a tree trunk, not an ounce of excess flesh on his body. His broad chest was matted with red hair, and the bush of hair at his groin was also flame-red. Sarah tore her gaze away from the awesome sight of his erect manhood. As Jeb stepped out of his breeches, she made a belated move to flee from the assault on her virtue she knew was coming. With the speed of a jungle cat, he came down on the bed, pinning her there with his big hands on her shoulders. His mouth was open, his breath hot, and the green eyes had a glazed look.

With one knee he forced her legs apart. Sarah used both hands in an effort to keep the towel spread across her loins. With an impatient snarl, Jeb removed one hand from her shoulder long enough to bat her hands and the towel out of the way.

Then she was spreadeagled and helpless before his assault. With one fierce thrust he was inside her, aided by the wetness of her excitement. Sarah felt a sharp stab of pain, and she cried out.

Jeb ignored the cry, if indeed he heard it, and thrust himself again and again into her body. In a short time the pain receded. His kisses nearly smothered her, and Sarah felt a strange warmth spread throughout her lower body. Not exactly pleasurable, yet not unpleasant either, it puzzled her. And even more strange, her body seemed to have a will of its own, wanting to move, wanting to meet his thrusts.

Sarah forced herself to remain still. She lay with her face turned aside. She tried to think of something else, anything but what was taking place. Into her mind came images of the Saint Elmo's fire she had observed playing about the masts. In some strange way, the wild beauty of that remembered sight connected with what was happening to her, and she found herself moving again. She turned her thoughts to the indignity she had suffered being brought aboard this man's ship, and anger took her in its grip. In her rage she began to beat Jeb about the chest and shoulders with her fists, which had no more effect on him than insects pestering a bull. In fact, it seemed to goad him on to greater effort. He drove at her with a frenzied fury now, his face contorted, and the part of it she could see, as red as his beard.

Then, all at once, it was all over. A moan was wrenched from Jeb, and his body went rigid. After a moment he expelled his breath with a sigh and relaxed atop her, his great weight crushing her into the bed.

Sarah could scarcely breathe. She said coldly, "Are you finished, sir?"

Jeb raised his head to say dazedly, "What?"

"Having taken me by brute force, sir, I was wondering if I now might return below to my cabin? There, at least, I will be safe from being further violated."

He mumbled something inaudible and moved to sit on the edge of the bed, his back to her. He combed his fingers distractedly through his beard. "I'm sorry, Sarah. I don't know what made me act in such a manner."

"Indeed, sir?"

"You must admit that you fought me little."

"You had informed me that fighting or screaming would avail me nothing. A captain is master of all on his ship, you said. At least with Giles Brock, he does not bother to conceal his lust. And when I refused him, he did not ravish me, but turned his vile attentions to Meg Fields!"

"What? What are you saying?" Jeb turned his head, and his gaze was riveted by the spots of blood on the bed clothing. "By the Lord Jehova, you were virgin!"

"Does that please you, sir, deflowering a virgin?"

"Please me? Of course not!" He reared up, staring down at her with a stricken look. "But it's not possible!"

"Is not the evidence enough for you, Captain? Did I not tell you that I had never lain with a man?"

"But if that is so, that means that all you have told me is true!"

"Yes, Captain. It would seem so, wouldn't it?"

"My most humble apologies, madam. I did not know. Certainly, not for a moment did I dream . . ."

Feeling strangely vindicated by the dazed look on his face, Sarah said, "Somewhat tardy for regrets, is it not? A woman's maidenhood is her most prized possession, the ultimate gift she brings to her husband on her wedding night. Now you have taken that from me, by force, and left me soiled and used."

"Believe me, Sarah, I am indeed . . ." Suddenly he straightened, something of his old stern demeanor returning, and he scowled. He managed to look dignified, though unclothed. "I *am* sorry, as I've made clear. But do you not dramatize the situation unduly? Surely you could not have retained your maiden state long once ashore on New York Island!"

Angered, Sarah sat up in bed. "You'd like to think that, I'm sure, removing the onus of guilt from yourself. But I have no intention of serving as a doxie for the soldiers in New York!"

Jeb's stare turned curious. "Just how do you intend to avoid that?"

"I don't know, but I'll find a way," she said spiritedly. "You can be certain of that."

A faint smile curved his mouth. "By Jehovah, I believe you will, madam, I believe you—"

The cabin door crashed open. With a stifled cry Sarah darted a glance that way. Giles Brock stood framed in the doorway. He carried a pistol in each hand. Behind him loomed one of the guards. Quickly, Sarah pulled the covers up to hide her nakedness.

"Well, lookee here!" Brock said with a sneer. "I've caught the captain with his breeches down! Not only that, but our pious captain has sneaked a doxie into his bed!"

"What is the meaning of this, Mister Brock?" Jeb roared, taking two steps toward Brock.

The pistols swung his way, centering on his chest. "That'll be far enough, Captain, else you'll get a pistol ball through the heart. I have no compunction about killing you, my word on it. As for what I'm about, I'm taking over the *North Star*. Listen!" He motioned with one of the pistols.

Listening, Sarah heard a sudden eruption of sound aboard the ship—shouts, pistol shots, and screams of agony.

"The crew is being given a choice, Captain Hawkins. Either join me and my men, or die. If you haven't surmised as much by now, the doxie guards are mine, sir. Their loyalty is to me. When the *North Star* is secure, all will be under my command." Brock gestured with one pistol. "Search the captain's quarters, Jack. Gather up any weapons."

For a moment Jeb looked stunned, his gaze following the man named Jack as he began his search. Then his face flamed red as his beard, his eyes turning to green ice. "This is mutiny, sir!"

Brock gave an indifferent shrug. "Give it whatever name you like, Captain—" He laughed. "Rather, *Mister* Hawkins, since you are no longer master of this vessel."

"I'll see you hanged for this, sir, when we reach New York Island!"

"Aye, I'm sure you'd like that. But you are in error in one respect. You see, we are no longer bound for New York." Brock was grinning now, a grimace of malicious amusement. "The moment I leave this cabin, I intend to change our destination."

"To where?"

"Down the coast of the Carolinas and across the Gulf. We are sailing for the Spanish port of New Orleans." At that moment Jack came toward him, carrying two pistols and a cutlass. "That the lot, Jack?"

"All I could find, sir."

"Good." Brock looked again at Jeb. "And now, I must leave you. The cabin door will be locked behind me, and this man or some other will stand watch outside around the clock. Should you try to get out, they have orders to put a bullet into your heart. I will leave your tart behind." He grinned over at Sarah. "Dally to your heart's content, Jeb Hawkins. 'Tis a lengthy voyage to New Orleans."

Chapter Seven

As the door closed behind Giles Brock and his cohort, Sarah said fearfully, "What is going to happen to us, Captain?"

Jeb Hawkins stood with his feet planted wide apart, glowering at the cabin door.

Sarah said, "Captain Hawkins?"

"Damnation, woman, how do I know?" he roared. He glared around at her, then softened slightly. "I'm sorry, Sarah. I'm as befuddled by this as you are. Probably more so, since you seem to have divined Giles Brock for the blackguard he is, while I, believing myself to be a great judge of character, was fooled; taken in by his smooth manner."

Jeb glanced down at himself with a start, as though he had forgotten his naked state. He gathered up his clothes where he had scattered them in his haste. Pulling on his sea boots, he said, "Whatever happens, Sarah, I wish you to know that I realize the error in judgment I made as concerns you."

"Giles Brock intends to kill us, doesn't he?" she asked, as steadily as she could.

"Not if I can help it, he won't, madam."

Quietly he moved to the cabin door, bending down to place an ear to it. While his back was turned, Sarah began dressing hurriedly. Without looking at her, he turned away from the door and toward a port. He muttered, "One of the mutineers is there, right enough. I can hear him pacing."

He stood for a moment peering out the porthole. "Black as tar. I can see naught. Damnation!" He smacked a fist into his palm. "If only I had some inkling as to his purpose! If only I knew how many members of my crew remained loyal! If any. The threat of death will make even good men become turncoats!"

He began to pace, head sunk in thought. Dressed now, Sarah stood quietly beside the bed, watching him.

Finally he seemed to remember her presence. He stopped to stare at her. "Why the clothes, madam? The hour grows late. You should be abed. You may need what rest you can get, before this nightmare is finished."

Sarah glanced at the bed. She drew herself up. "If you think that I am going to share that bed with you . . ."

"I said nothing of that. What sort of man do you think I am?"

"I doubt that you would care for my answer to that, sir."

He brooded on her, then sighed, nodding. "True, you have every reason to think harshly of me. But you need have no fear. I will not touch you again, my promise on it. Besides—" He gave a short bark of laughter. "I have things on my mind other than tumbling a wench, you can be sure!"

"But where will you sleep, Captain?"

"I will make a pallet on the deck, if I sleep at all."

"But sir, you should take the bed."

"Your concern strikes me as belated and false. Do not provoke me further, madam!"

"I only meant that if anyone can save us from this predicament, it will have to be you. Therefore, your need for proper rest is more important."

"Ah, now that is the Sarah Moody I am coming to know." He comtemplated her with amused eyes. "My comfort as such does not concern you, eh? Only how it may ultimately affect you?"

Sarah felt herself flushing. "That wasn't my meaning, sir!"

"No matter." He shrugged. "An instinct for self-preservation may stand you in good stead in the trying days ahead. And a few nights on the deck will be good for me. It seems I have grown soft and coddled. Many nights in my early days at sea I spent sleeping on the—" He broke off, his face assuming that fierce scowl. "For the love of Jehovah, madam, abed with you and stop your chatter!"

He crossed to a sea chest against one wall and rummaged in it for a sheet of sailcloth, which he then proceeded to hang around the bed, curtaining it off from the rest of the cabin.

"Thank you, Captain," Sarah said gratefully.

For this, she received a grunt. Long after she was abed, she heard him prowling the cabin, muttering, and she finally went to sleep with the pungent odor of his cigar in her nostrils.

She was awakened early the next morning by the cabin door banging open and the sound of a high voice she recognized as belonging to Tim, the cabin boy. Having slept in most of her clothes, it didn't take Sarah long to make herself decent. She stepped around the sailcloth curtain and saw Captain Hawkins at the table. Tim was putting food on the table, setting two places. Sarah noticed that the cabin door was closed, and she wondered briefly why they would allow Tim in here alone with them. Then she concluded that they probably thought there was little to fear from him at his young age.

Sarah sat at the table across from Jeb. The odor of food made her aware that she was hungry. She said, "Good morning, Tim."

"Morning, m'lady," Tim mumbled, not looking at her.

She saw that Jeb was glowering at the lad. Then he said heavily, "Have you joined with the mutineers, too, boy?"

"That I have, Captain," Tim said loudly. He shot a furtive glance at the door. Then he set up a great clatter of dishes and said in a whisper, "Mister Brock gave us a choice, Captain. Join with him or be shoved overboard. I played him false and said I was with him. But my loyalty still lies with you, Captain Hawkins. We must pretend that I am with them, so they will leave me free to come and go to your cabin."

"Good lad, Tim," Jeb said, equally low. "And the others? How many of them joined the mutiny?"

"Most of them, I fear, Captain. But some have sought me out in secret and whispered to me to pass the word that their hearts remain loyal to the ship's master."

"And the ones who did not fall in with Brock?"

Tim shook his head in sorrow. "A couple were killed by pistol fire when Mister Brock and the dox— the men guarding the women took over the ship. The others, those who refused to swear fealty to him, were thrown overboard. Some half-dozen, Captain."

Jeb struck the table with his fist, opened his mouth to bellow, then changed his mind with a glance toward the door. In a low, tense voice, he said, "That blackguard! If I ever get my hands on Mister Brock, he'll pay dearly for his perfidy!" He glared down at the food on his plate, but didn't touch it. "He said that our new destination is the port of New Orleans. Is that true, lad?"

"I know not, Captain. But he did change course during the night, and the ship now sails south."

The food was considerably better than that served the women below decks, and Sarah had been busily applying herself. Now she stopped eating and said bluntly, "He means to kill us, doesn't he, this man Brock?"

"I know not, m'lady," Tim said with averted gaze.

"Come now, I can abide the truth, Tim! But what is a puzzlement to me is why he has not done so already."

"I overheard a remark to the effect that—" Tim hesitated. "That he intends to lay the blame for the ship's fate to Captain Hawkins, should it come to that."

"But what *is* the ship's fate?" Jeb demanded. "What in the devil's name does the man intend doing with her?"

"Again, I know not, Captain—"

The cabin door banged open, and the man called Jack stuck his head inside. "Why are ye tarrying so long, boy? Shake it up!"

"Yes, sir. Right away, sir," Tim said nervously.

When the guard withdrew, leaving the door open slightly, Tim leaned close to Jeb to whisper, "I will find out what I can, Captain, and pass the word."

"See if you can smuggle me in a pistol or two, lad," Jeb whispered back.

"I'll do my best, Captain, depend on it."

"That's a good lad." Jeb gripped his arm and squeezed. "But take care now. Do not give them an excuse to feed you to the fishes."

With a nod, a dip of his upper body to Sarah, Tim hurriedly left the cabin. Jeb sat listening, head cocked, until he heard the click of the door being locked. Then he sighed and stared glumly down at his plate.

Sarah was attacking her food again. She said between bites, "Be of good cheer, Captain. I have confidence in you to extricate us from our predicament."

Jeb said dryly, "My thanks for your faith, madam. I wish I was as confident."

As the days passed, Sarah found the confinement of the cabin galling, luxurious as it was compared to her cubicle below decks. Most of all, she missed the freedom of being on deck. They were never allowed outside, and the only persons they saw were Tim and the door guards. Tim came three times a day, bringing food and water and emptying the necessary jar. He had little news of good cheer to impart. Apparently Brock and his cohorts, although allowing him to come and go almost at will, were still careful of what they said in his presence.

He did bring word of one happening. "Brock, Captain, he has let the seamen have free access to the females below." He flicked a glance at Sarah. "Almost all the sailors have their own women now."

Jeb and Sarah exchanged glances. Sarah said,

"That explains the sounds of merriment we have heard these past two nights, Jeb."

Jeb Hawkins seemed not to notice that she had addressed him by his given name for the first time. He said grimly, "It explains a number of things, madam. It means that Giles Brock is using the women to insure the loyalty of those seamen still harboring hatred for him." He looked directly at Tim. "Is that not true, lad?"

Tim's gaze dropped away. "I know not what you mean, Captain."

"Lad, lad, you are not dense," Jeb chided. "Those seamen who swore secret loyalty to their captain—are they not silent these days, content to dally with the wenches?"

Tim sighed. "I fear so." His glance came up. "But I am still with you, Captain."

"Stout lad." Jeb smiled at him. "The pistols—have you been able to acquire weapons as yet?"

"Not yet, sir. But I will keep trying."

After Tim had left, Jeb said wryly, "We are fortunate that he is not yet of an age where wenching has its lure for him, or we would have no one at all to look to for help!"

It was Sarah's private thought that a boy of fourteen was old enough to dally with women, yet she voiced none of her thoughts. Jeb had already turned away to stride over to a porthole where he stood staring out. He was like a great caged beast, pacing, muttering great oaths under his breath. His temper was always foul, and he usually snarled at Sarah whenever she made a comment. In many ways being locked up alone with him was worse than having Meg Fields as a cabin mate.

But Jeb had held to his promise. He had made no effort to share the bunk with her. She could well have been another man for all the notice he gave her. And as her fears of him receded, Sarah found herself a trifle piqued by this. She had to laugh at herself for this reaction. Yet no matter how hard she tried, time and again she caught herself thinking back to those few minutes in bed with him. In retrospect, it hadn't been all that terrible, and she had to admit to a strong curiosity, remembering that one moment when her treacherous body had responded to him. Was it possible that a second time would not be unpleasant at all, might even bring her some pleasure?

Not that she had any intention of finding out. Never again would he touch her in lust; she was determined about that. And she wasn't about to forgive him; she still hated Jeb Hawkins with all her being.

The few times that Jeb did not stand at one of the ports gazing out gave Sarah an opportunity to look out. Since the ports opened to the east, all she could see was the rolling ocean. From what Jeb told her she gathered that they were sailing within sight of land most of the time. Before long she could smell it. As they sailed farther south, the weather grew warmer, and at night she could smell the heavy, cloying odor of tropical flowers and plants wafted on the warm breeze.

One evening, as she stood looking out on a calm sea, peaceful and lovely under the glow of a full moon, Jeb spoke behind Sarah, causing her to jump.

"It is my estimation that we are now sailing down the east coast of the peninsula known as Florida. Soon we'll round the string of islands they call the Keys and come into the Gulf of Mexico."

"Are you familiar with these waters, Captain?"

"No, I have not sailed here."

"One thing mystifies me: Why has not this ship been challenged?"

" 'Tis my understanding that most of the rebel ships ply the shipping lanes farther north, where they can intercept British ships bound from England to New York. This distance south would either be infested with privateers, those vessels attacking our merchant ships for their cargoes, or out-and-out pirate vessels; and I would hazard that Mister Brock, with his fiendish cleverness, is well supplied with the flags of various countries. No doubt he passes the *North Star* off as a colonial ship one time, a Spanish vessel the next, whatever the occasion demands."

"But is that not illegal, Captain?"

"Aye, that it is, madam," he said, "but so too is the act of mutiny illegal. I misdoubt that illegality much bothers our Mister Brock."

Twice they encountered storms of hurricane force, the ship tossing and heaving terribly. Sarah wasn't overly frightened. She stood at one of the portholes until the waves became so high they washed over the decks and poured sea water into the cabin.

Jeb closed and battened the portholes, muttering, "I hope that damned Brock is a good enough seaman to weather a gale such as this. Seas of this nature could swamp the *North Star*."

He paced the cabin, smoking furiously, sometimes stopping to shout directions to an unseen Giles Brock. Sarah found it amusing that Jeb Hawkins was far more concerned, in that moment at least, with the safety of his ship—what had once been his ship—than with his personal welfare.

They went through both storms in good shape, as far as Sarah could judge. Three days later Jeb informed her that they had rounded the southernmost island of the Florida chain and were now sailing west and north toward New Orleans. And they had yet to learn of their fate. They had not seen Giles Brock since he locked them in the cabin, and Tim had been able to learn very little.

But two days before Jeb judged they were to reach New Orleans, Tim came into the cabin with their supper trays, napkins spread over the food.

As the guard closed the door, Tim whipped the napkin off one tray with a dramatic flourish. He whispered, "Here's something for you, Captain." He held the tray out. Instead of food, two pistols nestled on the tray. Tim smiled broadly. "The captain will have to go without his supper tonight."

Jeb's eyes caught fire, and he grinned widely. "Far more welcome than food, Tim lad, most assuredly." Eagerly he reached for the pistols. "Loaded?"

"Yes, Captain, and on the morrow I will fetch you spare powder and balls."

Jeb hurried across the cabin and buried the pistols deep in his sea chest. As he returned to the table, it was obvious to Sarah that his spirits had lightened considerably.

"Now I don't feel so damned defenseless. At least I can put up a fight." He sobered. "Will this spell trouble for you, Tim?"

"I think not, Captain. We are to reach New Orleans the day after tomorrow. I waited until now to sneak them. Mister Brock had searched the ship for all weapons possessed by the seamen, leaving only his guards armed. From this store of weapons I sneaked the pistols. I misdoubt they will be missed now. This close to port, they have relaxed their vigilance somewhat."

"You still have no inkling as to what Brock's intentions are regarding the *North Star?*"

"None, Captain. I did overhear the woman, Meg Fields, telling another that Mister Brock had told her that he intends to set the women up in a sporting house in New Orleans and put her in charge of it."

"A whore master! 'Tis a fitting trade for Giles Brock. Aye, that it is!" Jeb said in a sneering voice. "If I have anything to say about it, he will never sail aboard a ship again. Certainly not one sailing under a British flag." Jeb stopped short, staring at nothing.

"What is it, Jeb?" Sarah demanded in some alarm.

"That's it, of course." He focused on her. "He's here to sell the *North Star* to the Spanish! He can get a fortune for her! The Spanish, I understand, are sorely in need of ships, and they are not taking sides in this war, neither with King George nor the Colonials. They hate each equally, as it was told to me. By Jehovah, that's it!" He struck the table with his fist. "That scoundrel! And I can do naught to prevent it!" His voice rose to a full bellow.

The door popped open, and the guard stuck his head in, a cocked pistol in his hand. "What's the clatter in here?"

"Nothing amiss, sir," Sarah said hastily. "The captain dropped something on his foot and was voicing his vexation."

Jeb's shrewd guess was correct. Giles Brock had indeed taken the *North Star* to sell to the Spanish. They were not particular from whom they bought ships, and Brock had his story all ready. He had seized the *North Star* as a prize of war, boarding her as a privateer. Who would give the lie to him? Not the guards, certainly. And the seamen would be turned loose in New Orleans, happy to escape with their lives. The women would be situated in a sporting house, under his supervision, and were most happy with their promised lot, more content here than they would have been servicing King George's Redcoats in the Colonies.

There were many opportunities in New Orleans for a man with capital, daring, and few scruples. With the money he got from the sale of the *North Star* to invest in some enterprise and the anticipated income from the brothel, he should be in excellent shape. Never again would he have to go to sea!

Brock had few scruples against killing, although he had never been personally responsible for the death of another until this voyage. Consequently he had felt no qualms about having seen to it that those of the *North Star*'s crew refusing to bend to his will were tossed into the sea.

Also, he knew that he wouldn't have turned a hair had it been necessary to eliminate the women in the same manner. Yet he was just as glad that he had found a way to keep them alive and make a profit from them. True, the suggestion had come from Meg Fields, a desperate measure Brock realized Meg had thought up as a means of saving her own hide. He smiled to himself, remembering the way she had broached it to him.

When he informed Meg that he had taken over the ship and was sailing for New Orleans instead of their scheduled destination, she knew at once that he had it in his mind to rid himself of them.

"That's good, lovey," she had whispered to him, at the same time fondling his body into arousal as they lay abed. They were in his own bunk now; no longer was it necessary to play the sneak with her. "I know what you have in mind. New Orleans is a sinful village, 'tis my understanding. You will use the women on board to stock a sporting house. Is that not right, ducks?"

"It might be a project worth some thought," he said, chuckling. "But I've no experience with such a trade. I would need someone to run it for me."

"I know someone."

"And who might that be?"

"Me, ducks. Meg knows all there is to know about the whoring trade. We've got the wenches. You provide the with-all to set us up in a place, and I'll run it dandy for you."

An arm under her ample body, his other hand absently stroking her breast, Brock thought on it. Cleaned up a little and put into proper clothing, Meg might make a fine madam. She certainly should be familiar enough with a whore's trade, and it would be a means of making use of the wenches. Brock hated to see anything go to waste.

Making up his mind, he said, "We'll see what happens in New Orleans. If it doesn't interfere with my other plans. . . ."

She sighed gustily, and Brock realized that she had been holding her breath for his answer.

"You'll never be sorry, lovey, my word on it!"

She half-turned, burying him under her heavy flesh, raining kisses on his face. With a grunt Brock pushed her roughly over onto her back and mounted her. She cooperated eagerly in her gratitude, using all her skills to satisfy him.

Brock's mind was only partly on what he was doing. His thoughts were above decks, in the captain's cabin and on the wench, Sarah Moody. Should she be situated in the sporting house? Somehow Brock knew it would never work with Sarah. He would dearly love to see her tamed, beaten until she begged for mercy. Yet he doubted that she would ever submit to the sordid existence of a whore.

He had made a grievous error with Sarah; he could admit that to himself now, now that his scheme was working as smooth as silk. From the moment he had clapped eyes on her, prodded on board by those two clods, Bart and Corky, Brock had recognized Sarah for the lady that she was and should have immediately sent her on her way. But he had never known a fine lady up close, never bedded one, and the chance to humiliate and degrade such a lady had been too tempting to pass up. Brock would still dearly love to be able to do just that, yet he knew it was a personal indulgence he could ill afford.

When it was all over, Jeb Hawkins would either be publicly disgraced or dead; Brock hadn't decided yet which it would be. It all depended on how matters went in New Orleans. And the wenches would be herded like a flock of hens under Meg's wing, content to be told what to do.

Sarah Moody now, there was a different kettle of fish. She could pose a real threat to his future security. If she were let go free and managed to deck herself out in proper finery, it was quite possible that she could find someone willing to listen to her story.

And even in a raw frontier city like New Orleans, the abduction of a proper lady in an attempt to force her into whoredom would not be looked upon with favor. If she found a champion, such a champion might come looking for one Giles Brock. Brock understood that dueling was becoming a popular pastime in this city on the river, and he had no wish to be shot down in a quarrel over a wench, right when he was finally making his way in the world.

No, as much as he disliked sending such a juicy morsel down to Davy Jones' locker, Brock knew that Sarah had to go. He would see to it that she never set a dainty foot on New Orlean's soil.

Chapter Eight

In 1782, New Orleans was a true melting pot, a hodgepodge of races, religions, and professions. The first arrivals had been the French, later followed by Canadians, Arcadians, Germans, Spaniards, Englishmen, Italians, Irish, and a smattering of American Colonials, mostly frontiersmen escaping King George's iron fist, seeking adventure and fortune provided by the fur trade of the vast wilderness and the burgeoning water commerce along the Mississippi River. When the Revolution broke out in 1776, many of them came fleeing the war.

In 1699, two Frenchmen, the Le Moyne brothers, led an expedition up the mouth of the muddy Mississippi, looking among the swamps and bogs and flooded bayous for a stretch of dry land where they could build a town, a stronghold that would assure France and her king control of the great river. They found it 107 miles from the Gulf of Mexico, a stretch of swamp forest a few feet above sea level, framed by a crescent of the river. On the site began what was to become, within a half-century, an oasis of cosmopolitan charm in the sprawling, brawling babe of a country to be called America.

The town was named New Orleans in honor of the royal rakehell, Phillipe Duc d'Orleans, Regent of France during the minority of the child king, Louis

7

XV. Later, many of the more straitlaced New Orleanians claimed that naming the city after such a debauched individual placed a curse on it and was responsible for its long history of sin.

It was not until 1718 that a village was finally built on the banks of the mighty river. In February of that year, the younger of the Le Moyne brothers, Sieur de Bienville, landed on the site with a labor force, consisting mostly of convicts sent from France, and began construction of a town. Streets were laid out in eleven straight blocks along the river and six blocks back into the encroaching forest. This original rectangle, destroyed innumerable times by fire and flood, was always restored to its original formation, surviving down through the years, until that particular section became known as the French Quarter.

The village grew slowly, fighting off raids by Indians and rebuilding after fire and flood; from a population of 400, living in mud huts in 1718, it grew to 8,000 by 1722, when the first respectable dwellings were built.

New Orleans was passed from the rule of one European country to another, like a poor, unwanted relation. France, finding it difficult and expensive to rule from such a distance, made Spain a gift of Louisiana in 1762.

New Orleanians were outraged by this cavalier treatment and several times petitioned the government of France to be returned to the mother country. But it availed them nothing. However, it was not until 1766 that Spain sent the first Spanish governor, one Antonio de Ulloa, to take formal possession of Louisiana. Ulloa was an astronomer with a chilly, disdainful manner, who had little liking for the chore before him and absolutely no knowledge of governing.

New Orleans rose up in near-rebellion, its citizens holding meetings, signing petitions, and arming themselves. The new governor became alarmed at the attitude of the residents and took refuge with his family aboard a Spanish ship anchored in the river. Late one night the ship was mysteriously cut loose from its moorings and floated downstream with the current to the Gulf. That was the last New Orleans saw of Don Antonio de Ulloa.

The colony of Louisiana was free, and the citizens began to talk of setting up some form of home rule. Thus, in 1768, New Orleans could legitimately lay claim to being the first colony in the New World to have considered achieving independence from the mother country.

Their freedom was short-lived. Ten months later an Irish mercenary, Alexander O'Reilly, was sent, along with 2,000 soldiers, mostly adventurers, and twenty-four men-of-war, to once again proclaim Spain as the seat of power.

The size of O'Reilly's force was too large to resist. He hauled down the French flag, which Ulloa had never taken the trouble to remove, and hoisted the Spanish colors in the Place d'Armes. He promised that all citizens who had offended the Spanish government would be forgiven. With this promise, the revolutionaries quietly dispersed. However, O'Reilly quickly arrested the leaders of the revolt and had six of them shot in a public display in the Place d'Armes. This earned him the hatred of New Orleanians and the title of "Bloody" O'Reilly.

Sean Flanagan was one of the adventurers O'Reilly had recruited to journey to New Orleans to bring order and obedience to the King of Spain and to control the raw, savage land. Sean was an accomplished soldier, fearless and skilled in all manner of weapons; fighting for and with anyone willing to pay well for his services. His allegiance could be bought, but rarely for long, and he could not be wooed by pleas of noble causes. To Sean, there *were* no noble causes, not in the context of governments and countries. He felt that he owed allegiance only to his fellow man, be he not villainous; and even that allegiance tended to weaken if it interfered with his full belly, his thirst, and his appetite for wenches. He had fought under several flags, brilliantly and bravely and always for good pay; and he had done many things during brief periods of peace, even a bit of piracy.

Such was his military ability and reputation that he was given an officer's rank in O'Reilly's "Bloody" Raiders, even at the young age of twenty-one.

But disgust had risen in his throat like bile as he witnessed the execution of the six rebels in the Place d'Armes, and he resigned not long after. Bloody O'Reilly tried to keep him, offering him a jump in rank and more pay as inducement, but Sean rejected him. Harsh words passed between them, and Sean came within a hair of being shot himself.

He could have returned to soldiering. When the American Revolution began, he learned that the Colonials were hiring mercenaries. But Sean had had his fill of wars. He had been a soldier-of-fortune since the age of sixteen, and he was sick unto death of killing. By that time he was happy at another trade anyway.

During the years after he left O'Reilly, Sean had to admit that New Orleans and the surrounding area were faring better under O'Reilly's reign, in tandem with a new Spanish governor. Gone were the constant political strife and crooked dealings all too often seen under the administration of the French. The town was growing by leaps and bounds, becoming a bustling, prosperous metropolis.

It certainly had enough attractions to draw Sean back every spring to spend the summer, as hot and steamy as the summers were. It was the only town along the Mississippi with any charm and sophistication, as well as offering every indulgence a man might desire. It had every game of chance ever conceived and wenches of almost every race and degree of morals, and Sean had a taste for both. He had spent six summers here now, coming in with pockets laden with the profits of a winter devoted to trapping beaver, otter, and other fur-bearing animals, whose skins were so coveted by the fine ladies of Europe that they were willing to pay dearly for them.

Once, Sean would have scoffed at the thought of spending six months out of a year alone in a virtual wilderness, fighting bitter weather and countless other dangers. He had always thought of himself as a social animal. But after resigning his commission with "Bloody" O'Reilly, he had to earn a living in some manner. First, he had tried gambling, but a professional gambler had to be cold and calculating, and Sean was impetuous by nature. He belonged on the other side, getting his sport from pitting himself against the house or against great odds and usually losing. Later he had tried other trades, but had not been happy in them.

Now he loved the life he had chosen for himself—the isolation, the complete separation from the human race, the reliance on his own ability to survive deadly winters and attacks by Indians and renegade whites.

The fur trade was still in its infancy, most of it done by representatives of the Hudson's Bay Company, chartered in 1670. It was the only fur-trading company in existence on the North American continent at the time. The company itself was an enemy of the independent trapper, not looking with favor on anyone trapping without its sanction. There were times when Sean either had to elude the company's men or fight them. So far, he had been successful at both.

Since the company had been granted what amounted to a virtual monopoly on the fur trade, it was also violently opposed to any trapper selling his catch to other fur buyers, the few that existed. Since it did have what amounted to a monopoly, the company tended to pay a mere pittance for furs brought in by independent trappers. Sean had scouted around until he found a fur buyer willing to take his winter's catches at top prices.

Sean could understand the company's concern. He knew that within a few years the fur trade would open up in the far reaches of the frontier, probably not long after the war between the British and the Colonials reached some sort of conclusion. For that reason, the company was trying to nip the free fur trade in the bud. At the moment, powerful as they were, they had the upper hand, but Sean was convinced they wouldn't be able to stem the tide. The West was rich in furs; the market was strong and could only get stronger; and the territory would soon be swarming with trappers. Sean figured he was fortunate to have had the foresight to get into it in the beginning. When the time came that there wasn't enough room to build a lean-to without having a neighboring trapper within shouting range, he would take up another trade.

At thirty-five, Sean Flanagan was a tall man, with handsome features and a charming smile. He looked out at the world with a cynical humor that was seldom dampened. He even went into combat with a smile, laughing aloud in moments of danger. At first glance he seemed rather slight, even frail. But under stress he could move with the quickness of a puma, and his lean body was tough as rawhide.

Normally, Sean left New Orleans with a fresh team of pack mules in mid-September, so he could make the long trek to the trapping grounds and set up his quarters before the onslaught of winter. This year, he had stayed in New Orleans too long, it now being early October. He would be fortunate to make it before the first winter storm. But there had been a pretty French wench with whom he had dallied overlong.

He shrugged all thoughts of Celeste out of his mind. That was over, finished, and good riddance.

At last he was finally ready to leave. His packs were crammed with what he would need for the coming months, and the four mules he'd bought were waiting at the stables up the street. It was now late afternoon. Sean would wait until nightfall to start out, wait until the heat of the day was gone. For the next week at least he would travel mostly during the cool of the night.

Sean was staying in a two-story boardinghouse close to the river, the same place he usually stayed while in New Orleans. In a chest in one corner were the fine clothes he wore in the city. During his sojourns in New Orleans, he was something of a dandy.

Now on the bed were laid out the garments he would be wearing for the next six months—new buckskins, smoked black and daubed with grease to make them as waterproof as possible. The hunting shirt, called the Kentucky model, was long and fringed at the seams so the water would run off instead of soaking in. His moccasins were modeled on those worn by the Plains Indians, with rawhide soles and a fur lining for winter. Under the hunting shirt he would wear a cotton shirt. There would be no trousers under the buckskins, merely a breechclout and thigh-length leggings, the lower parts made of nonshrinkable blanket cloth. On his head would perch a coonskin cap. Since Sean loved ornaments, the fringed shirt was decorated with glass beads, and the cap was adorned with bright feathers. And now he would let his hair grow long until it fell to his shoulders, but Sean, unlike most fur trappers, shaved as often as he could in the wilderness. Bathing, of course, was seldom possible in the dead of winter, but after a man had lived with his own stink for several weeks, it no longer mattered.

The smoking and waterproofing of the buckskins was usually done by a fur trapper's squaw, but Sean hired a local Indian woman to prepare his. He had never picked a squaw to winter with him. It wasn't for moral or racial reasons; he had bedded a comely squaw more than once. But when a white man took an Indian woman into his lean-to for the winter, she was forever after ostracized by her own people. Most trappers thought little more of their squaws than they would a pet dog and turned them loose to fend for themselves when the trapping season was past, taking a new one the following autumn. More often than not, the Indian women thus cast loose starved to death or simply died from grief. Sean couldn't bring himself to do that to another human being, and certainly he couldn't take a squaw into civilization with him. If he did such a thing in New Orleans, he would be ostracized along with the squaw. So he managed without female companionship during the long winters and made up for the lack on his spring return to New Orleans.

Standing at the window now, Sean took a last look out over the Mississippi. It was low at this time of the year. A number of ships from various countries were docked at the crude wooden wharves along the river bank, and numerous others were anchored out a ways. As he watched, Sean saw a new arrival, a three-masted frigate slowly making headway against the river current. What struck him as strange about the newcomer was the fact that, although she flew the Spanish flag, she was of Dutch or British design. Most vessels coming in here bore Spanish or French colors, with a few other countries mixed in. But these days no English or Colonial ships were allowed through the mouth of the Mississippi emptying into the Gulf.

To his further surprise, Sean saw the ship drop anchor out in the river, away from the main current. He found this curious, since arriving ships usually came directly to the wharves to unload their cargoes. Because the wharves were usually crowded, they might then move out a distance to anchor, but only after unloading.

Definitely intrigued now, Sean took out his spyglass and focused on the new ship. He made out the name *North Star*. Indeed strange. A merchant vessel flying a Spanish flag, while definitely British in origin and name. Sean decided that the master of the *North Star* must have slipped a hefty bribe to the guards at one of the three passes opening into the river.

There was much activity on board the strange ship. In a little while, a boat was lowered, and many tiny figures clambered down the Jacob's ladder into the boat.

Sean focused the glass again. He grunted softly. By God, the figures were female, a stream of them! He lowered the spyglass. For what purpose would a cargo of females be brought to New Orleans?

He remembered hearing about several shipments of whores being brought to New Orleans back in the 20's, also boatloads of "casket girls." The latter were proper young Frenchwomen brought to the village to serve as brides for the men. They had middle-class backgrounds and were known as "casket girls" because of the small chest, containing a dowry of clothing, given to them by the Mississippi Company. On arrival in New Orleans, they were well guarded, locked up at night, and brought out only during the day to be paraded before the matrimonial-minded men to make their choice. They all apparently married, because, as Sean read from a report of the time, "This merchandise was soon disposed of." What amused Sean most about the episode was the fact that New Orleanians born after that time all claimed to be descendants of the casket girls, none born of strumpet predecessors.

But there was no reason for women, either casket girls *or* strumpets, to be shipped into the city today. True, the population numbered more males than females, but most of the males were transient, like Sean himself.

Still smiling amusedly to himself, Sean turned away from the window and prepared to dress in his buckskins. It was a puzzle, true, but already late starting on his trek north, he couldn't linger to seek the solution to the mystery. He would find out on his return in the spring.

Sarah's first impression of Louisiana and the great river running to the sea was depressing. The only things she could see from the port were low-lying, boggy land and mud-red water, and the only buildings were flat, mud huts. When the ship finally anchored in the river and she had her first glimpse of New Orleans, it was equally disappointing. There were no buildings larger than two stories, and the village had a stink that reached them even out on the river, a stench that reminded Sarah of the alleyways of London.

"Why, I thought New Orleans would be a city," she said in dismay. "It looks nothing like London!"

Beside her, Jeb said dryly, "This is still a raw, primitive land, Sarah. I understand that New Orleans is actually considered a fine, cosmopolitan city for this area. But do not expect London or Paris."

"Would New York have been the same?"

"Not entirely. New York is older and of more permanent construction, although it may be war-ravaged at present. But I've heard that New Orleans suffers catastrophe regularly; either fire or flood destroys it every few years, and it must be rebuilt. Naturally, no builder would be willing to invest funds on a fine building that could be destroyed at any time. . . . Listen!"

Jeb fell quiet, staring out the port. A boat was being lowered into the water. A Jacob's ladder was dropped, and in a moment the women began gingerly feeling their way down, clinging to the ropes. Sarah saw Meg Fields among them. Meg was white-faced with fear and had to be prodded from behind.

"They're certainly not wasting any time," Jeb mused. "They've hardly dropped anchor."

Jeb and Sarah stood at the ports watching for the next two hours. No one came into their cabin. The boats had to make several trips to get all the women ashore, and after the women, the *North Star*'s crew was taken ashore. By the time the last boatload of seamen had left, it was full dark, and the ship was very quiet.

"Do you suppose the ship is deserted?" Sarah asked in a whisper.

Jeb shook his head. "I'm sure Brock would leave a few men behind to guard us."

"Why don't they come for us?"

"I don't know, and I'm not waiting to find out." He looked down at her. "You're a good screamer, madam. May I suggest you put your talent to good use?"

He crossed quickly to his sea chest and dug down to the bottom for one of the pistols Tim had gotten for him. He gestured with it. "Get behind the curtain, Sarah, and scream. Make a great fuss."

Jeb tiptoed to a position where he would be standing behind the door when it opened. He gestured again and mouthed the word, "Now!"

Sarah ran behind the sailcloth curtain. She knocked a jar to the floor, shattering it, stomped with both feet, and cried shrilly, "Help! Please help me!" She screamed.

A pistol butt rapped on the cabin door, and a rough voice called, "What's about in there?"

In answer Sarah screamed again. A key sounded in the lock, and the door opened. A guard stepped in cautiously, pistol held alertly. Jeb remained very still, hidden behind the partially open door.

Sarah rustled the curtain and screamed once more.

The guard lowered his pistol and advanced a few steps into the cabin. He laughed shortly. "Tumbling you, is he, wench? Mayhap you need some help holding her, Captain Hawkins? I'll gladly lend a hand, if it's turn about when you've finished."

Jeb, pistol held high by the barrel, crept up behind the guard. He raised his arm to club the man on the head. Then a deck board under his foot made a popping sound, and the guard whirled around. The pistol butt glanced off the side of his head, then off his shoulder.

The guard, a large, burly fellow, snarled in fury and started to bring his own pistol up. Using his weapon like a sword, Jeb knocked the man's pistol out of his hand. The man charged, wrapping Jeb into his arms in a bearlike hug. Locked together, they wrestled back and forth across the cabin.

Sarah darted out from behind the curtain just as the pair careened into the desk. The candle Jeb always kept burning to light his cigars was knocked off.

It bounced across the floor toward the sailcloth curtain and the bed, still burning.

Sarah, eyes on the two men, did not notice it. She moved around the struggling men, looking for something she could use to help Jeb. She picked up the guard's pistol from the floor, but she knew nothing of firearms. Hoping to use it as a club, she tried to get clear access to the guard's head. But the men were struggling so furiously she had no chance to use it.

Now, still locked together, the men wrestled across the cabin and half fell through the open door to the deck outside. Sarah hurried after them.

Fearful that the commotion would attract the other guards, she darted a frantic glance around. She saw Tim racing toward them. Sarah saw, too, that Jeb's pistol had slipped from his grasp, skidding along the deck and overboard.

As Tim ran up, breathless, Sarah said, "Can you do somthing to help?"

But even as she spoke, she saw that it was no longer necessary; Jeb was now on top of the guard, straddling him, his powerful legs holding him captive. As she watched, Jeb seized the prone man by the hair and thumped his head hard against the deck. The guard slumped. His face crimson with anger and exertion, Jeb raised the man's head and brought it cracking down once more. It made a sound like a splitting melon. He was lifting the man's head a third time, when Sarah ran to him and tugged ineffectually at his shoulder.

"Jeb! You're going to kill him!"

Jeb turned his face up, his eyes glazed with fury.

"Please, Jeb, that's enough! The other guards may be here any second!"

Jeb gave his head a great shake and climbed slowly to his feet. The guard lay without moving.

Tim kneeled beside him. After a moment he looked up. "The man's dead, Captain."

"The other guards, Tim—Where are they?"

"Only two, Captain." Tim got to his feet. "Brock left only the three on board. The other pair are somewhere about the ship."

Jeb saw the pistol in Sarah's hand and took it from her. He jerked his head. "The sea chest in my cabin, Tim. Fetch the other pistol. We may need it." He paced to the head of the steps leading down to the main deck.

A shout came from Tim, and both Jeb and Sarah whirled about to see him staggering out of the cabin. Greasy smoke billowed out after him.

"Fire, Captain! The whole cabin's ablaze!"

"Dear God in Heaven!" Jeb exclaimed in dismay. A sailor's greatest fear was a fire on board ship. Since the ships were wholly constructed of wood, there was no hope once a blaze got a good start.

He ran to the cabin door and peered in. Heat blasted out at him, and he threw an arm up before his face. The cabin was an inferno. It was too late; there wasn't a prayer of saving the *North Star*. Jeb spun around. "Tim, is there a boat left on board?"

"One, Captain."

From the railing Sarah cried, "Jeb! Come quick!"

He sprang to her side. Two of Brock's guards were racing toward the steps. Both carried pistols.

Jeb leveled his weapon and shouted, "Halt!"

The two men skidded to a stop, looking up with gaping faces. At the sight of Jeb, they started to bring their pistols up.

In a deadly voice Jeb said, "I have only one ball, true, but I will get one of you before you can kill me. Is it worth the risk to you? Now, which one of you chooses to die?"

Slowly, the pair lowered their weapons.

Jeb let his breath go and said, "The ship is afire. No hope of saving her. We're taking the remaining boat. I suggest you two devil's scum hit the water. It's not a long swim to shore. You can make it easily." As they hesitated, Jeb leveled the pistol again. "Now! Or by Jehovah, one of you is a dead man!"

The two men exchanged glances, then quickly moved to the side of the ship and leaped into the water.

"Tim, let's get the boat into the water. If you have any belongings below you wish to take, be quick about it. This ship will soon be ablaze to the waterline. Sarah, how about you?"

"I have nothing."

Jeb looked sadly at the blazing cabin. "And it's far too late for me to save anything."

Tim was back quickly with a kerchief-wrapped bundle. They lowered the small, remaining boat and clambered down the side of the ship. With Tim and Jeb at the oars, they started rowing toward the lights of the shore. Fifty yards from the *North Star*, Jeb gestured, and they stopped rowing. His prediction had been correct. Topside, most of the ship was ablaze. In the light of the flames of the burning vessel, Sarah could see the sadness on his face.

Impulsively she touched his hand. "I'm sorry, Jeb. I know how much you loved her."

"Yes." He heaved a sigh. "But it's not just that. Horace Cartwright will hold me responsible, and all I have in this world is in the company's strongbox. Cartwright will confiscate it in partial payment for the loss of his ship."

Shocked, Sarah said, "But surely he can't do that!"

"He can and will, madam. Horace Cartwright is a man quick to seize a chance to reduce his losses." Jeb's face turned bitter. "All those years of devotion to the sea and practicing frugality have made me a well-off man. Now it is all gone. My only possessions are what I have on my person. I don't have so much as a farthing in my pocket. I know not what we shall do for food and lodging on this night."

"I have some few pounds I've saved," Tim said unexpectedly. "You, Captain, and m'lady are welcome to share."

"Thank you, Tim." Jeb squeezed his shoulder.

Hoping to bring some comfort to Jeb, Sarah said, "But with your experience and captain's papers, you should have no trouble getting another ship."

Jeb gave a snort. "You think not?" His face hardened. "I will never command another ship for Horace Cartwright, you may be sure. And he will likely see to it that no other British line will employ me."

"But surely you cannot be blamed for what has happened!"

"I once told you that a ship master is accountable to no one for his actions while aboard ship. But should something happen to that ship, the blame lies with the captain, no matter its origin. My only hope would be to prove mutiny, and who would side with me on that? You perhaps, and Tim here. But who will accept the word of a woman and a cabin boy? The other women are all gone, God knows where.

The crew, as well. And the guards belong to Brock. That's why, I am now convinced, he wanted the *North Star* to sail with the cargo of doxies, so he could talk Cartwright into sending along guards, men Brock hand-picked for their loyalty to him. He intended all along to seize the *North Star* and sell her to the Spanish. Thanks be to Jehovah, that plan was foiled," he said harshly. "Much as I loved her, I'd rather see the ship destroyed than let Giles Brock profit from her." He took a last, lingering look at the burning ship. "We'd better start rowing again, Tim. When the fire reaches the powder magazine, she'll blow."

They had only proceeded a short distance when the *North Star* exploded in a great gush of flame, followed by a wave of rolling sound. Jeb didn't glance up but bent to the oars. Sarah watched in awe as the ship disintegrated in the explosion. Bits of burning wood rained down on them. Then there were only a few pieces of wood left floating on the surface of the water. Some were still burning. One by one the flames were extinguished, until only a few pieces of charred wood remained on the surface.

Sarah turned, looking toward the river bank. They were close enough to see the lights of torches and lanterns. There seemed to be a great many people gathered on the wharves.

Jeb gestured to a spot of darkness some distance from the group of people. "Let's head over there, Tim. I have no stomach for the questions we might face. Jehovah only knows what Brock has told them."

They changed direction. The place they finally selected was about a mile north of the city. At Jeb's instructions they ran the boat up onto a narrow stretch of sand, beaching her.

Jeb stepped out, then gave Sarah a hand. With Tim beside them, they faced around. The faint glow of the city was to their left. Jeb sighed and said, "We have no choice but to take our chances in the city."

They had taken only a few steps when a harsh voice drove at them out of the night. "Hold right there, Jeb Hawkins, or take a pistol ball!"

Sarah recognized the voice as that of Giles Brock.

Chapter Nine

The day had gone well for Giles Brock. He had found an empty house large enough to lodge the women and had left them under the supervision of Meg Fields. He had dispersed all the *North Star*'s regular crew, warning them that it would be to their benefit to keep their mouths closed. They were in a strange country, where foreign tongues were spoken, a country at odds with both England and the Colonies. If they ran about yapping mutiny, few would believe them, or even care. Here in this land ruled from afar by Spain, nobody had an ear for the troubles of an Englishman; most certainly not the bleatings of common sailors.

Best of all, he had found many who were eager to purchase the *North Star*, no questions asked; and he had finally sold her for much more than he had anticipated. The sale was to be consummated on the morrow, when he turned possession of the vessel over to the purchaser. Soon, he would be a wealthy man.

All that remained was to deal with Jeb Hawkins and Sarah Moody. Having told the other guards that he would pay them the next day, Brock headed for the river and the boat, accompanied only by Rhys Pommet, to return to the *North Star* and tie up the loose ends.

Now that he had sold the ship, he had no further need of Captain Hawkins. Since Brock had no intention of ever putting himself into a position where he might have to answer to British maritime law, he no longer needed someone to shoulder the blame. And the permanent elimination of Jeb Hawkins would be to his ultimate benefit. He wanted no more witnesses than absolutely necessary. Once aboard the *North Star*, he intended to send the three remaining guards off with some pocket money, and he and Rhys Pommet would end the lives of Jeb Hawkins and the wench.

He had no fear of Pommet ever blabbing. Rhys Pommet was a brutal, cold-blooded killer; he received joy from it, and he was as involved as Brock himself. Pommet had personally dispatched several of the sailors in the taking of the *North Star*, with Brock as a witness.

Brock had no forewarning when he reached the edge of the river with Pommet and saw the crowd of people watching a burning ship out in the river. He forced his way rudely through the throng to the river bank and was stunned into silence when he saw that the ship was the *North Star*. Even as he watched, she exploded and was no more. Everything he had schemed and labored toward for almost a year had been right in his hands, and now it was all gone, wiped away as though it had never been!

A black, seething rage filled him, and he snarled like a cornered animal as Pommet turned to him, his cadaverous face agape. "It's the *North Star*, Giles! What could have happened?"

"How do I know, you gibbering ass?" he hissed. "I know it's gone, all gone, and here we stand nigh as penniless as orphans!"

And then, in the dying flare of light from the exploding ship, Brock saw a small boat rowing hard for the river bank. In the boat were three people.

"By Satan himself, it's Jeb Hawkins and the wench!" He turned toward Pommet, fists clenched. "How did they escape?"

Brock's black rage mounted until he almost sickened and choked on it. "Somehow, somehow, that devil managed to shake the guards and set fire to my ship! I swear by all that's holy he shall die a slow and painful death! As will she, as will she!"

Even as Brock watched, he saw the boat change direction, veering north. "He's heading away from the crowd. Let's after them, Rhys! I must have the satisfaction of feeling his throat between my hands!"

He urged Pommet through the crowd. Once free, they started up the narrow strip of wet sand at a dead run. A thought struck Brock, and he seized Pommet by the arm, slowing him. "You stay back a little. Keep hidden in the darkness. I'll accost them, let them think 'tis only me they must face. If Jeb Hawkins managed all this, he must be armed."

Rhys Pommet slowed, staying back several yards. Brock pounded on, moving over to run alongside the rise of land, so that his silhouette wouldn't be visible to the occupants of the boat. There was a full moon just rising, and he could see the boat easily as it neared the bank. He saw the spot where they were headed and got there first, staying well back until they ran the boat up on the sand, and he saw Jeb Hawkins helping Sarah out.

Then Brock stepped boldly forward, pistol leveled, and said harshly, "Hold right there, Jeb Hawkins, or take a pistol ball!"

The woman screamed, and Jeb Hawkins skidded to a stop. He started to reach for the pistol in his belt.

Brock bared his teeth in a snarl. "Go ahead, Hawkins. Touch that pistol and you die. 'Twould give me great pleasure. Killing you will be poor payment for your putting the torch to the *North Star!*"

"I didn't torch her," Hawkins growled. "It was an accident. But I'm happy she burned instead of staying in your hands, you mutinous scum!"

"I had her sold for a goodly sum," Brock said. "And now because of you, I have nothing!"

"You will have even less when your neck is stretched for mutiny!"

"That day will never come. Who will charge me with mutiny? Not you, Jeb Hawkins. I intend to see to that right now." Out of the corner of his eye, Brock saw Rhys Pommet creeping up at an angle a few feet behind the trio facing him. Brock raised his voice. "Now, Pommet!"

Jeb Hawkins started to whirl, but he was too late. Pommet brought his pistol butt down across the captain's skull, and Hawkins dropped like a stone to the sand and lay still.

Sarah cried out and started to run to him. Brock took two steps and grabbed her by the arm. She turned, starting to fight him, and Brock rammed the pistol barrel into her side. "Shut your yap, bitch, or I'll blow a hole in you!"

The cabin boy broke, running up the sandy bank. Pommet cocked and fired his pistol. Tim kept running, and Pommet cursed vilely. He started after him.

"Let him go, Rhys!" Brock shouted. "He's naught but a boy and can do us no harm. But Jeb Hawkins now—put him in the boat and row out to where the current's powerful. Dump him, and we'll have no worry about explaining his dead body."

112

"No!" cried Sarah, trying to struggle free.

Again, Brock prodded her with the pistol. "You want to live a while longer, you'll close your yap. Go ahead, Rhys, do what I say. And get your arse back here. We've got things to decide. And you, Sarah Moody, you'll be coming with me." He headed for the bank above them, dragging Sarah behind.

Sarah held back as best she could, digging her heels into the sand. "Where are you taking me?"

Brock stuck the pistol in his belt, then struck her face with his free hand. Sarah's head snapped far to one side from the force of the blow.

"I'm going to have my due from you. I'm going to show you what a real man is, not at all like that pious, cold-blooded captain whose bunk you've been sharing."

Despite the pain, Sarah managed to keep her voice steady. "Jeb Hawkins is twice the man you are!"

"Is that right now? We shall see, we shall see."

Brock threw a glance toward Pommet and Hawkins. He saw that Pommet was tumbling the unconscious Hawkins into the boat. Brock nodded to himself in satisfaction. He would have preferred that Hawkins suffer a great deal before he died; he could think of any number of unpleasant things he could have done to the captain, but time would not permit him that pleasure. It was enough to know that Jeb Hawkins would soon be dead.

They were climbing up a steep, sandy incline now. Low shrubs grew on it. It took all of Brock's strength to pull Sarah along. Finally they were out of sight of both the bank and the town. Brock spun Sarah around and sent her sprawling on her back on the soft ground.

The fall drove the breath from her body and stunned her, yet she attempted to crawl away. With a curse Brock leaned down and clubbed her alongside the head with the pistol. She fell back on her side, semiconscious.

Breathing heavily, Brock said, "I like my wenches with spirit, but I haven't the time now to tame you proper." The struggle with her had inflamed his senses, and he was fully aroused. He dropped to his knees before her and pushed her dress up above her waist. Placing the pistol within easy reach, he began fumbling with his breeches. "When I'm done with you, you'll be most happy to join your captain in the river. 'Tis my understanding that the river here has catfish as big as sharks. They like to nibble on corpses."

Sarah could hear his voice only dimly through the painful throbbing in her head. She willed herself to move, but all power of movement seemed to have left her.

As her senses cleared a little, she looked past him and almost screamed aloud. Behind the kneeling Brock loomed an apparition—tall, lean, with fringes like long fur on his arms and legs, and a strange cap with feathers on his head. In his hands he carried something like a long stick.

A deep voice drawled, "What's about here? I heard a pistol shot."

Brock, startled, reared back, half-twisting around. He snarled, "This is none of your affair, stranger! Can't a man fuck his woman without being bothered?"

"We-ell now, that all depends. If she's willing and able, yes. But unless my eyesight is failing me, I saw you clout the lass with your pistol. That being the case, she's not so willing, now is she? Suppose we let her decide? How say you, madam? Are you willing for what the sculpin here has in mind?"

Sarah moved slightly, trying to speak, but only an unintelligible sound emerged from her throat.

Brock had fallen to his hands and knees, and one hand was creeping like an insect across the ground toward the pistol.

"I wouldn't try it, boyo. Not unless you want a split noggin."

Brock froze momentarily, then he made a lunge for the pistol. The thing that looked like a long stick came whistling down with the speed of a striking snake, and Sarah realized that it was a rifle. The heavy butt thunked into the back of Brock's head. Brock sighed and collapsed, falling prone on his face. The tall man in the strange garb stepped up to stand over Brock, the rifle reversed now. He nudged Brock in the neck with the barrel. Brock didn't move.

The tall man said in a dry voice, "I warned the sculpin, now didn't I?"

Sarah sat up. She felt as fragile as an egg; her cheeks and head both felt distended and painful. She hastily pulled her dress down, attempted to get up, then fell back weakly.

The stranger reached down and gently helped her to her feet. "Are you all right, lass?"

Leaning on his arm, Sarah could only nod. She felt the side of her head where Brock had struck her with the pistol and winced.

The stranger's hand followed her own and touched the spot gently. "Your friend was no gentleman," he said softly.

Sarah leaned against him for a moment, then suddenly jerked upright as she remembered Jeb. "Oh, dear God!"

She broke free of the man's arm and ran to the edge of the bank. Each step intensified the pain in her head, but that was no matter now. Frantically she looked out into the river and was filled with dismay. She could see nothing. During that brief span of time, a river fog had drifted in, blanketing the river. Sarah sagged, dropping to her knees. She knew deep in her heart that it was too late; Jeb was dead, drowned in the river. They would not meet again.

Her rescuer ranged alongside her. He *was* tall, as tall as Jeb, but not as broad. "What's wrong?"

He had to lean close to hear her answer. "There was a man with me, the captain of the *North Star*. A cohort of the man trying to rape me took the captain out in a boat to drown him. But there's nothing to be done. It's too late, too late."

The man gave her a hand up. "You came today aboard the ship, the *North Star?*"

Sarah nodded. "I did, yes."

The man stroked his chin. "I must admit to some puzzlement. I saw the ship unloading a group of females. And now the events here. . . ." He swept his hand around. "Were you one of those women?"

"No. I—" Sarah hesitated, at a loss as to how to explain. "It's a very long, involved story."

"Yes, and yon sculpin will be coming around soon. We had better depart at once. Shall I escort you back to the city? Oh, forgive my manners, madam. I am Sean Flanagan." Smiling, he doffed the strange cap he was wearing.

Sarah clutched his arm with both of her hands.

"Mr. Flanagan, you have already done me a great service; still, I would ask you one thing more."

Sean looked into her face. "And what might that be?"

Sarah paused for a moment, then hissed the words, "Kill him! Kill Giles Brock!"

Sean drew back, his smile fading. "Brock? The man back there?"

She nodded, not releasing his arm. "Yes. He is a murderer, a mutineer, and more."

Sean shook his head. "Sorry, lass, but I have only your word for that. A raper of women he may be, I can attest to that, but for *that* I cannot kill him in cold blood."

Sarah, against her wishes, began to weep. "But if he lives, he will kill me!"

Sean pulled his arm from her hands, reached to his side, then handed her a heavy, wicked-looking knife. "If you wish him dead, lass, and if what you say is true, then you must kill him yourself."

He put the knife into her hands. Sarah held it for a moment, still weeping, then thrust it back at him.

"Ah, yes, then," he said softly, replacing the knife in its sheath at his belt. "So come along then. What's your name, lass?"

"Sarah Moody," she said, willing herself to stop the tears.

"Well now, where shall I be after taking you? I must be getting about my own affairs now. A man can be spending only so much time rescuing damsels."

Sarah suddenly became aware of her predicament. She had no money with which to pay for food and lodging. She had not the callousness necessary to kill Brock, and when he returned to consciousness, he and

117

Pommet would almost certainly attempt to find and kill her, for she was obviously a danger to them, knowing what she did.

She looked up at Sean. "Do you live in the town?"

"We-ell, I do and I don't." Sean shrugged. "I spend part of the year there. Right now, I'm on my way north. My train of mules is out there a ways. I was heading out of town and heard the shot. Being of a curious nature . . ." His grin was lazy, self-mocking. "I came to investigate."

Her mind suddenly clear, Sarah realized there was only one way out for her. She reached out to touch Sean's arm. "Take me with you. Please?"

Sean drew back. "Whoa now, Mistress Moody. Where I'm going is not a place for a fine lady such as yourself!"

"I didn't mean all the way. Only out of this place, the next settlement. I'll be no trouble, I promise."

Sean shook his head. "No, 'tis out of the question."

Sarah drew herself up and pointed a finger at Brock. "When that man regains consciousness, he will come after me and kill me. He is a determined man. Would you leave me to such a fate?" Sean hesitated, and Sarah pushed her advantage. "I told you how he and his cohort have done away with Captain Hawkins. At sea this man led a mutiny. He took over the *North Star* and murdered several sailors in the bargain. If you leave me in New Orleans with Giles Brock alive, he will seek me out and kill me. My death will be on your head."

Sean paused before he spoke. "But madam, there must be some safe place you could stay. New Orleans is not that lawless a village."

"I would have no place to abide. I have no

funds. All I have is the poor clothing upon my back."

Sean gestured sharply. "I can't help you there, lass. I have no funds to hand myself." Then he sighed and shrugged. "All right, Mistress Moody. You may accompany me. At least for a distance. But do not expect any fancy villages on our way. All you'll find are poor settlements."

"They must be better than death."

"Then come, let us move along before your sculpin friend back there is with us again."

Sean led the way up the river slope. Sarah glanced back, remembering Tim. But he had gotten clean away, and they meant no harm to the lad. Sarah turned her face resolutely forward. In about thirty yards, she made out the shapes of four animals in the moonlight. Sean made soothing noises as the mules snorted at the presence of a stranger.

"I will have to shift the packs around, so you may have a mule to ride. I have only the one saddle. You may have use of that."

"I do not wish to inconvenience you any more than necessary, sir. I can manage well enough without a saddle."

"I have never been considered a great gentleman," Sean said curtly, "but I have better manners than that. So we'll say no more about it."

Sean quickly redistributed the load from one mule to two of the others. Then he helped Sarah up into the saddle and sprang nimbly onto the bare back of the fourth mule. He gestured with the long rifle. "Move out! You'll find a mule a stubborn creature, colleen. If he stops on you, drum your heels against his flanks. I think it best we put some distance between us and your friend back there, and quietly. If he doesn't know the direction you took, he will naturally conclude that you went into the city. By the time he learns differently, we will be well away."

They rode in silence for a time. Sarah found the gait of the mule quite uncomfortable. At first she kept trying to pull her skirts down. But it was not long before she stopped worrying about an unseemly display of limbs. Her inner thighs chafed, and her buttocks were pounded unmercifully. Soon it became almost unbearable. She gritted her teeth and endured, knowing she was going to be sore and stiff on the morrow.

After a lengthy time had passed, Sean, as though realizing her discomfort, said, "I think we have traveled enough for the moment. We will rest for a bit."

He pulled the mules off the well-defined trail under a towering cypress, with moss hanging from it like a shaggy beard. He slid to the ground and helped Sarah off her mule. Her legs almost gave way, and he had to catch her to keep her from falling.

"A mule is not a rocking chair," he said with a chuckle, "but you do get accustomed."

He led Sarah to the tree and eased her to the ground where she could lean back against the trunk. Before he joined her, Sean went to tend to the mules, allowing them to graze but hobbling them with long strips of rawhide so they could not wander far. Sarah noticed that he never relinquished his grip on the long rifle, and he often stopped with his head cocked, listening. Finally he left the mules grazing quietly on the short grass and returned to her. He leaned the rifle near at hand against the tree and sat down beside Sarah with a sigh. "Much as I am accustomed to a mule's back, even my backside suffers sorely after six months away from one of the beasts." He took a long clay pipe from a heart-shaped pipe holder, garnished with beads, which hung around his neck. "Mind if I smoke, colleen?"

"No, not at all."

She watched as he went through an involved process. He filled the pipe with tobacco from a pouch, then scraped together a small pile of dry twigs. From a pouch hanging on his chest, he took flint and steel, striking them together until he finally nursed a spark into a small flame among the scattering of twigs. He found a long stick, set the end afire, and applied it to the pipe. As the pungent smell of tobacco reached Sarah's nostrils, she remembered Jeb and his cigars. Tears filled her eyes. Angrily, she dashed them away. She was sorry he was dead, of course, but why should she weep for him? He had deflowered her by force, hadn't he?

While the small bonfire blazed, Sarah took her first good look at Sean Flanagan. He was a handsome man, if somewhat tall and on the thin side. Aside from the strange garb—buckskins and moccasins and coonskin cap—she now saw that there was a sort of harness that stretched over his left shoulder and down under his right arm. Hanging from it were two items she later learned were a powder horn and a bullet pouch, in which he carried rifle balls, flint and steel, and other necessary odds and ends.

Pipe going well, Sean settled back comfortably. "Now would you be so kind as to satisfy my curiosity? How came you in this country, Mistress Moody? You're English, 'tis little doubt of that."

Sarah was silent for a moment, gathering her thoughts. In the beginning she intended to relate

9

only the broad outlines, certainly omitting the loss of her virginity to Jeb. That was not something to tell this stranger. But she got caught up in the flow of her narrative, and she told it all, omitting nothing. Sean was a good listener, smoking on his pipe, not interrupting her once. When Sarah was finished, she felt a lift of her spirits, as though the telling of her misfortunes had acted as a catharsis. And then she tensed, wondering if this man would believe her, when no one else had.

The first thing he said surprised her. "It strikes me that your captain is something of a villian himself, the treatment he gave you, colleen."

"Well, he did save my life . . ." She broke off. Why on earth should she defend Jeb Hawkins, after what he had done to her? She glanced at Sean and saw that he was smiling amusedly.

"Could it be that he has a hold on your heart, Sarah Moody?"

"That's not true at all!" Sarah felt her face flush, and she looked away. "It's just that, to be fair, there was good in him, as well as bad."

"He could have listened to you in the beginning, and you would never have been placed in peril of your life," Sean pointed out.

Sarah was silent, stubbornly refusing to discuss it further. After a long silence, she said, "You have told me nothing about Sean Flanagan."

"There's not a great deal to relate. I'm a retired soldier and Irish adventurer, now spending my winters along the Arkansas, fur trapping."

"This fur trapping—I know nothing of that. What do you do?"

"I trap, or shoot, fur-bearing animals. A few beaver, otter, foxes, raccoons, muskrats, then sell their peltries."

"Does it pay well? I mean, who buys the furs?"

"Most of them eventually reach the fine ladies of Europe, to adorn their bodies. You are recently from England. Surely you have seen many adorned with fine furs?"

Sarah thought for a little, then shook her head. "I don't recall seeing such. Of course, as I told you, I had little to do with fancy society. Mistress Allgood was not one for adorning herself with fine clothes, jewelry, and such."

"Well, 'tis coming like a mighty tide. Most of the furs, I understand, are going to Paris and such great cities. The English, being a more austere race of people, are always tardy at such things, except for queens and the like. At least that's the way I've always observed them." His lazy grin flashed. "But mark me well. Within twenty, thirty years at the most, the wilderness west of the Mississippi will be swarming with fur trappers. All the way to the great mountins to the west I have yet to see, but have heard much of."

Sean sat up, knocking the dottle from his pipe. "Time we were moving on, colleen." He got to his feet and lent Sarah a hand up.

Sarah suppressed a groan. Her bones ached with pain and fatigue. "Why do you ride at night?"

"Two reasons. First, it's much cooler until we get farther north. And there are still some hostiles around."

"Hostiles?" Sarah felt a thrill of fear.

"Indians, lass. The Natchez and the Chickasaws have been sorely treated by the good citizens of

Louisiana. There have been several Indian wars over the past fifty years. Many of the Indians were wiped out hereabouts, but there are still pockets of them around. They'd like nothing better than to flush a lone man riding through with a mule train full of goods. They don't much favor attacking at night. Something about their gods not approving. But don't mistake me, they have been known to do so. That's why I'm never far from Katie here." He patted the long rifle propped against the tree.

"Katie?" she said in astonishment. "You give your rifle a name?"

"I do."

"Why is that?"

"Don't really know. I suppose it's because a man's life out here pretty much depends on his rifle. Oh, I carry pistols and a knife, but only a rifle is any good for distance. And when you need meat for the belly, you can't get close enough to game with a smaller weapon."

"I'm curious, Sean. Why a woman's name? Why not a man's?"

"Don't know that, either." Now he seemed embarrassed. He picked up the rifle and ran his fingers caressingly along the barrel. Catching her glance, he jerked his fingers away as though burned. Then he flashed that self-mocking grin. "Guess a man out here feels wedded to his rifle."

"A wedding of convenience, you might say," Sarah said dryly.

Sean threw back his head and bellowed laughter, so loud that one of his mules brayed in alarm. "You might say that, yes. I like you, Sarah Moody. I do admire a woman with good humor about her." Sobering, he turned. "Let's be on our way. Can't prattle the night away."

Sean gathered up the mules, gave Sarah a hand up, and mounted his own. He said off-handedly, "Kate was my sainted mother's name."

Then he rode out, taking the lead. As though he had talked himself out, he rode silently now. Soon Sarah was so tired, so aching and miserable, she took scant heed of where they were going and of the passage of time. The night seemed to go on forever.

Sean's cheerful voice snapped her out of a nodding doze. "We'll camp here."

Sarah lifted her head and gazed around. It was dawn, and cool, with mists swirling along the ground like smoke. She noticed that Sean had led them off the main trail into a small glade. With the mist, the moss hanging from the giant cypresses, and the gray dawn, there was an eerie quality about the scene. But Sarah was so near complete exhaustion she took little notice.

She saw Sean spread something on the ground near a tree. It was a strange-looking object, with fur on one side the color of rust.

Now Sean came to the mule and held his arms up. "Come along, lass, methinks you're worn out." She fell rather than climbed into his arms, and he half-carried her to the thing he had spread onto the ground, furry side up. He stretched Sarah out and kneeled beside her.

"What is this?" she asked.

"A buffalo robe, colleen. Pull it around you and you'll be snug and comforted."

He folded the robe around her, and Sarah settled down gratefully. The robe had a strong odor, rank, stinging to her nostrils, but she was too tired to care. Just before she drifted off to sleep, she was dimly aware of Sean still busy setting up camp.

Sarah awoke with a start. The sight that greeted her wrung a small cry from her lips. Two strange-looking men sat on small ponies a few feet away staring impassively down at her. They were slight and red-brown of skin. Obsidian eyes studied her with interest. Except for some pieces of cloth draped like a baby's diaper across their loins, they were naked and rode bareback. Each carried a bow strung across one shoulder and a quiver of arrows. Without once taking their eyes from Sarah, they babbled something in a language she found incomprehensible. She drew the robe tightly around her and looked about for Sean, but he was nowhere in sight. Another buffalo robe, empty, was spread on the ground a few feet away.

Had he deserted her? Sarah thought of trying to flee, but she was sensible enough to realize that she had no chance against the mounted men.

With shocking suddenness a bloodcurdling yell came from the trees behind her, and Sean burst out into the open, rifle held in his hands. It was the first time she had seen him in full light, and in his strange garb, he was a fearsome sight. And even stranger, she saw that he was grinning from ear to ear.

The ponies reared, pawing the air, and it took a moment for their riders to get them under control. Sean waited, rifle at ready.

Then he went into an exchange of the strange garbled language Sarah had heard the riders speak. Finally, without taking his eyes from the riders, Sean stooped and groped in one of the packs for two wrapped packages. He tossed one to each. The near-naked men caught them deftly, lifted them high, and screamed, "Eeei-ay!" Then drumming heels into their ponies' flanks, they rode off at a fast gallop into the woods.

Weak with relief, Sarah sat staring after them. When Sean turned to her, still grinning widely, she said, "I thought you had deserted me."

"I'm after thinking they gave you a fright, eh?"

She had noticed that, during moments of stress, Sean's Irish brogue thickened. She said angrily, "You're bloody right they gave me a fright! Waking up to see those two staring down at me would have given anyone a fright! What in Heaven's name were they?"

"Redskins. Indians. Part of the Natchez tribe."

"The hostiles you were telling me about?"

"Not that pair of sculpins." He shrugged. "Scavengers, beggars, probably outcasts from their tribe."

"Then why did you sneak off like that?"

"How could I know what they were until I had a chance to study on them?" he said with elaborate patience.

"So you sneaked away and left me to face them all alone!" she said indignantly.

"Colleen, if I had tried to wake you up suddenly, you'd probably have screamed, and if they *had* been hostiles, we'd've been hung out to dry. You were never in any danger. I wasn't that far away. If they'd made a move to harm you, old Katie here. . . ." He patted the rifle. "I had a bead on them."

Sean hunkered down and began to build a pile of twigs and sticks for a fire.

Sarah eyed this strange man curiously. "Sean, how did you know they were near?"

He said simply, "It's something you learn out here, if you have a hope of surviving."

After a moment Sarah looked around. "I need to . . ."

Without glancing at her, Sean gestured. "Plenty of trees and bushes, just a few yards away."

Blushing, Sarah said tartly, "I'd also like to wash. I'm grimy."

"There's a creek over beyond the first grove of trees. Use that." Now he looked around at her. A hint of annoyance glinted in the brown eyes. "We might as well get something straight, Mistress Moody. 'Twas your idea to tag along. So if the accommodations are not to your liking, that's your misfortune."

Sarah turned her back and marched off. The Indians were still in her mind, so she kept a wary eye out. But all she heard and saw were the chirping of birds in the trees and a few small animals scurrying away at her approach. Gradually, she relaxed her vigilance. It was peaceful here, and she had the feeling that there wasn't another soul within miles. It wasn't a bad feeling, she discovered to her surprise.

She found the meandering creek, little more than a trickle. She washed her face and hands as best she could and dried them on the hem of her dress. She examined herself ruefully. She was a mess—hair atangle, dress torn and filthy, pinned together here and there, the same dress she had worn all the way from London.

When she returned to the glade, Sean was crouched over a small fire, almost smokeless in the still after-

128

noon air. The odors of cooking food and brewing tea reached her.

She sat down across the fire from him. In one skillet he was frying a thick slice of ham, and in another, over a heap of coals, cornbread was cooking.

Sean leaned back on his heels and smiled over at her. " 'Tis sorry I am, colleen, for speaking harshly to you. I'm unaccustomed to having females along on my treks."

"I understand, Sean. I realize I must be a nuisance to you."

His smile broadened, eyes twinkling merrily. "But a beautiful nuisance, lass, a very beautiful nuisance."

Her color rose. "I don't know how you can say that, looking the way I do. This dress . . ." She gestured. "It's torn and filthy. And my hair—I don't know what I'm going to do with it!" She combed her fingers through it, working at a tangle.

"Squaws braid their hair. Might not be such a bad idea for you to do the same. I understand it stays cleaner that way, less tangles, less chance of collecting burrs and such."

"Squaws?"

"Indian women, colleen. In primitive country, you learn to adapt. As for the dress . . ." He studied her critically. "I don't see much can be done about that. I do have a pair of spare breeches and a hunting shirt. Both will be too big for you, but they'll be more comfortable, especially for mule riding. Course, a lady going about in breeches ain't considered proper." His glance was quizzical.

"I don't care about that. At least that way I can save the dress, such as it is, for later wear."

"Yep." His face smoothed out of all expression. He

bent to the fire. "Supper's ready. We'd better eat and be on our way."

After a few days they began to ride during the daylight hours. Sarah was more comfortable now. She had grown more accustomed to the mule's gait, and she had taken Sean's suggestion and was wearing his shirt and breeches. She was lost in them and looked somewhat clownish, but they were considerably more comfortable. She had also accepted his other suggestion and braided her hair. It now hung in long plaits, over her shoulders.

Riding by daylight now, Sarah discovered that the countryside wasn't as deserted as she had first thought. While they passed no villages, there were a good many farms along the river, some large enough to be called plantations.

"What crops do they grow, Sean?"

"Tobacco, rice, sugar cane, and lately, cotton."

The trail they were on stayed generally close to the river; most of the time it was in sight. Sarah noted a large number of rather odd-looking craft on the river, mostly heading toward New Orleans. They seemed to fall roughly into two categories. One was long and flat and looked like a number of planks lashed together. The other was also flat, but larger, more elaborate in design, with a long, low cabin, and seemed of a more permanent construction. All of those headed south were heavily laden. Sarah asked Sean about them.

"The smaller, all-flat ones are flatboats. They are floated downriver loaded with goods, unloaded in New Orleans, then broken up, the lumber sold. The others are something we've just recently seen on the river. They're called keelboats. They're far better built, have large crews, even living quarters on board. River traffic has increased considerably in the last year or so. It's only the beginning, I'm after thinking. And before you ask. . . ." He held up a hand. "No, few sailing vessels venture up the Mississippi. The river is wide, deep in many places, but it is full of sandbars and has never really been charted. Only craft drawing very little water dare use her."

Soon, the contours of the countryside began to change. It became hillier, much less settled. The cypresses and moss were less in evidence. The weather became cooler. Sean pushed the mules harder now. They rode from sunup to sundown.

When pressed for an explanation, Sean said shortly, "It's tardy I am. If I don't reach the hunting grounds before too long, winter will already have set in."

One day he told her they were in what was known as Upper Louisiana. "It's still Spanish territory, of course. But it's more lawless. The Spanish exert little real authority here. These people pretty much govern themselves."

One afternoon Sean drew his mule up short on a rise of land. As Sarah ranged alongside him, he pointed down into a valley. A small village squatted on the banks of the river.

"There it is, lass. The only village of any size we will be after seeing."

She looked down on the collection of mud huts and wooden shanties in dismay. "But it looks as primitive as can be!"

"That it is, Mistress Moody," he said dryly. "And teeming with the choicest collection of cutthroats and thieves to be found anywhere." He added shyly, "As well as whores."

"What will I do there?" she said, almost to herself.

"Don't be asking me. You refused to remain in the only real city along the river, and as you yourself said, 'It's better than death.' Of course . . ." He pointed down to a number of keelboats bumping against rickety wharves. "You might be able to beg a journey on a keelboat back to New Orleans."

"I can't do that!" she exclaimed. "I've explained why. Is there no other city near?"

"The only decent town north along the river is St. Louis. And I am not going there. From here I go north and west. To journey to St. Louis would take me weeks out of my way."

Sarah stood quietly looking down at the cluster of huts. Sean was right. She had begged him to take her to the nearest settlement, and he *had* warned her. He had done more than was fair. She must not burden him further.

She looked up at him and tried to smile. "I'd best change my clothes. You will need these, and it wouldn't look well for me to arrive in men's britches."

He sighed and eyed her thoughtfully. "Do you know how Indian women make their deerskin garments? The fur is scraped away very carefully, then they chew it inch by inch to soften it, so it will be suitable for wear."

"Ugh! Sounds disgusting!" Sarah shuddered. Then she stared at him. "But why tell me this?"

He sighed again. "Most fur trappers find a squaw to winter with them. I have never done so."

"Why not, pray?"

"That, Mistress Moody, is my own affair. The work is hard, the food has a sameness that begins to pall.

132

The winters are dreadful beyond belief, and the dugout acquires a stench like a charnel house ere long."

"Again, why relate this to me?"

"You have few choices, I'm after thinking. Try your furtune down there. Return to New Orleans on a keelboat." He paused. "Or accompany me on my winter's trapping."

"But that is a life I know nothing of. And you, sir, have been careful to detail the many hardships."

"All true. But I have been observing you, and you have adapted well to life on the trail, much better than I would have thought any fine English lady could. You are a strong woman, Sarah Moody."

"But wouldn't I only be a nuisance and a hindrance?"

"You will soon learn to be useful. I have been giving it much thought these past three days. It seems the only answer to your situation. And . . ." His gaze turned bold. "It does grow lonely for a man out there."

When his meaning sunk home, Sarah felt her cheeks burn.

"I will certainly treat you better, madam, than your rough sea captain. I am a man of much experience and—we-ell—delicacy in such matters." Then he added, deliberately callous, " 'Twill be far better then you would have fared in New York at the hands of soldiers. Or in a sporting house in New Orleans."

Sean paused. After a lengthy silence, he continued, "There are two other factors you might consider. By winter's end, the sculpin we left back there on the river bank will have given up the search for you. And if you make yourself useful, and if the winter's catch is fruitful, I will share with you, a quarter."

Sarah gave him a look of astonishment. "You would do that?"

"Foolish of me, I know." His glance slipped away. "But I believe in paying for value received. Besides . . ." Now his tone was self-mocking again. "I will only roister it away during the summer on wenches and games of chance. That is my usual custom."

"You argue persuasively, sir, but why you should bother, I do not know."

His bold look was on her again. "Should you be a man, colleen, you would understand."

Sarah ignored the implications of his remark and said, "I will go with you, Sean. It will be new to me, but it cannot be worse than the alternatives I am faced with. I hope I do not cause you much trouble."

"Then it is settled, Mistress Moody," Sean said briskly. "We start our journey now. We have a long, hard ride before us."

He clucked to his mule and led the way down the spine of the ridge. Sarah turned to look back once, for a last view of the river and the sorry village there. Then she turned her face resolutely forward. She tried to push any apprehensions of the future from her thoughts.

But one thing she could not avoid thinking about. This tall, strange man had made it clear that he would expect her to share his buffalo robes with him. She let her thoughts dwell on how it would be, on what would be expected of her. To her own amazement, she found the prospect not so displeasing as she would have thought.

PART TWO

The Wilderness

Chapter Ten

During the first few days, Sarah waited apprehensively every night for Sean to ask to share her buffalo robe. When he did not, she began to think that she had been mistaken about his intentions, that lying with her had not been in his mind at all.

They rode long distances every day, from sunup until dark, Sean driving the mules hard. Sarah was exhausted by nightfall, barely able to stay awake long enough to eat. But the long, hard riding and the pure, clear air gave her a ravenous appetite by the end of the day.

On the evening of the third day after they turned inland from the Mississippi, Sarah was watching Sean build a fire and start supper. "I do know how to cook, you realize," she said. "Before I entered the Allgood household, I cooked most of our meals at home, poor mother being so tired at the end of the day."

Sean smiled across the fire at her. "Out in the open, you cooked? Over a campfire?"

"Of course not!"

"It's an entirely different bit of business, lass."

"But I feel that I must do something to earn my keep."

"You will earn your keep, Sarah Moody. I will see to it. But as for cooking, I'm after thinking you'd better watch a while and learn. A man gets a growl-

10

137

ing belly after a long day such as this, and I don't care to have my supper mucked up, if you'll pardon me for saying so, colleen."

Sarah retired into a sulking silence, but she ate heartily enough when it was time, and she had to admit to herself that Sean made their limited fare tasty.

Soon the character of the land changed even more. Mountains loomed blue in the distance, and autumn brushed the foliage red, brown, and gold. Sarah had never seen a mountain before, and she said in awe, "How beautiful!"

Riding slightly in front, Sean glanced back. "What's beautiful? The fall colors?"

"That, of course, but I had reference to those mountains."

"Mountains? The Ozarks? Nothing but hills." Sean laughed. "If you ever clap eyes on the great mountains to the west, you'll know what I mean."

If possible, Sean tried to camp near water every night. Sarah was used to the grueling daily rides now and had a little more energy at the end of the day. She would retire out of sight of Sean at his cooking fire and bathe. The weather was changing rapidly, and the nights were chillier. The water in the streams and rivers was icy, and she finished her ablutions blue with cold, teeth chattering. She also noted another change in herself. Her skin, daily exposed to the sun, was turning a deep tan. Fortunately, with her dark coloring, she didn't sunburn easily.

Sean commented with a grin, "Won't be long before you'll be dark enough to pass for a squaw."

One afternoon, shortly before sundown, they rode into a small valley, with a meadow at the bottom. As they rode out of the trees, Sean reined his mule to a halt and held up his hand. "Shh, don't even breathe, Sarah," he whispered.

"What is it?"

Without speaking he pointed. In the center of the meadow, a deer grazed. Sarah had seen pictures of deer; this was the first one she had ever seen in the flesh. It was beautiful, graceful as a poem in motion. She was aware of Sean sliding off his mule. She glanced around just as he kneeled to one knee, leveling the long rifle.

Sarah started to cry out in protest, but she was too late. The rifle cracked, disturbing the quiet of the meadow. Birds flew up from the trees in wing-beating fright. She looked back around in time to see the deer give a great leap as though starting in flight, then fall to its side.

"Oh, how cruel!" she cried, glancing at Sean. "Killing such a lovely creature."

Getting up, Sean stared at her in open astonishment. "Woman, you constantly amaze me. Where we're going, we will live off wild creatures such as that. Or starve to death. Now we'll have fresh meat for days. And . . ." He grinned. "You can start chewing on the hide to make yourself a decent garment."

Sean unloaded the mules, staked them out, then went toward the dead deer. Sarah refused to go near as he kneeled beside the dead animal. Taking out his hunting knife, Sean carefully slit the hide up the belly and began to peel it off.

As he began to cut up the deer, Sean called over to her, "We'll camp here for tonight. If you are too finicky to help me, make yourself useful some other way. Gather wood for a fire, if nothing else."

Sarah collected firewood and stacked it underneath a large oak tree. It was growing dark. Glancing over at Sean, she saw that he was still busy with the deer. She washed in the stream, then came back and rummaged through the packs until she found the spare flint and steel. She had watched Sean start fires for two weeks now; she was sure she could do it. But it wasn't as easy as it looked. Stubbornly, she kept at it. Twice, she had a small blaze going, but each time she tried to blow it into a larger blaze, it went out. On the third try, she got it burning and soon had a nice fire going.

Sean came carrying the deerskin and hung it over a branch of the oak. He faced her, hands on hips. "Well, good for you, colleen. I knew you'd turn out to be useful."

Sarah felt herself flushing with pleasure.

Sean went back for the meat he had hacked off and hung most of it on the tree as well. Then he chopped off some long, green branches and trimmed them. Using four, he staked two branches on each side of the fire, lashing them together in the shape of an X. He sharpened the end of yet another stick, rammed it through a haunch of venison, and propped it in the apex of the crude spit. His hands were red with dried blood, with some splatters on his buckskins.

"I'm going down to the branch and wash. Think you can watch the meat and turn it slowly so it will brown evenly?"

"I can manage," she said, not daring to tell him that she felt revulsion at having to eat the flesh of the beautiful animal she had just seen killed.

Sean went to one of the packs and removed a fresh shirt, then disappeared in the direction of the stream.

Sarah tended to the roasting meat, and soon the mouth-watering odors coming from it overcame any reservations she had. Sean was gone a long time. By the time he returned, the meat was done to a turn, and Sarah had made a pot of tea.

Sean squatted beside her, rubbing his hands together briskly before the flames. "You've done fine, Sarah."

She looked at him curiously. Not only was he in a clean shirt, but he had shaved away the day's stubble of beard.

"How did you do that, shave away the beard? In cold water, and in the dark?"

"As I think I've mentioned, a man learns to do many things out here, if he's to survive."

With his knife he sliced off chunks of venison, spitting them on small sticks. He gave Sarah one. The meat was hot; she was so hungry she ate it before it had cooled sufficiently.

After she had surfeited herself, Sarah looked over to find that lazy smile of amusement on his face. He was handsome in the dying firelight.

"What do you find so humorous?"

"You, colleen. A while ago you were scorning me for slaughtering a beautiful creature. But I notice you've eaten your fill."

"A woman has to learn to do many things if she is to survive out here," she retorted.

Sean looked startled for a moment, then threw back his head and laughed. "*Touché!*"

"But I must agree that it tasted bloody marvelous," Sarah admitted shamefacedly.

His look was sober. "Regretting your decision, Sarah?"

"Well, not really. Not yet. I do admit to having shivers thinking about what I may be facing. But, as you so cleverly pointed out, I had little choice, did I?"

Sean was filling his pipe. "And *I* will admit that I have been wondering all this week if I would regret my offer."

"And have you?" she asked, in a much softer voice than she had intended.

Half-smiling, he looked at her over the pipe. "Not as yet. But I'm after thinking that 'tis only the beginning."

They fell silent then. Sean smoked, sunk in thought. Sarah pulled her buffalo robe around her and sat quietly staring into the dying fire.

Some time later, she heard Sean stir. He knocked out his pipe, got to his feet, and headed into the dark without a word to her. Sarah made herself ready for sleep. For the first few nights she had slept in the shirt and breeches Sean had given her. But she had found them uncomfortable for sleeping. Now she slipped out of them, put on her torn petticoat to serve as a nightgown, squirmed about until she found a soft spot, pulled the robe around her, and was asleep at once.

She awoke with a start, crying out. She was no longer alone in the robe.

"Shh, Sarah darlin'. It's all right. 'Tis only me, Sean."

He was naked as Adam. Before Sarah was fully awake, he had slipped her petticoat up above her waist and was caressing her body with gentle hands.

Sarah, still sleep-fuddled, instinctively started to protest. She had the feeling that underneath Sean's pretense of being a rogue and a rakehell, he was a true gentleman, and no matter how much he might desire her, he would not take her against her will.

But her half-formed protests were never voiced. After all, they had made a bargain, unspoken though it had been. She had to earn her keep, and what better way for a woman to pay a debt that with her body?

Also, she had to confess, the touch of his hand was pleasant upon her flesh. He was an attractive man, and she was not immune to his charm. As his hands tenderly explored her body, she did wonder why he had waited until tonight to come to her. Why wait until after he had made a kill? Sarah recalled reading that one way primitive man wooed a female was by killing game and making of it an offering to the lady of his choice. Was that what Sean had done, perhaps without consciously thinking of it in that way?

By now the stroking of his hands had made her breath quicken. There was none of the rough urgency Jeb Hawkins had exhibited. A warmth like a low fever suffused her. Now his hands found her breasts, and she felt a sweet ache in them. She felt her nipples harden. He kissed them, teasing each nipple with his tongue. As he turned, shifting, she felt the hardness of his manhood against her thigh.

Remembering the pain with Jeb, Sarah shrank away. Sean made a soothing, murmuring sound deep in his throat, much like the sound he made to the mules when they acted up.

"I'm not one of your bloody mules!" she said sharply.

"Then don't act like one," he said just as sharply.

Sarah went tense with anger, then relaxed as laughter overcame her.

Sean laughed along with her. "Just relax, colleen. I won't hurt you, I promise."

All the while, his caressing hands had never left her body. The sensations thus created smothered her fears, and she did relax, giving herself up to his ministrations.

He found her mouth. His breath had a sweet, faintly tart odor, and she knew that he not only had bathed while away in the woods, he had chewed on some fragrant plant.

For the first time she took note of his body. While not as broad and muscular as Jeb, he was well-muscled, his slender body hard yet smooth-skinned. Sarah opened her lips to him and was soon lost in the kiss. Waves of pleasure flowed over her, causing an ever-mounting heat that set up a wanting in her and burned away the last of her fears of what was to happen.

Almost involuntarily, she put her arms around him and pulled him closer. Her hands danced along the rippling muscles of his back.

"Sean . . ."

"Yes, darlin'?" he murmured.

"I want . . ." She broke off. "I don't know!"

Sean laughed softly. His fingers stroked her inner thighs, and Sarah was on fire. She began to toss and moan, head rolling back and forth on the robe.

Suddenly, his hands left her, and for a moment she was suspended in a timeless moment of need. Then he loomed over her, spreading her thighs.

Sarah tensed with a startled cry.

"Easy, colleen. Easy now. I'm not after hurting you."

She felt him inside her, not a brutal lunge, but a

tender probing. There was no pain, only a sensation of pleasant warmth that spread rapidly. He filled her completely and began to move gently, with exquisite slowness.

Sean waited until she started to move also, rising to meet his slow thrustings.

"Fine now, darlin'?"

"Yes, oh yes! Wonderful," she said hoarsely.

His movements increased in speed and force, and she matched him, movement for movement. Pleasure raced through her body like a series of tiny shocks.

Abruptly she experienced a new and wholly strange sensation, a gathering, an unbearable tension that she felt would bring her to the brink of madness if it did not ease. Then it did ease, an explosion of ecstasy, and she cried out sharply, cleaving to him.

Sean gave a joyous shout, his lean body rigid against her.

The shudders of ecstasy continued for a moment without time, receding in intensity, and Sarah finally fell back, knowing surcease.

Sean lay beside her, breathing heavily. "How does my loving match up to your captain's, lass?"

"That's not a question a gentleman would ask!"

Sarah tried to move away, but he caught her by the arm, holding her close. "Now, I don't be remembering that I ever made myself out a gentleman." Then he let her go with a sigh. "But I am begging your forgiveness, colleen. 'Tis none of my affair, your feelings toward the captain, especially him being no longer with us."

"I have no feelings for him," Sarah said stiffly. "None at all."

"Of course you don't," he said almost under his breath.

Sarah lay next to the warmth of his body, trying to sort out the sensations and feelings she had experienced in the past few minutes. It was a puzzlement, a pleasurable experience totally unexpected. But even as she puzzled over it, she drifted into sleep.

Sometime later, she awoke, instinctively feeling for Sean. He was gone. She raised her head. He was dressed again in his buckskins, squatting by the fire which he had built up again, smoking his pipe. His profile as he stared into the fire had an unusually solemn, brooding expression for him.

Sarah had the feeling that it was very late. "Sean," she called. "Are you all right?"

Without looking around, he said, "I'm fine, Sarah. Best go back to sleep. Soon time to be on our way."

Chapter Eleven

The character of the land continued to change. Sean guided them through a portion of the mountains he called the Ozarks, but they seldom climbed high, following low passes and riding through valleys. The wild beauty of the land enthralled Sarah. There was plenty of game now, and when their supply of fresh meat was low, Sean could always find another deer. She had gotten over her first revulsion and ate the meat he killed without qualms.

Besides, as he explained to her, "At home you ate meat, I'll wager. Pork, lamb, beef. That all came from living animals. The only difference is that they were tame creatures, bred for the slaughter. So where is the big difference?"

Sarah had to admit that he was right. She was doing most of the cooking now, and Sean complimented her. For the first few nights he worked on the deerskin, removing the hair from it and softening it considerably.

One night he gave it to her with an impish grin. "Now, colleen, if you want to get out of those breeches of mine, chew. Chew a bit at a time until it's soft enough to sew. There are other, mayhap more pleasant ways to do the thing, but I happen not to have the necessaries. But I do have an awl and strips of rawhide, things you'll be needing to make a garment from it. You *can* sew, I presume?"

"I can sew."

Before much time had passed, gamely chewing according to Sean's instructions, she had the deerskin soft and pliable, and had sewn it into a garment similar to that worn by the Indian women. She had long since thrown away the shoes she had worn all the way from London and now wore deerskin moccasins Sean had shown her how to make.

And now, almost every night, he shared her buffalo robe. Sarah looked forward to it now. Out here, it seeemed fitting to shed her gentility like a second skin and let her emotions and passions have free rein. She welcomed Sean into her embrace eagerly.

This pleased Sean immensely. "Ah, darlin', my judgment was sound, bringing you along. 'Twill be the best winter I have spent out here, us snug as two bugs in a buffalo robe while the winter rages away outside the dugout."

A tumble to Sean was a matter of joy and laughter. Often, they rolled and tossed on the ground like playful animals. Sarah found delight in teasing, fleeing from him, laughing, forcing him to chase and catch her. Many was the time they did this in broad daylight. In the moccasins she was, indeed, as fleet of foot as a deer, but naturally she always allowed him to catch her.

And, catching her, tumbling her to the ground, Sean would shove up the skirt and enter her, laughing all the while. " 'Tis far easier, you wanton lass, without the breeches!"

Never once did he profess anything more than generous affection for her. He talked not of love, nor of a future beyond the winter's trapping. Sarah was just as happy not to press it. She liked Sean very much, having developed a strong feeling for him, but she did not love him. She could not envision a life together with him. She knew him well enough by now to realize that he would chafe at a life where he was tied to a spouse and a family. He was a man born to be wild and free, to come and go as he pleased. If by some whim or artifice, she lured him into wedding her, Sarah knew intuitively that they would both be miserable within a very short time.

The weather as well as the terrain was changing. The farther north and west they traveled, the colder the nights became. Even the days, when the sky was overcast, were chill. Often, an icy, driving rain fell, and Sarah could see the true value of the buckskins and her deerskin dress: the garments shed water very well. If she had been wearing Sean's shirt and breeches, she would have been soaked to the skin, since he refused to seek shelter during the rain.

For almost a month now they had been riding, and Sarah had not once glimpsed a settlement or a dwelling of any sort, nor a white man or woman.

The only living things she saw, aside from the wild creatures, were Indians from time to time, astride their ponies at a distance, seldom more than a half-dozen at once. They never came close, just rode along for a time, keeping pace. Then they would vanish as they had come. For all the heed Sean paid them, they might as well not have existed.

After one group of eight had ridden parallel to them along a ridge for miles, then abruptly disappeared, Sarah said, "Are those the redskins you said were hostile, the ones we rode at night to avoid?"

"No, lass. The Indians out here are seldom hostile. They have had little contact with the white man and have no reason to hate or fear us. Most tribes on the Plains are peaceful. Oh, the Comanche and Apache tribes are warlike, and fight among themselves, or lead raids against other tribes, but contrary to most beliefs they rarely bother the white man. 'Twon't last long, I'm after thinking," he said dryly. "When the white men begin to swarm over the prairies and mountains in great numbers, cheating the Indian and slaughtering his game, and the Indian as well, he will turn on us. Fur traders have been cheating him for years, trading cheap beads and such-like for his furs. At the present time, the red man doesn't know he's being cheated, but he'll learn."

"Fur traders? I thought you told me you trapped your furs?"

"That I do, Sarah. But there are many out here who make their livelihood by trading for furs the Indians have trapped. But their furs aren't of good quality. The Indian has little knowledge of how to cure the pelts for sale. My way, it's more lucrative, and I don't have to bother with trade goods. Also . . ." He grinned lazily. "It's more fun my way, more sporting you might say. It's me against the beasts, not like I'm engaged in commerce, in haggling."

A few days later they wound down out of a pass and came upon a swift-running river.

"It's called the Arkansas. It's where I've trapped these two winters past, many miles up of course, where the tributaries run into it. Otter, beaver, muskrat, foxes— They're thick there. I built a dugout. If it's still there, it's where we'll winter."

"How much farther?"

"A distance yet, colleen. Two weeks hard riding, at least."

At the end of the first week, the mountains were behind them, the country flatter, the few hills lower. But they still rode along the north bank of the Arkansas; the river bottom was wide, with high bluffs on either side.

Late one afternoon, they came upon another, smaller stream emptying into the Arkansas from the north. A grove of alders, the few leaves left on their branches golden, stood at the bottom of the bluff.

Thirty yards from the grove, Sean drew his mule to a halt and raised his hand for Sarah to stop. Cupping his hands around his mouth, he shouted, "Halloo! J.J., you got company!"

Sarah, puzzled, could see no sign of any habitation.

Sean said, "Always remember, Sarah, when approaching someone's dugout or camp, call out first, or you might end up gutshot." He saw her look of puzzlement and pointed.

She looked in the direction he was pointing and saw a man emerging from the side of the bluff. He was enormous, with a flowing white beard, and carried the inevitable long rifle cradled in his arms. He ambled toward them like a great bear.

Then he threw his arms wide and yelled, "Hurraw, you Irish coyote!"

Sean slid down and went to meet the big man. They embraced fervently.

Then the big man stood back. "Late this year, ain't you, Sean? This child thought you wasn't coming for plew. Thought mebbe that lodge down there on the Missip had a bear trap's holt on you. Wagh!"

"Got a late start, J.J." Sean faced about. "I'd like you to meet Sarah, J.J. Sarah Moody. Sarah, this bear that walks like a man is J.J. Reed."

J.J. Reed squinted fierce brown eyes at Sarah. "You finally trapped a squaw, did you? This ole hoss thought you never would. She some punkin, too. Wait now . . ." His eyes widened. "She ain't Injun!"

"That she is not, J.J.," Sean said with his impish grin. Then, with a perfectly straight face, he added, "Mistress Moody is a lady's maid just off a ship from England."

"Lady's maid! From England! Wagh!" Eyes bulging, J.J. stared at Sarah in vast astonishment. "Hoss, you trying to fool this child! Tell me that you are!"

"No fooling, J.J.," Sean said solemnly. " 'Tis the Lord's holy gospel I'm after telling you."

"Wal now, hyar's damp powder and no fire to dry it!" Then J.J. Reed shrugged as though to dismiss Sarah from his mind, and thereafter he generally ignored her. "Whyn't you unload those critters of yours, stake'em out down there? Still some good grazing left. Then jine me. We'll smoke a pipe and swap a few yarns. Might have some victuals later on. I'll tell Many Tongues to toast up some boudin for us'uns to chomp on."

The big man turned away and disappeared into the side of the bluff.

Sarah stared after him open-mouthed, then turned on Sean to find him convulsed with laughter.

"Thought you might be a mite shaken by J.J."

"That's hardly the word for it." Sarah was full of questions, but the first one was: "What's boudin?"

152

Still laughing, Sean said, "Sure you want to know?"

"I wouldn't have asked if I didn't!"

"It's the intestines of a buffalo. Considered a great delicacy out here, when toasted lightly."

"Aaagh!" Sarah made a face. "And Many Tongues—I suppose that's his, uh, squaw?"

"His Indian wife, right. An Arapaho." Sean laughed again.

"Now what's to laugh about?"

"You'll see, colleen."

Sean started to unload the mules, stacking the saddle and the packs against a tree. Sarah helped him. Then he led the mules down to the small, triangular meadow formed by the juncture of the two rivers. After a glance at the hillside, Sarah scurried after him.

"J.J., you know, is unique amongst fur trappers," said Sean. "He's been here in this same spot for as long as I've been coming out here. And he's never once been back to civilization. He traps enough furs to purchase sugar, tobacco, the few other necessaries he can't get out here, sends the furs along with a trapper he can trust, then waits until the trapper returns with his necessaries. I've been that trapper for these two years past. I have some things for him in my packs."

"You mean he hasn't seen anyone but his, uh, wife and a few trappers in all that time?"

"That's right, Sarah. Oh, a few Indians, of course. He gets along just fine with the Indians. For one thing, they think he's a little addled in the head, a notion he's after deliberately cultivating. The Indians are leery of a man they think mad. But J.J. is far from mad. A little eccentric, perhaps. But he's sharp

II

as a fox." Sean grinned. "Some say the J.J. stands for Jackass, he's so stubborn. But I wouldn't advise calling him that to his face."

"I should think he'd *go* mad from just plain loneliness."

"Not J.J. He says he's seen all the civilization he ever wants to see. He's happy as a bee in clover here. I like the old coot, granting you'll think him a little strange."

Sarah noticed a small cleared area off to one side, which showed signs of having been tilled, with some dead stalks remaining. She motioned. "What does he grow?"

"Oh, that's Many Tongues' vegetable garden. And . . ." He grinned. "Corn. For cornmeal, of course, but mostly for J.J.'s corn liquor."

"He makes liquor from corn?"

"He does, and wait until you taste it. Tastes like ambrosia and has a kick like a mule." As they started back toward where the packs were, Sean said, "A word of caution, Mistress Moody: Out here, people don't take kindly to their guests refusing whatever fare is offered them. Many Tongues especially might not take to it if you spurn her cooking." With a straight face, he added, "Has been told to me that she has a mean streak of temper, with a knife always somewhere on her person."

From the stack of packs, Sean selected one, and they started toward the hillside. Sarah could still see no sign of a habitation, but then Sean pushed aside a curtain of thick shrubbery, and she saw a low doorway, framed with logs. The heavy door stood open. Sean made a mocking half-bow, and Sarah preceded him inside.

It was so dim inside she could see nothing at first. The immediate thing that struck her was the rank odor; a smell of mingled wood smoke, various and stale food odors, animal hides, and unwashed humans. As her eyes gradually became accustomed to the dimness, Sarah saw that she was in a sort of cave dug back into the hillside. The low ceiling was of rough-hewn, smoke-blackened logs. The front and the back were also of logs, the other two sides and the floor nothing but earth. On the back wall was a crude fireplace, in which a fire blazed. There was some sort of chimney, but it seemed to Sarah that most of the smoke escaped into the one room, the air stale and heavy with it.

The dugout was a great clutter, with scarcely room to move about. Traps and hides and haunches of smoked meat hung on the walls. A few buffalo and bear rugs were scattered haphazardly about on the tamped-down, dirt floor. And in one corner Sarah saw what she supposed was a bed—many willow branches crisscrossed within a log frame, with two buffalo robes tossed carelessly atop it. There were no chairs. J.J. Reed sat cross-legged on a buffalo robe before the fire, and a small female form was bent over something cooking in the fireplace.

Sean said, "Brought you a few things, J.J.," and tossed the pack which J.J. caught deftly.

"Bacca?" the big man said eagerly. "I been out these past two moons."

"Oh, did you be after needing tobacco?" Sean said with that innocent look. "Sorry, I forgot."

"Irish pissant speak with forked tongue." J.J. was already digging into the pack. He came up with a large leather pouch. He sniffed, a beatific smile on his face. "Wagh!" He heaved his bulk upright. "I'll go fetch the corn squeezings, Sean."

As he went out of the dugout, the woman turned from the fire, and Sarah was amazed to see that she was tiny, delicate, very lovely, and young. It was hard to guess J.J.'s age, yet Sarah judged that this woman was less than half as old.

"Many Tongues," Sean said, "this is Sarah, Sarah Moody."

The Indian woman giggled behind her hand and darted off into the dimness of one corner without a word.

"Doesn't she speak English?" Sarah whispered.

"Better than J.J. Or so he claims. She talks his ear off when they're alone, but I've never heard her speak a single word. Not even in her own language. That's why J.J. calls her Many Tongues."

"That's not her real name?"

"No, it's one J.J. hung on her."

"Here we be, Sean!" It was J.J. returning, carrying an earthenware jug. "A jug of my own special horse piss. This child keeps it cooling in a spring alongside the dugout."

Many Tongues brought four huge mugs. J.J. tilted the jug up and filled the mugs to the brim. Many Tongues gave Sean one and came to Sarah with another, ducking her head shyly, doe eyes shining.

Sarah gazed dubiously down into the mug. It looked harmless enough, as clear as spring water. The others all sat before the fire. Sarah arranged herself awkwardly on the ground beside Sean.

J.J. held his mug up in a toast. "Hyar's to a winter of fine peltries, Sean."

"I'll drink heartily to that."

Both Sean and J.J. drank, and Sarah noticed that Many Tongues also drank. Well, if she can do it, Sarah thought, so can I!

She drank from the mug, too much, too quickly. It went down smoothly enough. But a second later her throat was on fire, and the liquor exploded in her belly. She coughed wrackingly, almost strangling. Laughing, Sean pounded her on the back. Even in her distress, Sarah experienced a flash of poignant memory—of Jeb doing the same on board the *North Star* when she'd gulped down too much brandy.

She gasped out crossly, "Leave me alone!"

Sean gave her a puzzled glance, then desisted, turning back to J.J. Thereafter, Sarah drank sparingly of the fiery liquor.

After a little Many Tongues got up and forked something from the coals onto pewter plates. Sarah, already warned by Sean, knew what it was. She scarcely dared look at the object on her plate. The others ate with sounds of delight. When Sarah caught the Indian woman's gaze on her, she hastily nibbled at the boudin. Despite its unsavory appearance, it had a smoked, tart taste that was flavorful on the tongue. Still, Sarah couldn't help but think of what it was, and her stomach heaved. Fearful she might vomit, she quickly washed it down with a sip of the whiskey.

The combination of weariness from the long day's ride, the warmth of the fire, and the effects of the liquor soon put Sarah into a rosy, sleepy state. Sean and J.J. were talking animatedly, with much rough laughter; their voices reached Sarah as from a distance.

Many Tongues was busy now about the fire. Sarah

watched her graceful movements and wondered anew what combination of circumstances had placed this lovely young woman into the buffalo robes of such a primitive as J.J. Reed. Into the buffalo robes! Sarah laughed softly to herself. She was beginning to sound like a trapper's woman!

The food, when served, was very good. Buffalo steaks, Sean told her. It had about the same taste as the deer meat, if somewhat stronger in flavor. Along with it, Many Tongues served boiled potatoes and carrots; vegetables she had grown herself, Sarah assumed.

After the meal was finished, Many Tongues started to collect the dishes. Sarah whispered in Sean's ear, "Should I offer to help her?"

Sean shook his head in the negative. Many Tongues scraped the dishes into the fire, which didn't help the odor inside the close dugout. Now J.J. poured two mugs of whiskey, not offering the women any this time. Sarah didn't want any, yet she thought it rather rude of him. Now both J.J. and Sean got out their pipes—J.J.'s was made of cottonwood bark—and filled them from the leather pouch of tobacco. To Sarah's amazement, Many Tongues squatted on the other side of J.J., filled and lit a pipe of her own. Soon the smoke from the fire and the three pipes was overwhelming. Sarah realized that it would do no good to complain, which left her with a choice of staying or going outside, so she kept her mouth closed.

Without preamble, J.J. said, "Ten years this child has trapped along the Platte and the Arkansas. Reckin I will die out hyar. I've thought of going back to my old state, but who's left thar to member me? Been thinking I'll soon move on to the big mountains to the west, Sean. No more settlements for this child. And it's getting too crowded around hyar."

Sean laughed. "J.J., you haven't got a neighbor for miles! I'll probably be the closest, and that's a week's ride from here."

"Even that's too close for comfort, hoss. I recollect a time when I didn't see a white face for years on end. Sent my peltries in by Indians, friends of Many Tongues here. I ever come to tell you how I came by her, hoss?"

"At least once a year you tell me."

Ignoring him, J.J. rambled on, "This child knew she was some punkin when I first clapped eyes on her. And she took to me right off. Her pap, Swift Eagle, wanted a dozen horses for her. Took my whole year's catch to buy them horses. But it turned out not to be so easy. Seems the son of the chief had his eye on her, too. And this old chief didn't lean much toward the white man. Seems some Spanyard bastid caught one of his squaws out in the bushes and taken her at the point of a knife. But this child had already struck a bargain with Swift Eagle. A brownskin's honor is sacred, you know that, hoss. But the old chief was a sly one. He said his son, Little Elk his name was, he says Little Elk's heart would be broke forever unless he didn't at least contest for her. And the chief also decided that the fight would be on horses, bareback, and with tomahawks. Wagh!" J.J. spat into the fire. "You know I never been on friendly terms with them critters. Much rather walk than ride. The old brownskin knew this, o'course. But wasn't much this child could do if I wanted Many Tongues. By that time we'd snuck off into the bushes a few times." J.J. grinned, and beside him Many

Tongues giggled. "I was younger then and some hot-blooded. Knew I have to have her to share my buffler robes. So I figgered out something made it more even. You know what that was, hoss?"

"I'm after thinking you're going to tell us, J.J."

"The only rules set up by the chief was that we would ride at each other. The first one to whomp t'other off his horse would win Many Tongues. So I cut me some long strips of rawhide and had Many Tongues tie my feet together under the horse's belly. Know why that was, hoss?"

When Sean didn't respond, Sarah, who had been caught up in the tale, leaned forward to say, "So you wouldn't fall off the horse!"

Beaming, J.J. spoke directly to her for the first time since they'd entered the dugout. "In a way, Sarah Moody. But that ain't the whole of it. You see, some years back I had found one of them suits of armor down south a ways, left behind by a Spanyard soldier under that Coronado feller way back in 15 and 40, somewheres around there. It was a curiosity, and I lugged it back to my lodge. It had rusted some and was a tight fit. Seems them Spanyards back in them days was all little fellers. But I got the top part on me, protecting my upper parts, and that there metal headpiece. Purty hard to see out of them little bitty slits, but I managed her. Reckon I was some fearsome sight to them brownskins." J.J. spat again and laughed uproariously. "That Little Elk probly shat his breechclout at the first sight of me. But he had gumption, did that Injun. So we had at each other. I was some awkward, carrying all that iron on me, and like to wore that Injun pony out. Little Elk stuck to his horse like a burr, and he whacked me with that

160

there tomahawk agin and agin, but always he hit that iron chestplate or the iron face thing. This child's ears was ringing, 'til I couldn't've heard it thunder. But otherwise he didn't hurt me none. He just kept coming, and this child kept swinging away. My guess is that the thing went on 'bout an hour. I'd get in a half-assed lick now and then and had him bleeding some. But I finally did her. Holding that tomahawk in both hands, this child took a mighty swipe at Little Elk as he came riding by and knocked him ass over tumbleweed off'n his horse. Wagh! He was bleeding some, but not hurt bad. And that's how I won Many Tongues hyar!"

J.J. looped an arm around Many Tongues and hugged her fiercely. Roaring laughter, he said, "You know what them Arapahos called me after that? Iron Rider!"

J.J. filled his and Sean's mugs again, and within minutes was deep into another yarn. Sarah was yawning, barely able to keep her eyes open. Sean, noticing this, said, "You'd better bed down, Sarah. I'll go fetch our buffalo robes."

In a little while Sarah was bedded down in one corner of the dugout. Many Tongues had also retired to the willow bed. Almost asleep, Sarah heard J.J.'s rumbling voice. "Sean, what for you bringing a female like that out hyar? She probly fine in your robes, but what good she gonna be to your trapping?"

"But you see, J.J., I didn't have to pay twelve horses for her." Sean laughed softly. "Did have a little tussle, but didn't amount to much. Otherwise, you see, she came free."

You're going to regret that remark, Sean Flanagan, Sarah thought drowsily and went to sleep.

She didn't know how long the two men sat up talking. Some strange noises woke her much later. The fire had died down, and Sean was in his robe close beside her. She raised her head, trying to identify the noises. Then she figured it out. J.J. and Many Tongues were thrashing about on their bed. Sarah was shocked. Making love right in the room with two strangers! Didn't they have any sense of decorum?

Riding out early the next morning, Sarah said, "Do you know what J.J. was doing to Many Tongues last night?"

Sean grinned. "Knowing how randy the old codger is, especially when well stoked with that white lightning of his, I can well imagine."

"But that's shocking! With guests, strangers at that, in the same room! They woke me up!"

"Went at it good, did they?" he said. "Too bad I was so weary or we could have joined in the sport."

"We certainly would not have, not in the same room with other people!"

"'Tis a common thing in an Indian tepee."

"Well, I'm not a savage, not yet! And that reminds me, Sean Flanagan. I heard what you told J.J. last night. Got me for free, did you?"

"We-ell, it's true, ain't it?" he drawled.

"We'll just see, Sean Flanagan! You can sleep in your own robe tonight!"

She drummed her heels in the mule's flanks and startled the animal enough to send him into a trot for all of twenty yards. Sean's soft laughter followed her, and Sarah's face flamed.

Her resolution didn't last long. They had to camp

early that evening. The day had grown sullen, sultry, very warm for the time of the year.

Sean said, "We'd better find a dry place to camp early tonight. A thunderstorm is on the way, I can feel it."

A few miles farther on, Sean located an overhang along the river bluff, a huge rock jutting out, forming a near cave. While Sarah quickly unloaded the mules and stored the packs under the overhang, Sean scrounged up enough firewood to last for the night. For supper they had steaks J.J. had given them from the buffalo he had recently killed. Supper was finished and Sean was sitting back with his pipe going, when the storm struck. It was an awesome sight. Lightning crackled in blinding flashes, and thunder rolled like continuous cannon fire. Rain came down in solid sheets, churning up white froth on the river. Sarah saw lightning balls rolling along the prairie across the river. And directly across from them a huge cottonwood tree was struck by lightning. It splintered and burned fiercely for a few minutes before the driving rain put it out.

The closest Sarah had ever come to a storm of this magnitude was the display of Saint Elmo's fire on board the *North Star*. The thunder and lightning both frightened and excited her.

She retired to her buffalo robe, head propped up so she could still watch. Sean knocked out his pipe, piled wood on the fire, and unrolled his robe a distance from hers. He made no move to come to her.

In a small voice Sarah said, "Sean?"

"Yes, colleen?"

"Aren't you coming over?"

"Just this morning you said . . ."

163

"Damn you, Sean Flanagan!" she said hoarsely. "Come over here!"

Sean, realizing this was no time to laugh or tease her, rolled over onto her robe without a word.

She came against him, her mouth hot on his. She made love with a wanton intensity he had never seen in her before. Gone was the genteel lady who approached lovemaking with shyness and some trepidation. True, there had been times these weeks past when she had entered into it with abandon and laughing enjoyment. But tonight there was a sultry, demanding passion he had not glimpsed in her. She entered into the bout of love with the raging fierceness of the storm, her face briefly seen in the lightning flashes wild and sightless.

When it was all over, Sarah gave a great sigh and went immediately to sleep in the crook of his arm. Sean lay sleepless.

He had suspected it for some time, but now he could no longer avoid it. He was in love with Sarah Moody. He, Sean Flanagan, who had taken wenches where he could find them, of all races and over most of the world, going his merry way afterward without a qualm or regret. Never once had he considered wedding any colleen. He had thought himself a free spirit, never a man to be tied down to one woman for the rest of his life. Now, within a matter of short weeks, that had changed.

Of course, he had absolutely no intention of telling Sarah. She was in love with Jeb Hawkins. She didn't realize it herself, yet Sean was convinced of it. And how could he compete with a dead man, with the memory of a dead man? If she could never be wholly his, he would not be happy. He couldn't live with

Sarah with a ghost haunting her. The way she had made love just now—she hadn't been making love to Sean Flanagan, but to Jeb Hawkins!

Some time during the night, the rain turned to hail, then to snow, and when Sarah awoke at sunrise, there was a dusting of white over everything. The still unmelted hailstones glittered like jewels in the first rays of the rising sun. Everything looked new and fresh and white, and Sarah remembered the winter snows in London. Only short hours after a snowfall there, the pristine snow would be fouled with a peppering of soot. The sky here was cloudless, and so bright when the sun came up, the glare hurt her eyes.

Sarah sat up, yawning. Sean was already up, stoking up the fire. Hearing her, he glanced around. "Sleep well, did you?"

"Quite well, thank you."

"I shouldn't be after wondering."

"And what exactly does that mean?"

"I'm after thinking that anyone would sleep well following the exercise you had last eve." His bold gaze moved down.

Sarah realized that she was completely naked to the waist. In a rush of memory she recalled in detail the events of last night, and she felt herself turn a fiery red.

She snatched the buffalo robe up to her shoulders. "You have a guttersnipe mind, Sean Flanagan!"

"All too true, darlin'. Me and J.J."

Laughing that soft laugh, he turned back to the fire. Sarah hurriedly pulled on her clothes. The marvelous air gave her a good appetite, and she ate everything on her plate. By the time she was finished packing away the cooking utensils, Sean had the mules ready to go. They mounted up and rode along the river bottom. Before long the sun had melted all the snow from the ground. As they crested a small rise, Sarah drew in her mule with a gasp of awe. To the west towered great mountains, their peaks white with snow.

"My God!" she exclaimed. "What's that?"

"The western mountains I told you about. They call them the Rockies."

"They look so close, not more than a day's ride."

"The air is deceptive out here, Sarah. I assure you they are many leagues distant. It would take us many days of hard riding to reach them."

"I've never seen anything so—so beautiful, so awe-inspiring!"

"That they are, lass, that they are."

They pushed on, riding hard again until dark every night. Midway on the fifth day, they came to another fork in the river, a smaller stream tumbling down from the north into the Arkansas. The surrounding area reminded Sarah very much of the place where J.J. Reed had his dugout.

Sean held up his hand, signaling a halt. He slid off his mule. "You stay here, Sarah."

Carrying his rifle at ready, he approached the bluff about fifty yards distant with caution. A heavy growth of shrubs obscured the bottom of the bluff. Sarah blinked as Sean suddenly vanished from sight.

Minutes passed, and she grew apprehensive. Then he reappeared, smiling as he came toward her.

"It's all right. You never know when some sculpin has moved in and taken over your digs. But from the look of it, nobody's been around."

He led the mules up to the shrubbery and began to unload the packs. He gestured. "Go ahead, colleen." He grinned slyly. "Have a peek at where you'll be spending the winter."

Sarah got stiffly down off the mule and forced her way through the thick shrubbery until she saw logs set into the bluff and the open door. She went in and stopped, appalled. It was similar to J.J.'s dugout, except it was empty—empty of everything but dust, piles of debris, and cobwebs. Cobwebs hung like thick nets from every corner. The interior had a rank, musty odor.

At a sound from behind her, Sarah whirled. "This place is filthy, not fit for human habitation!"

"Then it's your task to make it fit," he said curtly, dumping the packs he was toting. "I'm going to be busy from dawn to dusk. Late in the year as it is, I have to gather as many otter, fox, and muskrat furs as possible before we're snowed in."

During the next few days, Sarah worked until she was tired enough to drop. She made a broom of twigs bound to a willow limb and swept until she slowly brought some neatness and order to their quarters. Sean was out every day with his rifle and traps, and the only thing he did to help her inside, was construct a bed of soft, sweet-smelling boughs in one corner, over which he spread their buffalo robes. The outside wall of the dugout was soon hung with animal pelts of various kinds, drying and stinking to the heavens. Finally Sarah had done all she could. At least the place was livable. The hardest chore of all was clearing it of the rats that had moved in during the summer.

Only the nights, on the bed Sean had made, gave

her any pleasure. Sean was still the gentle, skillful lover she had come to know so well, and she grew more and more fond of him.

One morning into their second week, Sean, rising with the dawn as usual, called to her from the doorway. "Sarah lass, come look!"

As Sarah got out of the robes, she suddenly noticed how cold it had become overnight. She threw on her clothes, draped one of the buffalo robes around her shoulders, and went outside. She found Sean just beyond the bushes screening the dugout entrance.

He made a sweeping motion with one hand. "Look! Winter's here."

Everywhere she looked the earth was covered with a thick blanket of white. It was a beautiful sight, yet Sarah felt a sudden ache of sadness.

The snow did not lay evenly on the prairie, but in long wind-rows where the storm had blown it. The undulating snow reminded Sarah of the ocean—of course different in color—but it still brought back the memory of those nights on board the *North Star* when she had stood at the railing and looked long at the heaving sea.

It reminded her of the *North Star*—and of Jeb.

Her heart ached with grief, and yet she was angry at herself.

Would there never come a time when something would not suddenly remind her of Jeb? Jeb was dead; she would never see him again. But the undeniable truth of this did nothing to ease the dull ache of loss she felt.

Chapter Twelve

The first thing Jeb Hawkins noticed on regaining consciousness was cold, cold seeping into his very bones. He was shivering and wet, his clothes sodden. The next thing he noticed was movement, movement like that of a ship sailing in smooth waters.

Jeb opened his eyes and tried to move. Pain rocketed in his skull, and he recalled the moment on the river bank and the blow on his head from behind. He groaned.

"Captain Hawkins?" A face leaned over him. It was very dark, a mist shrouding everything, and he had to squint before he finally recognized Tim.

"Tim? Where are we?"

"You're to lie still, Captain. You suffered a terrible knock on the head, then Rhys Pommet rowed out to the middle of the river and rolled you overboard."

"What saved me?"

"I did, Captain," Tim said diffidently. "When he struck you down, I seized my chance and fled. They let me get away. I hid in the reeds and watched Pommet row away from shore with you. Then I swam out. I was a few yards away when he rolled you overboard. The river was clogged with mist and he could not see me. I went down and brought you to the surface."

"And Sarah? Sarah Moody?"

"I know not what happened to her, Captain," Tim said dolefully.

Jeb was swept by a great sense of loss. If Giles Brock had tried to murder him, he certainly would not have hesitated to kill Sarah. Alone, a woman, who would have defended her? Undoubtedly she was dead.

Jeb experienced a flood of guilt and pain. If he had believed her story and left her behind in London, she would be alive now.

He sighed and struggled to sit up. "Help me up, lad."

"Captain . . ."

"Damnation, boy! So I got a knock on the head and almost drowned! By the Lord Jehovah, that doesn't mean I have to lie on my arse for the rest of my life!"

Tim helped him up. There was some sort of low structure behind Jeb, and Tim maneuvered him until he was propped against it. Jeb fumbled in his pockets for a cigar, then laughed at his stupidity. If there were any cigars on his person, they were ruined.

For the first time he tried to take stock of his surroundings. They were on water, no doubt of that. The low, thick fog prevented him from seeing much. The craft was wide and flat, and he could hear a slapping sound, like oars in the water.

"What kind of a craft is this, Tim?"

"I'm not sure, Captain. It's not a ship exactly," Tim said cautiously. "But be grateful for them, sir. They came along just in time to save us. My strength was nigh gone, and we would have sunk together. . . ."

"You're aboard my keelboat, Captain," said a cheery voice.

Jeb looked up to see a rolypoly man of about fifty emerge from the swirls of fog. Wearing rough clothing, he had an unruly mop of ginger-brown hair streaked with gray and a round face with ruddy cheeks. Brown eyes twinkled merrily.

"You have the advantage of me, sir."

"Charles Clayborne, Captain. I suppose you could call *me* captain, but we don't go in much for fancy titles." Clayborne threw back his head and laughed. "Nothing fancy about my boat either. Built strictly for hauling cargo up and down Mrs. Sippi."

Jeb said, "You have my gratitude, sir, for saving my life."

" 'Twas nothing more than any Christian man would do. Although I must needs admit there be many scalawags working the river who'd not bother to take on nonpaying passengers. And your thanks should go to your lad here." Clayborne ruffled Tim's hair. "Without him, you'd be feeding the fishes about now."

"Speaking of paying passengers, Mr. Clayborne, my pockets are empty."

Clayborne shrugged. "No matter. You'll take up little space, since we're going back north with the decks mainly empty. Of food, we have plenty, and you and the lad are most welcome to it."

"Perhaps I could do some work aboard your, uh, keelboat, to pay our way?"

"We can always use an extra pair of hands for poling and such. It's a long, hard haul up Mrs. Sippi, when she's low as she is this time of the year. We average a mile an hour, and we're fortunate."

"What's your destination, Mr. Clayborne?"

"St. Louis, Captain Hawkins." At a hail from a voice in the fog on the other side of the boat, Clayborne turned his head and bellowed, "Hold your water, blast you! Be right there." He spat on the planking, "Have to watch'em every minute." He nodded to Jeb. "You'd better get below, friend Hawkins, and dry out. Have a cuppa tea and some hot soup. There's a fire down there." He bent down to tap Jeb on the shoulder, then strode briskly off into the mist.

Jeb got to his feet and followed Tim around the structure he'd been leaning against. There was a glow of light from an open doorway, an opening so low Jeb had to stoop almost double to pass under. Down a short flight of steps, they found themselves in a long, low room, with a small fire burning in a stone hearth in the center. Jeb realized that the room—or cabin—was half-below, half-above the waterline. It was not furnished; sleeping robes and bedding were strewn about, and there were a few cooking utensils around the smoking fire. The low ceiling was smoke-blackened.

A gnome of a man squatted by the hearth. He glanced up as Jeb and Tim approached. "You be the pair snatched out'n the river, I'd gather," he said in a grumbling voice. "Not enough to have to feed the louts we have on board. Have to go and hoist aboard a pair of strays, wet as water rats."

"Mr. Clayborne said to come below to get dry and have a bowl of soup," Jeb said stiffly. "But if it's too much trouble, I will go and inform Mr. Clayborne that he need not go to the bother."

"Not so, not so, Squire," the gnome said hastily. "If Cap sent you down, he would have my arse in bloody bits if'n I turned you away. Cap is a man well known for his hospitality."

Jeb's curiosity stirred. "Then Mr. Clayborne *is* a captain?"

The gnome turned a wizened monkey's face. It wore a grimace Jeb supposed was meant to be a smile. "Not by sailor's terms, he ain't. But we'uns call him that. He's known up and down the river as Cap."

Tim and Jeb squatted on their haunches by the meager fire, while the gnome poured tea into great mugs and ladled thick soup into wooden bowls from a pot suspended over the fire. The tea was hot but bitter. Jeb made a face at the taste, but he sipped, seeking warmth in his belly. Then the gnome picked up a rum bottle and splashed a dollop into Jeb's mug. He raised an eyebrow in Tim's direction, and Jeb nodded. The small man tilted the rum bottle sparingly over Tim's mug.

Jeb took another sip of the tea. The rum had improved the taste a great deal. Heat went through his blood like a fever. And the soup, surprisingly, was very good. It was thick, with chunks of potatoes and other vegetables, as well as morsels of well-cooked beef floating in it.

The gnome took an odd-looking pipe from his pocket, stuffed tobacco into it, and lit it from a coal scooped from the hearth between calloused fingers. Jeb's shivering had decreased. The cabin, if such it was, smelled foul and was filled with eddies of smoke from the fire. There was a hole in the roof directly above, but little of the smoke escaped that way.

The odor of the smoking pipe made Jeb long for a cigar. He asked, "What sort of pipe is that? I have never seen such."

The gnome gave a cackle of laughter. " 'Tis of my own making. Call it a corncob, I does. I made it from a hollowed-out corncob and a reed. Draws well and has a fine flavor once 'tis well used."

"I don't suppose there would be any cigars on board?"

"Afraid not, Squire. When we get to St. Louie, you might buy some seegars there."

A cheerful voice broke in, "Feeling better now, friend Hawkins?"

Jeb glanced around at the rotund figure of Cap Clayborne.

"We are indeed, and much thanks to your hospitality, sir."

"'Tis my privilege." Cap squatted down beside them. Rubbing his plump hands together briskly, he said, "How about a cup of that witches' brew you call tea, Ezra? And don't forget the tot of rum. Ezra likes to hoard the rum portion for himself. A sot, he is. Without rum to sweeten it, his tea would gag a man." He accepted a mug of tea and rum and took a sip. "Have you met our cook, Ezra Boggs, friends Hawkins? Leastways, he calls himself such."

"Ha, make sport of me all you like, Cap. None of these other river rats can put together victuals fit to eat!"

"True, Ezra, true." To Jeb, Cap said, "Ezra here has been with me since I started keelboating on the river, some two years now. The only one who has stayed. I have to scratch up a new crew every trip, Captain. Work on a keelboat is hard, and most get a bellyfull of it on one trip."

"I am afraid I am no longer entitled to be called captain, Mr. Clayborne," Jeb said gloomily.

Cap's brown eyes turned serious. "And why is that, sir?"

After a moment's hesitation, Jeb told him an edited version of what happened.

At the finish Cap nodded. "It would seem you have indeed been ill-used by villains. I can understand your predicament. As a lad, I sailed the oceans of the world. The life is too hard for the likes of me. And many's the time I have seen a ship's master deprived of his livelihood for a reason not his own doing. But look on the bright side, friend Hawkins. Did you ever think you might be the better free of it?"

"I have known naught but the sea since an early age."

"That doesn't mean you cannot make your way in another trade, man. This is a land of great opportunity for a stout fellow of sense and enterprise. Soon as this fuss with King George is settled, this old river out there will be busy the likes of nothing nobody has ever seen before. And after all . . ." Cap's eyes twinkled. "Just because a wench has been a whore does not mean she cannot change her colors."

Cap's words brought the image of Sarah full-blown into Jeb's mind. The remark was queerly timed, considering the fact that he had mentioned nothing of Sarah in his tale.

His face must have taken on a set, harsh look, for Cap said hastily, "No offense meant, friend Hawkins."

"And none taken, Cap." Jeb sipped at the tea and rum. "One thing puzzles me. Why do you travel at night?"

"Oh, yes." Cap grinned. "It would be natural such a thought should occur to a seafaring man. The Spanish have set up a rather loose blockade by edict. They have forbidden either British or Colonial boats to bring goods to New Orleans. Yet they are in sore need of the goods my keelboat carries, as well as a means of shipping their own goods north. So they wink at our comings and goings. Still, it *is* forbidden, and sometimes they capture a boat running the blockade. But they are always careful to wait *until* we have unloaded at the wharves in New Orleans. Since most of the cargo is brought down on flatboats, which are broken up, their lumber sold in New Orleans, only them of us running the keelboats have need to worry. So I always make it a habit to sneak out under the cover of darkness, until I'm well away from the port. The dirty Spaniards have another blockade farther upriver, with small river boats and guns. They give chase and oftentimes sink one of us. But they know little of riverboating, and a man shrewd in its ways can easily elude them." Cap drained his mug and stood up. "I must prowl the boat, kick the arses of the lollygaggers. You and the boy better get your rest now. On the morrow, you might, if you still feel so inclined, give us a hand poling, friend Hawkins. I am sorely shorthanded. Most of my crew downriver remained behind to taste the fleshpots of New Orleans, and a ragbag bunch it is I scrounged up to replace them."

"I will be most happy to assist in any way I can, Cap, ignorant though I am."

Cap's ready grin flickered. "Needs no knowledge, friend, only a strong back."

"Again, my heartfelt thanks, sir."

Cap waved a hand and waddled out the cabin door.

Looking at Tim, Jeb saw that the lad was already asleep, curled up in a fetal knot. "Where shall we bed down, Ezra?"

The gnome grunted. "Take any pallet you can find, Squire. This is not a fancy inn, and I cannot vouch for the lack of vermin."

Standing up, Jeb nudged Tim with a toe. Half-awake, the lad stumbled to his feet, and Jeb led them to a far corner of the cabin, where it was darker and the smoke was less. He saw one figure rolled up in blankets, snoring slightly. He found a place near the far wall, made a pallet for Tim, who lay down and was asleep again at once.

Jeb stretched out on his back, but he found sleep hard to come by.

His situation was dire. Without any funds, or the slightest prospects for any, without employment, in a land foreign to him, where the languages and the customs were strange—he could hardly have been in worse straits. Still, he knew that he could manage well enough; he was confident of his ability to survive in any environment. Jeb was truthful enough with himself to admit that it was being reduced from the master of a mighty ship, lord of all he surveyed, to a penniless wanderer that galled him. That, and the likelihood that he would never again sail the seas as a ship's captain, was what tried his spirit.

And inevitably his thoughts moved to Sarah Moody and her possible fate. The thought that she was probably dead by now grieved him far more than he would have ever thought possible. The woman had gotten to the heart of him, he could admit that to himself now, in the dark hours of the night and the spirit. He had loved the wench! If events had gone the other way, he would have had an opportunity to make amends for the cruel treatment he had given her. Now it was too late!

He twisted and turned on the rough planking for what seemed hours before a troubled sleep finally claimed him.

Accustomed as he was to the movement of a water craft, of whatever sort, he awoke instantly when he felt the keelboat cease all movement. Daylight seeped in through the cracks in the crude cabin. Sitting up, he saw other forms asleep around him. The fire had died to coals on the stone hearth, and Ezra Boggs slept where he sat, his chin resting on his chest.

Jeb got up, careful not to rouse Tim, and went through the low door. As he stepped outside, he was amazed to hear a high, sweet voice singing, accompanied by the sawing of a fiddle.

> *We are a hard, freeborn race,*
> *None to ever fear a stranger;*
> *Whate'er the game, we join in the chase,*
> *Despising toil and danger;*
> *And if a daring foe annoys,*
> *No matter what his force is,*
> *We'll show him that Kentucky boys,*
> *Are alligator-horses.*

The voice was coming from above him. Jeb craned his neck and saw an aged Negro seated atop the cabin, singing the ditty, and playing the fiddle. His crinkly hair was snow-white, and his eye sockets were nothing but scar tissue.

Jeb heard Cap's now-familiar voice behind him and turned.

"That's Blind Bob," Cap said. "He was a slave on a plantation down south a ways. He kept running away, until one day his owner flew into a rage and had both eyes put out. 'Course, then he was no longer any use to the man. Some folks are real mean, you know that, friend?" Cap sighed, then brightened again immediately. "Blind Bob sings us awake in the morn, sometimes sings us asleep at night. And when we be having a mite of trouble rowing upriver against a mean current, he warbles a ditty to help the polers or those manning the oars to forget their misery."

"What are alligator-horses? It's an expression unfamiliar to me."

Cap laughed heartily. "It's what rivermen call themselves. They like to think they're half-alligator, half-horse. Some are mean enough to be both, and sadly smell like both. . . ."

As Cap prattled on, Jeb had time to look around. He saw that the keelboat was snuggled against a river bank. The sun was up, showing the broad, mud-red sweep of the Mississippi and a stark bluff rising high from the narrow, muddy bank where they had stopped. It wasn't all mud, however. There was a stretch of dry ground at the foot of the bluff. There amid a small grove of willows, some of the keelboat crew had camped, with a fire going.

As Cap talked, Jeb took his first good, daylight look at the keelboat. It was about eighty feet long and probably ten feet in the beam, with a shallow keel. It was sharp at both ends. The long, low cabin took up most of the center portion of the boat, stretching back almost to the stern. All around the gunwales ran a cleated footway, eighteen inches wide, where Jeb knew the crew must walk while poling the boat. He was later to learn that these cleated footways were called running boards. In the bow were ten seats to accommodate the rowers when oars were used.

The steering, Jeb saw, was done by means of a long oar pivoted at the stern, extending approximately twelve feet beyond the stern end of the boat. Under the long oar, there was a sort of round stand, resembling a barrel half, and Jeb assumed that was where the steersman stood. He supposed that Cap did most of the steering.

"... decided to lay up here today and tonight, get an early start in the morning," Cap was saying. "We're far enough from New Orleans so that it's reasonably safe to travel by daylight. Let the crew rest, have their compliment of whiskey tonight. Hungover they'll be, but I'll soon work that off them."

Jeb noticed that the boat's cargo was meager, only a few canvas-covered bundles lashed atop the long cabin. "You are indeed light of cargo," he said.

"Aye, that I am." Cap sighed. "We can load her good going south with the current, furs and such, but fighting back upriver is a far different thing."

"What are you hauling back?"

"Mostly cotton. Some sugar cane and rice from the plantations. Many cotton plantations are just beginning along the lower reaches of old Mrs. Sippi, since the introduction of the hand cotton gin back in 1751. 'Tis only the beginning, to my thinking." Cap waxed enthusiastic. "Soon the river will be crowded with keelboats and flatboats."

"No sailing vessels venture this far?"

"Few, friend Hawkins, few. They draw too much water. The river is wide and deep in many places, but she is full of sandbars and has never been truly charted. Only craft drawing very little water dare use her. We have a square sail we can hoist. Seldom do we get a strong breeze from the south."

Interested now, his mind busy, Jeb said slowly, "Then to make it a well-paying proposition, you need some way to make good headway up the river with larger loads, is that not correct?"

"You've hit the nail smack on the head, friend!"

"You usually propel by either oars or poling?"

"Or cordelling."

"That I do not understand."

"A cordelle is a towline, several hundred feet long, sometimes as much as a thousand. The cordelle is attached to the bow, and the crew goes ashore, if there be some kind of towpath, and they tow her by hand. Towpaths ain't often the best along Mrs. Sippi. The men have to wade through muck and bushes. Oftentimes, when the undergrowth is too thick, I send a few men ahead with axes to clear a path. There be times when the towers walk along a high cliff. Other times, when the bottom of the river is too soft for poling, filled with silt, and the men can't tow from the bank, we warp her along. I send a skiff up ahead with one man in it, carrying one end of the cordelle. He fastens the end to a stout tree limb, and the men still on board pull us along hand over hand. That way's a bitch, friend Hawkins. Fortunate we make a mile a day that way."

"Have you ever thought of using mules on shore to pull this cordelle you speak of, instead of using your crew?"

"Mules?" Cap stared. *"Mules?"*

Jeb nodded. "It seems to me it would be much more efficient."

"Mules would be expensive, and 'twould mean hiring men who know mules."

"The mules could be bought in New Orleans for the trip back, then sold at your destination. Likely for a profit."

"There be much of this old river where mules couldn't find a towpath."

"No worse than for your crew. On how much of the journey would that happen?"

Cap hesitated, calculating. "Hard to guess. Mebbe a third of the distance."

"Even so," Jeb pointed out, "you'd still come out ahead, making much better headway for the other two-thirds of the distance."

Cap stared at Jeb thoughtfully, fingering his chin. "You've a head on your shoulders, friend. It's worth a deal of thought. 'Tisn't all that new, of course. I've heard of it being done on smaller, less stubborn rivers. But never has it crossed my mind to do it on Mrs. Sippi."

"Captain Hawkins?" Tim came out of the cabin, yawning. "What's happened?"

"Nothing, lad. Cap has tied up his boat for the day."

"Captain . . ." Tim hesitated. "I'm hungry."

"Course you be, boy." Laughing, Cap scrubbed Tim's head briskly. "And that can be fixed in a hurry, your belly filled. My men on shore are busy preparing to breakfast right now. S'pose we join them?" He yelled up. "Blind Bob, time to go ashore!"

He helped the blind man down from the cabin roof, Blind Bob carefully cradling his fiddle. Cap picked up a thick hickory stick, longer than he was tall, from the decking. The stick was worn smooth from much handling. With Jeb and Tim following, Cap guided the blind man down the wide plank bridging the boat and the river bank. The ground was marshy underfoot. Leading the way, Cap used the end of the stick to probe for firm ground, and they followed in the path he picked out for them. Finally they reached solid land and strode toward the grove of willows where the rivermen were squatting around the fire. They had lugged a keg of whiskey ashore, and each had a cup of the whiskey and one of water, from which he sipped.

The rest of the crew, apparently aroused by Blind Bob's singing, were trooping off the keelboat now. They were a rough-looking lot—tall, gaunt and big-boned, and sunburned a dark brown. Their breeches were either of linsey-woolsey or buckskin. None wore shirts, being bare to the waist. Their language was rough, profane, and Jeb wondered if it was fitting for Tim's tender ears. Then he laughed at himself. A sailor's language among his fellows was little better. A ship's master, keeping his distance from the seamen, was apt to forget that fact.

The rivermen tended to ignore the strangers in their midst. Cap poured himself a cup of whiskey and moved among them easily, drinking and joshing with them.

Jeb had to wonder how the round, easy-going man, smaller than any of the rivermen, managed to maintain discipline among this rough bunch.

Being master of a keelboat, at least the way Cap managed it, was far different from being captain of a sailing vessel. No ship's captain would ever think of mingling with his crew as Cap was now doing. Yet, in some ways, Jeb thought, it might be a pleasant way of life.

He accepted a cup of whiskey from Cap and drank sparingly of it. Blind Bob was introduced to Jeb and Tim, and he sat down next to them. The food was ample, if simple—an appetizing stew liberally dotted with beef chunks and potatoes, cornbread, and the strong tea.

"I spose the victuals we eats is not what a ship's captain is used to?" Blind Bob remarked.

"It's different, but filling. There are times at sea when we must get by with meager fare."

"Cap sees to it that we'uns eat good. Most keelboat men have to make do with sorry victuals. Corn, potatoes half-raw, hardtack, and what meat served often be spoiled."

"I've noticed an odd thing, Bob," Jeb said. "The men fill one cup with river water, another with the whiskey, taking a sip of whiskey first, then water." Jeb shuddered. "That water looks mostly mud."

Blind Bob laughed. "'Tis the custom of rivermen. Water from this old river's not that bad. There's a saying along the river, 'The sand in the water scours out the bowels, and the more a person drinks, the better he be in health.'"

Jeb had been curious all along as to the function of a blind man brought along on trips where hard labor was required of all. How could Cap afford a man along who could only play the fiddle and sing? Out of the kindness of his heart? Jeb figured it would be discourteous of him, as well as unkind, to ask Blind Bob, so he kept his silence and continued eating.

Most of the keelboat men, once they had finished their meal, stretched out under what shade they could find and were soon asleep. A few smoked a pipe first. The smell of tobacco disturbed Jeb. He moved with Tim some distance from the others and sat back against a tree trunk. Tim curled up on the ground and was very soon asleep. Jeb didn't feel sleepy, since he had just gotten up. But it wasn't long before the combination of the cup of whiskey, the food, and the warmth of the sun made him drowsy. He stretched out beside Tim and went to sleep.

He awoke to the smell of burning tobacco. Opening his eyes, he found Cap Clayborne squatting beside him, pipe fuming. Jeb was amazed that he had slept the day away. It was nigh to sundown. But he did feel rested, the soreness in his bruised limbs and head much eased.

He sat up. "Are we about to depart, Cap?"

"No, no, Friend Hawkins. We'll spend the night here. Let the men have a time for themselves. Some of them didn't even go ashore in New Orleans. They have a night of sport coming to them. 'Twill be a long and arduous journey to St. Louis."

"Sport? What kind of sport can they enjoy here, on a sorry river bank?"

Cap smiled and winked. "You will see, friend Hawkins, you will see!"

Jeb did indeed see. And he also learned at least one reason why Blind Bob was along.

By dark they had all eaten again. Two more kegs of whiskey were brought ashore from the keelboat, and wood was piled on the fire until the flames roared high.

Then Jeb witnessed a ritual he would never forget.

One of the keelboat men jumped to his feet. From somewhere he had produced an apron. It was about twenty inches in width at the top where the strings attached, and approximately two feet from top to bottom. It was a bright red in color. He tied it deftly around his waist and yelled, "Blind Bob, strike us a jig!"

Blind Bob obliged, beginning a merry jig on the

13

fiddle. The man with the apron seized the hands of another riverman. He put his arms around the man's waist, and they began to dance. The men around the fire sang lustily, with much clapping of hands.

"Ye dance like an old maid, Jack!" shouted the man with the apron and pushed him away. He selected another man and pulled him to his feet. The strange couple danced with a grace that astonished Jeb. After some minutes of this, the man with the apron shouted, "A polka, Blind Bob!"

Blind Bob began playing a polka. The two men bounded around the clearing with incredible agility, and the men cheered loudly when they finished. The man with the apron bowed, grinning from ear to ear. He accepted a cup of whiskey and one of water, drinking heartily from both.

Then he minced around the circle, chin resting on fingertip, pretending to be very particular about his next partner. Finally he selected one and pulled him up to dance. Soon, others of the men paired off, and all were eventually dancing.

It continued for an hour, two hours, while Jeb watched in amusement. Cap didn't join the dancers; instead, he stood off to one side, leaning on his stick. He steadily drank whiskey and shouted encouragement to the dancers, grinning broadly all the while.

At the end of two hours it seemed to Jeb that the rivermen were as fresh as when they began. They were growing drunk, true, but only a few dropped out to sit watching.

Occasionally Blind Bob would sing a ditty. Only then would the rivermen cease dancing, listening respectfully.

One short verse brought a roar from them:

Dance, boatmen, dance,
Dance, dance away;
Dance all night till broad daylight,
And go home with the gals in the morning!

A riverman yelled, "That we will, Blind Bob!"

"What gals? Don't see any gals around!" bellowed another man. "Except'n you, apron man!" He seized the man with the apron, and the dancing began again.

And then, suddenly, it all came to a stop. One man, six-four at least, with shoulders as broad as an ox, loosed a great roar and stomped on the ground for attention. "This is me, don't ye mistake it! Johnny Bearcat, in the flesh. Cuss me if I cain't whup anybody here! I'm spileing for a fight. Ain't had one for nigh onto a week! I'm cock o' the walk and ain't never been whupped!" He threw back his head. "Cock-a-doodle-doo! Reckin ye ain't heard 'bout the time a horse kicked me and throwed both his hips out of jint? If'n that ain't the Lord's own truth, slice me up for catfish bait! When I was a babe without my eyes yet open, I spurned my ma's milk and asked for a bottle of Kaintuck whiskey! One drop of my piss on a bull's heel would raise a blister!" Now he began to strut up and down before the campfire. "I kin out-pull, out-jump, out-swim, out-drink, and out-fuck any man alive! And I kin whup any man here! Ain't any of you yellowbellies got the craw for to try me?"

"I'll try ye, damn ye for a windbag!"

A man with a scraggly brown beard, slighter and slimmer than Johnny Bearcat, jumped into the cleared space, facing the big man. One of the challenger's hands, Jeb noted, was held behind his back.

Johnny Bearcat roared happily, and the two men came together with enough impact to shake the ground. They clawed and gouged at each other like cats. Then the bigger man had the other in a bear hug. He squeezed mightily.

Jeb saw the flash of firelight on metal, and the big man screamed, staggering back. Blood streamed down his face from several deep, parallel gouges. The smaller man stood in a crouch, waiting, right hand extended now. On that hand Jeb saw metal fingers like claws, attached in a sort of glovelike arrangement.

And now Jeb saw how Cap Clayborne kept discipline among this rough crew. He moved silently up behind the man wearing the claw and brought the thicker end of the hickory stick whistling down on his head. The man collapsed without a sound, lying face down on the ground.

Johnny Bearcat charged with a snarl of rage, drawing back his foot to kick the prone man. Cap rammed the end of the hickory stick into his belly and sent him reeling back.

"You've had your fun now, you bastards!" Cap said in a harsh voice. He squatted and tore the claw attachment from the unconscious man's hand. Standing up, Cap gave a great heave, and in a moment came the sound of the iron claw falling into the river.

Cap glared around the circle. "You all know I don't approve of any man of mine using a devil's claw. If I ever find any of you with one again, your arse is mine. Now, 'tis time to bed down, fun's over." He gestured with the stick. "You, Johnny, go aboard and rouse Ezra, see what he can do to fix your face. The rest of you rowdies, bed down. Hard day coming up tomorrow. I'm rousting you all out at daybreak."

Chapter Thirteen

Giles Brock shifted his weight in the saddle, but the movement did little to ease the painful aching in his hips and thigh bones. With only one horse, he and Pommet rode what was known as "whipsaw fashion." One rode for an hour, then got off and walked while the other rode the horse. They had stolen the horse in the outskirts of New Orleans and were now riding north, up the Natchez Trace.

Brock didn't much take to riding a horse, but then he didn't care for walking either. The trail was boggy, overgrown with vines and bushes, and clogged with fallen logs.

Before the day was far advanced, Brock was doing most of the riding. When Pommet complained, Giles drew his pistol and aimed it. "Shut your yap and walk, damn you! Else I'll put a ball through you and have this bloody horse to myself the rest of the way!"

"To carry out our plan, you'll be needing me, Giles," Pommet whined, then had the good sense to be quiet.

Brock was in the blackest of moods. He could not keep his thoughts away from the loss of the *North Star* and what had happened back there on the river bank with Sarah and the odd-looking stranger who had butted in. When Brock had regained consciousness from the knock on the head, Sarah Moody was gone and Pommet was shaking him.

"What happened to you, Giles?"

"Never mind, Pommet!" Brock had snapped. "Did you take care of Jeb Hawkins?"

An evil smile had blossomed on Pommet's face. "At the bottom of the river, Giles."

That at least was to the good, but it did little to make up for pockets empty of money and no immediate means to accumulate more. Brock knew he dared not return to New Orleans. He had promised the other nine guards their share of the bounty from the sale of the *North Star*. Now that the ship had gone up in smoke, they would be angry enough to kill him, being the bloody cutthroats they were.

So, what to do?

It was Rhys Pommet who came up with the hoped-for solution to their dire predicament. Pommet had a ferret's nose for sniffing out ways and means to garner ill-gotten gains. He had learned quite a bit about the ways of this new country, even during the brief time they had spent in New Orleans.

It seemed that flatboatmen coming down the Mississippi to New Orleans had a choice of three ways to return north after their flatboats were broken up and sold. They could take a ship around Florida for Baltimore or Philadelphia and then return to their point of origin. But travel by sea was perilous during these times of the Revolution. Or they could sign on a keelboat beating its way back upriver. But that way usually meant working as a keelboat man, and also had an element of risk, especially for the flatboat owners carrying monies back to the shippers in the north. The third way, and the most often used, was the

Natchez Trace, a trail leading from New Orleans to Nashville, a distance of some 700 miles, with no white settlements for most of the distance.

"What we need to find is a flatboat captain or cargo owner returning north, their mules loaded with the silver and gold, or specie, they got in exchange for their cargoes in New Orleans," Pommet explained. "Since the flatboatmen themselves usually stay in New Orleans until their wages are spent, the owners usually travel in twos, or mayhap three at the most. We'll find a good spot for an ambush, lay in wait, and then shoot'em down. Should we be fortunate enough, we might seize a goodly sum."

"Just the pair of us?" Brock was dubious. "We carry little fire power."

"We have three pistols. Yours, mine, and the one I took from Hawkins. True, we ain't much powder and balls, but enough. They'll likely have pistols and rifles we can arm ourselves with after we kill'em." Pommett leaned forward. "Giles, I saw a number of heavily cargoed flatboats unloading in New Orleans. There will be fortunes for the taking moving up the Trace."

Brock didn't much like the odds; yet he knew, if he was to wield control over Rhys Pommet, it would not do to show fear before the man. Pommet, so far as Brock had been able to tell, feared neither man nor the devil. Besides, what choice was there?

So here they were, trudging up this poor excuse for a trail, existing on hardtack, rice, and corn, which they had purchased in Natchez with the last of their money. Travel on the Trace was light. All they had seen so far going north were large groups of men, groups far too big for their purpose.

A week out of Natchez, Brock had had enough. "Let's find this ambush you've been yakking about and rest our arses until some likely victims come alone. I've had my fill of this."

Pommet agreed readily. "We should be far enough now. I'll scout ahead and find a likely spot where we can lay in wait."

Pommet took the horse and was soon out of sight. Brock plodded along, weary of limb and low in spirit. Walking along with his head down, he almost jumped out of his skin when Pommet suddenly appeared before him like a ghost.

"That's a damn good way to get your head blown off!" Brock snarled.

Pommet was grinning broadly. "But you didn't see me, did you? I've found the perfect spot. A mule could pass within a foot of us and naught would anyone see of us! Come, I'll show you."

Pommet turned, pushing his way through the thicket of underbrush until they were about two yards from the edge of the trail. "Watch your step now, Giles."

The warning was timely, else Brock would have plunged headfirst into a ditch about two feet deep and several feet across. The bottom, covered with a carpet of leaves, was soggy. Apparently, it was a small stream during wet times.

"You see, Giles, we can lay up in here, snug as two bugs, and not be seen from the trail. We can hear the approach of animals in plenty of time and peek out to see if they be likely victims. Lookee, I've already tried it."

Pommet got down on his belly, head just above the level of the ditch. Hesitantly, Brock joined him. Pommet parted the vines and bushes carefully and quietly. "We can see fifty-some yards straight down the trail. Plenty of time to make up our minds."

Brock peered out. It was true; they could see a goodly distance.

"And we can wait until they're almost close enough to spit on afore firing." Pommet chortled gleefully. "We can't miss!"

"I guess 'twill do," Brock said grudgingly. "Where's the damned horse?"

"Oh, I tied him to a tree back a ways, so he can't be heard. He'll be content, good grazing there."

They settled down to wait. It was a long wait and an uncomfortable one. Pommet's comment about snug as bugs was truthful in more ways than one. The ditch teemed with insects of every sort. They got under Brock's clothing, biting and crawling. Soon, he was scratching like a madman, temper as short as a bomb fuse.

They had to wait three days. The only travelers they saw in all that time were either in too large a group to attack or looked as destitute as they were. Their meager supply of food was growing short. And the mosquitoes attacked in droves at night; sleep was almost impossible.

When Brock got up at sunrise on the third day, stiff and sore, his skin welted by mosquito bites, he snapped at Pommet, "If we land nothing today, we're going to have to come up with another way. I'm damned if I will endure this discomfort another day, not another day!"

But shortly past noon they had their victims. Brock was dozing when Pommet, ever alert, nudged him awake. "I think we've got what we been looking for!"

Brock parted the bushes and took a look. Coming up the trail was a party of three, better-dressed and more prosperous-looking than any they had seen so far. All rode horses, and in addition, they were leading two pack mules with saddlebags thrown over them.

In a tense whisper Pommet said, "See them saddlebags, Giles? See how heavy they hang? I'll wager my life they're full of what we're looking for."

Tired of the long waiting and thinking that Pommet was probably right in his estimate of the party's booty, Brock said, "All right, we take them."

"Wait until they be almost abreast of us, about ten feet. I'll take the two on the right, riding together. You give the other'un your pistol ball."

"You're that accurate with both hands?" Brock asked doubtfully.

"Wait and see, Giles," Pommet said with his evil, death's-head grin.

Pommet quietly cocked both pistols. Brock did likewise with his. Brock lay tense with apprehension. This was a situation new to him and was, he knew, fraught with peril, despite Pommet's cockiness.

The riders loomed larger and larger in his vision. Then Pommet nudged him with an elbow and went boiling out of the bushes, Brock two steps behind him. Both of Pommet's pistols barked, and Brock fired a moment later. He saw his target bowled backward off his horse. He darted a quick look at the other two men and saw they had also been shot from their mounts.

Both men ran to the prone figures. Brock's man was dead, shot through the heart. One of Pommet's men was still alive. Pommet quickly reloaded one pistol and fired a ball into the twitching man's head.

Brock was already at the two mules, wresting the saddlebags off with trembling fingers. The horses, startled by the pistol fire, had bolted a few yards up the trail but were now standing quietly.

Brock opened one saddlebag, and gold and silver coins tumbled out in a gleaming cascade.

Behind him Pommet said gloatingly, "What did I tell you, Giles? We've hit it rich! No more hardtack and rice for we two!" He fell to his knees beside Brock and opened the other saddlebag. It also was full of coins and specie. Pommet ran his stubby fingers through the heap of coins, then threw back his head and howled like a wolf.

A deep voice said, "Well, now what do we have here? It would seem that you two fine lads have done the Lord's work for us."

Brock wheeled about with a startled yelp, groping for the pistol in his belt before he remembered that it was unloaded.

Confronting them were over a dozen men, all carrying pistols and rifles, but the one who drew Brock's attention was the man a step in front, undoubtedly their leader. He was a slender man, with black, fierce eyes, black hair, mutton-chop whiskers, and a lantern jaw. What was most odd about him was his all-black, ministerial garb and his black, wide-brimmed hat.

It took Brock a long moment to find his voice. "Who—Who are you?"

"I am Blessing Johnson, pilgrim, and these with me are my flock, my congregation."

"You're a minister?"

"I am that." Blessing Johnson drew himself up,

195

eyes flashing. He swept a hand around in a gesture, but the other hand, holding the pistol, remained centered on Brock's chest. "And this, this wilderness of Our Lord God, is my church. Our Lord has spoken to me, counseling me to go forth in the wilderness and relieve the money-changers of their ill-gotten gains." Just then two women, both comely wenches, stepped out of the bushes to stand on either side of him. "And these are my wives, Purity and Chastity."

"Your wives?" Brock gaped. "*Two* wives?"

"The Good Book says that man is put upon this earth to be fruitful. Did not Solomon have many wives?" The black eyes took on a mad glitter. "That is why I was turned out of my church. Over east I had my own church. When I took unto myself a second wife, the nonbelievers that were then members of my congregation, may God forgive the misguided souls, turned me out. But their loss was the greater. Now I have the Lord's own cathedral for my church." Again the grandiloquent sweep of his hand. Then Blessing became brisk. "Brethren, will you be so kind as to collect our offering?"

Several men moved forward for the saddlebags.

Pommet spoke for the first time, "You're robbing us!"

"It seems you still do not understand, pilgrim," Blessing said benignly, at the same time casually moving his pistol to bear on Pommet. "The monies there are the proper dues for my church. Perhaps 'twould be best, brethren, if you relieve our two pilgrims of their weapons."

Two of the men took Pommet's two pistols, then Brock's.

Brock had collected his wits now, and fear chilled his blood. "What do you intend doing with us?"

"Ah, there is that problem." Blessing stroked his long jaw with the pistol. "Your fates are indeed in the balance. It will require some thought, and perhaps prayer, before I reach that decision. It is possible that the Almighty shall instruct me to use the Right Hand of God."

Befuddled, Brock asked, "The Right Hand of God?"

"This, pilgrim. This is the Right Hand of God." Blessing flourished the pistol in his right hand. "However, we have more pressing matters to attend to now. We must give these poor misguided souls a proper burial."

While Brock watched in amazement, spades were fetched, and three graves were quickly dug off the trail. The three travelers they had killed were placed into the graves.

Blessing removed his hat, placed it over his heart, and bowed his head. "Our Lord Who art in Heaven, it is written in the Good Book that man is on this earth for but a brief time. Dust he is, and to dust he shall returneth. Forgive these poor sinners, Dear Lord, for spending their brief span on this earth doing naught but gathering riches unto them. Forgive them, for they knew not what they did. The final judgment is Yours, Dear Lord. Shall they burn in eternal hellfire or shall they be granted absolution and allowed to enter the Gates of Heaven? Should You decide that they shall suffer hellfire and damnation, our prayers go with them. Amen. May their souls forever rest in peace."

Blessing gestured, and the men began shoveling dirt into the graves.

Blessing turned to Brock and Pommet. "You shall accompany us and sup with us. We owe you at least that small debt of gratitude for performing the Lord's work for us."

Within a few minutes, the horses and mules of the dead travelers, as well as the one Brock and Pommet had stolen, were collected, and Blessing's flock was on its way. Pommet watched with open hostility as the saddlebags were loaded onto the mules, but what concerned Brock the most was their eventual fate at the hands of this band of cutthroats. Blessing's sanctimonious manner didn't fool him for an instant. Brock knew he would kill them without blinking an eye, then pray over their graves.

A short distance up the Trace, the group turned off onto a dim trail winding westward. They had to travel single file now. But an armed man rode behind and in front of Brock and Pommet, and they had no chance to escape.

An hour's ride from the Natchez Trace, they came upon a small clearing in the thick woods, and Blessing gave orders to make camp. It was already growing dark. Campfires were built, and the two women threw chunks of meat and numerous vegetables into cooking pots. Soon the smell of the stew reached Brock's nostrils, and he was reminded of their poor rations these past few days.

He and Pommet sat glumly side by side, under close guard. Pommet grumbled, "I could sure use a tot of something."

Overhearing him from nearby, Blessing turned a black scowl on him. "Drinking of the devil's spirits is strictly forbidden among my flock. I will not countenance it. We live by the commandments laid down by the Good Book. And there is no wenching either. To have a woman with him, any brother here must wed her."

Pommet subsided, mumbling under his breath. Brock could only stare at this strange individual, Blessing Johnson. There was no doubt in Brock's mind that the man was more than half-mad. Yet he was shrewd, and there was no denying his ability to command men. If he could prevent this motley crew of cutthroats from drinking and wenching, he had to rule with an iron hand.

The stew was done, and the two women ladled it out into wooden bowls, along with chunks of freshly baked cornbread. Brock accepted his gratefully, other concerns forgotten for the moment. Mouth watering and belly grumbling, he sat down and started to dip into the bowl. The man guarding him nudged him with a pistol, and Brock started, looking around. The man indicated with a jerk of his head for Brock to wait.

In a moment Brock learned the reason. When everyone was served, Blessing Johnson bowed his head. "Brethren, join me in a prayer of thanks. We thank thee, Dear Lord, for providing us sustenance for our bellies. We ask Your everlasting Grace, and pray for Your Divine intervention in all future endeavors we might undertake in our labors in Your behalf here in the wilderness. Thank thee, Dear Lord, and amen."

At a gesture from Blessing, all began eating. For a fleeting moment, Brock wondered what evil endeavor this crew had performed to get the food they were about to eat. Likely it had been taken from other travelers along the Trace. Then he began to eat with gusto, forgetting everything else in the desire to fill his belly.

When everyone was finished, Brock and Pommet were summoned into Blessing's presence. He sat before his own campfire, the two wives on each side, like handmaidens to a king.

"I have decided about the pair of you," Blessing said. "It was first in my mind to kill you in the name of Our Lord. The Good Book says, an eye for an eye, a tooth for a tooth, and death to thine enemies. However, you did perform our work for us. Most efficiently, I might say. Therefore, we do owe you a debt of gratitude. My flock . . ." He swept his hand around in that grand manner. "My flock is somewhat depleted at present. I have sore need of good and able brothers to carry on the Lord's work. So if it is your desire to do so, you may become as one with us."

Pommet said bitterly, "Or else you will kill us. That be the choice you're giving us?"

Blessing said serenely, "Aptly put, pilgrim."

"Join you in what exactly?" Brock asked. "Robbing, uh, relieving the money-changers along the Trace?"

"No, that has been merely a means toward another end," Blessing said. "A means to help us toward our final goal."

"And what is that?"

"River traffic along the great river called the Mississippi is growing steadily. Many valuable goods are being shipped down to that city of sin, New Orleans, by way of flatboats and keelboats. These goods are being shipped by avaricious merchants in the north, from cities such as St. Louis, even as far east as

200

Philadelphia. This presents a golden opportunity for us to do the Lord's work. These rivermen are not shrewd fighters and are ill-equipped to defend their cargoes. From here I intend to lead my flock up to Cave-in-Rock, below St. Louis, and establish my headquarters." Blessing paused, eyeing them keenly. "Well, what say you?"

Brock hesitated, thinking hard. All his instincts and the information about river traffic that Pommet had gathered in New Orleans told him that this man had hit upon a lucrative scheme. And as Pommet had pointed out, they had little choice.

He said cautiously, "What happens if we agree to side with you, then watch for our chance and flee?"

"I will accept your word as Christian gentlemen. But if in that you fail me and desert . . ." Blessing's eyes turned hard and cold. "In that event, I will send some of the brothers to track you down and kill you. There are a few with me who are loyal to the death. Certain other brothers have chosen the path you suggested and sorely regretted their despicable action."

Again Brock hesitated. Now he recognized how Blessing ruled this motley crew—through fear. But why did they not turn on him and kill him, since they far outnumbered him? There was an answer to that, of sorts. Brock knew that most men, even the lowest, conscienceless scum, shrank away from killing a man of God. Even if they did not believe in a Supreme Being, something in their black hearts quailed at the thought that retribution might somehow fall on them. Brock had no such qualms; neither, he knew, did Pommet. When the proper time came, they would scheme together, kill this pious madman, and take

14

over his crew. River pirating, Brock thought, could well be the way he could make his fortune after all!

Finally he said, "We are with you, Blessing Johnson."

Blessing's eyes sparkled, and he smiled broadly. He reached out to clasp both men's hands, saying, "Bless you, brothers. And welcome to my flock! Together, we shall prosper mightily, while doing the Lord's work!"

Chapter Fourteen

Before the end of the long, severe winter, Sarah had learned a great many things, many of which were of vital importance to her survival in this new and strange land. One thing she learned, however, while not useful in that sense, did help her to confront the deadly boredom imposed by confinement in the small dugout during the heavy snows.

The first time they were snowbound in the cliff dugout for over a week, Sean said to her. " 'Twould no doubt astonish you, lass, how many men go mad out here when buried in their lean-tos or dugouts for weeks on end. Of course, some, those with little foresight, starve, but they are the stupid ones. A far greater number have ample supplies, but lose control of their minds. Every spring thaw, a number are found wandering the prairie, bereft of their senses. That's why so many take squaws. Not only for physical comfort, but simply for company, someone to talk to, even if only to quarrel. Fortunately . . ." That wry, self-mocking grin. "My greatest sin, gambling, has spared me that fate. I am a confirmed gambler, and when I am snowbound, I spend my time trying to improve my skill."

Sarah studied him with amusement. "And does it help?"

"Not overmuch. I still end up losing everything I

take to New Orleans with me. Fortunately, I always have funds left on deposit with Jacques Fortier, the Frenchie fur buyer in St. Louis I deal with. A sort of reserve to fall back on, you might say. Late every summer, without even being asked, Jacques sends a letter of credit to me in New Orleans, so I can outfit myself for the winter." He cocked his head, eyes twinkling. "I had a sudden thought. With you here this winter, perhaps I should teach you how to gamble. 'Twould help idle away the time, and in the teaching I might learn something."

During the time prior to the first great snowfall, Sarah learned how to help Sean in a number of ways. Every day the weather permitted, he was out with his traps. He trapped or shot a great many otter, foxes, and muskrats. Usually he would skin the animals on the spot, and then bring the hides back to the dugout. But there was still work to be done. All the flesh and fatty substance had to be scraped away from the underside, the pelts then stretched over a wooden framework and hung on the front of the dugout to thoroughly dry.

With determination, Sarah overcame her initial repugnance and took over this part of the operation, freeing Sean for more trapping. Sean was dubious at first, but she watched closely as he worked, and soon she performed the task almost as efficiently as Sean. By the time they were first snowed in, one wall inside the dugout was stacked high with bundles of pelts.

She learned to handle the long, heavy knife and carried it in the belt around her waist until it became a part of her.

Sean shook his head in admiration. "Lass, you continue to dazzle me!" He reached a hand out as though to caress her cheek, then drew it back. "You are going to be a great help!"

Their personal relationship had remained unchanged. In the robes at night, they were compatible, and Sarah enjoyed their romps together immensely. Yet she kept her secret self in rigid reserve, and Sean, as though sensing this, never expressed his true feelings.

On her part, Sarah suspected that his feelings were nothing more than finding pleasure in her body. She somehow could not conceive of Sean Flanagan giving of himself wholly to any one woman.

Their only serious disagreement was over the matter of body cleanliness. No arguments occurred until the rivers and creeks froze, and they were snowbound. But after the first big blizzard hit, lasting three whole days, Sean couldn't force the door open more than a few inches. He had to dig his way out to get down to the crude corral he had built against the bluff for the mules, so he could feed them.

Sarah insisted they both wash as best they could in the pans of water she heated in the fireplace, water made from melted snow.

"I'm after thinking you're going to drive me mad before the winter is out, woman," he grumbled. "This thing you have for cleanliness is out of place here. Wintering alone, I have gone for weeks without bathing. 'Tis one of the hardships you learn to accept." He grinned. "After a man lives with his own stink for a time, he no longer notices it."

"Well, you're not living alone now, Sean Flanagan," she retorted. "If you don't bathe more often, you can spread your robe across the room from me. As far away as you can get." She gestured. "Over by your peltries. You have the same smell!"

" 'Tis a hard woman you are, colleen. My suspicions have been confirmed. The English are indeed a finicky race."

"I've heard it said in London town that the Irish bring their yard animals into the house with them in winter. Why don't you remain true to *your* race and bring those bloody mules in here with us?"

"I did, twice, during dire winters. And don't be after making sport of it. It not only saved the mules, but probably my life as well. Many a trapper has been saved by having his animals in with him, when he was snowed in and couldn't get out to gather firewood."

"Hah! I'd rather freeze!"

"You only say that because . . ." Again he grinned, good humor surging back. He could never remain angry with her for long. "Because you have me to snuggle up to and keep you warm, darlin'."

"Not if you don't bathe. No bathing, no snuggling!"

So, with a put-upon sigh, Sean washed in the tiny pans of snow water she heated.

Sean taught her the rudiments of cards—poker, faro, euchre, seven-up. To her vast surprise, Sarah found herself fascinated by the games. Her long fingers, even work-reddened and winter-chapped, proved to be very adept at handling the cards, and she had a near-total recall of a card displayed and discarded minutes earlier.

"By the Lord above!" Sean whispered in awe. "If I had that memory of yours and your skill at handling

206

the cards, I'd never have to come out here again!" He grinned across the blanket upon which they were playing. "I have a thought. When the winter's past, come with me to New Orleans, lass. I'm after thinking we could do as well at gambling together as at trapping."

Sarah sniffed. "By the time this winter's over, it's my thought we'll be sick to death of each other."

"Ah, now, and I was after thinking we were growing fonder of each other."

"Speak for yourself, Sean Flanagan."

Since she was doing so well, Sean taught her everything he knew about the subject, all the rules of the games, how they should be played, and his ideas on how to win. "Conceding, you understand, that I seldom win."

Although Sarah could not foresee any earthly use such knowledge would ever be for her, it did while away the time. Before long she could easily beat him at any game, and she soon found herself the mentor, her quick mind devising means of winning. She even tried to teach Sean how to retain the memory of cards played, but it was a wasted effort.

"Your mind is like quicksilver, Sean!" she finally said in exasperation. "It darts here and there, like a rolling pebble, never lingering on any one thought for long. If you'd bloody well concentrate for longer than a minute!"

"Only one thing I can concentrate on for long, darlin'," he said with that grin and took her to the bed in the corner.

When she finally lay back exhausted, flushed rosy with pleasure, Sean raised up in the dimness to smile down at her. "How was that for concentration, lass?"

So how could she stay annoyed with him? Laughing, she pulled his head down and kissed him with open mouth.

There were a few days, widely scattered, when the weather would clear, the snowfall stopping. Sean would then dig his way out and see to the mules. If the sun came out, melting the top snow into a hard crust, Sean was able to accomplish some trapping and hunt for game. During much of the winter, they existed on dried meat and the like, a fare that Sean had warned her she would grow weary of.

He made a pair of weblike objects he could fasten onto his feet and wear on the snow without sinking to his hips. They were constructed of rawhide strips laced onto egg-shaped frames made of green wood.

About all he could trap were foxes and a few muskrats, and although their furs were valuable, their meat did not make good fare for the table. However, on one occasion he shot an elk, and they ate well for days. And another time he found a half-grown buffalo which had evidently wandered away from the herd. Quickly gutting the animal and skinning it, Sean carved up the carcass, saving the tastier parts. He was grinning when he came back to the dugout, lugging the meat, still steaming in the cold, behind him on the buffalo hide.

"We'll eat good tonight, Sarah. Buffalo tongue is considered a delicacy out here."

"Like J.J.'s boudin?" she asked suspiciously.

"No, no. This is mouthwatering. I'll show you how to prepare it."

They ate well that night. First, they had hump ribs cooked brown, juice oozing and dripping into the flames with a sputtering noise. They ate the tender meat from the rib bones with their fingers. Earlier, Sean had buried the buffalo tongue in the ashes of the fire. Now he removed it with a long stick, raked the ashes from it, then sliced it in half, giving Sarah her portion. Carefully, she took a bite. It was well-baked, soft and sweet, and had an exquisite flavor.

"This is marvelous!" she exclaimed.

Sean beamed. "Didn't I tell you?"

One morning, at the beginning of April, Sarah awoke to a strange new sound. She lay listening for a moment, puzzling over it. Beside her Sean stirred, yawning. She nudged him with an elbow. "Sean, listen! What is that sound?"

He listened, head cocked. Then his face split wide in a grin. "It's water dripping from the eaves, Sarah! Wagh! The herald of spring! Oh, we may have a blizzard or two yet, but the worst is over. Now I can get busy. This is the time of the year to trap beaver. When the creeks and rivers thaw, Mr. Beaver comes out of hibernation, out of his lodge."

"Sean, there's nothing much for me to do here now. Can I go with you to trap beaver, at least for the first few days?" she asked. "I promise not to get in your way. But I need to get out and around."

Sean studied her guardedly, remembering her reaction to his killing the deer back in autumn. "You won't turn finicky on me? Trapping any kind of varmint is not for the weak of stomach."

"I promise, Sean. If I get out of hand, you can beat me, like a trapper does his squaw if she misbehaves. 'Lodge-poleing,' I think they call it."

"Where'd you hear that?"

"Many Tongues was not so silent as you thought," Sarah said, smiling. "The morning before we left J.J.'s dugout, we had a little talk."

"Why, you sly wench! All this time you knew and didn't so much as mention it!"

"Why should I have? You didn't beat me."

"There've been times I have been sorely tempted." He paused to draw on his pipe. It was the night of the first mild thaw now, and they were basking before the fire. "And speaking of squaws . . ."

"Yes?"

He took a deep breath. "Now that spring is nigh, fur traders will be coming through, trading their beads to the Indians for beaver plews. No doubt, several will pass this way. They know I'm usually here. They will expect my hospitality, and I can't very well turn them away."

"Why should you?"

"Many of them are mean sculpins, lass." He sighed. "So I must warn you. When and if a fur trader is invited to spend the night in our dugout, you are a squaw. You heed me well. You're brown enough now to be one, and with the deerskin and the mocassins . . . If a trader directs a word at you, do nothing but grunt in reply. Never speak a word of English."

"But why?" Sarah was bewildered.

"Because I say so, dammit! Woman, will you listen to me for once?" Then he softened, taking her hand. "Sarah, if they think you are my squaw, they won't touch you. They can find a squaw to tumble anywhere. But a white woman is a different matter. Many of them never see a white woman from year to year, and certainly never lie with one. If they learn

210

you're white, they'd find a way to catch you alone and rape you. They might even go so far as to backshoot me to get at you."

Sarah shivered slightly. "All right, Sean, I'll do as you say." She grinned suddenly. "Or you'll lodge-pole me, right?"

"Sarah, I'm damned serious. If they get at you," he said grimly, "you'd be glad to exchange a beating for what they'll do to you. Take my word on it."

A few days later, the spring thaw was indeed upon them. The creeks flowing into the Arkansas began to run full, and the ice on the river itself began to break up, making cracking sounds like rifle shots.

Sean said, "This day I go looking for beaver sign. You still determined to come along?"

"I am."

"Then let's be off."

Sean took along one mule, loaded down with the heavy steel traps. From one of his packs he also took a small bottle of liquid.

"What's that?" Sarah asked.

"The bait. There are others that can be used, but this is the best kind." He uncorked the bottle and let her smell the glandular, yellow substance.

Sarah wrinkled her nose. "Ugh! It smells!"

"It's supposed to. The smell is what attracts Mr. Beaver."

"What is it?"

"The proper name is castoreum. It comes from the beaver itself. The beaver has a sac, extra glands, which secretes castoreum. It gives the beaver the musky smell peculiar to the animal. Any foresighted trapper is always careful to carry home a bottle of it

211

from last season's trapping. Soon as I catch my first one, I will open up Mr. Beaver and replenish my supply of castoreum."

Already, Sarah thought, I don't like this whole business. But she had promised to behave, so she grimly set herself to accompany him.

Some snow still remained on the ground, but most of it was gone. As they walked along beside the mule, Sean explained what he was looking for.

"I'm searching for a tree across a creek, gnawed down by a beaver, which would mean he has built a dam, and his lodge will be nearby. Or if they are out, and they are, they'll be hungry, and we'll find smaller trees gnawed down for food. Mr. Beaver will be hungry after his long winter's hibernation."

It took Sean most of the day to find ideal spots for traps, yet he didn't set them immediately. "The best time to set the traps is between sunset and dark." When approaching a likely place for beaver sign, he waded in the water, instead of walking on the creek bank. He left Sarah and the mule behind. "Mr. Beaver is a wily creature. If he hears some unusual sound, or smells anything out of the ordinary, he won't come near the trap."

He kept up a running commentary, as though delighted to have an audience, and a novice at that. When the day was done, Sarah had received a thorough lesson in beaver trapping.

Before sunset Sean had located enough promising places to set all of his traps. "You set the traps about four, five inches under the surface of the water, then you fasten one end of the chain to the trap, the other to a stick of dead wood. If the wood is not dead, the beaver will stop to eat on it. Then you put another dead stick in the bank, so it's hanging over the trap. Like this . . ." First, Sean dipped the end of the stick into the bottle of castoreum, and then hung that end over the trap in the water. "Mr. Beaver will smell the castoreum, and he can't resist coming to investigate. But to reach the end of the stick for a good sniff, he has to put his feet right into the jaws of the trap. Whap! The jaws snap closed on his feet, and he takes off for deep water, trying to shake the trap, and drowns. Hopefully, when I come in the morning, I'll have me a beaver. The stick of dead wood will be floating on top of the water, locating Mr. Beaver for me." Standing ankle deep in the water, Sean grinned up at Sarah, who was making a face. "Has been said that the beaver is like a dog: He always seeks out a place where one of his own kind has loosed a stream of piss."

"Ugh!" Sarah said.

"Just remember, lass, if we end our winter's work with a goodly number of beaver plews, it means that much more to stow in your reticule."

It was long after dark when they returned to the dugout, and Sarah was dead tired. They ate a quick supper and retired early at Sean's suggestion. "I want to get to the traps early in the morning, before some predator comes along and chews up the pelts. Still going with me?"

"I'm going," said Sarah stoutly.

Before the morning was well along, she wished she hadn't accompanied him. Sean's traps yielded a rich harvest, beavers caught in all but two. But watching Sean expertly skin the beaver wasn't a pretty sight. He made a quick cut from neck to anus, then four quick cuts about the feet and he had the skin off. He loaded both skin and carcass onto the mule.

"Why the animals, too? Why not just the skins?"

"Because beaver makes good eating. We can use some fresh meat, I'm after thinking. A beaver, lass, exists on the bark of trees and shrubs. As a result the flesh tastes very fine. But an otter, for example, eats fish and reptiles, and the meat is offensive to the taste." Sean squatted on his heels, smiling up at her. "A beaver tail, for instance, is considered a great delicacy out here." He held up the tail, flat and oval in shape, and about ten inches long; it was covered with scales like a fish.

"Boudins, buffalo tongues, everything strange is a delicacy to you!"

"You'll see. You liked buffalo tongue, didn't you now?"

When they returned to camp, their mule laden with pelts and carcasses, Sean and Sarah, now used to the procedure, scraped away the flesh and fatty substance, then stretched the pelts over the wooden framework.

Sean nodded in satisfaction. "Another week or two, and we'll have all the peltries the mules can tote."

That evening, after they had returned from resetting the traps, Sean cooked two beaver tails for them. He thrust long sticks through each tail and held them before the fire with the scales on. After the fierce heat of the fire had penetrated enough to roast the tails, large blisters rose to the surface. But these were easily removed, and the remaining meat was very white.

Sarah found the meat delicious. "This is better than anything I've ever eaten."

Sean was firing his pipe. "I told you so, didn't I?"

"Must you always be so right, Sean Flanagan? I hate a man who is always right!"

Sean was proven right again, three days later, when they had late afternoon visitors. Sarah was working on the beaver pelts. She had stopped going out to the traps with Sean, remaining behind to tend to the pelts. Sean had just returned from his day's catch and was busy pressing the dried pelts into bundles, binding them tightly with rawhide strips.

Suddenly, he stopped what he was doing and stood absolutely still.

"What is it, Sean?"

"We've got company coming. Go inside, Sarah, and stay there until I tell you to come out. Could be hostile Indians. Bolt the door."

He was already reaching for the long rifle leaning against the log wall as Sarah darted inside. She closed the door and dropped the thick wooden bar into place. Heart thudding wildly, she put her ear to the door. She could hear nothing.

Time stretched painfully, and Sarah was so tense and apprehensive, she jumped as Sean's knuckles rapped on the door.

"It's all right, lass. You can come out now."

Sarah unlatched the door and stepped outside. Sean gestured east along the river bottom. Glancing that way, Sarah saw two horsemen approaching, leading two pack animals.

"Fur traders." Sean grunted and spat on the ground. "A pair of mean boyos, for sure. I know them. One's called Walleye, the other one's Frenchie."

Since the riders were still a half-mile distant, Sarah

wondered how he could recognize them, but she had learned not to question his eyesight or hearing. Or perhaps it was some sixth sense he possessed.

"Remember what I told you, Sarah. You're an Indian squaw, naught else. If they speak to you, and they likely won't, just grunt, or gobble something under your breath. Since they're used to that, they won't be suspicious. And now get inside. A squaw never comes out to greet visitors."

Sarah complied, but she kept the door cracked and stood listening. She heard the sounds of horses approaching, and then the sound of voices.

"Howdy, Irisher. We were wondering if ye'd be here again this year. How's the sign?"

"Walleye, Frenchie. Sign's good. A fine year. Welcome to my lodge. Stake your animals down beyond the corral. The grass is just beginning to come to good graze."

As Sean led the way down toward the grazing spot, Sarah sneaked a quick look out the door. From what she could see of them, they were as unsavory a pair as she had ever gazed upon. Their buckskins were ragged and black with dirt. Straggly beards sprouted on their faces like rank weeds, and their hands and faces were grimy from wood smoke. One was tall and lean, the other short and dumpy. Since they were walking away from her, leading their animals, Sarah couldn't see their faces. She noticed that Sean carried the long rifle along with him.

She went about preparing supper for four. They had ample beaver meat on hand, even some beaver tail. She didn't ready any of the tail. She was sure that Sean didn't like them enough to share that delicacy with them.

A few minutes later she heard them coming, the two newcomers talking volubly. One spoke in a language she recognized as French, with a few English phrases thrown in. He was almost incomprehensible.

Sarah was bent over the fireplace when they came in. She heard a grunt from one.

"By damn, Irisher, ye've turned squawman! Finally got too much for ye, did it?"

Sarah turned, ducking her head, but not so much she couldn't see them. Their rank smell reached her even across the dugout. She knew immediately that the tall one was Walleye. The reason for his name was obvious. His left eye rolled up and to the side in its socket, showing mostly white. It gave his face an evil cast, and his bony countenance reminded her unpleasantly of Rhys Pommet. And the other, the shorter man had a zig-zag knife scar across one side of his face.

Now the short one spoke. "By gar, Irisher, Frenchie, he could lofe that one!"

"She's mine," Sean said shortly. "So, paws off, boyos."

"O' course, she's your'n, Irisher," said the man called Walleye, clapping Sean on the shoulder. "Me and Frenchie, we ain't ones to be poaching on another man's squaw. She is some punkin, though. What do ye call her?"

Without seeming to, Sean stepped away from the other man's touch, leaning his rifle against the side of the fireplace within easy reach. Hiding a grin so that only Sarah could see it, he said, "She's called Deerskin Chewer."

"Deerskin Chewer? Wagh! Funny name, even for an Injun." Walleye laughed raucously. "Brought

15

along some drinkin' likker, Irisher, knowing ye have a taste for it."

"That panther piss you trade to the redskins?"

"Naw. Now would we do that to ye?" Walleye said with a wounded look. "Frenchie here brought it down from Canada way."

"By gar, fine Canadian whiskey," Frenchie said, beaming.

Sean fetched cups, and Walleye poured them full. They toasted each other, Sean drinking sparingly.

Sarah, busying herself fixing their food, thought that Sean's warning had been unnecessary. For all the attention the visitors showed her the rest of the evening, she could have been a piece of furniture. They spent their time getting drunk. She did notice that Walleye slanted his one good eye at her curiously a time or two, but for the most part they drank, told extravagant lies about their accomplishments at fur trading, and ate with their fingers until their faces were slick and shiny with grease.

She found the pair of them revolting in the extreme. She noticed that Sean drank very little and was never far from his rifle, and she was glad of that. She felt safe with him there, convinced he would let nothing bad happen to her.

After eating his fill, Walleye leaned back, belched, and rubbed the back of his smoke-blackened hand across his mouth. His glance slid to the stacks of pelts against one wall. He said slyly, "Looks like ye had a good winter's catch, Irisher. How about we take them peltries off your hands? Save ye from lugging them all the way to St. Louie."

Sean laughed shortly. "And have you cheat me, Walleye? Like you do the Indians? No, thanks, I have no use for your pretty beads. I'll handle the sale of my own pelts, like I always do."

Seemingly unoffended, Walleye bellowed laughter. He reached for the whiskey jug and drank directly from it.

Sarah didn't bother cleaning up the mess they had made. She was glad to retire as quickly as possible. But not to sleep. She lay awake, listening to their roaring voices and raucous laughter. They told coarse jokes and stories, as if she was not within hearing.

Sean took small sips as the jug was passed to him and kept urging the pair to drink up. What he had hoped for happened before long. Walleye gave a huge yawn and said, " 'Bout time we was getting slumber, Frenchie. We got a long ride afore us on the morrow."

He got up, staggered, and had to catch at the wall to keep from falling. He careened off into the dimness, Frenchie stumbling along after him. They sprawled right on the dirt floor, and the dugout soon resounded with their loud snores.

Sean sat hunkered before the dying fire, smoking a last pipe. He was sure they were both drunk and out cold for the rest of the night, yet he knew it wasn't beyond them, especially Walleye, to pretend slumber, then get up, murder both he and Sarah in their sleep, and make off with their catch of furs. Finally satisfied that they were indeed asleep, yet knowing that he would sleep lightly this night, Sean moved toward the bed. He took Katie with him, placing the rifle close at hand. He removed only his moccasins. He was surprised to find Sarah still awake.

She rolled against him, and he felt her shiver. "They're an awful pair of—sculpins, Sean."

"That they are, lass," he said gravely. He put his arm under her, so she could lie with her head on his shoulder.

She did, snuggling close. In a whisper she said, "Sean, what are their real names?"

Sean smiled in the darkness. "I've known those boyos for years, but never heard them called aught but Walleye and Frenchie. They're probably charged with all sorts of vile crimes under their real names."

"Well, anyway, I can sleep now, with you here, Sean," she said drowsily. "I feel safe with you near me."

Unexpectedly, his throat closed up, and he couldn't speak for the life of him. He felt a wave of great tenderness flood over him.

Sleeping lightly the rest of the night, Sean was up with the dawn, stirring up the fire. Walleye and Frenchie were still snoring in the corner. Sean aroused Sarah, quietly told her to prepare a quick, skimpy breakfast. Then he prodded his guests awake with his toe and got them moving. Hungover, glum, the pair had little to say and rode out as soon as they had breakfasted.

Standing with Sarah outside the dugout, Sean said with a sigh, " 'Tis glad I am to see the last of that pair."

"Me, too, Sean."

"Well," he said briskly, "I have to check out my traps." He looked down at her. "Wish to go with me?"

"No, I have plenty to do here. For one thing, I have to clean up the mess our visitors left inside. They're a pair of pigs, Sean!"

Sean threw back his head and laughed. "That they are, lass, that they are."

A short time later he left with the mule, and Sarah went inside to clean. She had the mess cleaned up in a couple of hours. The day was warm and sunny, the warmest yet of spring. A walk on such a day would be nice, and Sarah decided she would do just that. She wandered down along the river bottom, delighted to see a few spring flowers in bloom. She would pick a bouquet to freshen the dugout. Sean would be pleased, when he returned.

Kneeling amid a cluster of wild flowers, she heard a sudden sound behind her and wheeled, starting to her feet.

But the man rushing at her was only a few steps away. He pounced, knocking Sarah sprawling on her back. It was the man called Walleye. He came down on top of her, straddling her belly with his legs, knocking the breath from her.

"Injun, be ye! No more Injun than I am, girlie!" he said gloatingly. "Not with them violet-colored eyes. I spotted ye for a white gal right off. Old Irisher thought he'd run a sandy on me. I ain't had me a white gal in a coon's age!"

Her breath back, Sarah struggled, trying to free herself. But Walleye was much stronger than he looked, and he kept her pinned to the ground.

"I'll scream for Sean!"

"Scream your pretty head off, girlie! Your Irisher ain't within hearing distance. I watched from atop the bluff, saw him leading his mule downriver. And then what'd I see? I seen his *squaw* come sashaying out all on her lonesome." He leaned down, face close to hers, and she noticed that he had several rotting

221

teeth. His breath was horrible. She turned her face away, mind racing in an effort to devise a way out of this predicament.

"And old Walleye thinks to himself, now there's a juicy little piece o' white meat all to myself. And I'm going to have it!"

His hands were working the deerskin garment up around her waist even as he talked. Thinking his attention momentarily distracted, Sarah tried again to squirm away. With the speed of light, one hand fastened on her throat, squeezing.

"Now ye lay still and be a good gal, or I'll squeeze the life out'n ye. Dead or alive, it's all the same to me. It's been years since I've humped a white gal, by God, and nothing's stopping me now!"

He had the dress up around her waist now. His mouth hung open, spittle drooling from it. But for all his state of passion, he still had her neck in a firm, cruel grip. With his free hand he was fumbling with his breeches, mouthing a steady stream of obscenities.

Sarah felt vomit rising toward her throat, but swallowed it back. He was easily the most disgusting creature she had ever seen, and the thought of his penetrating her body made her flesh crawl. God knew she had been mistreated in the past, but to have this man use her was a horror she could not countenance. She felt a terrible anger drive out her fear. He *would not* possess her—at least not alive. She knew she would have to pick the right moment, if she was to save herself. With her right hand Sarah felt along her belt until she found the handle of the knife she wore there. Her fingers closed around it, and she stealthily slipped it free.

"Ahh!" Walleye had finally freed himself from his breeches.

Sarah felt the prod of his manhood as he sought entry into her body. The stench of him almost made her gag again, yet she willed herself to lie still for just a moment longer.

The pressure of his fingers around her neck relaxed slightly as he moved, just enough for her to raise up and strike, driving the knife to the hilt in Walleye's back. He screamed, arching high. She pulled the knife free, then drove it into him again, relentless in her outrage and fury. Walleye's breath left him in a long, rasping sigh, and he went limp, all of his weight falling on her. Sarah felt the slickness of his blood on her hand.

Shuddering with revulsion, she shoved with all her strength and managed to push his inert weight aside enough so she could slide out from under him. She came up on her knees, staring down at him, breathing hard.

Gingerly she touched him, and he rolled over onto his back. The one eye stared sightlessly. He was dead.

The enormity of what she had done struck Sarah like a blow. She had killed a man! True, it had been in self-defense, and the death of a man like Walleye was no great loss to the world. Still, it was the first thing she had ever killed.

Reaction set in, and she began to cry quietly. Later, she got hold of herself and gave some thought as to what to do. She remembered Walleye's companion, Frenchie. She darted a fearful look at the woods around her, but saw nothing unusual. Then she noticed Walleye's rifle on the ground nearby, and she recalled Sean's telling her to fire a pistol if she ever needed help when he wasn't around. He had taught her how to fire a pistol, but he had not ever given her instructions on firing his beloved Katie. Still, she had watched him use the rifle a number of times and thought she could manage one.

She checked to see if Walleye's rifle was ready to fire. Carefully, she held the butt against her shoulder, aimed at the sky, and fired. The recoil knocked her flat, and she landed on her back on the ground. For a moment she feared she had broken something in her shoulder, but she could move her arm and decided that it was just bruised.

Squatting a few yards away from Walleye's dead body, she waited. In a very short time she heard Sean calling from the dugout, "Sarah? Lass, where are you?"

She stood up, waving her hands. "Here, Sean. Here I am!"

Sean came at a dead run. Reaching her, he skidded to a stop at the sight of the dead man. "God in Heaven!" He looked at Sarah, then back at Walleye. "He attacked you." It was a statement, not a question. "Ah, colleen, 'tis sorry I am that you had to go through this." He reached for her, and she ran into his arms, crying.

He said gently, "All right, darlin'. Dry the tears. Walleye was not worth one of your tears. The world will be better off without the sculpin!"

"But I killed a man, Sean!"

"Yes, and you'd better thank your God you had the courage for it. He would have used you foully, you can be sure of that."

"His companion—Do you suppose he's nearby?"

"Frenchie?" Sean shook his head. "I very much

doubt it. This one, villain that he was, had some guts about him. Frenchie now, he has about as much courage as a rabbit. I doubt Walleye even told him what he was about. He probably sneaked away. Anyway, Frenchie will be just as happy to be without him. Now the trade goods are his, and the furs he trades for will all belong to him." He pushed her away, gently kissing her cheek. "You go back to the dugout. I'll bury this boyo, and nobody'll ever be the wiser. He will not be missed by a soul on this earth."

When Sean returned to the dugout, he found Sarah composed. She had come to terms with what she had done and knew that as soon as the memory of it had receded a little, she would feel few regrets.

Sean said, "It's about time we moved along, Sarah. We have all the pelts the mules can tote. We're going to have to walk out as it is, with the catch we've got. Think you can walk it, lass? At least to the Missouri, where perhaps we can board a flatboat on down to St. Louis."

"After what happened today, I can do anything required of me," she said strongly.

Chapter Fifteen

It took them three days to dry and bale the last of the furs. Sean nodded in preening satisfaction. "By far the best winter's catch I've had. And much of the credit goes to you, Sarah Moody." He smiled. "When we reach St. Louis, you will no longer be penniless. That should tickle your fancy."

"It does. . . . Sean," she said, suddenly serious, "where do you go from St. Louis?"

"Why, to New Orleans, naturally. I always do. And you?"

"I've been giving it a great deal of thought. New Orleans, too, I suppose. If you'll have me along with you."

"As to that, I would be most delighted." He touched her cheek. "But you look troubled. Why is that, lass?"

"Giles Brock—Do you suppose he'll still be there?"

"That I doubt, colleen. I'm after thinking the boyo will be long gone. A villain such as your Brock would not linger long in New Orleans. Not if he's done the things you've told me. And don't worry. . . ." His lean face took on that grim, deadly look of purpose she'd seen more than once. "I'll see to it that he does not harm you. Of that, you may rest assured."

Aside from the furs and his traps, the only things Sean took along were what was necessary for their journey. The rest he buried some distance from the dugout. "Just in case some sculpin comes along and steals everything in sight. My traps I don't dare leave behind. They're too valuable, too hard to come by."

It was dark when they finished preparations for the journey. They ate a cold supper, and Sean smoked a last pipe. "We'd better bed down early, lass. An early start in the morning. We have a long, hard journey before us."

Sarah had mixed feelings about leaving the dugout. Despite the hardships she had endured, it had not been a bad life here with Sean. The important thing was, she *had* endured; she had survived, even the attempted rape by Walleye. She rarely thought of his death now. She had come to accept the fact that life was cheap in this fierce land. But aside from a certain sadness at leaving what had, in effect, been the first home of her very own, she was excited about returning to civilization again.

That night, in Sean's arms, she was ardent and demanding, and they made love with such a fierce intensity that both were exhausted when it was over.

Sean chuckled in the dark. "It's wondering I am, darlin', if you will still be as ardent, when we return to where folks are more genteel."

Sarah didn't answer, because she had no answer for him. She curled up against him and went to sleep.

It was still dark when Sean routed her out of bed. "Up, up, lay-abed! The mules are loaded and ready. I've been busy for an hour, while you've been warm and dreaming."

They left the dugout shortly after dawn. Sarah looked back once, not sure if in nostalgia or good-bye. Although Sean had not inquired of her, Sarah had often wondered if she would be coming back here with him again next winter. She thought not. Surely she could find something in New Orleans more befitting a woman.

She was fortunate in one respect. The long, hard days of labor had toughened her physically. Sean set a hard pace, and she often longed to be astride one of the mules. But the mules were carrying all the load they could tote, and the idea of dumping off even a few of those rich furs was unthinkable. Sean had told her to make several pairs of moccasins before they left, and Sarah soon saw the reason. She wore out a pair within a week's walking.

At least most of the terrain was flat. The only difficult times they had were while fording the streams, all overflowing with the spring run-off from the mountains to the west.

Sean was able to find enough game to keep their stomachs filled. He shot an antelope a few days from the dugout, and later a buffalo on the fringe of a small herd. Twice, they detoured around small Indian villages.

"We'd probably be received with a warm welcome, but no need to take chances. And even if we were welcomed, it'd mean we'd have to spend a few days with them, delaying us further. Indians are offended if you accept their hospitality for only one day."

Finally they reached the Missouri River. It was a wide, swift-running river, flooding the lowlands in many places. The water was muddy, dull red in color. Sean followed the river east now, walking as near to it as possible. He kept a lookout for some river craft that they could board for portage down to St. Louis. Sarah saw many small water craft, mostly canoes.

"Fur traders mostly," Sean explained. "Hauling their pelts to St. Louis. Many fur traders travel by canoe. Easier getting their peltries to market. But it has its bad side. They have to hide their canoes and walk inland most times to find Indian tribes to trade with. And oftentimes, when they return, they find some sculpin has stolen their canoes and furs."

Two days later, they saw a flatboat making its way down the river. Sean stood on the river bank, waving his hands and yelling. One of the men on the boat waved back and indicated a spot almost a half-mile farther down, where there was less flooding.

Using long poles, the rivermen began maneuvering the ungainly craft in toward the bank. Sean used a willow switch on the mules, hurrying them a little. By the time they had reached the designated spot, the flatboat was beached, the front one-third resting on the mudbank.

"Sean!" yelled the big, burly man who had waved. "Ain't seen you in a dog's age!"

"How about portage on down to St. Louis, Thorny?" Sean shouted back. "Pay you when I sell my pelts."

The man called Thorny scrubbed at his chin, looking around with a shake of his head. The flatboat was piled high with baled furs. "Like to accommodate you, Sean, but we're pretty full up, as you can see."

"I have fresh meat I'll share. Killed a young buffalo. Much of it is left."

"Hurrah! That does her. We need fresh victuals. See if you can crowd your pelts and woman on board."

Sean unloaded the mules first and handed the bales of furs to the crew members, four in number in addition to Thorny. The mules were skittish about clambering onto the swaying, partially submerged boat. By dint of much lashing with the willow switches, cursing by Sean, and shoving by both Sarah and Sean, they finally had the animals on board and staked out, so they wouldn't fall off with the motion of the flatboat.

Thorny eyed the mules doubtfully. "You know, Sean, I don't much favor animals on my boat. If they panic, they could swamp the lot of us, boat and all."

"These mules will be valuable in St. Louis, Thorny. You know I couldn't leave them behind," Sean said. "They'll calm down, soon as they get used to it. I'll see they give you no trouble."

"Ah, well, what the hell! I've been flopped over on a flatboat afore." Thorny glanced at Sarah. "Picked yourself up a squaw, did you?"

Before Sean could answer, Sarah, weary of passing for an Indian squaw, said tartly, "I am not a squaw. My name is Sarah Moody."

Sean glared at her, then grinned slowly, spreading his hands.

"A white woman, is it! Well, I'll be skinned for a polecat!" The big man guffawed. Then he turned and bellowed, "All right, you river rats, let's get this thing moving!"

With Sean helping, the six men lined up with the long poles poking into the bank. With grunting effort, they slowly inched the flatboat out of the mud. In a few minutes it was caught by the swift current and spun almost completely around, before two men could station themselves on each side and get it headed downriver again with the aid of the poles.

When the flatboat was underway to Thorny's satisfaction, he came over to Sean and Sarah. "Been out all winter, have you, Sean?"

"That I have."

"Then I expect you haven't heard the news?"

"What news is that?"

"The War for Independence is over!"

"Who won? But that's a silly question. The Colonists, of course."

Thorny stared. "How did you know that, if you haven't heard the news?"

"Because the puny English aren't hardy enough to survive in this frontier country." He slanted a sly glance at Sarah. "With mayhap an exception or two."

St. Louis had grown some since last Sean had seen it, and the streets were bustling with many people; most of them, he was soon to learn with sorrow, heading west—fur trapping or fur trading.

Sarah was impressed with her first sight of the village, built as it was on a bluff thirty feet above the waters of the Mississippi.

"A wise man did that," Sean told her. "A Frenchman by the name of Pierre Leclede founded the settlement in 1764. He was sharp enough to realize that towns built on low ground would flood out every spring. But here St. Louis stands high and dry. It's had quite a history, first belonging to the French, then to Spain. Officially it is now Spanish territory, supposedly under Spanish rule, but 90 percent of the inhabitants are French, especially the businessmen in the fur trade. Even the present governor is French."

The river was high, but the waterfront landing was free of silt, enabling the flatboat to tie up without trouble. There were a great number of river craft tied up at the busy landing. Sean quickly herded the mules off, then loaded his furs onto them for the hike up the bluff into St. Louis proper.

As Sarah trudged up the slope behind the mules and along the streets of St. Louis, at first she was inclined to cringe away from the bustle of people. She very well knew the appearance she must give. Then she scolded herself and walked straight and proud. She noticed that no one paid her any heed anyway. Then it occurred to her that, after almost a year spent in the New World, this was the first village of any sort she had set foot in. Landing on the outskirts of New Orleans, she had seen none of it, except for that brief glimpse from the *North Star*. So now she stared in wonder. True, it was a primitive settlement, yet it was a town, it was civilization of a sort, and it seemed to have an energetic, throbbing heartbeat.

Sarah walked along, taking in everything she saw. And now that she was walking with head erect, she saw a number of Indian women, dressed much as she was, walking along behind their men.

Sean brought the mules to a sudden halt, in front of a long, low, rambling structure with a crudely lettered sign across the front: "Fortier's Trading Post—Furs Bought and Sold—Ladies' Garments a Specialty."

Sean was coming toward her. "This is my fur buyer's establishment, lass. Since I already have funds on deposit with Jacques, I'm thinking you'll be wanting to purchase some garments more befitting a lady, before we travel on to New Orleans. You'll not have to wait until after my dealings with Jacques. So . . ." He spread his hands, grinning.

"Oh, Sean, may I?" She asked eagerly, eyes spar-

16

kling. "Then will I be able to find lodgings where I can bathe and change?"

"I'm sure you will find an inn to your liking, Mistress Moody," he said dryly. He extended his arm. "Now, shall we visit Monsieur Fortier's emporium?"

Inside, they were met by a bouncy, little butterball of a man, with gleaming black eyes and a happy smile. "Sean! *Mon ami,* my friend!" He threw his arms around Sean, standing on tiptoe to kiss him on both cheeks. "*Mon Dieu,* I am most delighted to see you!"

He looked in question at Sarah, and Sean said, "This is Sarah Moody, Jacques. And this little Frenchie, Sarah, is Jacques Fortier."

"I am deeply honored, mademoiselle." He took her hand and bowed over it.

"The lady, Jacques, is much in need of new garments. May she be catered to while we conduct our business?"

"*Naturellement, mon ami.* Follow me, mademoiselle."

Jacques Fortier led Sarah down the long room toward a door at the far end. As they went along, Sarah gazed curiously at the contents of the room. There were trade goods of every sort, as well as rifles, pistols, knives, blankets, buffalo robes, etcetera. There was such a profusion of things that Sarah's head was spinning.

Then they were in the next room, and she drew in a breath of astonishment. Many beautiful dresses hung on racks. One whole counter was taken up with ladies' wigs, another with shoes, dainty and exquisite.

Fortier called, "Marie, my sweet!"

A large, plump woman waddled from the back.

Fortier beamed. "My wife, Marie. Marie, meet Sarah Moody. She needs fittings." He threw his arms wide. "She is to have anything her heart desires." He winked broadly at Sarah. "I took a peek at Sean's mules. With that winter's catch, he can afford the best for you, mademoiselle."

As Fortier left, Sarah wondered aloud at the wide selection of ladies' garments for sale in a frontier village.

"Since we are so far from the fashion centers, Mistress Moody, we can keep the garments for a long time without the ladies realizing they may be out of fashion. And it might surprise you. Many fine houses are being built on the hill, and many fine ladies come in. And the Indian women now . . ." Mrs. Fortier grinned broadly. "When they accompany their trapper men—not many trappers do that, you know. But when they do, they demand the best of clothing. I would imagine the garments do not last overlong in the wilderness out there. The same squaws come back, in the spring, wearing their deer or elk skin garments, clamoring again for fine lady attire."

Sarah liked one dress of velvet particularly well. Mrs. Fortier commented, " 'Tis a close match in color for your eyes."

"I must show it to Sean!" Sarah cried. Barefooted, she ran into the other room, where Sean and Jacques Fortier were engaged in what appeared to be a bitter argument, with loud voices and much waving of plump hands by Fortier. "Sean! Look!"

Sean turned to look. Smiling, Sarah turned around slowly.

Staring at her, Sean was stunned by her beauty. He realized that this was the first time he had seen Sarah dressed in something befitting her. She was a great beauty, one of the loveliest women he had ever seen.

"Well?" she demanded impatiently. "What do you think?"

Sean cleared his throat, finally finding his voice. "I think, colleen, that I have never seen a more beautiful wench!"

Blushing, she said, "The dress, Sean Flanagan, the dress!"

"Oh, the dress." Chin propped on his hand, he circled her, making a great show of frowning concentration.

Sarah saw Jacques Fortier leaning on his arms on the counter, chortling in open delight. Sarah said sharply, "Sean!"

"We-ell, I'm thinking that the dress becomes you, darlin'. Not, however, nearly as much as the squaw dress you made yourself."

"Oh! You're impossible!" She flounced off, but she began to smile the moment her face was out of his sight.

Back in the lady's section, she told Mrs. Fortier that she would take the dress, as well as a wine-colored traveling outfit; a blue bonnet, almost the exact shade of blue as the velvet dress; underclothing; shoes, including evening slippers; a cape; gloves; and toilet articles. She then bought a small trunk in which to store her purchases.

When she finally returned to the main room, carrying a large bundle of clothing, the scene there seemed a continuation of what she had observed earlier—both men talking at once at the top of their voices. Fortier waving his hands violently.

"Sean?" she said tentatively.

Sean turned, smiled, and said in his normal voice, "Done already, Sarah?"

Jacques Fortier beamed at her. "I hope mademoiselle found the items offered by my poor shop adequate for her needs?"

"Most adequate, thank you, sir," she said. "Sean, when will you be ready to go?"

"Oh, not for some hours yet. You have to haggle with this Frenchie boyo for a long time to reach a fair bargain."

"But I can't wait that long!" she said in dismay. "I sorely need a bath."

"No need for you to wait, lass. The Foster House is the best in town. Clean rooms, good food served. And Dulcie Foster, the lady who owns it, is grand. Come along, I'll hail a carriage for you." He took her arm and led her outside. "Sarah, you might do something for us. I'm not after knowing how long I'll be occupied here. And I have other things to do as well." His glance slid away. "After you've bathed and dressed, would you mind taking a carriage down to the landing and see about arranging passage for us on a keelboat for New Orleans? You'll be safe enough in daylight. A rough lot, those rivermen, but they'll not harm you by day. 'Twould be better for you to do it than me, so you may select accommodations to your liking." He handed her some coins.

"All right, Sean. Would you see that the trunk and the other things I bought are sent along later?"

"Yes, darlin'." He kissed her cheek. "I'll bring them along myself."

The Foster House was, as promised, clean and comfortable. After the primitive dugout, the room she was shown to looked like the ultimate in civilized living. There was a large brass bed with a white coverlet, two comfortable chairs, a dresser and mirror. She asked for a tub of hot water, and after several trips by Mrs. Foster's young son, who gaped at her each time he returned with the bucket, she slipped out of her grimy deerskin dress and into the hot water. Sarah couldn't remember when anything felt so good.

By the middle of the afternoon Sarah was dressed in the blue velvet. Using the new brush she had purchased, she coiled her hair at the base of her neck and fastened it with pins. The woman looking back at her from the mirror seemed a stranger. Her sun-darkened skin accented the violet of her eyes, and her face, thinner now, looked more mature. Pulling on the blue bonnet, which framed her hair flatteringly, she picked up the cape and reticule, and went downstairs for her first civilized meal in months.

After her meal, she hired a carriage to take her to the river landing. At the landing, flatboats and keelboats were docked in great numbers, so thick that they backed up out into the river, forming an island of sorts. Men were busily engaged loading and unloading the boats. They were rough men, dirty and sweaty, cursing in loud voices.

She received a few curious, admiring glances, but no one approached or directed a crude remark at her. She was disappointed by the condition of the keelboats she saw at first. They looked ill-kept, hardly seaworthy. Then, down the line a ways, she saw two tied up end to end. They looked much better than the others; the long, low cabins even had fresh coats of paint. A tall, broad-shouldered man, his back to her, was overseeing bales of furs being loaded on board one of them.

Sarah approached the big man, stopping behind him. "Your pardon, sir, could I . . . ?"

The man gave a soft snort of impatience and wheeled about with an annoyed gesture. "Yes? What is it?"

"I wish to . . ." Sarah's voice faltered, and she stared at the man's face, at his full beard. It was impossible!

"Captain Hawkins? Jeb?" It was; it must be!

The man's face broke wide in a smile, and he stepped toward her, hands held out. "Sarah Moody? By the Lord Jehovah, it *is* you!"

Chapter Sixteen

Giles Brock learned the fundamentals of his new trade, river piracy, quickly. Within a short time he learned that there were a number of ways to take a river boat and its cargo. One way was to have a member of the pirate crew, preferably a woman, stand on the river bank and hail the passing boat, under the pretext of asking for passage downriver. The instant the boat touched the bank, the hidden pirates would boil out of the underbrush and storm it. A second method was to wait until the boat tied up for the night, then entice the rivermen into a card game, ply them liberally with liquor, and make off with their cargo. Another means was to wait until the boat came into the bank for the night, then sneak up and bore holes in the bottom or knock out some of the caulking. When the boat began to sink, the pirate crew would rush up on the pretense of rescuing the cargo.

Blessing Johnson's method was a direct assault on the boats, whenever possible.

This method was the most difficult, resulting in greater physical danger for the pirates and often a heavy loss of life. It did not appeal to Brock, not in the least.

But Blessing scorned the easier ways. "I will not be a party to employing my wives as Circe's scarlet women, even if only playacting. And I will not resort to the devil's twin evils, gambling and liquor." Blessing's eyes took on that staring, half-mad look. "I will not employ my flock in such evil ways. We shall descend upon the money-changers with the wrath of God as our weapons. Our Lord says, 'All that take up the sword shall perish with the sword!' "

According to Blessing's reasoning, the use of the sword by his own crew was on the side of the Lord. Brock felt like pointing out that many of his "flock" also perished by using Blessing's way, but he knew it would be a waste of breath. There was no reasoning with Blessing Johnson. Whatever he did was the Lord's work, the Lord was *always* on his side, and who could argue with that?

Blessing Johnson must be killed; Brock had already decided that. He had early grasped the fact that a pirate crew such as this could profit mightily by raiding the river boats, if done in the proper manner.

The only thing that remained was to figure out the manner of doing it, a safe way. Brock was convinced that the other members of the crew would be most happy to follow a leader who could point the way to more booty, who would allow them to wench and gamble and drink. Even Blessing's most loyal coterie, Brock was convinced, would fall in behind a new leader once the old was no more.

He and Rhys Pommet were in complete agreement on this and had gotten their heads together many times considering ways and means. A pistol ball in the back or a knife in the heart while Blessing slept were the two simplest and most direct. Yet Brock soon saw that would be too great a risk. The half-dozen loyal followers were never far from Blessing

Johnson, even while he slept. And one or two always had an eye out.

"There's only one way I can see to do it proper," Brock said during one of their sessions. "Lure him into a duel. You know how he likes to 'execute the Lord's will' himself, using . . ." He sneered. "The Right Hand of God! We've seen him duel three men already for breaking one of his rules. There's only one thing wrong with that. The bastard's a dead shot!"

"I'll do it, Giles. I'm not afraid of him," Pommet said eagerly. "And I'm as good a shot as he is, damned if I'm not!"

"No, Rhys, it has to be me." He didn't elucidate further. But the man who killed Blessing Johnson would be the undisputed leader of the band, and Brock intended to have that position. "There has to be a way," he mused.

Suddenly Pommet grinned. "I know how to manage it! You know he keeps that pistol, his Right Hand of God, in that fancy case of his'n. Ain't that right?"

"So how does that help us?"

"I'll sneak into the case when he ain't watching and foul up his priming powder."

Brock felt a thrill of hope. "That might do it. One thing— The challenge will have to come from him, so 'twill appear a sudden thing."

Pommet frowned in puzzlement. "How will you arrange that, Giles?"

"I think I know a way. It'll fire him up so he'll *have* to call me out."

Brock had noticed that the youngest of Blessing's two wives, Purity, had eyed him boldly a number of times. He had a suspicion that Blessing Johnson, at least in his late fifties, had not the virility to keep two young wives content between the blankets. So far, Brock had not encouraged the wench by even so much as a wink, having already learned that Blessing was murderously jealous of his wives.

Purity was by far the comeliest of the pair; buxom, sturdy of limb, and full of breast, a look about her black, snapping eyes as bold as a strumpet's strut. Brock well knew that he was not unappealing to wenches, so he had no doubts about his being able to coax the wench into the bushes for a lusty tumble. Timing, that was the important factor.

Finally, his chance came. After capturing a flatboat and its cargo by Blessing's usual direct assault, the pirate crew found a secluded spot where they could rest for a few days and allow the wounds of those still alive to heal. They had lost four men in the attack. Blessing squatted by the campfire, shouting prayers to the Almighty to have mercy on the souls of those of his flock just killed. Brock noticed that Purity took advantage of Blessing's inattention and made bold advances, brushing a full breast against Brock's chest.

Brock seized the opportunity. He winked and whispered, "How about it, love? I'll meet you down by the big oak past the bend of the creek."

"I don't take your meaning, sir," Purity said, with a flirty roll of her eyes.

"You take my meaning right enough," he growled. "Wander down there. I'll follow."

She gave him a saucy toss of the head and walked off without replying. But Brock, watching, saw her edge out of the firelight a few minutes later and casually stroll off in the direction of the stream.

Brock sidled up to Pommet. In a low voice he said, "Did you fix the powder?"

"It's fixed, Giles," Pommet replied with an evil grin. "With the powder now in his horn, Blessing couldn't kill a mosquito."

"Give me about ten minutes, then whisper to Blessing that his wench, Purity, is dallying with me under the big oak."

It didn't really take that long. Purity was ready and willing, so hot and eager in his arms that Brock was aroused despite himself, and the thought crossed his mind to give her a quick tumble. Yet it would not do. Since it was Blessing's practice to have his "duels" staged before the others of the crew as an object lesson, Brock knew that ordinarily the man would not shoot him on sight, but if by chance he found Brock already copulating with Purity, such might be his rage that he *would* shoot on the moment.

Brock had Purity on her back on the ground, her skirts tossed up above her waist, and was fumbling with his breeches, Purity urging him to hurry up, when Blessing's great voice thundered behind him. "What is this I see! One of my own flock cuckolding me! An adulterer in my congregation! The wrath of Our Lord shall descend upon you, Giles Brock! You shall be punished forthwith!"

Brock got quickly to his feet, feigning great terror, cringing away. In a whining voice he said, " 'Twas not my doing, Blessing. She enticed me, did your wench. She lured me here and . . ."

"That is no excuse, sir!" Blessing roared. "The Good Book tells us, 'Yield not to temptation.' " He gestured to the men behind him. "See to it that he does not flee, brethren. Escort him back to our camp and I shall mete out retribution with the Right Hand of God."

Blessing turned and strode away. The men gathered around Brock and herded him back to camp.

At the camp Blessing was directing that more wood be dumped onto the fire. Soon, the flames were leaping high, and the clearing was almost as bright as day.

Blessing ordered his pistol be brought to him. Then he glared at Brock. "Prepare to defend yourself, sinner. The hour of your retribution is at hand!"

Rhys Pommet brought a pistol for Brock. As Brock primed the weapon, he shot a glance at Blessing, who was overseeing the preparation of the Right Hand of God. In a whisper Brock said, "You're sure things are right?"

"Right as rain. Trust me, Giles."

"Trust or not, his pistol better misfire. If not, not only will I be dead, but you as well. You think he'll let you live after killing me?"

Blessing thundered, "Ready, sinner?"

"I'm ready."

"Then let us about it. We stand back to back. You, Seth, will count off as we take ten paces. On the count of ten, we shall turn and fire."

Midway through his ten paces, Brock had a powerful urge to wheel and fire. But he knew it would never do. If he killed Blessing Johnson in such a manner, the others would turn on him. It had to have the appearance of a fair duel. He had to trust Pommet and wait.

At the count of ten Brock whirled. Already Blessing's pistol was aimed. Before Brock could even bring his weapon to bear, there was a puff of smoke from the other's pistol. Brock steeled himself against the shock of a pistol ball. It never came. As Brock brought his own pistol up, he saw Blessing's eyes flare wide in disbelief, and then go dark with the awareness of his approaching death.

Brock took careful aim and fired. His aim was true. The ball knocked Blessing Johnson backward. There were exclamations of awe from the others. One man dropped to a knee beside Blessing. He looked up, mouth agape. "He's dead. Blessing's dead!"

Brock faced the others, raising his voice. "You all saw it happen. All fair and square. This time, Blessing Johnson found his own retribution. Your leader is dead, and I am your new leader! It is my right and due. Those of you not caring to follow me may leave now. But for those of you who remain and take your orders from me, I promise that pickings in the future will be richer and much easier to come by. You'll not need to be afraid of dying each time. There are easier ways than Blessing's way. And I promise you all the liquor, wenches, and gambling you desire. No more of Blessing's rules." He paused to take a deep breath, his hard gaze raking over them. "Now, who'll join me?"

There was some muttering, many looks exchanged, and then Brock saw the two women come boldly forward. They ranged on either side of him, taking his arm. Purity let a breast press against his arm.

Then, one by one, the others stepped forward, until they were all beside him.

Jeb Hawkins had taken Cap's long rifle and gone hunting. They could use some fresh meat. That morning, the keelboat had rammed into a floating tree stump, knocking some of the caulking loose from a seam, letting in a seepage of water. Since they had a heavy cargo, Cap had decided it would be prudent to haul the keelboat partway up onto the bank and re-caulk the seam.

Jeb had known little of rifles, but these months with Cap's crew, always in peril of attack by river pirates, had taught him that it would be a good idea to familiarize himself with weapons of all kinds. Cap had given him a few lessons with the rifle, and Jeb found he had a knack for it.

He walked upriver for quite a distance without spotting any game, but he was enjoying the stroll. Although it was mid-December, the day was sunny and warm. He was several miles from the keelboat when he heard the distant sound of gunfire. Cocking his head intently, he realized that the firing was in the vicinity of the keelboat. It was under attack!

Cursing himself for leaving the keelboat, Jeb began to run, heart thudding with apprehension.

The hard work on the keelboat had toughened him considerably, yet he couldn't run at full speed the entire distance. For one thing, he often had to force his way through the thick underbrush, which slowed him down. And it wasn't long before he developed a stitch in his side, and he had to rest for a little, his lungs on fire, his legs like leaden weights.

In a short time he was up and running again. He already knew that whatever had taken place at the keelboat was long since over. Either the pirates had been driven off, or the boat looted, those on board either dead or chased off.

Two hundred yards from the boat's location, he

slowed and began to approach more cautiously. Reaching the last growth of underbrush, he got down on his hands and knees and crawled until he could part the bushes and see the boat.

His heart sank. The keelboat was more than two-thirds submerged in the river, with just the bow sticking up. The decks were clean of cargo. They had been heavily laden with rich furs from St. Louis and other valuable cargo. It was all gone. And from where he was, Jeb could see no sign of life.

Holding the rifle ready to fire if the need arose, Jeb went forward warily, his gaze darting about as he plodded along the soft sand toward the sunken keelboat. The smell of gunpowder and the sick-sweet odor of blood was strong. He found the first body ten yards from the boat. It was one of the rivermen, dead, a gaping hole in his chest. A few feet farther Jeb found another. Blind Bob, the back of his head crushed. A black rage filled Jeb. What manner of men would needlessly kill a blind man who could do them no harm?

Jeb was at the bow of the boat now. He saw another man sprawled in death on the deck. A part of the long cabin was out of the water, the door ripped off its hinges.

As Jeb started to climb on board, a voice hailed him. "Captain Hawkins!"

Jeb wheeled, falling into a crouch, the rifle coming up. Then he relaxed as he recognized Tim running toward him.

Breathless, Tim hurled himself against Jeb. Jeb leaned the rifle against the keelboat and held the boy in his arms. "Thanks be to Jehovah you're alive and safe, lad!"

"It was awful, Captain!" Tim sobbed. "Just bloody awful!"

In a moment Tim had himself under control, and he stood back, dashing tears from his eyes.

"Now tell me what happened here, Tim."

"Well, the men and Cap were busy caulking the boat. I had to go into the bushes. Suddenly I heard gunshots. I started running back, then stopped and hid where I could watch. There was nothing I could do, Captain. I had no weapon!" Tim's eyes sought his pleadingly.

"You did right, Tim. Nothing you could have done. They would have killed you."

"There were about twenty of them, armed to the teeth. They caught all on board by surprise, and the men had little chance to fight back. They killed four, maybe five. The others managed to escape into the woods. Then the pirates loaded everything onto a flatboat they must have had hidden around the bend, chopped a hole into the bottom of the keelboat, and sunk her."

"And Cap?"

"They killed him and threw him overboard. He's long gone down the river, Captain."

"Dear God," Jeb said softly, almost in prayer.

"There's something else, Captain."

"What, lad?"

"The leader of the river pirates was Giles Brock!"

"What! Are you sure?" Jeb seized Tim by the shoulder and shook him. "You could not be mistaken?"

"I saw him, Captain, plain as day. Him and Rhys Pommet. I swear. The others were taking orders from Brock."

"But how did he . . . ?" Jeb broke off, his gaze coming to rest on Blind Bob. "Blind Bob—why did they kill him? He could have done them no harm."

"For the sport of it, I think. It was just as they were leaving. Blind Bob was stumbling around on the bank, scared I be sure, not knowing what was about. It was Giles Brock. Laughing, he came up behind Blind Bob and hit him in the back of the skull with the butt of a rifle."

"That murderous, mutinous scum!" Jeb said angrily. He clenched his fists. "Some day we'll meet face to face and he'll pay for all his villainy." He turned away abruptly. "Let's see what damage was done to the boat."

He hoisted Tim aboard the tilted keelboat. They found one man alive on board. Peering into the cabin, the lower end slowly filling with water, Jeb saw Ezra Boggs lying crumpled and still, water lapping at his feet. Quickly Jeb ducked inside and pulled him out. There was a raw pistol wound in his left shoulder, but he was still breathing.

They got Ezra off the boat and onto the bank. Jeb said crisply, "Quickly, Tim, gather as much firewood as you can, while I see what I can find in the cabin before it fills with water."

When Jeb returned to the cabin, he realized something that, in his agitation, he had not noticed before. There was no settling motion; the keelboat was resting firmly on the bottom. Which meant that there was some hope of saving her and little danger of the cabin flooding further.

Awkwardly clambering around on the tilted decking of the portion of the cabin that was still dry, he found an armload of blankets, a few knives, and, most fortunately, Ezra's rum jug.

Climbing off the boat, Jeb saw that Tim had already collected a pile of dry driftwood.

"Good, lad, good."

With one of the knives Jeb made a small pile of wood shavings, then fumbled out his flint and steel and started a fire. Just as it was going good, Tim called urgently, "Captain! Som'un is coming!"

Jeb spun around on one knee, snatching up the rifle. Then he recognized one of the crew members, coming toward them with hands held out in supplication. Jeb recalled his name was Marlowe. "I be sorry, Jeb Hawkins, for running away like a scared horse, but I didn't have nary a weapon to fight back with."

Jeb snorted softly. "Don't grovel, Marlowe. Just be glad you saved your own skull. I can use a hand here. We have to remove a pistol ball from Ezra's shoulder."

Just then Ezra groaned, twitching. His eyes opened, and he muttered something. "Here." Jeb gave the rum jug to Marlowe. "Feed him rum until he's senseless. This is going to pain him considerably."

Jeb tested the knives for sharpness. The blade of the sharpest knife he heated by turning it over and over in the flames.

He looked around. "Is he rum-sotted?"

Marlowe grinned, showing missing teeth. "Drunk as a skunk."

"You hold him by the unwounded shoulder and head. Tim, you hold his feet. Hard now, hold him hard."

Jeb took the rum jug, now almost empty, and

splashed rum liberally onto the wound. Ezra Boggs screamed and struck out with his arms and legs.

"Hold him!" Jeb snapped.

Without further ado, Jeb probed into the wound with the knife point. Fortunately the ball wasn't buried deep. He found it almost at once. He dug deeper. Ezra screamed again, then slumped back in a faint.

With a twist of the knife, Jeb flipped out the pistol ball, then poured more rum on the wound. "Tim, go aboard the boat and see if you can locate some spirit turpentine and sugar. We'll make a poultice of that, then bind up the wound. I think he'll be fine."

Jeb stood up, looking around. "Marlowe, let's gather up the dead and bury them."

After that onerous chore was completed, Jeb stood studying the keelboat, absently searching his pockets for a cigar. He had bought a fresh supply in St. Louis, but there was none on his person. With a curse he hurried aboard the boat where he found the fresh cigar supply still high and dry. Jeb lit the cigar, and then stood on the tilted bow, smoking, thinking of the future. He knew what he was going to do now.

Charles Clayborne had had no family. Once, in a moment of confidence, he had said, "I have no one, friend Hawkins. Neither kith nor kin. Should something dire befall me, the keelboat is yours."

By nightfall, three more members of the crew had returned. Jeb had a feeling that was the lot, that the others had kept running. But the six of them would be enough. They found enough food on board to make a scanty supper.

After they had eaten, Jeb stood before them. "In the morning, at first light, we will use the cordelle and warp the boat out of the water. We can use that tree over there." He pointed to a giant oak on the bank, dimly seen in the flickering firelight. "Then we will repair her and make for St. Louis for a new cargo."

One of the men said sullenly, "And who made you captain, Jeb Hawkins?"

"I did," Jeb said flatly. "Cap Clayborne had no family. I am taking the keelboat as mine. Any here to say me nay?"

He stared hard at the man who had spoken. He looked away, grumbling under his breath.

Marlowe said eagerly, "I'm with you, Jeb Hawkins. I'm glad to have you as captain any day."

One by one the others chimed in their agreement, even the early dissenter.

"Excellent!" Jeb said. "There is good money to be made keelboating, if it's done right. Cap's way was fine, but it can be improved upon. Eventually, you will earn better wages. My promise on it."

Jeb Hawkins was a contented man when he stretched out on the ground to sleep. He was grieved that Cap Clayborne was dead, he had liked the man, yet it was a grand feeling to know that he would be the master of his own vessel again, even if only a keelboat!

Over the next few months Jeb drove himself night and day, and he soon prospered. He prospered very well.

He came up with several innovative ideas. After repairing the keelboat and struggling upriver to St. Louis for a new cargo to take to New Orleans, he had enough profit to invest in the idea he had proposed to Cap—a team of twelve mules to tow the keelboat back up the river. It speeded the boat's progress by more than half. The mules he sold in St. Louis for a profit and immediately set about getting a new cargo. He also began putting together a permanent crew, one that would remain with him for trip after trip. To do this, he paid his men more money. This caused some grumbling from other keelboat operators, but he ignored them and went his own way. He hired men who were good fighters, proficient with weapons of all kinds, and drilled them in ways to defend the boat. And every time it was necessary to tie the boat up on the bank for any reason, he posted guards around the clock and sent out scouts in both directions along the river, with orders to hie themselves back to the boat at once should they spy any suspicious characters in the vicinity.

Even these precautions did not save them from being attacked by river pirates. Three times they were set upon, but in each instance his men drove the pirates off, without a single loss of life among the rivermen. Each time, when the pirates finally fled, they left dead men behind.

During the third attack, Jeb was positive he saw Giles Brock leading the pirates. At the sight of Brock, a murderous rage filled him. Forgetting caution, he vaulted from the deck of the keelboat onto the ground and started for the man, pistol cocked and ready.

But the pirates were already in full flight, and Brock was too far away for Jeb to get to him. In frustration, he dropped to one knee on the sand and aimed his pistol at the fleeing Brock. But the distance was too great, and the ball fell harmlessly to the ground.

Swearing under his breath, Jeb turned and plodded back to the keelboat. It was common knowledge along the river now that Giles Brock led a gang of river pirates, a villainous crew given the sobriquet of Brock's Bloody Bastards.

At the boat Tim scolded him. "Captain, that was a foolish risk you took. They could have killed you."

"I know, Tim, I know. But I saw Giles Brock among them, and I could think of naught else but to kill him." He shouted to the crew, "Let's get this scow underway!"

Lighting a cigar, he stood ready at the steering oar until the boat was caught by the current, then guided the keelboat downstream. He performed the chore automatically, his thoughts still on Giles Brock.

With the end of the Revolutionary War, traffic along the river increased as Cap Clayborne had predicted. Not only was more cargo being shipped, but now the passenger trade began to pick up. People were willing to pay well for water transport both ways along the Mississippi. Jeb's keelboat, as well as all the others, provided poor quarters for passengers. Certainly it was sorry housing for women, and many ladies were accompanying their husbands up and down the river now.

Jeb could see only one thing to do. He drew up his own plans for another keelboat, a *passenger* keelboat, and had it built. It had a larger cabin area and was larger overall. The big cabin he had partitioned off into a number of smaller cabins. They were hardly large enough to accommodate two people, yet this was far better than communal sleeping in one large cabin, and he could charge higher fares, too. In addition to the passengers on the new boat, there was also room on top of the cabin for a goodly amount of cargo.

There was one additional feature—a sop to his vanity, Jeb was honest enough with himself to admit. He had one larger cabin added to the new boat, a near-duplicate of his cabin on the *North Star*. He would be the only keelboat captain on the Mississippi with his private quarters, which would be certainly luxurious by most standards.

Jeb intended to operate the two keelboats in tandem, running them together up and down the river.

And now, in St. Louis, the new keelboat was ready for her maiden voyage, spanking new and bright with fresh paint. Jeb was departing for New Orleans the next morning. Due to the newness of his passenger boat, plus the fact that he had not yet had time to advertise passenger accommodations, he would be leaving with only about half the cabins occupied, but he had no fears that he would attain full capacity on the next trip.

That was when he heard a female voice behind him and turned to see a beautiful woman staring at him dazedly. It took him a full moment to recognize Sarah, and when he did, he was staggered by the shock of it.

Chapter Seventeen

"Sarah?" Jeb said again. "By the Lord Jehovah, it *is* you!"

"Jeb?" Sarah said in bewilderment, seeing what she thought was the impossible. "I thought you were dead!"

"And I you!"

"It seems we were both wrong then, doesn't it?"

Jeb looked startled for a moment, then burst into laughter.

Sarah also started to laugh but such was her joy at seeing him alive, at seeing him at all, that she became dizzied with it, and the laughter edged dangerously close to hysteria.

"Ah, Sarah. Love!" He took a step, opening his arms, and she went into them, beginning to weep softly.

"Thank God, Jeb," she whispered against his chest. "Thank God that you're alive!"

"Don't cry, Sarah love. Don't cry." He smoothed her hair. "Does that mean that I am forgiven then?"

With tear-wet eyes she looked up at him, truly bewildered. "Forgiven for what?"

"Oh, for bringing you to this country, for not believing you. For what I . . ." He cleared his throat and suddenly remembered where he was. He looked up and saw all his men stopped at their work, gaping at the sight of their captain holding in his arms a beautiful, well-dressed lady, the likes of which was rarely seen on the landing.

"What are you staring at?" he roared. "Get back to your labors, you lollygaggers!"

The men immediately returned to work, gazes carefully averted.

At his bellow, Sarah had started, stepping back. Eyes downcast, she murmured, "They probably think I'm some strumpet down here to see you."

"Whatever they may think, Sarah, 'tis not that you are a strumpet. You are every inch a lady. And a wondrous beauty at that." His gaze grew intent, and her color rose. "Speaking of that, what in Jehovah's name *are* you doing down here? It's hardly the place for a lady, a lady not in the company of a gentleman."

"I—I came down to engage passage to New Orleans on a keelboat."

Jeb smiled broadly. "Now there, madam, I can be of service. I am the proud owner of not one, but two keelboats. One will be on her first voyage and is especially fitted to carry passengers."

He turned, motioning to indicate the two keelboats of a better class that Sarah had already noted. She stared. "Those belong to you?"

"Indeed they do," he said with pride. "Not, of course, in a class with the *North Star*, but they are mine, and none can take them from me. Although Giles Brock and his ilk have tried hard," he added grimly.

"Giles Brock?" she said in apprehension. "Is he still around?"

"Aye, that he is. The blackguard has now turned

river pirate, a bloody plague along the river, plundering and murdering at will. . . ."

A voice broke in. "Mistress Moody? Is it really you?"

Sarah turned to see Tim staring at her. The lad had grown taller since last she had seen him; he would soon be a man. She smiled. "Yes, Tim. It's me, in the flesh."

Tim dipped his head shyly. "'Tis glad I am to see you safe and sound, m'lady."

On impulse she hugged him against her, running her hands over his head cradled on her bosom.

Stepping back, she saw that his face was flaming red, and she knew that she had embarrassed him. She suppressed a smile.

"Tim," Jeb said briskly, "see to it that these laggards keep at it. I am going to show Sarah our new keelboat."

As he lent an arm to help Sarah up the long plank onto the keelboat, he explained, 'Tim is my good right hand now, my first mate, you might say. And good at it he is, too, despite his tender years."

On the boat he escorted her into the long cabin. His plans had called for a higher cabin than was the norm, and it was possible to walk upright in this one. There was a corridor running the length of it, with doors opening off. Jeb opened one and showed Sarah the interior of the small cabin.

"Not the most roomy, but 'tis adequate for sleeping two." It was in Jeb's mind to inquire if she was seeking passage for two, but at the last moment he decided to hold his tongue.

Instead, he said, "But there is something else I wish

you to see. A touch of vanity on my part, I am aware, but I think it will be a surprise to you."

He guided her to the last door on the right, opened it, and motioned her inside with a flourish.

Two steps inside, Sarah stopped short with a gasp. "Why, it's just like . . ."

Jeb said, "Yes, a close replica of my cabin on the *North Star*. As I said, an exercise in vanity and a loss of revenue, but . . ." He shrugged expressively.

Sarah's gaze jumped across the room. And yes, there it was! "Even the same . . ." Remembering, she felt her cheeks turn scarlet.

Jeb pretended not to notice her discomfiture. "Yes, the same large bed. Another sop to vanity and an additional expense. But it is a comfort. I slept here last night for the first time. On most keelboats, you know, you sleep on decking as unyielding as stone. This, I should think, is one luxury I will not regret . . ." Jeb realized that he was talking too much and too fast. He forced himself to slow down, taking a deep breath. "Perhaps I could offer you a brandy, Sarah?"

To his astonishment, she nodded. "I could use a tot of something, after the shock of finding you alive."

Hiding his surprise, Jeb seated her at the bolted-down table. As he fetched the brandy bottle and mugs, it crossed his mind that she had changed; Sarah Moody had become more a woman of the world. The Sarah Moody he had known on the *North Star* would never have so openly accepted the offer of liquor. And on the heels of that came the thought: If she has changed in that respect, in what other ways might she have changed?

He poured the brandy and sat down across from

her. He raised the mug in a toast: "To a return to life. And to our reunion."

Sarah hesitated; for the first time since the shock of seeing Jeb alive, she thought of Sean. Then she smiled, pushed all consideration of Sean from her mind, and said, "A fine toast, Captain Hawkins, sir, and one I'll drink to."

They drank, and Jeb set his mug down with a thump. "Now, I'm anxious to know what befell you, Sarah Moody."

Again she hesitated, wondering how much to tell him. Slowly, she began, from the moment Jeb had been struck down on the river bank, and told it all. Or most of it. It wasn't necessary to tell him that she had spent the winter in the arms of another man; the set of his face told her that he knew that.

He said carefully, "Are you in love with this man, this Sean Flanagan, Sarah?"

Flushing, she tossed her head. "I fail to see that that is any of your affair, Captain Hawkins!"

"Perhaps not. But I'm asking anyway. Are you?"

"No. I'll be honest. I am not in love with Sean. I feel much affection for him, a great deal of affection, and I owe him my life. In many ways."

Jeb smiled then and drank from the mug. "I must meet this Flanagan fellow and offer my heartfelt gratitude as well."

At the moment Sarah didn't wish to pursue the subject of Sean Flanagan. She said hastily, "Now it's your turn. What happened to you?"

"It's a long tale, and a grim one at times," he said gravely. "But it seems to have reached a happy conclusion, as all fairy tales should. For it is a fairy tale, in a manner of speaking."

Once, as he talked, Jeb got up to refill their mugs with brandy.

When he was finished, Sarah said musingly, "So Giles Brock is still around and would probably welcome another chance to kill us."

"That he is, and more villainous than ever." Jeb's face flushed with anger. "And kill us he would, yes, if he ever gets the chance. But he is a coward, is our Mister Brock, and would never dare face me."

Sarah suddenly realized that it was growing late. Sean might be looking for her at the Foster House. She said, "I didn't realize how long I had tarried. I must go, Jeb."

"No, Sarah." He leaned forward, face intense. "Don't go."

"I must, Jeb."

Not aware of how much brandy she had consumed, Sarah stood up and staggered, almost falling. Jeb was at her side in a flash, catching her.

"Stay, Sarah. Stay a while."

His face was very close to hers, his breath warm on her cheek. Then he kissed her, a hungry, demanding kiss.

"No, Jeb, no. You mustn't." She pushed against his chest, but already a weakness had invaded her. She didn't have the strength to fight him; she didn't *want* to fight him. All winter she had thought of a moment like this, longing for it, all the while convinced that it could never happen.

His mouth was on hers again, and this time she returned the kiss with growing ardor. His hands roamed over her body, and even through the thickness of her clothing, Sarah's flesh shivered wherever he touched.

She thought it strange that Jeb could arouse passion in her with just a touch, a kiss, while Sean, a skillful, more artful lover by far, had to devote some time to it.

Then all reasoning power left her in a great blaze of passion. Certainly this was no time to be thinking of Sean!

Jeb had maneuvered her to that great bed of his. As the backs of her knees struck the bed, Sarah fell athwart it. Jeb came down on the bed and immediately started to push her skirts up.

"Oh, no!" She pushed at him. "You're not going to tear this dress. It's the first decent garment I've had in almost a year!"

She squirmed away from him and off the bed.

"Women! By Jehovah, the vanity of women!" he said.

Sarah said indignantly, "I've had this dress on for two hours, and you're about to tear it. And speaking of vanity, who spent all the money to re-create the captain's cabin of the *North Star*, right down to the bed?"

"You're right, of course, love." He dissolved into laughter, doubling over, and was still laughing when Sarah, naked now, tumbled into the bed again.

Jeb sobered and got out of bed to quickly undress. Sarah felt heat rush through her at the sight of that magnificent body of his. Then he faced about, and her breath escaped her with a sigh at the sight of his erect manhood.

Remembering that other time, she expected a hasty, rough assault on her body. Jeb surprised her. He was gentle and made very tender love to her until

18

she was tossing with need. She tugged at him, urging him over her.

He rose, hovering, staring down into her face. I have missed you, Sarah Moody. Jehovah, how I have missed you! Not a night has passed that you were not in my thoughts." His voice lowered to a whisper. "I love you, dearest Sarah."

She drew a breath. "And I love you, Jeb. Oh how I love you!"

Before the last words were out, he was inside her, so that his entrance into her body seemed an unexpected surprise. Sarah cried out softly at the suddenness of it. As he thrust again and again into her, Sarah initiated a responding thrust of her own.

And she said breathlessly, "Ah, yes, Jeb, I love you!"

The pleasure of it was deep and intense, almost unbearable, and a tiny part of her mind compared this with the times she had lain with Sean. And while those times had been pleasurable, there was a difference, a great difference, a difference she could not put a name to.

Ecstasy broke over her in waves, and she said again, "Dear God, yes, I love you!"

A while later, she lay drowsy and content in his arms, her head on his shoulder. He stirred, one hand idly stroking her back. "It was true, my dear, what I said. I do love you."

"I know, I know that now."

"The question that follows, is what do we do about it?" There was a certain note of demand in his voice.

And that shattered the idyllic spell that had had Sarah in its grip since they had come aboard the keelboat. It brought thoughts of Sean flooding into her mind. Although she did not love Sean, and she was still convinced that he did not love her, there was a powerful bond between them. And he had planned for them to go to New Orleans together. In fact, while she had idled away the afternoon here, he had probably gone to the Foster House looking for her. The cabin had grown dark.

"We will talk later, Jeb. On the way down to New Orleans. Now I have to go."

She skidded a kiss off his cheek, hopped out of bed, and began getting dressed.

"Going to meet this Flanagan fellow, are you?"

She darted a quick glance at him, surprised yet secretly pleased at the touch of jealousy in his voice. "Yes, Jeb, I am. But I will come back to you. I promise. With Sean, it is mostly business. After all, we have trapped many furs, and I am to receive a share of the profits," she added proudly.

Jeb's face took on a look of astonishment. "You are to share in the profits? What did you, a woman, do to earn it?"

She held out her hands, slim and brown, but bearing the marks of physical labor. "I treated pelts, I cooked and cleaned. I earned my share, never fear."

"Where? In bed?"

She wheeled on him, ablaze with anger. "Yes! I shared his bed! But he was a gentleman about it and did not take me by force! He saved my life, and I had no money, no place to go, so out of the kindness of his heart, he took me along with him into the wilderness, instead of leaving me to die! Is that so terrible then?"

Jeb, staring at her, made a strong effort to get himself under control. Even though his mind was afire with images of this woman he loved in the arms of another man, the rational part of his mind told him that he was being unjust. What had taken place during the period of time since they'd last seen each other was no affair of his. What else could he have expected her to do? A lone woman, in a strange country, without money or hopes of getting any, her only other course would have been to become a whore. Sarah certainly had not done that, at least not in the usual sense, and she was, if anything, more of a lady than ever.

Still, there was that small, painful jealousy in his mind.

He shook his head to clear it and got out of bed. "My apologies, madam. I was wrong to say what I did." He started to dress. "I will see you back to your lodgings."

"No!" Sarah said sharply. If Sean happened to be waiting there . . . In a softer voice, she said, "Thank you, Jeb. But you have work to do. I made my way here, I can make it back. Honestly, Jeb, I would much rather return alone." She stood on tiptoe and brushed his cheek with her lips. "Your return from the dead has left me shaken and confused. I need a little time to accustom myself to it."

He nodded, his face unreadable. "At least let me find you a carriage."

Outside, the men were still loading the keelboats. Even though it was dark, the landing was illuminated by bonfires. Tim was keeping a close watch on the workers.

Jeb said, "Tim, trot up the hill and fetch a carriage back for Mistress Moody."

With a nod Tim was off at a trot. Jeb lit a cigar at

one of the fires, then stood with Sarah. They were strangely silent now, at a loss for anything to say. Within a very short time Tim came riding back in a carriage.

Jeb helped Sarah into it. "Where shall I direct the driver, Sarah?"

"The Foster House."

"The Foster House, driver." Jeb took Sarah's hand. "Then I will see you in the morning? I will reserve a cabin for you and—your friend. We depart at eight sharp."

"Yes, Jeb, I will be here." She smiled, adding, "And I believe you should make that two cabins, not one. I will not be sharing one with Sean."

Earlier in the year when Giles Brock, leading an attack on a keelboat, had glimpsed Jeb Hawkins in charge of the defenders, he had been stunned speechless. Later, after the pirate crew had fled to safety, he had cuffed Pommet across the face, snarling, "You told me Jeb Hawkins was dead!"

"I thought he was, Giles. I swear! I don't know how he could still be alive!"

And now, on the wharf of the St. Louis landing, he and Pommet disguised as wharf workers, Brock could only stand and gape in amazement when he saw Sarah Moody, every inch the fine lady, engaged in animated conversation with Jeb Hawkins.

Pommet whined in his ear, "You railed at me about Captain Hawkins being still alive. How about the wench there? 'Twas my understanding you snuffed her out on the river bank back in New Orleans."

"I never told you that!" Brock hissed. "Just shut up and get back to work, before someone suspicions us."

They resumed the laborious chore of loading cargo onto a flatboat. The reason they were here was very simple. Twice now, Brock and his men had attacked Hawkins' keelboat, and both times they had been routed in ignominious defeat. Brock had learned from a spy in St. Louis that Jeb Hawkins was docked there for cargo, and that he now had a second keelboat, fitted out for carrying passengers. So it had been Brock's idea that he and Pommet slip onto the landing, disguised as common workers, to see if they could pick up some information that would be useful to them in their next attack on Hawkins' boat.

And now here was Mistress Sarah Moody, large as life! What infuriated Brock the most was the finery with which she had adorned herself. What had she been doing these past months to be able to afford the clothes? When he'd last seen her she hadn't a penny to her name and looked like a ragamuffin right out of the alleyways of London.

Even as he watched, he saw Hawkins guiding her up onto his new keelboat. Then they disappeared from sight.

Pommet whispered, "What do you plan to do, Giles?"

"Quiet! I'm thinking on it."

He would sell his soul to get his hands on the bitch again. As he and Pommet labored for the next hour, Brock let his thoughts roam ahead, dreaming of what he would do to Sarah Moody, should he be able to snatch her. All the while he kept a careful watch on the keelboat, but neither reappeared.

Finally they finished with their arduous labor and were paid off. Brock picked a spot some distance from Hawkins' keelboat, a place where he and Pommet could rest, partially hidden, and still keep an eye on the boat.

Then, there they were! Brock's breath left him in a hiss as he saw them. He leaned forward, watching intently, motioning Pommet quiet. He saw the pair pause and saw Hawkins motion to that young bastard of a cabin boy. They exchanged a few words, then the cabin boy was off at a trot, up the bluff road leading into town.

Brock's mind leaped to a conclusion. To Pommet, he said, "He's sent the boy after a carriage for the Moody bitch! Quick now, and be careful we're not seen!"

"What are we about, Giles?"

"We are going to sneak quietly up to the top of the bluff, then hide in the bushes. We'll find a likely spot, just where the carriage will labor to the top, and waylay it, taking the wench."

Pommet had more questions, but Brock motioned him silent and started at a slant up the cliff road. There was little fear of their being seen now in the darkness. Panting from the climb, Brock slowed at the top of the carriage road, just where it ran level again. And there, growing close to the narrow, dusty road was a thick clump of bushes.

"Ah, there. Just the spot. The carriage will be going slow from the climb, and we'll be able to leap aboard with ease."

They crouched in the bushes, far enough back to screen them from the road.

When Pommet got his breath back, he said, "How do you know this carriage, if such the boy went for, will be for Sarah Moody?"

"We will see, Rhys, we will see."

"And what if Captain Hawkins accompanies the wench?"

"Then we'll kill him and be rid of him for once and for all," Brock said harshly. "But it's my thought he'll be sending her back to the village alone. Why should he go with her? He's had his afternoon's dalliance with her—Listen!" He held up a hand for silence. They could hear the plop-plop of horses' hooves and the creak of an ungreased wheel. In a moment a small, open carriage came along the road, candle-lanterns glowing, picking up speed as it started down the incline. The only passenger was the cabin boy.

"You see?" Brock said in satisfaction. "I knew he'd gone to fetch a carriage. And who could it be for but Sarah Moody?"

"You're a sharp one, Giles," Pommet said admiringly.

Brock was tempted to preen at Pommet's praise, but there was no time for that. He stepped out into the rutted road, trying to peer down the bluff. But it was too dark now, too far, to make out anything except the flicker of the fires on the landing.

He returned to crouch beside Pommet. "Now we know there's only one carriage down there, and since it has a squeaking wheel, we can hear it coming. As it draws abreast, we'll spring out of the bushes and jump up onto the steps. It'll only be creeping along. You make for the driver; club him off the seat with your pistol butt. Don't fire unless you have to; we don't want to arouse any more attention than necessary. I'll take care of Sarah Moody. Once the driver's dumped, take the reins and hie us to the tables where we left our horses. We can't take the carriage out of town; no roads fit for it."

"You'll take the wench, you say, but what if she's not alone? Like I said, what if Captain Hawkins is with her?"

"He won't be, I told you!" Nonetheless, Brock felt a shiver of apprehension. As much as he wanted Hawkins dead, he didn't much care to confront the man face to face. He snarled, "And stop calling him captain, for Satan's sake! He's no longer captain of the *North Star*, but the owner of a lowly keelboat!"

Then he heard it—the creaking wheel, the snap of the driver's whip, and his harsh voice cursing the team.

Brock said in a tense whisper, "Be prepared, here they come!"

Both men pulled their pistols. Brock waited until the carriage had just crested the rise and reached level ground, so the carriage wouldn't roll out of control back down the slope once the driver was disposed of. Then he said urgently, "Now!"

They took two running steps and leaped into the carriage steps, Pommet clambering immediately upon the driver's seat. There was enough light to show Brock that the woman was alone in the carriage. With a feeling of relief, he grasped the carriage door with one hand, stuck his pistol back into his belt, then vaulted into the seat just as Sarah Moody cried out.

Brock threw an arm around her shoulders. He saw her eyes widen with shock and fear.

"It's you!"

"Aye, Mistress Moody, 'tis your old friend, Giles Brock!"

As she opened her mouth to scream, he clamped a hand over it, stifling any sound of alarm. She struggled wildly in his grasp, but he held her firmly wedged into the corner of the seat. He risked a glance at the driver's seat, just in time to see Pommet shoving the driver's inert body off into the road. Pommet took the man's seat, picking up the reins, then turned about with that skull-like grin.

"You got her, Giles?"

"I've got her. Now head for the stables. But take it slow and easy, so we don't raise suspicions."

He turned his attention back to Sarah. "I've got you for good this time. This time, no stranger'll be butting in, I wager!"

Sarah's struggles grew wilder, and he tightened his hand over her mouth, pinching off her nostrils as well. In a few minutes she slumped in his grip. He held her mouth and nostrils covered a while longer, not enough to kill her, just enough to insure that she would remain unconscious for a spell.

He looked up to see that they were traveling down a side street in the village now. There were a few people about. Brock bent over Sarah, his face hiding hers, so that if anyone noticed, they would dismiss it as a swain out with his lady love. That gave him an idea. Grinning, he ran his hands over her, fondling her breasts through the material of her dress, then pushing the dress up to run his hands over the silky smoothness of her limbs. Ah, she was a fine-bodied wench! Brock was breathing heavily when Pommet swung the carriage into the stables.

A quick glance told Brock that no one was about. "Saddle our horses, Rhys. On second thought, steal another one and saddle it as well. But keep a watchful eye out for the stableman. If he comes poking about, take care of him."

In an empty stall nearby, the stableman supposed to be on duty stirred, aroused by the commotion; he awoke just in time to hear Brock's threat. He lay still, listening, feeling blindly for the bottle of wine he had been sucking on before he fell into a drunken slumber.

Shortly Pommet led three saddled horses up to the carriage. "Now that we got her, what we going to do with the wench, Giles?"

"We'll lash her to the extra horse and head out at once. I know what I'm going to do with her, all right. But first we'll have our fun with her, you and me. Then after that, we'll sell her to an Injun I've heard about. 'Tis my understanding he pays dearly for white slaves, most especially a juicy wench like Sarah Moody. Yes, 'tis an Injun slave she is going to be. That, I'll wager, she'll not take to at all, at all!"

PART THREE

The Slave

Chapter Eighteen

At 8:30 the next morning, Jeb was striding impatiently up and down the landing, cigar fuming. The cargo was loaded, the meager collection of passengers was on board, and the crews of both keelboats were standing by.

However, Sarah had not put in an appearance.

Finally Tim approached him timidly. "Captain, should I hurry up to the Foster House and see what's delaying Mistress Moody?"

"No, you will not!" Jeb wheeled on him. "Damn the woman anyway! She well knows what time we depart. Why should I dally here for her?"

Yet he made no move to board, but continued to pace. A few minutes later, a carriage came rolling down the bluff road, trailing a plume of dust.

Jeb heaved a sigh of relief. "There she is now. Women! They're always tardy."

But to Jeb's dismay, the carriage rolled right past him and on down the landing. He stared in disbelief as it disgorged a big man who staggered drunkenly out, a man he recognized as another keelboat operator. Jeb clamped on his cigar in frustration as he watched the drunken man fumble coins out of his pocket to pay the driver.

Then as the carriage made a wide, sweeping turn,

and started back, Jeb suddenly waved frantically, emitting a shrill whistle. The carriage stopped.

"Tim, try to keep the crew and passengers placated. I'll only be gone a short while. Either I bring the contrary wench back, or we depart without her!"

Climbing into the carriage, he told the driver to take him to the Foster House.

The streets of St. Louis were abustle as the carriage made its way through the business section—to a quiet side street. The Foster House was a wooden, two-story structure. A sign in front said: "Food and Lodgings. Ladies and Gentlemen Welcome."

Jeb told the carriage driver to wait and mounted the front steps. He rapped on the door. In a moment a shuffling sound came from within, and the door opened a crack. One eye peered out at him, and a female voice said, "What do you want, sir? You're not one of my guests, and this is not a sporting house."

"Sarah Moody." He cleared his throat. "I'm seeking Mistress Sarah Moody. I understood she is lodging here?"

"She has rented quarters, yes. But I've not seen her this day."

"Well, would you be so kind as to inform her that Jeb Hawkins is here for her? Captain Jeb Hawkins."

"Captain, is it?" The door opened grudgingly. "You may step in while I go to her room."

The vestibule was dim, so dim Jeb could barely make out the bulky shape of an enormously fat woman, who was just starting up the narrow stairs. She stopped and turned ponderously about. "You remain right there, now. My name is Dulcie Foster, and I own this house. I have certain rules, and one is, ladies only on the second floor. No gentleman allowed."

Jeb remained where he was, chewing on his impatience. It was a long time before Dulcie Foster came heavily back down the stairs. His spirits dropped. She was alone.

Before he could speak, she said, "Mistress Moody is not in her room. It is empty. From the looks of it, she has not spent the night there. And now that I think on it, I did not see her return last evening."

"Not return! But she must have!" Then something else she had said sunk in. "Empty, you say, madam? But surely she must have some baggage."

"No baggage. She came with none. Naught is there but that . . ." The broad face grimaced with distaste. "That Injun garment she was wearing. Stinks of the Lord only knows what."

By now she had reached the bottom step, stopping there.

Jeb took a step forward. "Perhaps if I looked? Perhaps she left some message. . . ."

"No message." She folded her arms over an ample bosom and stood stolidly. "And no, you may not look. My word on it, Captain, or whatever you are. There is nothing. No message. I looked."

Shoulders slumping in defeat, Jeb turned away and let himself out. He stood on the steps for a moment, thinking. Absently, he took a cigar from his pocket and put it in his mouth.

Should he search for her? But where? Where else could she have gone but here? A disturbing thought intruded into his mind. He tried to push it out, but it would not go away.

She had decided to stay with this fellow she had

19

spent the winter with. What was his name? Flanagan, something like that. Probably a handsome, dashing, Irish adventurer, from the sound of him, and a man who had beguiling ways with women.

Not like a blundering, insensitive clod of a sea captain, Jeb thought glumly, who had so let his lust overwhelm him that he had practically raped her at the first opportunity. Practically? He *had* raped her! Why deny it?

So why should she chose Jebadiah Hawkins over someone like this Irishman?

Yesterday afternoon, she had been overcome at seeeing a dead man returned to life, and then allowed him to have his way out of simple kindness, not wishing to offend him.

True, she had declaimed her love and sworn to return to him. There was a ready explanation for that. She had wished to escape his clutches. He recalled now that she had been in a flurry of haste to get away.

It was barely possible that she had meant what she said at the time, but had changed her mind after meeting her other lover again. She had said herself that Flanagan had been kind to her, and that she was beholden to him for saving her life. It was obvious now that she had thought things over and decided in favor of this Flanagan.

Sunk in a mood of anger and despondency, Jeb strode down the steps and climbed into the carriage. "Back to the river landing, driver. And hurry, please."

Although he hadn't slept a wink all night, Sean Flanagan was humming gaily to himself as he got out of the hired carriage before the Foster House. Another open carriage was just pulling away, the passenger a tall, bearded man.

Sean said to his driver, "Wait, Andrew. You'll be taking me and a lady down to the river landing shortly. I'll leave the trunk and the other things with you."

Sean stood a moment, brushing and straightening his new clothes, the finest Fortier's Trading Post could provide a gentleman—black, highly polished boots; soft, dove-colored breeches; and a white, ruffled shirt. He had bought them last night before getting into the card game, wanting to show Sarah that he too could wear something other than buckskins.

He straightened his shoulders and went blithely up the steps. He knocked on the door.

It opened almost at once, and the querulous voice of Dulcie Foster said, "Now what do you be wanting? Oh, it's you, Sean Flanagan."

"In the flesh, Dulcie lass."

"Well, if it's the lady you sent here yesterday, using your name, you're looking for, she ain't here." Dulcie Foster opened the door wide, but stood blocking it with her bulk.

Sean frowned at her. "Not here? Where did she go?"

"On that, I have no inkling." She crossed her arms over her bosom. "Didn't spend the night here, either."

Sean felt the first tremor of alarm. "But she must have, Dulcie! Where else could she have stayed?"

"On that, I have no inkling, either. She dressed herself up in fine clothes, ate my victuals like a starved person, and left in a carriage. Ain't seen hide nor hair of her since."

Sean shook his head to clear it. He had dallied the night away at cards, having his fill of good French brandy, and he was still somewhat fuzzy-brained from the liquor. His good spirits this morning came from the fact that he had won at cards; he had won heavily, more money than at any one time in his life. Now he said slowly, "I simply do not understand. . . ."

"I can be of no help to you there. And don't be asking to see her room. There's nothing there but the filthy Injun garments she wore. There was another . . ."

Sean said alertly, "Another what, Dulcie?"

She shook her head. "Never mind, it's nothing of importance."

"We-ell, I guess I'd better set up a search for her. If she does by chance return, tell her I was here, Dulcie."

"That I will." As he turned away, she gave vent to a cackle of laughter. "Looks like you may be losing your charm for the ladies, Sean Flanagan. I knew one would soon see through the blarney of yours!"

"Ah, but not you, I'm after thinking," he said, chucking her under the chin. "Not you, Dulcie lass."

She was still laughing as Sean walked down the steps, his mind buzzing. Now that his head was clearing, he sensed something awry. Could Sarah have taken a keelboat to New Orleans without him? No, she had no money; she wouldn't leave without her share of the proceeds from the furs. And there was the trunk of clothes. . . .

No, he was certain that he knew her better than that. If Sarah hadn't wanted him to accompany her to New Orleans, she would have said so right out. That was her way. Something had happened to her, he was sure of it!

Back in the carriage, he said, "Andrew, did you by chance drive a lady away from here yesterday? A lady with black hair, wearing a blue velvet dress?"

"Not me, Mr. Flanagan, sir. First time I've been to the Foster House all week."

Sean sat for a moment, pondering. There were only four carriages for hire in St. Louis, and they all operated out of the same stable. One of the drivers *must* have driven her to the landing. "Take me right to the stable, Andrew. And hurry!"

"Right away, sir!" Andrew cracked his whip, and the carriage rumbled away.

Busy with his own dire thoughts, Sean was aware that the driver was talking, but he paid scant heed until he heard, ". . . found poor Eli dead with his head bashed in."

Sean said urgently, "I was wool-gathering, Andrew. What was that about someone dead?"

"One of our drivers, Mr. Flanagan. Eli Thompson. He was found dead this morning on the edge of the landing road, just at the crest of the slope."

A chill went down Sean's back, a feeling he had experienced before, warning of something amiss. "Nobody has an idea who or why?"

"Not's far as I know," Andrew said chattily. "Probably some ruffian riverman conked him for what few coins he had. They're a rough lot, those river rats."

"The carriage—Did they steal it?"

"Nah, the team brought it back to the stable on its own."

"Doesn't that strike you as odd? Usually a team will

panic and bolt when losing the driver, but soon as the horses run a while, they stop and graze at the first good spot they find."

" 'Tis odd, I agree, sir, but Samuel swears that's what happened."

"And who is this Samuel?"

"Samuel Fisher, the fellow who keeps watch on the stable at night."

Sean saw that they were approaching the stable now. "This Samuel you speak of. Is he still around the stables?"

"Likely he is. He ain't got no home that I know of." The carriage drew up at the stable entrance. "He sleeps in an empty stall by day."

Sean climbed down quickly. "If he's here, where would I likely find him?"

"First empty stall on the right, Mr. Flanagan."

"All right, Andrew. Wait for me. I'll be needing you again shortly."

Sean strode purposefully into the dimness of the stable. There were two men working in the back, but he ignored them and searched out the empty stall Andrew had mentioned. There, in a huddle on a pile of straw, a man slept. Sean went in, bent down, and hauled the man upright by his shirt front.

Samuel Fisher was an aging skeleton of a man. His clothes were torn and filthy, and he stank of sour wine and stable filth. Sean shook him, and the man opened bleary eyes.

"Samuel Fisher?"

The man swallowed convulsively, looking at Sean out of red-streaked blue eyes suddenly filling with fear. "I be Samuel Fisher, squire. What is it ye want of me?"

"I want you to tell me about the carriage that came back empty last night after the driver was killed."

"Why, squire, what's to tell?" The scrawny man tried to shrug out of Sean's grip. "The team just brought it back."

There was something shifty, evasive, about the man's manner, and Sean's instinct told him that he was lying. "You're lying, Samuel! Now I'll be after having the truth from you, or I'll shake you till your teeth fall out. On the other hand, tell me what I want to hear, and there'll be coins in your pocket, enough for a bottle."

"But I know nothing, I tell ye," Samuel Fisher whined.

"I'm wagering you do, boyo. I can smell fear in you like corruption. Now why should you be afraid?"

Sean shook him hard, then slapped him lightly across the face with the back of his hand. "Now I want the truth, or you'll be the sorrier for it!"

"All right, all right!" The man was close to tears. "I'll tell ye. The carriage, it came back with three people. I was napping here. Hearing it, I thought 'twas Eli. Then I heard strange voices and lay listening. They were armed and mean. I was afraid to make a peep. Then, after they left, I was afraid to tell the stablemaster, fearing I'd be let go. . . ."

"I'm not interested in that!" Sean snapped. "Three people, you said. Was one a woman?"

"I—I think so. But I didn't hear her utter nary a word. The men spoke of a woman."

"The men—Any names?"

The man hesitated. "One name was used. All I heard anyways. Giles, I think it was."

"Giles Brock!" Sean swore. "The sculpin has his dirty hands on Sarah! What happened then?"

"They took three horses. Two was theirs, it would seem. The other they stole."

"But where to, man! Did you overhear mention of their destination?"

"All I heard. . . ." Samuel Fisher swallowed, eyes rolling wildly. "I heard mention of selling the wench to an Injun chief as a slave."

"What Indian chief? What tribe?"

In his anguish Sean had unconsciously tightened his grip on the man's shirt until it bound his neck like a noose.

Samuel Fisher waved his hands frantically, making choking sounds. Sean loosened his grip slightly.

"I swear that's all I know, squire. They mentioned no names, no Injun tribes. Not in my hearing."

"You heard nothing else then?"

"All, all, I swear on my poor old mother's grave!"

In a spasm of disgust, Sean loosed his grip. Then, with the flat of his hand, he gave the man a shove, sending him sprawling on his back. Sean dug into his pocket for a handful of coins and threw them into the dirt. With a cry Samuel Fisher scrambled about on his hands and knees, searching for the coins.

Sean spun away, took three steps, then turned back. "Tell your stablemaster that Sean Flanagan wishes to buy two of his best horses. Have them saddled and waiting. I will be back within the hour."

Outside, Sean flung himself into the carriage. "To Fortier's, Andrew. And whip them up, I am in a great hurry!"

Sean's thoughts were black on the brief trip to Fortier's Trading Post. He had never experienced such anger. He should have heeded Sarah's plea on the river bank outside of New Orleans and slain Giles Brock. Now, because he had not, Sarah was on her way to a horrible fate. Poor lass, was she doomed to severe hardship and degradation forever? He was swept with a feeling of love and longing for her, so poignant that he wanted to weep.

Also, he felt an aching compassion for her. No matter what her ultimate fate—and becoming a white slave woman with Indians was harsh enough—there was no doubt in Sean's mind that she would suffer foully at the hands of Giles Brock.

Before Fortier's Trading Post, Sean again told Andrew to wait for him. As he started inside, Sean glanced ruefully at his new clothes. Even guzzling brandy and playing cards last night, he had been careful to keep them clean. Sarah never had a chance to see his new clothes.

Behind the counter, Jacques Fortier glanced up in surprise as Sean burst in. He frowned at the look on Sean's face. *"Mon Dieu, my friend, you look like a thundercloud! I have never seen you so. What has happened?"*

"Sarah Moody was taken last night whilst I spent my time at cards. The sculpins who seized her are on their way to sell her as a slave to some Indian tribe. I'm going in pursuit, of course, but I may be too late."

"Mon Dieu!" Fortier slapped his plump cheeks. "The poor woman! I am most sorry, *mon ami.*"

"I'll need supplies, Jacques. And my buckskins and rifle I left with you last night. And here . . ." From his pockets Sean dumped all the money he had won at cards. "I want to leave this on deposit with you,

Jacques, along with the proceeds from the sale of my furs, and the other funds you are already holding for me."

Fortier's full mouth pursed in a whistle. "That is a substantial sum, my friend."

"I know. If I fail to return from this journey, if something dire happens to me, but Sarah Moody *does* return, all the funds you have on deposit for me are to go to her. Is that understood?"

"It will be as you say, Sean." Fortier's face showed distress. "But what if neither of you return?"

"Then I'm after thinking it won't matter, will it?" Sean grinned tightly. "Then it's all yours, Jacques, old friend. Just spend a part of it holding a good, old-fashioned Irish wake!"

When Sarah regained consciousness, she found that she was face down across a saddle. Her hands and feet were bound together with thongs running under the belly of the horse she was on, and there was a gag tied around her mouth. It was night, and they were riding hard.

Memory came back to her with a rush, and black despair filled her. Once again she was at the mercy of Giles Brock, and God only knew what he had in mind for her. Of all the alternatives she could think of, death would no doubt be the most merciful. But clearly he had something else planned, or she would be dead already.

What had Jeb told her? That Giles Brock was now the leader of a band of river pirates? Was that his intention, to take her to his pirate cohorts to serve as a whore for them?

Outrage overcame her despair, and she began to

struggle. She soon discovered that she was also tied to the saddle. She might as well have been a sack of grain for all the chance she had of rolling off the horse. Her ribs ached from the pressure of the hard saddle, and her wrists burned as the rough thongs pulled and chafed with the movement of the horse.

She remembered now. There had been *two* men leaping aboard the carriage. The attack had been so unexpected and sudden that she'd had no opportunity to see who the second man was.

Realizing that any effort to escape while tied to the horse was useless, she subsided, feigning unconsciousness, but listening closely all the while.

Her efforts were eventually rewarded.

A voice complained, "My arse is getting sore, Giles. How long we going to ride?"

"Until we're a goodly distance out of St. Louis. I very much doubt it, but there is always a chance someone is on our tail. You think I like it any better than you, Rhys? You know how I hate horses. I'm always more comfortable with my feet planted on solid ground, not bouncing around atop some beast."

Rhys Pommet is the second man, Sarah thought. She should have known. Whatever enterprise Brock was about, Pommet would naturally be a party to it. The twins of evil, she named them in her mind. Or, as Sean would say, a rare pair of sculpins they are, colleen.

She experienced a deep wave of despair at the thought of Sean and of Jeb. What would they think in the morning when they couldn't find her anywhere? Would each think she had gone off with the other? If they did think that, she could expect no pursuit, no help from them to escape this pair. If she got away from them, it would have to be through her own efforts.

It was an arduous ride. Head down as she was, Sarah soon became nauseous and feared that she would vomit, and with the filthy rag tied around her mouth, she might choke to death. She managed to control her upset stomach, turning her thoughts toward what she would do to Giles Brock for this indignity, should she ever have the opportunity.

The longer they rode, the more her discomfort increased. Soon the pain was almost unbearable; the circulation was practically cut off in her hands and feet by the bonds.

Just as dawn turned the night to gray, Brock called a halt. "We'll stop here for a spell. Now that it's daylight one of us can keep watch while the other sleeps."

Brock and Pommet dismounted and led the horses off the dim trail behind a screen of bushes.

While Pommet unsaddled their two horses and staked them out to graze, Brock came over to Sarah's horse. She kept her eyes closed, pretending to still be unconscious.

"You're awake and aware, missy. I heard you thrashing around a long ways back. So open your eyes and have a look at your old friend, Giles."

Sarah kept her eyes shut. Then she felt him fumbling beneath her. He found a breast and pinched hard between thumb and forefinger. The pain was excruciating. Her eyes flew open, and she was only inches from his grinning countenance, so close she could smell the foulness of his breath. She struggled, trying to cry out.

Still grinning, Brock ceased pinching and ripped the gag from her mouth.

Sarah drew in a deep breath of sweet, fresh air, and then exhaled it, along with the anger she could no longer retain. "Bloody bastard!" she heard herself saying in a dry, harsh whisper. "Sculpin! Ship rat!"

Brock glared at her with a look of malevolent fury. He made a fist and clubbed her alongside the head. The blow dazed Sarah. Bright dots of light danced before her eyes.

Dimly she heard Pommet's chuckle. "You going to let her get away with that, Giles?"

"Not for long, I'm not," Brock snarled. "Untie her from that damned horse. Then dump her under the tree over there. She's going to suffer for that little bit of defiance."

"Now, Giles? We're going to take her now? I haven't had a wench in a week."

"You can have her after I'm finished."

By the time Pommet had her off the horse, half-dragging her to the spot indicated and dumping her, Sarah's head was clearing. She opened her eyes just enough to see Pommet standing over her, that evil grin in evidence and Brock approaching, unfastening his breeches.

Sarah realized this would be her only chance; she was on her feet running before either man could react.

Brock yelled, "Catch her, Rhys, or I'll have your head! Damn, I told you to watch her!"

Sarah, her limbs stiff and awkward from the long binding, made for the horse she'd been tied to. The saddle was still on the animal. If she could make it into the saddle before they reached her, she had a chance of getting away.

She was just reaching for the saddle when she was seized by the shoulder from behind, jerked roughly backward, and sent crashing to the ground.

"Tie her up again," Brock said.

Sarah fought with all her strength, but soon she was bound again, flat on the ground.

She closed her eyes as she felt her skirts being pushed up.

Brock said in a thick voice, "Now we'll see, missy. Now you'll have a small taste of what's in store for you."

"Hurry up, Giles!" Pommet said. "I'm so randy I can't wait much longer."

"You'll wait, Rhys, you'll wait, till I'm finished with the wench."

When Sarah felt Brock's full weight upon her bruised body, she almost cried out, but bit her lip to keep the sound in, not wanting to give them the satisfaction of knowing her pain. As Brock made his brutal entry into her, she had no recourse but to suffer the cruel thrusts. She tried to turn her thoughts to something else, yet the obscenity being inflicted on her could not be willed away.

When Brock was done, and she felt his semen running down her thigh, there was no respite. Pommet took Brock's place, and Sarah's eyes flew open involuntarily. At the sight of his skull-like face, like death itself looming over her, Sarah screamed. Pommet closed her mouth with a slobbering kiss.

Repugnance convulsed her, and her stomach heaved. Pommet, mistaking it for a response to his thrusts, cried out, "You see, Giles! She's learning! She likes it. Strikes me maybe you weren't man enough for her!"

Sarah knew that in time the damage to her body would pass, although she would remember the indignity of it for the rest of her life. The damage to her very soul and the outrage to her sensibilities and womanhood would leave a scar that would never heal.

When Pommet, sated, finally lay gasping beside her, they let her be. She was propped up against a small tree trunk, bound to it tightly by a rawhide strap around her chest and the tree. It was an extremely uncomfortable position, and Sarah didn't know how she would be able to get any rest; but she would be eternally damned before she would complain to these two animals!

Her dress, the fine dress she had bought in St. Louis, was torn and filthy, and would never be decent enough to wear again. Since she had no other garments with her, there was no telling when she would get another.

Brock and Pommet were quarreling about who should take the first turn at watch. Brock won out, sending Pommet to keep watch on the trail. Then Brock stretched out on the ground and was soon snoring.

An intriguing thought came to Sarah. Was it possible that she could cause bad blood between the two men? If she could bring about a fight between them, and one was killed, it would go much easier for her, and her chances of escaping would be doubled.

Despite the discomfort of her position she did sleep a little, dozing off and on. Once, she dreamed of the time Walleye attacked her. Only in her nightmare he succeeded, and the copious flood of blood from the wound in his back was hers. She woke up with a scream.

The scream aroused Rhys Pommet, who was asleep on the ground close by. He raised his head and snarled, "Shut your yap, wench, or I'll come over and shut it for you!"

Sarah stared at him with utter loathing, hating him with every fiber of her being. Somehow this feeling of hate gave her strength. She must stay alive, if only to have her revenge upon these two, who had caused her, and others, so much pain.

The journey seemed endless. The torture of riding head down across the saddle, with her hands and feet tied together, grew greater with each passing day. The indignities, the insults to her body, continued without letup. Many times, Sarah, despite her resolution, found herself wishing for death. She even thought of ways in which she could kill herself. Yet always something within her recoiled at the thought. The memory of what she had endured and survived during this past year rallied her spirit. She devised a trick to ease matters a bit. When either Brock or Pommet was raping her, Sarah thought of Sean, of the hour with Jeb on the keelboat; she thought of the clean, white sweep of prairie when wearing its thick blanket of snow; she thought of the joyous times with Sean, of his patience with her, his unfailing kindnesses.

Her efforts at causing dissension between her two captors failed. Once, when Brock was out of hearing and Pommet was grunting and heaving out his ecstasy on her body, Sarah seized a moment when he was inert and breathing hard to whisper in his ear, "It could be good with you, Rhys." She tried to make her voice soft and beguiling. "Just think of how wonderful it would be, just us two, without Giles Brock around, abusing you. If he was out of the way, we could . . ."

Pommet raised his head and stared down at her with those pale eyes, very intent and grave, and for a breathless moment Sarah thought she had succeeded.

Then he threw back his head and bellowed with laughter. Getting up, he fixed his breeches and yelled, "Giles! Come arunning!"

In a moment Brock burst into the clearing to come to a breathless halt before them. "What is it, Rhys? Something amiss?"

"Nope," Pommet said, grinning. "It's just that it seems the wench here likes me better. You know what she just told me? How grand it would be, just me and her, without you around. What do you think about that?"

Brock looked at Sarah with narrowed eyes. "Here's what I think." He leaned down and, almost casually, struck her across the face with the back of his hand. Sarah had grown so hardened to abuse from the pair that she scarcely felt the blow.

"You're a clever one, now ain't you, missy? Thinking you'd set up a rumble betwixt me and Rhys here. Thinking maybe he'd kill me over you, and you'd have a better chance to get away?" Brock smiled venomously. "Clever, yes, clever, but not clever enough. You see, Rhys would never kill me. Oh, not that he'd be afraid to try, or that he'd have any scruples, if it be to his advantage. But the thing is, my death wouldn't be to his advantage. He's got a soft life now, mostly. All the wenches he can lay, all the liquor he can drink, and it's all coming about through me. He well knows that. Rhys may not be the smartest man in the world, but he knows where the goodies are coming from. Don't you Rhys?"

"That's about the way it is, Giles," Pommet said without rancor.

"You see, my fine lady?" Brock said. "That's the way it is, so don't go wasting your time at clever games."

Several times Sarah inquired of Brock where they were headed and what his intentions were toward her.

Each time she received a chuckle and the same response: "You'll know soon enough, Mistress Moody. Count yourself fortunate that you *don't* know!"

Sarah could not conceive of anything much worse than her present situation. The painful horseback trip each day, Brock and Pommet slaking their lust on her body every night—the whore of a dozen men could hardly fare worse. Brock wouldn't even allow her to perform body functions in private. They kept her ankles hobbled, and one stood by, watching, usually Pommet. Perhaps the most demeaning thing of all was the fact that they would not let her wash. She'd had no bath since they had taken her; they would not even allow her to wash her hands and face.

So whatever was in store for her, she could not believe it would be more painful or unpleasant than what she was enduring.

She was puzzled by the fact that they traveled in a generally northwest direction, bearing away from the

Mississippi. If Brock was the leader of a band of river pirates, why were they heading away from the river?

Then, one afternoon after a week of traveling, Brock, riding in the lead, held up a hand for them to halt just as they crested a ridge. As Sarah and Pommet ranged alongside him, Brock pointed to the hollow below. "There, there's the village, Rhys. The one we're looking for."

Sarah painfully turned her head. All she could see was a collection of tepees. An Indian village? What in Heaven's name were they going to do there? Sarah was more mystified than ever.

As she was thinking about it, Brock had already turned the horses, leading them back down toward a small stream they had crossed only minutes before.

He motioned as they halted at the stream. "There, wench. You've been yapping about a wash. Well, wash to you heart's content." He got down and untied her.

Sarah stood on unsteady legs, rubbing her wrists. "Why allow me to bathe *now?*"

"Never mind the questions." He gave her a shove toward the stream. "Just wash. And we'll be right here, watching. So don't try to flee, missy. You'll be afoot and us with horses. You wouldn't get far."

Sarah was so eager to clean the accumulated grime from her skin and hair, that she didn't question him further. It didn't bother her too much that they would be watching. They'd seen her naked body every night for a week; at least this time they wouldn't be touching her.

Her back to them, Sarah removed her clothes and slipped into the water. It was icy. She ignored the cold and sat down in the shallow water. Teeth chattering, she luxuriated in the water. Having no soap, she used clean sand from the bottom of the stream to scrub herself. After her body was clean as she could make it, she proceeded to wash her long black hair. She kept washing long after she was clean, prolonging it as long as possible.

Finally Brock, squatting on the bank, growled, "That's good enough. We haven't got all day. Come on out now."

Reluctantly, Sarah emerged dripping from the water. Brock tossed her a piece of rough muslin to use as a towel. As she quickly dried herself, Pommet made a guttural sound in his throat and started toward her.

Brock caught him by the arm. "No, Rhys."

"Just one more time, Giles. I got an ache that needs easing!"

Smiling, Brock shook his head. "I know, the look of her like that makes me randy, too, but no more."

As they argued, Sarah hastily slipped her dress over her head.

Brock continued, "We have to have her clean and ..." He laughed. "... pure for Chief White Buffalo. That's why I wanted her washed and clean. The Injuns like their white women clean, pure, and sweet-smelling. Why they should, I don't know." He made a face. "To me, an Injun always stinks like sheep shit. But we'll get a better price for her clean, a better price indeed."

Suddenly cold with apprehension, Sarah stared at him. "Chief White Buffalo? A better price?"

"We're selling you to Chief White Buffalo, great chief of the Pawnee. He often buys white slaves, especially comely wenches. You'll fetch a good price in fine furs, Mistress Moody."

Sarah uttered a small sound, and without even thinking about it, started to run.

"Fetch her, Rhys."

Within a few yards, Pommet came up behind Sarah. He got a grip on the long hair streaming behind her and jerked her cruelly to a sudden stop. The pain was terrible. Sarah thought her hair would be ripped out by the roots. Pommet pulled her along by the hair back to where Brock waited.

"Tie her onto the horse, Rhys," Brock said. "But upright in the saddle this time, hands tied behind her, feet tied to the stirrups. We want to give the chief a good impression, show that she has *some* spirit, not that it's necessary to bring her in for sale thrown over a horse like the carcass of a deer."

Chapter Nineteen

Brock went first, leading the horse Sarah was riding; Pommet followed behind. They were greeted by a chorus of barking dogs, nipping at the heels of the horses. As Indians began emerging from their tepees, Brock said out of the corner of his mouth, "Easy does it, Rhys. Don't spook. Just take it slow and easy, and we'll be fine. If one of them Injuns makes a sudden move, just ignore it. They like to scare a white man, if they can." Now Brock raised his right hand over his head, palm out.

As they made their way deeper into the Indian encampment, Sarah saw what he meant. Children ran yelling at them, circling the horses, throwing stones. One hit Sarah on the shoulder. She didn't flinch, but rode staring straight ahead, head held high.

Indian women lined up on each side. They stared at her in open, cold hostility. A few Indian braves also lined up. They stood with arms folded, faces stoic. All together, they formed a human lane toward the tallest, most elaborate tepee in the very center of the village—Chief White Buffalo's tepee, Sarah assumed. It towered several feet above the others.

Suddenly, one brave stepped directly into their path. He carried a bow. He fitted an arrow into it, pulled the bowstring back, aiming in their direction.

He loosed the arrow, but it flew harmlessly over their heads.

Now, from the large tepee, stepped a tall, handsome Indian brave. He was the color of bronze, with midnight-black hair in plaits on either side of his strong-boned face. He wore deerskin leggings and moccasins, while the other braves Sarah saw wore only breech cloths. A white buffalo robe was draped around his broad shoulders. He stood silently, waiting for them.

Any doubts Sarah might have had that this was the Pawnee chief were dispelled when Brock said in a low voice, "There's Chief White Buffalo. I met him once before, when I sold him that load of liquor we got off the flatboat, Rhys. See that white buffalo robe? A white buffalo is a rare creature, and an Injun who kills one is powerful medicine. Probably why he's the chief and named as he is. Could even be the reason . . . He smirked at Sarah. ". . . that he's partial to white women." Brock reined his horse in. "We'll stop here, and I'll go forward to powwow with him. You stay, Rhys, and keep a sharp eye on missy here."

Brock slid down from his horse, advancing toward the waiting chief. The Indian women gathered around Sarah's horse. Giggling, they pointed to her bonds. They fingered the torn material of her dress, talking rapidly to one another in Pawnee. One or two pinched Sarah cruelly on the legs. She ignored them as best she could.

Brock had reached Chief White Buffalo now, and they were talking together, in sign language apparently. Then Brock turned and pointed a finger at Sarah.

Since the moment by the stream when Brock had

told Sarah of her fate, she had tried to keep from thinking about it. Now full awareness of her predicament crashed in on her. What kind of a man was this Indian chief? Could he possibly be more brutal than Brock and Pommet? But whatever his nature, Sarah knew that she was in for an unpleasant time. The open hostility of the Indian women was evidence enough of that.

Already her thoughts were turning to plans for escape. Surely the Indians wouldn't keep her tied up all the time, as had Brock and Pommet.

Now Brock and White Buffalo turned and went inside the tepee together. Sarah and Pommet remained on their horses. After a time the Indian women grew tired of tormenting Sarah and withdrew. In fact, soon she and Pommet were ignored altogether. The Indian women went about their business; the braves sat cross-legged before their tepees or disappeared inside; and the children scattered about in play.

Pommet squirmed uncomfortably in the saddle. He grumbled, "Damn that Giles! My arse is getting tired, and he sits in there, probably guzzling that Injun's firewater. Or his food. My belly is empty as a drum. Eating dog, probably. Did you know that Injuns consider dog meat the finest of victuals, missy?" He laughed. "That's what you'll be eating soon."

Sarah paid him no heed whatsoever, staring straight ahead. She ached in every muscle, and her neck was a solid mass of pain from holding it erect. She would give anything to be able to slide off the horse, curl up on the ground, and go to sleep. But she'd be bloody damned if she'd give Pommet, *or* the Indians, the satisfaction of letting them know the extent of her weariness!

Finally, just short of sundown, Brock emerged from the chief's tepee and came toward them, grinning, rubbing his hands together.

"Well, I made a trade for you, Mistress Moody. From this moment on, you're the wife of White Buffalo. His fourth wife, I think he said. I have trouble with some of that Injun sign language." To Pommet, he said, "A good trade for us, Rhys. After haggling, he agreed to part with a bundle of pelts that will fetch a pretty penny." He turned to Sarah. "A little advice to you, missy. White Buffalo, 'tis my understanding, has had white wenches before. His other wives killed the last one. So I'd advise you to keep a civil tongue around them. Course . . ." His grin was cruel, self-satisfied. "They'll kill you in the end, anyway. Soon as they see White Buffalo growing tired of you in his robes, they'll seize the first chance to get rid of you."

Sarah saw White Buffalo striding toward them, followed by several braves carrying armloads of furs. Hastily Brock helped Sarah off the horse.

When White Buffalo reached them, he gestured imperiously. "Untie woman."

Brock complied, then belatedly gaped at the chief. "You speak the white man's language! Why did you let me go through all that folderol with the sign language?"

"White man who sell own woman like dirt under White Buffalo's feet." He spat into the dirt. "White Buffalo not stoop to speak language of such a man."

"Then what does that make you?" Pommet said in a snarling voice. "You bought her, you heathen Injun!"

The chief grew very still, his eyes coming to rest on

306

Pommet. They glittered like cold, black stones, and as if on signal, all the Indians gathered around suddenly fell quiet. Sarah could feel the menace in the air.

"Hush your yap, Rhys!" Brock said quickly. He aimed an ingratiating smile at White Buffalo. "My companion knows little of Indian ways and spoke hastily, not meaning it."

White Buffalo stared at Pommet for a moment longer, then nodded to Brock. He gestured to the braves with the furs and said a few curt words in Pawnee. To Sarah, he said, "Come."

As she started off, she heard Brock say, "You want to get us killed, you bloody arse?"

"What gave him the right to say that about us?" Pommet said in a whining tone.

"He doesn't need any right. He's chief here and could order us slain with a snap of his fingers. Now, help me load these furs, and let's get the hell out of here; hopefully, with our whole skins!"

Sarah followed White Buffalo into his lodge. It was roomier inside than she would have thought. There was a cooking pit in the center with a small blaze going, the smoke rising straight up to the tiny hole at the apex of the tepee. There were several narrow beds, but it was the one that White Buffalo went to at once that caught Sarah's attention. It consisted of a low, wooden frame, upon which rested a mat made of smoothed willow sticks. She later learned that each one had been pierced at the ends, so that antelope sinews could be poked through and tied off onto the wooden frame, thus keeping the willow mat firm. On top of the mat were spread two buffalo robes, carefully tanned and pliable.

On the tepee wall behind this bed hung another

buffalo robe; it had been tanned and worked on until it resembled parchment. And on this robe someone had painted scenes with a variety of colored pigments. White Buffalo appeared in all the scenes: shooting a buffalo with bow and arrow; engaged in hand-to-hand tomahawk combat with another Indian; standing tall in full battle dress and war paint; and slaying yet another buffalo, a white one, with a feather-tipped lance, astride a big horse at full gallop. Whoever the artist had been, Sarah thought, he or she was good. The horse somehow gave the impression of running on the parchment.

Yet the object that held Sarah's interest the most was the bed. It was different from the others in that the willow and antelope sinew mat extended for three feet at the farthest end, the extension bent and held upright by two stout wooden poles driven into the ground. It formed a backrest and, as White Buffalo sat in it now, he gave the appearance of sitting on a throne. The poles were polished until they glistened, and a number of the strands were gaily colored. Together with the handsome man on the throne, it was very impressive.

Sarah heard sounds behind her and turned. While she had been absorbed in studying the throne, three Indian women had filed in behind her. They stood glaring at Sarah in open hatred.

One spat on the ground and said in barely understandable English, "White squaw!"

White Buffalo spoke angrily and at length in Pawnee, clearly lecturing the women. When he was finished, he gestured royally, and the women, eyes downcast, moved around Sarah. While one piled more wood on the fire, the other two busied themselves preparing food.

"You," said White Buffalo. "What your white woman name?"

"Sarah, Sarah Moody."

"I call you . . ." He stared at her face, looking deep into her eyes, then smiled slightly. "Sky Eyes. Come." He motioned to the ground on his right beside the throne. "You sit here, Sky Eyes."

Not knowing what to expect, Sarah was fearful, yet she knew it would probably be a mistake to show hesitancy. She stepped forward and slowly lowered herself to the ground. An involuntary sigh escaped her; it felt wonderful to sit down, no matter what was going to happen.

White Buffalo reached out to stroke her hair. The chief of the Pawnee muttered in satisfaction and ran his fingers through her hair as he would a fall of water. Sarah sat tense, expecting him to touch her elsewhere. To her surprise, he did not.

Instead, he leaned back, closing his eyes. "White Buffalo will sleep until food is ready. Do not move, Sky Eyes."

Sarah dared not move, although the thought crossed her mind of making a dash for the opening in the tepee. Yet some instinct warned her that it would be a fatal error. White Buffalo was sleeping, true, a soft snore coming from him, and the Indian women were not looking at her directly; but Sarah was certain that they were very aware of her and would like nothing better than for her to make an attempt to escape, so they, collectively, could kill her.

The smell of food cooking was delicious, and it made Sarah almost ill. Brock and Pommet had kept her on poor rations during the past week, feeding her only enough to keep her alive, and she had been constantly hungry. Now she was starving.

What they were to eat was not dog, as Pommet had told her. It consisted of some wild greens, which she could not put a name to, and pemmican, which Sean had told her about. Pemmican was lean meat, dried, pounded fine, and mixed with melted fat.

When the food was done, it was served on curved plates made of cottonwood tree bark. As chief, White Buffalo was served first. Then the women got portions for themselves and retired to one wall of the tepee to eat, ignoring Sarah.

Sarah made a move to get up and serve herself. White Buffalo grunted, placing a hand on her head. "Stay, Sky Eyes." In Pawnee he rattled off several angry words.

One of the women finally got up and placed the food on a bark plate. With a sullen countenance she came to Sarah with it. They had no utensils, but ate the food with their fingers. Sarah was hungry enough to emulate them without giving any thought to it. It was not the tastiest of food, yet it was plentiful.

When all were done, a dish of water was brought to White Buffalo, who washed his hands and face. Then another of his wives brought him a pipe with a long stem and a wooden bowl. While he smoked, the three women retired to their beds against one wall. The fire was allowed to die. Sarah, not knowing what was expected of her, sat on. Very weary, stomach full, she became quite sleepy, and was dozing where she sat when White Buffalo stirred.

"Come, Sky Eyes. Now you share my robes."

Once again Sarah thought of fleeing. Or refusing

his request. Afraid to do either, she stood up to comply with his command.

With a gesture of disdain, White Buffalo hooked strong fingers in the bodice of her dress, and to her dismay, ripped it all the way down the front. Then he used both hands to tear it all the way off, and Sarah stood naked before him, trembling.

White Buffalo said, "White man's dress. Wear Indian dress here, Sky Eyes." He motioned for her to lie down on his bed.

Sarah did so, and a moment later White Buffalo joined her. She hadn't the least idea what to expect. She lay tense, thighs clamped together. However he went about it, she had no intention of aiding him in any way!

White Buffalo went about it in a businesslike manner. There were no preliminaries of any kind. His manhood was already erect. With powerful hands he spread her legs apart and went into her with a lunge. He was enormous, and Sarah felt a sharp agony. She closed her eyes and turned her head aside. Although he said nothing to her, White Buffalo was quite noisy, making grunting sounds of delight, his breathing making a slight whistling sound.

Sarah was humiliated and embarrassed. She knew that the other three women were awake, listening, well aware of what was happening. She supposed they were accustomed to their husband taking one of them in the presence of others, but Sarah knew she would never become accustomed to having an audience.

Fortunately, it was over quickly enough. The chief grunted once more, loud in the tepee, then shuddered out his passion. In a moment he moved away, unceremoniously shoving her off the bed onto the ground.

He was snoring within seconds. Since she had no robes, Sarah tried to make a bed for herself as best she could with the ruined dress. At least the weather was warm. Her last thought before she went to sleep was about what she would wear in the morning. If the Indian women, in their spite, didn't provide her with a garment, would she have to go about naked?

Indian tribes were nomadic by nature and inclination, as well as by necessity. They struck camp and moved often, following the buffalo throughout spring, summer, and fall, remaining stationary only when the winter snows hit. The Pawnee, while not as nomadic as some tribes, the Arapaho for instance, moved often and sometimes for great distances.

White Buffalo's tribe chose the next morning to begin one of their long treks. Sarah, weary as she had been, slept soundly and was awakened early the next morning by the sound of much activity. Somewhat bewildered, she sat up and found that the hides had already been stripped from the sides of the tepee. The chief's bed had been dismantled, and his three wives were busily packing items into boxlike carrying cases made of heavy, partially tanned hides, which Sarah was to learn were called parfleches.

It was a moment before Sarah was fully awake and realized that she was nude, with nothing to put on. White Buffalo was not present. In desperation she called to the busy women, trying to make her need understood.

They spared her not a single glance. Frantically wondering what to do, she tried to hide her nakedness with the torn dress. Indians, both men and women, were passing by the stripped tepee; she noticed with relief that they paid her no heed. Still, that did not solve her problem.

Just as she was growing really desperate, a young, slender, very pretty Indian girl stopped just outside the frame of the tepee, then ducked down and came inside. Sarah noticed, hopefully, that she was carrying a worn deerskin dress and a pair of moccasins.

To Sarah's surprise, the girl spoke to her in English. "I Prairie Blossom." She smiled shyly, and Sarah thought fleetingly of J.J. Reed's squaw, Many Tongues. "Chief White Buffalo say you have need of clothes." Still with that shy smile, she held out the garments.

Sarah reached for them gratefully. "Thank you, Prairie Blossom. Dear God, yes, thank you!" She smiled brilliantly and impulsively reached out to press the girl's small brown hand.

The Indian girl squatted before her, looking furtively at the wives. "They— How I say? Mad with you, with Chief White Buffalo. Be watchful."

"I will, Prairie Blossom. Thank you again."

"You need talk— You not know something." Prairie Blossom made vague gestures with her hands. "Do not be afraid. Ask me. I tell."

"I will." Sarah smiled wryly. "It seems there are many things I do not know."

Prairie Blossom bobbed her head in that shy manner and scooted out of the tepee. Sarah began putting on the clothes. They were a rather loose fit and had a rank odor, clearly some Indian woman's cast-offs.

Even before she was dressed, the three wives were taking down the shorter tepee poles. Sarah got out of the way just in time before they took down the three taller key-poles. If she hadn't ducked quickly, they would have crashed down on her head.

Now the women used the poles to make three travois, onto which they loaded the parfleches. Glancing around, Sarah saw that the entire village was leveled now, each family's travois being attached to ponies. Three horses were led up by Chief White Buffalo, who didn't once glance at Sarah. The wives lashed the three travois to the horses, then mounted bareback.

There was no horse for Sarah, and she realized that she was going to have to walk. But as the tribe began to depart, forming a straggly line, she saw that a few other Indian women were walking, including Prairie Blossom. Many of the children also walked, but all the men, Sarah noted, rode ponies, with their chief in the lead.

As they strung out across the prairie, Sarah glanced back at the site of the Indian village. The only things left to indicate that a village had ever been there were the tepee firepits and a few odds and ends scattered about. Everything else had been packed on the travois or on horseback.

The prairie stretched endlessly before them. Sarah hadn't the slightest idea where they were. Chief White Buffalo had placed no guard on her, but even if Sarah had had any thoughts of trying to get away now, she knew she wouldn't get a hundred yards before one of the braves on horseback would run her down. As far as she could ascertain, the Indians paid very little attention to her.

No one even spoke to her, until Prairie Blossom, a few miles from camp, dropped back to walk alongside her.

Sarah was already tired of walking. "How long will we walk like this?"

"Until we find buffalo. Reason we leave. Meat gone." Prairie Blossom shrugged. "Many suns. Walk until find buffalo herd."

"The men— The braves, I notice leave all the work to the women."

"Braves hunt. Find food. Go on warpath," the girl said gravely. "Women carve up meat braves kill. Cook meat. Put up tepee. Tear down tepee."

Sarah, remembering the hard labor of the winter with Sean, sighed. "The lot of the female in this country is hard. It seems the lot of the Indian woman is harder still."

Prairie Blossom looked at her with comprehension. "This 'lot.' Prairie Flower not know."

"Work. Indian women have to work hard."

"Yes, hard!" The girl smiled. "Better now."

"Better? How, for heaven's sake?"

Prairie Blossom explained that tales coming down through many generations told of how it had been with the Indian women before the ponies came to the prairies. In the old days the women not only walked everywhere, but also pulled the travois. "Now use pony. Ride pony."

"But not you. Why is that?"

Prairie Blossom smiled shyly. "Not have husband. Only woman with husband have pony to ride."

"Then I hope you find a husband soon," Sarah said absently.

"I find," the girl said with her shy smile, yet with a note of confidence. "Not long."

A thought came to Sarah. "Prairie Blossom, do you

know of the big river— That way." She motioned in the direction she thought was south.

"Big river?" Prairie Blossom said dubiously. Then her face broke wide in a smile. "Fast water? Red like blood when snow melt?"

"That's it! The Missouri." She had been right in that at least; they were north of the Missouri River. "How far?"

"Oh, many suns. Three, four suns walking."

Sarah's spirits sank. That meant three or four days of hard walking. But she could do it; she had walked farther than that with Sean. If she could reach the Missouri, she would at least have a direction in which to go. Remembering the heavy traffic on the river, Sarah was sure she would be able to get passage back to St. Louis.

All that remained was to pick the proper time.

They made camp just at sundown. No tepees were erected. The horses were staked out to graze, and several large cooking fires were started. The Indian women quickly prepared the meals.

Chief White Buffalo and his wives had a fire all to themselves. He spoke to Sarah for the first time since the evening before, gesturing her to his side. "Come, Sky Eyes. Sit here."

Sarah sat beside him, enduring the touch of his hand as he sat stroking her hair. She couldn't help but notice the venomous glances directed at her by the three women around the cooking fire.

Sarah knew that Prairie Blossom's warning was true. These three women would welcome a chance to do her harm, if it could be done in such a way that

White Buffalo would not know. And if the time came when she fell out of favor with him. . . .

The food was again pemmican and a cooked wild vegetable. The night was a repeat of the one before, except, of course, that there was no tepee, and what with being away from water, no one, including the chief, washed his hands and face. Sarah furtively wiped her fingers on the hem of the dress; it couldn't make it much filthier than it already was.

The three wives retired to their robes outside the circle of firelight. White Buffalo smoked a pipe, clamping a firm hand on Sarah's shoulder as she started to move away to curl up on the ground. She was bone tired, her feet and legs sore from the day's walking.

The fire dwindled down. The Pawnee chief lay back on his buffalo robes, pulling Sarah back with him. He pushed her skirts up and mounted her, once again impersonal about it, except for the expressive grunts.

Like a bull mounting a heifer, Sarah thought rebelliously; and I'm no bloody heifer!

When he finished and pushed her off his robes onto the hard ground, she felt used, soiled.

Wakeful now, her mind cold with rage, Sarah considered what she was going to do. She had to get away, even if they killed her for it. Death would be preferable to this nightly humiliation!

She lay awake for a long time, scheming of ways to escape. She would not make the attempt tonight; she was far too weary.

The next day Sarah husbanded her strength as much as possible, waiting for the night. After the evening ritual was repeated, she waited until everyone

317

was asleep. She feared the dogs the most, but they had grown accustomed to her smell now, and she hoped they would not bother her. When she squirmed out of the circle of sleeping Indians on her hands and knees, Sarah held her breath for the sudden yelping of one of the dogs. No sound came. She considered taking a horse, yet she wasn't familiar enough with them and was fearful they would spook at her smell and set up a great racket.

She crawled almost a hundred yards from the encampment, before she dared get up and walk. There still had been no hue and cry raised. She was going to make it!

She headed in a southerly direction. Sean had taught her a little about using the stars at night as a guide. Fortunately, it was a clear night, quite dark, without a moon. Sarah located the North Star over her shoulder and traveled away from it, checking back every so often to get her bearings.

A wave of longing for Jeb swept over her at the thought of the ship, the *North Star*. Jeb darling, she said silently; I'm coming back to you!

She wanted to run; everything in her demanded that she break into a run and gain as much distance from the Indian encampment as possible. Common sense told her that would be a mistake. If she ran, she would eventually collapse from exhaustion. She held herself down to a fast walk, and by the time dawn broke, she estimated she had covered at least five miles. Desperately tired now, she longed to rest. Instead, she kept plodding ahead.

About two hours after sunrise, the sound of hoofbeats struck terror to her heart. Looking back, she saw four horses galloping toward her. Sarah broke into a staggering run, despair and fear giving her an extra spurt of strength.

The sound of the pounding hooves grew into thunder. Any second she anticipated an arrow or a spear to strike her in the back.

"Ai-iii!"

Sarah flinched at the shrill cry and tried to run faster. Then she was seized around the waist and swept off her feet into the arms of a Pawnee brave.

She struck out at the coppery face with her fists. Laughing, the brave turned her over onto her stomach and held her across the pony in front of him.

Chapter Twenty

The horse carrying Sarah wheeled smartly in front of White Buffalo, and the Pawnee astride the animal dumped Sarah onto the dirt before the chief.

With a swift motion the chief stooped and wound his fingers in Sarah's hair, pulling her up. He lifted her off her feet, raising her until her face was on a level with his. Those deep black eyes glittered with a cold fury.

"White woman foolish try to get away from Pawnee. Pawnee can track eagle in sky at night." He shook her, and Sarah bit down hard on her lip to keep from crying out. "White Buffalo give many furs for Sky Eyes. Belong to White Buffalo now. Do not run again." He flung her away from him, and Sarah struck the ground hard, the breath knocked from her.

Stunned, she barely heard him shout at the tribe in Pawnee. They had not left the camp when Sarah was discovered missing, Now, White Buffalo was setting the tribe in motion again. Sarah sat up, shaking her head dazedly. She heard mocking laughter and looked up to see White Buffalo's three wives converging on her. They hustled her up, then sent her reeling forward on her feet. For the rest of the day one of the three was never far from her, and whichever one was guarding her carried a willow switch, which was brought whistling down across Sarah's back every time she lagged behind.

She saw Prairie Blossom, but the girl kept her distance, not even risking a glance at her. Apparently, the girl had been warned to stay away, Sarah thought.

While with Sean this past winter, Sarah had several times experienced what she was convinced was the ultimate in weariness. Now she found that she had been wrong. With only a few hours rest the night before, the long flight on foot, and now the day's lengthy trek, she was so tired by the time they camped that night, she dropped in her tracks and went instantly to sleep.

She was awakened by a rude shake. With a small cry she sat up. It was night, the meal long since over, and the fires were low. In the light of their dying fire White Buffalo's face had a cruel cast, and his fingers dug into the flesh of her arm like talons. He dragged her to his robes, flinging her down on them.

Maybe I can just go back to sleep, Sarah thought with a flash of humor, and sleep through it.

Perhaps she could have, except that White Buffalo treated her roughly this time, punishing her, pinching her flesh—her arms, thighs, and breasts. As Sarah writhed in pain, the chief picked her up off the ground, his hands under her, then drove into her viciously, slamming her to the ground with all his weight. She hurt, hurt like the very devil, and she came fully awake, clawing and snarling in her outrage, on the edge of savagery herself.

White Buffalo laughed coarsely. "Sky Eyes got much spirit."

Then, without warning, his fist slammed into the side of her head, and she fell back in a dazed stupor, dimly aware of the chief's continued assault on her body.

A few minutes later, still partially stunned, she was pushed off the chief's robes onto the ground. Clumsily, she shoved the deerskin skirt down and raised her head to look around. Her glance caught the North Star. How ironic, she thought; and she knew then that she was going to make another attempt to get away. She would never give up.

The next morning, trudging across the prairie, Sarah thought deeply about it. She knew now that her biggest mistake had been in trying to get away on foot. The next time she would have to use one of the Indian ponies. How she would manage that, she had no idea at the moment. There had to be a way.

"You do wrong, run away," a soft voice said beside her.

Sarah swung her head around. "Oh, it's you, Prairie Blossom." She laughed shortly. "I'm not such a pariah today, then?"

The Indian girl looked bewildered. "I do not understand."

"It doesn't matter." Sarah motioned. "I'm just glad *someone* is talking to me." A few steps farther on, she said, "What was so wrong about it, my running away? These are your people, Prairie Blossom, but I am a slave, bought and paid for! And suffering cruel treatment at the hands of your chief."

"He not good in robes, Chief White Buffalo?" Prairie Blossom said, with shy humor.

"There are only two men, no, three men worse than he is. All are white men, and one is dead." Sarah recalled then, vividly, how she had killed Walleye, but White Buffalo was no drunken fur trader; he was strong and fierce, a mighty warrior. Even if she could somehow get her hands on a knife, Sarah doubted he would give her a chance to use it, and even if, by some small chance, she was able to kill him, the others would kill her before she could escape.

" . . . you say two suns ago, is true," Prairie Blossom was saying. "The life, you say, of Indian women bad. But is the way of the Pawnee," she concluded dolefully.

"Well, take heart, Prairie Blossom." Sarah squeezed the girl's hand. "The life of many white women is not too grand either."

Later that afternoon, Sarah edged casually up to a brown and white pony pulling a travois. A glance around told her that she wasn't being watched too carefully now. Apparently they had concluded that her futile effort at escape had taught her a lesson, and close surveillance was not necessary.

In a low voice she whispered words into the pony's ear, nonsense phrases spoken in a soothing voice, directed at getting the brown and white pony accustomed to the sound of her voice. At first the horse shied away, then settled back into its plodding pace. After a time Sarah reached out tentatively to stroke the animal's mane. Again, it shied, but before she finally walked away, it was suffering her touch.

Sarah did this several times during the next few days. By then, the pony was quite familiar with her voice and touch.

Late in the afternoon of the fourth day, she saw White Buffalo, in the lead as always, pull his mount to a stop atop a small rise, raising one hand in the air. There was an immediate stir of excitement among the other Indians. They all left their ponies and moved quickly up to join their chief. Sarah saw Prairie Blossom among them, and she hurried, catching up to the Indian girl just as she gained the top of the ridge.

Breathlessly, she said, "What is it?"

Prairie Blossom pointed. "Buffalo."

Sarah looked and gasped aloud with awe. Below was a long, shallow valley, with a small stream meandering through it. On the far side of the stream was a moving sea of brown. Almost as far west as Sarah could see, the heaving mass of buffalo grazed.

"Dear God, I've never seen anything like it! There must be at least a thousand buffalo!"

"I not know what thousand mean, but many, many buffalo," Prairie Blossom said simply. "Such herd Prairie Blossom never see."

In that moment White Buffalo spoke in Pawnee, his voice low but carrying. *"Wa-ti-hes ti-kót-it ti-ra-hah!"*

"What did he say?"

"He say, 'Tomorrow we will kill buffalo!'" Prairie Blossom glanced at Sarah with that shyly humorous smile she was growing familiar with. "Tonight, Chief White Buffalo not ask you share his robes."

"And why is that?"

"Save his strength for hunt buffalo. But going to do battle—How you say?—different. Brave might not come back."

Sarah said caustically, "Thank God for buffalo then!"

"Oh, night after different."

"How will it be different?" Sarah looked at her with suspicion.

The Indian girl laughed softly. "Kill many buffalo, chief will lie with you all night!"

White Buffalo motioned the tribe back off the ridge. They retreated from the rise and traveled south for about two miles.

"This buffalo hunt tomorrow—" Sarah groped for the right words. "This is important— A big event, a busy time for the tribe?"

"It is— How you say? Big, important to Pawnee." She clapped her hands, happy as a child. "Tomorrow busy. Braves hunt buffalo all day. Then women takes off hides, carve up meat. Cook. Sun go down, we have feast!" Her face grew solemn. "Without buffalo, Pawnee die. Usual before hunt, have buffalo dance, pray to A-ti-us-ti-rá-wa, Spirit Father, for brave kill many buffalo. No time now. Buffalo here. Pawnee need food."

And tomorrow night, when their bellies are full, Sarah thought, is when I get away.

Now the Indians were crossing the crest again and moving down toward the stream.

"Set up tepees here," Prairie Blossom said. "Here buffalo cannot see, smell Pawnee."

As they began setting up camp, Sarah saw something she would never forget—the chief's three wives erecting the tepee. They did it with dispatch and efficiency.

Once, Sarah half-heartedly offered to help. She only got in the way, succeeding in stirring their ire, and they turned on her as one, chattering and gesturing. Sarah quickly retreated and watched from a distance.

First, the three women removed the parfleches and

dismantled the travois. The poles used to construct the travois now became lodge poles, the three longer ones employed as key-poles, which were laid out on the ground where the tepee was to be erected. The thin ends were lashed together with antelope thongs, approximately three feet from the tips, forming a tripod. The tripod was set into the ground, the thick ends of the poles wedged into the earth, placed far enough apart to make it stable.

Now the wives gathered up a dozen of the shorter poles and drove them into the ground, propping them against the point where the key-poles were tied together. This was the skeleton of the lodge, the base firmly wedged into the ground. Sarah noticed that it was indeed higher than the other tepees going up around it. Tanned buffalo hides were used to form the covering. These were hung by one of the wives who was held by the other two as she clambered up to the juncture of the key-poles and bound the skins to it. The skins were allowed to fall naturally, draped evenly over the pole skeleton. The opening through which the Indians would enter the tepee faced east. Sarah was to learn from Prairie Blossom that all tepees were erected so the openings faced east; it was unthinkable for it to face any other direction.

Last of all, the wives took two even longer poles and fitted the top points into the buffalo hides at the very top of the tepee. This pair of poles was not wedged into the ground, but left free so they could be swung to different positions and different angles, shifting the tanned hides about. In this way, they could regulate how much ventilation would come in at the top at any given time, ensuring both a warm and a healthy lodge.

Sarah was amazed at how fast the Indian women performed their task, and with little wasted effort; it couldn't have taken them much longer than thirty minutes.

All the while Sarah had been thinking longingly of the stream only a few yards away. Now that the three wives were busy inside, setting up the chief's throne, Sarah began strolling casually toward the water. If what Prairie Blossom had told her was true and she was spared the "honor" of warming the chief's robes tonight, it would be a grand feeling to be clean again, if only for a night. She watched closely to see if she was being observed, but the Indians were all quite busy. The braves were seeing to their arrows and lances in preparation for tomorrow's hunt, and the women were occupied erecting tepees. Sarah noticed that most of the tepees were being put up by one Indian woman, and none were so far along as the chief's wives. Being one of *three* wives had certain advantages, she thought with a smile; the work was divided up.

In fact, so unnoticed did her progress seem to be that Sarah thought briefly of fleeing again the moment she was out of sight. No, she would stick to her plan, foregoing any spur-of-the-moment flight.

At the stream she found a clump of bushes screening her from the Indian encampment and undressed behind it. First, she scrubbed the deerskin dress and moccasins with sand, getting as much of the dirt and grease out of them as possible. Then she slipped naked into the water. The stream was quite shallow, the water cold, and she had to lie on her back to be fully immersed. In the luxury of the water she hummed a little to herself, momentarily forgetting her plight, her surroundings. Last of all, she washed her hair. In the middle of it she felt, rather than heard, a presence behind her. She froze, turning her head slowly. An Indian brave stood on the sloping bank, arms folded, looking at her without expression. Sarah knew he had been sent to check on her whereabouts.

Sarah stared at him defiantly, making no attempt to cover herself. Then, contemptuously, she turned her back and resumed washing her hair. When she looked around again, he was gone, as silently as he had come.

Grass was luxuriant on the bank. After washing her hair, Sarah lay on her back on the grass, letting the sun dry her body. She lay there for a long time, drowsing in the warmth of the sun. She awoke shivering. The sun had gone down, and it was chilly. She found that the dress and the moccasins were almost dry, at least dry enough to wear. She quickly dressed and hurried back to the village and the chief's tepee. The tepees were all up now, pencil-streams of smoke from cooking fires emerging from the tops.

She ducked into the chief's tepee. White Buffalo was ensconced on his throne, and for all the notice any of them paid Sarah, she might never have been absent for two hours. She noticed that, when she took her accustomed place by White Buffalo's throne, he did not reach out to stroke her hair, the only sign of affection he had ever given her. Apparently he was still angry with her for running away. Wait until tomorrow night, she thought with satisfaction; then he will really be furious!

The only words he directed at her was when they

were served the tough pemmican. "Tomorrow, fresh buffalo meat. Will eat well, Sky Eyes."

As soon as the skimpy meal was finished, the fire was dampened down, and they all retired to their respective robes. Sarah sat for a moment, tense, expectant, but once again Prairie Blossom had been right. This night White Buffalo made no demands on her. His snores filled the lodge immediately. Sarah still had no sleeping robes, but it didn't really matter. She arranged herself for sleep, knowing she would need all the rest she could get, if her flight was to be successful.

The next day was an arduous one, beginning with the rising of the sun. At the end of the day, Sarah was of two minds about it. It was an unforgettable experience, no denying that, yet it was also an exhausting one. She would just as soon have remained behind in the camp, but that option wasn't open to her. Everyone, men, women, and children, went en masse on the buffalo hunt. Only those too old or infirm were left behind.

A line of the braves on the best horses went first, with White Buffalo on his big stallion in the lead. Many of the braves, to Sarah's astonishment and embarrassment, rode naked on their ponies to hunt buffalo, carrying only their weapons—bows and arrows and feathered lances. No rifles were to be seen. Come to think of it, Sarah couldn't remember seeing a single rifle or pistol since she had been with them.

The braves all rode bareback; a strip of rawhide was knotted around each pony's jaw, forming a bridle. Sarah had already stolen one of those and hidden it to use tonight. All the ponies from the encampment were brought along, of course, but she was relieved to notice that the brown and white pony was to be used only to tote the meat and hides back. The Indian women led this second line of ponies behind the braves, makeshift travois lashed behind each pony.

The buffalo herd had moved a short distance from where they had been the day before. When Sarah first sighted them this morning, most of the animals were lying down. A few bulls stood quietly chewing their cuds, while others were grinding their horns into the yellow dirt.

The buffalo paid not the slightest heed to the line of mounted braves riding toward them. The order for the initial charge had not yet been given. As the braves approached the herd, the ends of the long line curved out and inward slightly, so they could ride at the flanks. When the line reached a few outlying buffalo, the animals started to their feet in alarm, blowing and pawing at the ground, edging back toward the main herd. This finally attracted the attention of the whole herd, and they came to their feet.

In that moment White Buffalo raised an arm high and shouted, *"Loó-ah!"*

The braves drummed their mounts into full charge, yelling and screaming. Now all the buffalo were on their feet. Down went the huge heads and up flew every little tail, and the herd was off in a headlong stampede in the other direction.

The Indian riders on the flanks had far outdistanced the others, riding for the head of the stampede. Their purpose was soon clear to Sarah. They were attempting to turn the leaders of the stampede back. Later, she was to learn that the cows and heifers were always in the lead in a buffalo stampede, the bulls hanging back to form a sort of rear guard, and since the younger the buffalo, the tenderer the meat, the Indians always wanted to kill as many of the young buffalo as possible.

The outriders were successful. The leading buffalo were turned back into the main herd, and it soon became a milling, bawling mass. The braves rode into it on their ponies at full gallop, bows pulled back and arrows flying. Lance heads glinted in the morning sun, then disappeared as they were driven into the buffalo. Before long the herd and the slaughtering braves were hidden in a boiling dust cloud.

The women and the children waited patiently. The smell of blood soon reached them, and they uttered cries of exultation. The dust cloud was drifting slowly westward, leaving dead buffalo behind.

One of the Indian women gave a signal, and they moved in, falling like vultures onto the carcasses. Knives flashed as the women expertly removed the buffalo hides, piling them underside up to the sun. While about half of the women roamed ahead from buffalo to buffalo, stripping away the hides, the other half moved in and began carving up the skinned animals.

The stench of blood lay over everything, and flies hovered, buzzing. As much as she thought the winter's trapping had hardened her, Sarah felt sickened by it all. Yet she knew it meant the very existence of the tribe. Survival was all, and without the buffalo meat and hides, the Pawnee would cease to exist.

Sarah felt helpless as she stood watching, generally ignored. In the distance the braves were still riding in and out of the herd, killing with deadly efficiency with arrow and lance. They rode fearlessly into the thick of the herd, ignoring the danger of tossing horns as the enraged buffalo charged at them. It was a terrifying sight, yet there was a raw, primitive beauty about it, stirring some atavistic instinct even in Sarah herself.

She saw Prairie Blossom working industriously over one buffalo carcass, and she walked over.

"Is there anything I can do to help, Prairie Blossom?" she asked.

The Indian girl, hands smeared with blood, looked up with a happy smile. "Can help load travois." She gestured to the patient pony beside her. "I cut, you tie meat on so will not fall off."

The girl was very skilled, very fast, cutting off the best parts of the buffalo meat. As Sarah helped, she noticed with stomach-turning disgust that many of the other women would stop from time to time to devour some of the innards, especially the boudin. She did not look at them again. She busied herself loading chunks of meat onto the travois, lashing them on it with rawhide thongs so they wouldn't fall off on the way back to camp. The buffalo hides were tied across the pony's back.

Prairie Blossom explained to her that only the tender young cows were completely butchered. From the older animals only the tongues and the softer cuts around the hump were taken. But all the guts were collected for making pemmican, and to give that winter ration a good flavor, some of the tougher meat from the older animals was also taken.

The slaughter and the work continued into late afternoon, Prairie Blossom and Sarah made two trips back to camp with the laden pony and returned again to the killing grounds. Sarah, despite all her efforts, was now bloody from fingertip to elbow, and the Indian girl had blood smeared on her face like paint.

Finally, the killing stopped. The prairie was dotted with the dark carcasses of dead animals. The herd had vanished over the horizon. The braves began coming back in ones and twos. One brave stopped by Prairie Blossom, raised his bloody lance high and shouted something in Pawnee; then raced on toward camp.

"What did he say, Prairie Blossom?"

"He say Chief White Buffalo kill most buffalo of all braves. Kill . . ." The girl held up all her fingers.

"He killed ten buffalo?"

"As you say, ten. Most buffalo of all braves. Reason White Buffalo, your husband, is chief. You be— How you say? Proud?"

"Hah! That'll be the day!" Sarah snorted and turned away.

Into her mind sprang a vivid memory of the day Sean had slain the doe in the meadow. It had been that night that he had come to her for the first time.

The strong, almost visual imagery of that night produced such a mental anguish that Sarah dropped the meat she was carrying into the dirt and doubled over.

Ah, Sean! Rogue, adventurer, lover, where are you? Have you given me up for lost?

It had been over two weeks now, and no sign of Sean. He had probably decided that she had fled from him.

"Sa-rah? What wrong?"

Sarah straightened up to look into Prairie Blossom's concerned face. It was the first time the girl had tried to use her name. Sarah forced a smile. "I'm all right, Prairie Blossom. Just a stomach cramp."

"Stomach cramp? You mean, hurt here?" The Indian girl folded her hands over her stomach and doubled over, expressing pain. "Woman pain? Prairie Blossom feel that two moons back first time. Older women say I am now woman." She beamed proudly.

Sarah said, "No, not that . . ." Then she stopped, knowing there was no way she could explain. "Yes, Prairie Blossom. Woman pain."

It was not long before sundown when the Indian women straggled back to the encampment with the last load of hides and meat. Sarah watched carefully to see where the brown and white pony was taken. The Indians had erected a crude corral at the south end of the camp, and she saw the spotted pony turned loose in there with the other animals. It was located some distance from the main village; if she could sneak that far without being detected, Sarah was sure she could get away on the pony.

Sarah hurried down to the stream and washed the blood off. By the time she returned to the village, two huge fires were blazing in the center of the encampment, and the braves were squatting around the fires, drinking from a keg of whiskey.

When she could get Prairie Blossom alone, Sarah asked the girl were they had gotten the whiskey.

"Fur traders came. Pawnee trade for firewater." The girl made a face. "Braves now get addled in the head."

Sarah felt a lurch of dismay at this news. If she had been here when the traders came, she might have been able to beg their help.

She asked, "How did the traders find the tribe?"

"Heard buffalo stampede. Knew Pawnee hunt buffalo."

Sarah remembered something Sean had said once: "Fur traders have some kind of sixth sense for when Indians are thirsting for that skull-bustin' concoction they peddle. I've seen it happen time and again."

After thinking about it, and remembering Walleye and Frenchie, Sarah cheered up. If these fur traders were anything like *that* pair, she was better off without them. Already she saw signs of drunkenness among the braves. Even White Buffalo was drinking. If they all got drunk enough and fell into a stupor, it would make it much easier for her to slip away.

The cooking was not done in individual tepees tonight. It was all done around the roaring fires. There was much feasting, drinking, and merriment. Sarah noticed that the women were not allowed to drink.

Marrow bones were tossed into the red embers of the fires to cook, buffalo calves' heads were baked in the hot earth, and plump ribs were roasted over the flames. Most of the boudin, and even some tongue, was eaten raw while the rest cooked.

Sarah sat quietly beside the chief, although he paid her not the slightest heed. The men, steadily getting drunker, told tales of hunting and battle prowess. Even the usual sober-faced White Buffalo was gay and laughing tonight.

When the food was done, everyone fell on it ravenously. Sarah ate all she could hold, knowing she had a long trek before her without food. Watching her chance, she managed to secret quite a bit of meat in a small bundle she made of a scrap of deerskin, then hid it along with the rawhide bridle in the tepee.

Not long after the food was devoured, the braves began to stagger off to their own tepees, their wives following. Many of them fell asleep right on the ground where they had been eating, their wives with them. Sarah realized that she need not have worried about the women not drinking. Having gone for weeks without rich food such as this feast, they had gorged themselves into a torpor, and for her purpose, it served as well as if they had been sodden with drink.

White Buffalo was one of the last to give in. Abruptly he got to his feet, pulling Sarah up by the arm. "Come."

Staggering a little, he dragged her along to the tepee. Sarah was glad about one thing. The three wives had fallen asleep on the ground, and they had the tepee to themselves.

The chief shoved her back onto his throne, clumsily got out of his leggings, and mounted her without ceremony. Even full of drink as he was, he was like a bull in its prime. The excitement of the day's hunt had aroused him to the fullest. His ruttings continued without slackening, even after he had grunted out his first pleasure. He continued driving into her without pause until a sharp cry issued from his open mouth, and he slumped down on her. Instead of shoving her off the cot, as was his wont, White Buffalo went to sleep at once.

Sarah waited for a little, enduring the heaviness of his body, the revolting odor of buffalo blood still on him. Finally, slowly and with infinite care, she squirmed out from under him. It did not disturb the rhythm of his snoring.

Curled up on the ground near the throne, Sarah

had to fight against falling asleep. The long day's labor and a full stomach made her yearn for rest; yet she realized that if she succumbed, she would probably sleep through the night. She lay tense, occasionally pinching herself awake, for what she judged to be two hours, until she was certain that the whole camp was asleep, even the dogs.

Then she retrieved her small bundle of food and the bridle and crept carefully out of the tepee. The fires had died down to coals, and the sprawled bodies of the Indians lay unmoving.

Everything living in the encampment seemed to be sleeping soundly. Even the horses, Sarah found when she reached the corral, were either lying down, or asleep on their feet. She congratulated herself on selecting the brown and white. He was easy to pick out even in the dark, and fortunately, he was one of the few on his feet.

Sarah slipped into the corral and made her way to the animal. The others backed away at her presence, but they were apparently too weary to make any great fuss. Sarah threw an arm around the neck of the spotted pony and whispered in his ear, "I'm sorry, Brownie. I know you're tired, but I desperately need you."

The pony sleepily nudged her with his nose and made no protest when Sarah slipped on the rawhide bridle. She led the pony to the gate, lowered the two poles, tugged the animal outside, then replaced the gate poles.

Sarah didn't mount up at once. She got a fix on the North Star, breathing a prayer of thanksgiving for the cloudless night, and led the pony in a southerly direction, moving slowly and quietly. She did not get onto the pony until she judged they were at least two miles from the Indian village. Even when she was astride the animal, she allowed him to proceed at a walk, knowing how keen were Pawnee ears. There was one problem she hadn't considered. All the other times she had ridden, even on Sean's mules, Sarah had used a saddle. This was her first experience bareback, and she found it difficult to keep her seat. She dreaded to think what would happen to her if she had to ride hard and fast. Since she was unfamiliar with the terrain, she let the pony pick its own way, using the reins only when she thought he was veering in the wrong direction.

When dawn finally came, Sarah was relieved to see that they were still close to the stream. Evidently it wandered south, eventually emptying into the Missouri. At least she wouldn't be without water.

At sunrise, she reined the pony in, looking back. The land here was quite flat, and she could see behind her for miles. There was no sign of pursuit. Sarah heaved a sigh of relief. The pony stood with head hanging, sagging with weariness.

Sarah slid off, led the animal to the stream, and let him drink. She got down on her knees and scooped water up with cupped hands, drinking thirstily. When the pony had drunk its fill, she turned him away to a small tree, tying off the long reins. The grass here was lush and thick. Sarah sat down with a weary sigh, leaning back against the tree trunk. If fortune favored her, the Pawnees would not stir much before mid-morning and likely would not miss her until then. The urge to travel on, to put as much distance behind her as possible, was strong. Yet, if she drove the pony too hard, he would drop from exhaustion, and she would be afoot. Already the animal had sunk to the ground, having grazed very little.

The need for slumber was heavy on Sarah. She dared not, she knew. She forced herself to remain awake, looking always northward. She let the pony rest for what she judged to be at least three hours, before she prodded him up and mounted. The pony seemed freshened by the rest and started off at a brisk pace.

When Sarah judged it to be noon, she stopped again and ate part of the buffalo meat from her small store. All morning she had frequently turned to look back, but the landscape was still empty behind her. The farther she traveled, the more her spirits rose. Hopefully, she had too long a lead to ever be caught. It was even possible that White Buffalo, in his disgust, would decide to let her go.

She stopped at full dark, staked the pony to graze, and ate the last of her food. If Prairie Blossom's estimate was correct, she should be a third of the way to the Missouri by now. She could go hungry for two days, if need be. Tired as she was, Sarah slept well that night, even on hard ground. She was up at first light and riding again. The country was more broken now, with ravines and small, narrow valleys.

The sun was warm on her face, and such was her growing feeling of safety, she was dozing on the pony's back by the middle of the morning. Then she heard a sound that caused her to start in fear. She darted a look back and saw six Indians on horseback about a mile behind her, strung out in a ragged line. They were coming fast.

Sarah drummed her heels into the pony's flanks and urged him into a gallop. Her heart beating wildly, she clung desperately to the pony's bare back. Yet she knew in her heart that she was doomed to failure; she would never outrace them.

This time, when she was dumped onto the ground before the scowling chief of the Pawnee, he said nothing to her. Instead, he motioned and spoke a few harsh words in Pawnee. Two braves with rawhide thongs converged on Sarah. Before she could even move, they had her by both arms and had lashed her wrists together behind her back. Then one of the chief's three wives approached, grinning with huge enjoyment. She carried a knife, which she gave to White Buffalo.

He squatted, seizing Sarah from behind by the hair. Horrible images flitted through Sarah's mind. Sean had told her stories of Indians scalping people while they were still alive. She screamed, struggling in complete terror. White Buffalo spoke in Pawnee again, and the two braves grasped her limbs, holding her still.

Sarah closed her eyes, tensing herself for the bite of the knife blade on her scalp. It didn't come. Instead, she felt a tugging at the roots of her hair, and she realized that he was cutting it off. She slumped, almost fainting in her relief. When White Buffalo was finished, she had only a short stubble of hair on her head. He stood up, the knife flashing in his hand as he drew it back. Sarah flinched as the knife drove into the earth between her legs, buried to the hilt.

White Buffalo said contemptuously, "Sky Eyes no longer favorite wife. Now see what happen to foolish white squaw."

Sarah was tied to a tree stump, only her legs left

free. She was tormented incessantly the rest of the afternoon and into the evening. The women taunted her, pinching her flesh, pulling at her short hair. Children threw sticks and small stones at her. They circled her, high-stepping, emitting war cries, imitating their elders. Two even had tomahawks. Every time they passed, they swiped at her, the tomahawk blades coming so close Sarah could feel the rush of air. She flinched away, until finally she was too weary, too sick at heart, to care any more.

Sarah thought her humiliation was complete, but with the morning, she found there was yet another indignity in store for her.

The tribe stirred with the dawn and quickly began taking down the tepees. They were moving again. No one approached her until it was time to leave.

Then White Buffalo came, leading his stallion. From it he took a length of knotted rawhide, some thirty feet long. He made a noose in one end and looped it around her neck. He untied her hands from around the stump, and Sarah managed to stagger to her feet. Then he retied her hands behind her back.

"Now white woman learn," he said impassively. "Will be led like dog of white man. Will work like white man's black slave."

He handed the end of the rawhide rope to one of his wives, gave Sarah a fierce, unyielding glare, and vaulted onto his horse.

Chapter Twenty-one

Sean Flanagan realized from the very beginning that, if he didn't catch up with Sarah's captors before they sold her, he would have a difficult time of it. They had at least a twelve-hour start on him, and he had no firm idea of what direction they were taking. He had only one thing in his favor. He knew that the two Indian tribes most likely to purchase a white slave were the Cheyenne and the Pawnee; the Cheyenne were noted for it. The other Indian tribes within reasonable riding distance of St. Louis did not keep any slaves. They did not even make slaves of other Indians taken in battle.

Most of the Pawnee and Cheyenne tribes roamed the prairie to the north and the west, and Sean had a strong feeling that Giles Brock would be reluctant to venture far from the Mississippi. Jacques Fortier had told Sean, while he was outfitting him for travel, that he was familiar with the name of Giles Brock. Over the past year the name had gained much notoriety as a bloody river pirate. This gave Sean some hope. Brock would be out of his element on the prairie and among the Indians; so the odds were heavy against his going far from the river.

So Sean headed north, out of St. Louis. He rode hard for several days, even at night, stopping only to rest the horses and catch a few hours sleep. He had some faint hope of coming across someone who had seen Sarah and her captors. The hope soon dimmed. He asked everyone he met riding south if they had seen a woman and two men, but none would admit to it. It was entirely possible that the three hadn't come this way at all. Of course, they would try to avoid any contact with others. Knowing Sarah, Sean was certain they had to keep her tied up, and two men with a bound woman traveling with them would certainly arouse curiosity.

By the end of the third day, with no sign or word of them, discouragement weighed heavily on Sean. He knew now that he would not catch up to them before they had sold Sarah to whatever tribe they had in mind.

He could not keep the thought out of his mind—the picture of Sarah in the rough embrace of an Indian brave. How would she fare? With her fire and spirit she would not tame easily, and Sean knew that Indian men had little patience with disobedience. How long could she survive in such an environment? He must find her before her spirit or her body was broken. He would keep up the search if it took all year, or even longer; he would continue until he had visited every Indian tribe on the prairie.

That is what he proceeded to do. Staying north of the Missouri, until the river itself turned north, he traveled in a zig-zag pattern across the great prairie, stopping at every Indian encampment he could find, asking if they had seen a white woman slave or had heard rumors of one.

Many rumors were passed on to him. Most, he suspected, were made up on the spot, for even the friendly Indians took great delight in bedeviling the white man. Doggedly, Sean tracked down every rumor to its source, all without success. Any time he came into contact with a Pawnee or Cheyenne tribe, he was circumspect, never asking the direct question, but simply wearing out his welcome until he'd had a look at every person in the village.

Following this erratic course, he moved slowly westward through the tag end of spring and into the dust and heat of summer.

By the end of summer, Sean realized, from the sly glances he was receiving, that many of the tribes now had advance warning of his appearance among them and his purpose. He knew that most of them considered him mad—a lone white man searching the endless prairies for a white squaw. Sean smiled to himself, knowing what they were thinking. Why fur trapper spend much time hunting white squaw? Must be other white squaws!

Sean let none of this deter him. In fact, his determination only grew stronger as he ran down every rumor and still failed to find Sarah.

By the middle of October, he was approaching the North Platte region. The autumn leaves had turned golden, and the air had a chill bite to it. Sean had to rest oftener now. Not for himself so much as for the animals. They had been ridden hard and long, and were gaunt and weary. Since it appeared certain that his search was going to stretch into winter, Sean knew that he had to rest the horses. One day, he found a small glade, with a lake fed by spring water. Despite the lateness of the year, the grass around the lake was still lush and green. Sean set up camp. He staked out the animals to graze and went hunting on foot, shooting a couple of fat quail for his supper.

He rested there for several days, letting the weariness ease out of him. The weather turned warm, and he and the animals basked in the luxury of the brief Indian summer, soaking in the heat of the sun. Within an amazingly short time, the horses filled out, becoming sleek and frisky, and Sean grew restless, anxious to continue his search. It was time to go.

But first he must hunt. He would need larger game this time; so he would have food to last for a few days. The last rumor he had picked up told of a Cheyenne tribe along the North Platte with a white captive.

In a draw about a mile from camp, scouting ahead of the horse he had taken along, Sean came upon a small herd of antelope grazing. He settled down on the lip of the draw, drew a bead on a half-grown antelope, and killed the animal with a shot through the heart. The rest of the herd took flight, stampeding. Sean went back a hundred yards to where he had left the horse, leading him down into the draw. Quickly he skinned the dead antelope and cut off the choice pieces of meat, loading it onto the horse. Sean walked back to camp, leading the horse.

Shortly before sundown he made a fire, spitted antelope steaks on sticks, and propped them over the fire to roast. He smoked a pipe, now and then leaning forward to turn the meat.

All of a sudden, he was alerted by the sound of hoofbeats. He came to his feet, snatching up Katie, and moving out of the firelight. Looking in the direction of the sounds, he saw two riders top the rise to the east, then send their mounts plunging down the slight slope. They were leading two pack animals laden with furs.

Sean's keen eyesight told him that they were white, likely fur traders. Since they were coming in openly, he sensed no danger. He stepped out into the firelight, but he didn't relax his guard enough to place Katie out of reach. He leaned on the rifle and waited.

They drew to a halt a few yards away, hands upraised to show they had no weapons ready. Fur traders, right enough, Sean thought. And about as scroungy a pair as he'd ever seen. There was nothing unusual in that, of course; most fur traders were a ratty-looking lot after some months on the prairies.

"Hello, stranger!" said the larger of the two. "Heered a rifle shot some distance back. Figgered maybe there was a white man around. Wagh!" He grinned cheerfully, teeth white in a graying straggle of beard.

"Shot an antelope for my supper," Sean said laconically. "You're both welcome to share. I'm Sean Flanagan."

"That's right kind of you, Friend Flanagan." The big man slid off his horse. "I'm Buck, Buck Ketichum. This here's my pard, Canniberry. We'll be happy to jine you. Ain't had fresh meat for days. Been riding hard to make the Missouri before the snow flies."

The pair staked out their animals to graze, stacking their furs where they could keep an eye on them. While they were busy at this, Sean brewed a pot of strong tea.

Ketichum returned carrying a jug. When Sean handed them cups of the steaming tea, Ketichum held the jug over his cup, then his partner's, and glanced questioningly at Sean. "How about a splash of our firewater? The last jug left." He grinned.

"That's one reason we're heading out. All our trade goods are gone."

Sean managed to conceal his distaste. He considered fur traders who swapped cheap liquor to the Indians for furs the lowest of the low, yet it was commonplace enough. He shrugged and held out his cup. "A dollop might go well with the antelope."

Ketichum poured liberally. "Here's to good fur prices in St. Louie! Wagh!" He hoisted his cup, and they drank.

Sean grimaced slightly. The liquor taste came through the tea, raw and potent.

Ketichum grinned broadly, smacking his lips. "Wagh! Powerful strong, huh, friend? After we'uns give the redskins a sample of our wares, they fall over themselves bringing out peltries to trade."

Sean moved away to turn the meat; it would soon be done. With more liquor in his belly, Buck Ketichum became loquacious and vulgar, relating with relish their success in bilking the Indians and going into detail about how many comely squaws they'd tumbled that long summer. His companion, a tall, thin, bony man, with a lugubrious face, seldom spoke beyond a grunt. Sean finally concluded that he was either too stupid to have anything to say, or Ketichum never shut up long enough for the other to speak.

Sean was thoroughly sick of the pair before long. They were a fine pair of sculpins. They ate and drank like two hogs at a trough, and as accustomed as he was to the stories of fur traders and trappers, even Sean was revolted by some of the things Ketichum told him.

After the meal was finished, Sean excused himself

and went down to the lake to wash and see to his animals. His visitors didn't stir from the fire.

When Sean returned, Ketichum began again. Sean filled and lit his pipe, and squatted cross-legged, staring into the fire, scarcely listening to the man's talk. Then he caught a phrase that alerted him. Careful not to show undue interest, he said casually, "I'm sorry, Buck. I didn't quite catch that last."

Ketichum looked momentarily confused. "What was that, friend?"

"I thought you said something about trading with a Pawnee tribe just recently?"

"Yah." Ketichum made a face. "Onliest thing they had to trade was buffaler hides. We had about all of them we could—"

"No, not that. Something you said about a woman on a long leash."

"Oh, that!" Ketichum laughed, slapping his knee. "Gol-darnest thing I ever seen. I tell you, them Injuns know how to handle a female, be she white or red of skin."

Sean said, "This one was white, you say?"

"Couldn't really tell, she was so dirty, face and hands black with smoke. Reckon she was white, though. Claimed she was, and she had blue eyes, almost the color of prairie violets. Her Injun name is Sky Eyes. Ain't that a pistol?"

Sean was hard put to contain his excitement now. Was his long search at an end? "You spoke to her, did you?"

"Wasn't our doing. Jest as we was about to be on our way, she runs out in our path, gobbling something about us taking her along with us. Can you figger us doing that, all them Injuns ready to plant an arrer in our backs?"

"She tell you what her white name was?"

"Nah. Didn't have a chance for that. There was an Injun on the other end of the rope. When he spots her yakking to us, he gave a jerk and sent her ass-end over teakettle. Damned near snapped her neck, it did!"

"This Pawnee tribe—what's the chief's name?"

"White Buffalo, so he tole us." Ketichum seemed to sober a little, and he gave Sean a probing look out of small black eyes. "What all the curiousness about this white wench and the Pawnee tribe, Friend Flanagan?"

Sean was slow in answering, his mind racing. Had this pair heard of the crazy man wandering the prairie looking for a captive white woman? In an offhand manner, he finally said, "Oh, it's not the woman I'm interested in. But this White Buffalo now— That's the sculpin I'm after trying to find. Like you two fellows, I was traveling along with my last load of firewater some two weeks back. A Pawnee tribe ambushed me, caught me with my breeches down, so to speak." Sean forced an embarrassed laugh. "They stole my pack animals, furs, liquor, and all. I'm looking for the sculpins."

Ketichum nodded, his curiosity lessening. "Wondered why you was out here all alone, with nothing but two horses, no furs nor trade goods. Say now . . ." He gawked at Sean. "You ain't thinking of going after that whole passel of Pawnee on your own, are you?"

"We-ell, they stole my trade goods."

"Friend, you're addled! You'd be better off taking

out for St. Louie with what furs you have and put that bunch of Pawnee right out of your head."

Sean shrugged. "I may be addled, but I'm also a stubborn cuss." He stared into the fire, thinking of Sarah. By all the saints, he would kill the man that had done this to her!

Ketichum said anxiously, "Say now, you ain't thinking that mebbe me and Canniberry here are going to side with you agin a pack of Pawnee, are you? If you be, forget it! Appreciate your friendly nature and your antelope steaks, but we got to get on south afore the snow flies."

"No, no! It's my problem. I'll handle it." Sean gestured without looking at the man. "Did you pick up any hint as to where they might be headed, White Buffalo's tribe?"

"I heered some talk about wintering near the North Platte, not far from Rattlesnake Buttes. But you take a word of advice from me, friend, you forget it."

With a quick toss of his head, Buck Ketichum drained his cup of whiskey, and he and his partner retired to their robes without even a word of goodnight, settling down some distance from the fire. Sean sat on for a while, smoking a last pipe, brooding on the dying fire. He knew Ketichum's advice was sound. What chance did he have going up against a large tribe of Pawnee by himself? Still, he had no choice, as he saw it. If the white woman with the Pawnee was Sarah, he couldn't leave her there, and his gut instinct told him that it *was* Sarah.

He rolled up in his robes, rifle near, and both his pistols in the robes with him. As always when strangers were nigh, he slept lightly. He was awake instantly when he heard the pair of traders stirring. Sean turned his head slowly, so he could observe them. It was just dawn. They were already saddling their horses. Taking off without a word, Sean thought wryly; just like I'm some plague carrier.

Then he saw that they didn't mount up at once. They were standing with heads together, talking in low voices, looking in his direction. Buck Ketichum was motioning with both hands.

They're thinking of killing me while I sleep and stealing my horses and what little gear I have. Oh, what a fine pair of sculpins!

He sat up abruptly, letting the top robe fall back. His hands in his lap both held pistols, pointed casually in their direction.

Smiling, he said cheerfully, "Good morning, gentlemen. Thinking of leaving without even a farewell, without a bite to put in your bellies?"

Ketichum started. He smiled ingratiatingly, his gaze on the brace of pistols. "We're in a great rush, Friend Flanagan. Hoped we'd get off without waking you."

"Now I'm thinking that's right considerate of you, Mr. Ketichum," Sean said dryly.

"Well, good-bye, friend. And good luck." Ketichum gestured to his partner. The two men mounted up and rode away with a great clatter, leading their pack animals.

Sean laughed heartily. He got out of the robes and stoked up the fire from the few coals remaining. His laughter died as he remembered his mission, and the possibility that this rumor of Sarah's whereabouts had an authentic ring to it. A sense of urgency drove him. He ate a cold breakfast, except for a cup of tea, then quickly collected his gear. He saddled the horses and set out at a brisk pace.

It was going to be a long trek to Rattlesnake Buttes, those twin peaks near where the North Platte River was joined by a dark, swift river flowing in from the northwest. Sean had never been that far west, but he had heard many tales of it and had a crudely drawn map of the area. Trappers who had been that far spoke of it as one of the loveliest spots in the west, with the majestic Rockies always in view. Rattlesnake Buttes were aptly named. The area at the foot of the pillars was infested with thousands of the poisonous snakes.

But the place where Sean suspected the Pawnee were headed was at the confluence of the North Platte and the western river. It was said that it teemed with beaver; wild turkey and deer were plentiful, as well as ducks and elk. Buffalo favored it as a watering spot.

Sean knew that when he finally reached the area, he would be some 900 miles from St. Louis. He had been surprised during his search to find Pawnee tribes so far east. Pawnee territory was generally north of the Platte and west of the Missouri after that river swung north. He would have to cross the Missouri before he reached his destination, and there would be some difficulty locating White Buffalo's tribe, since there would be many Pawnee tribes in the area.

After crossing the Missouri, the Rockies in view on clear days, Sean proceeded with caution. He generally followed the flow of the North Platte River now, toward the dark, swift-running river from the west; the name he didn't know, remembering only that it had been named after some French fur trapper who had discovered it.

When he was into Pawnee country, Sean left his horses staked out and reconnoitered on foot, ranging several miles ahead. During a period of four days, he found three Pawnee villages. Each was located near water, down in a small valley. Sean lay on his belly on a nearby ridge, studying each encampment through the spyglass he had been wise enough to tote along. He was familiar by this time with the many different tribes, so he could spot a Pawnee easily enough. However, after a full day's watch on each of the three Indian villages, he never once saw Sarah. He was aware enough of Pawnee ways to know that, if Sarah was in disfavor enough to be on a leash, she would certainly be visible, doing the lowest form of work around the camp. So Sean was confident by the time he left each village behind that Sarah was not there.

On the fifth day, he spotted another camp, smaller in population than the others. He discovered it late in the afternoon, too late to set up surveillance. He made a cold camp three miles distant, not daring to risk a fire. The nights were quite cold now, and already he had ridden through snow flurries. If he managed to find Sarah and spirit her away, they would have to ride hard to get out before the prairie was locked in the grip of winter.

Grass for the horses was growing sparse, and he had taken to feeding them bark from certain trees, as the Indians did when the grass was gone. The horses didn't take to it in the beginning, but they eventually gave in when they became hungry enough.

Before sunrise the next morning, Sean was situated

on top of the ridge to the east of the village, screened by low bushes. Making himself comfortable, he adjusted the spyglass and aimed it at the village, which was just beginning to show signs of life, smoke rising from the tepees, straight as a string in the cold, still air.

A brave with a buffalo robe across his shoulders stepped from a tepee, stretching and yawning. He moved a few feet away from the tepee, then threw back the robe and calmly urinated. The spyglass was so strong Sean could even see steam rising from the frosty ground. A movement on the periphery of his vision caused Sean to swing the focus of the spyglass, just in time to catch another brave doing the same thing as the first.

With a grunt of impatience Sean swept the entire village with the glass. Finally he settled the glass on the tallest tepee in the village. Was this the tribal chieftain's tepee? Sean winged a brief prayer heavenward.

As if in answer to that prayer, the robes folded back over the entrance, and a shuffling figure emerged, carrying a wooden bowl. The figure was clearly female. As she moved along, Sean could make out what seemed to be a rope around her neck leading back into the tepee. Frantically, he tried to adjust the glass for a clearer picture. Yes, undoubtedly the woman was tethered to the end of some kind of a leash.

But Sarah? Could this be Sarah Moody? The shuffling, defeated gait, the tattered and filthy deerskins, the black hair she had been so proud of shorn as short as a freshly sheared sheep! And her face and hands were as smoke-blackened as a chimney. Could this be Sarah, the Sarah Moody who had been so finicky about cleanliness? Then she straightened, throwing her shoulder back as with a great effort, and turned her face toward the warmth of the rising sun.

It *was* Sarah! By all the saints above, what had they done to her? His heart went out to her, his emotions a mixture of love and pity.

And yet, there was that stance she had just taken. At least some of that fire and indomitable spirit still remained. At that moment an Indian woman came out of the chief's tepee, the end of the leash in her hand, and instantly Sarah slumped again into the posture of defeat. She emptied the contents of the bowl onto the ground and returned to the tepee in response to a tug on the rope, her footsteps dragging.

It took all of Sean's willpower to stop himself from rushing down to her. But that way would be disastrous for both of them. He watched until Sarah had disappeared into the tepee, then wormed back out of sight below the lip of the ridge.

He started back to where he had left his horse. The question now looming before him was, how was he going to get her out of there? He had very little to trade for her, only the two horses. Even if the Pawnee chief would swap Sarah for the two horses, the odds against their walking out of this prairie wilderness with winter coming on, were prohibitive. Besides, Indians had their pride. If they had failed to break her spirit, as was obvious, they would not wish a white man to learn this. In all likelihood, if he walked boldly into their camp and offered to trade his horses for their white woman captive, they would kill both him and Sarah.

No, he had to use his wits. He had to devise some

way to sneak her out of the village and make good their escape. Sean was reasonably certain that the tribe had made camp for the winter and would not be moving again until the spring thaw. All he could do was keep watch on the village, have patience, and figure a way to get her out.

One thing did mystify him. If Sarah was out of favor with the chief, why had she not been killed? That was what usually happened in such instances. It was a puzzle. He was only grateful that she *was* still alive, for whatever reason.

Sarah attributed her still being alive to two factors. First, the Pawnee had not succeeded in breaking her spirit, not completely. The hardships she had endured since her second attempt to escape were enough to break anyone, and many times Sarah had almost given in to the urge to give up, to die; but always a small spark remained, a spark that would catch fire from time to time and cause her to show defiance to her captors. This defiance earned her beatings and abuse. She was tied outside in all kinds of weather, the last time all night during a snowfall. Always after such episodes Sarah had learned to feign compliance to their will, obediently performing the most menial of chores.

The second reason she learned from a whispered conversation with Prairie Blossom. Sarah was a complete pariah now; Chief White Buffalo had forbidden any of the Indians to speak to her, unless it was to give an order to perform some chore. Yet Prairie Blossom still managed to sneak in a few words on occasion. "Chief say he not have his due from Sky Eyes. Sky Eyes must work until worth of furs are repaid.

Chief has forbidden wives to kill Sky Eyes until that happen."

Sarah had tried to beguile Prairie Blossom into helping her escape again, but the Indian girl was too frightened to do that. "Chief would kill Prairie Blossom, I help Sa-rah get away."

Sarah had made one attempt to escape after they put the leash around her neck. Awaiting her chance, she had worked it loose and run. She got less than a mile from the camp before they caught her.

This time, after the rawhide loop had been placed around her neck and knotted, they had poured bowl after bowl of water on her neck, until the rawhide had shrunk, the knot becoming like iron. No matter how she picked at it—and she did until her nails were broken down to the quick—Sarah could not loosen it. There was only one way it would ever be removed now. It would have to be cut off, and they never allowed her a knife. She tried a few times to saw through it with a piece of shattered glass, once a dull, discarded tomahawk blade, and only succeeded in cutting her neck. Sarah finally desisted, fearful she would sever an artery. Any thought of killing herself was long past. She was grimly determined that she would survive and somehow manage to escape.

One indignity she had not suffered. She had been positive that, once White Buffalo no longer demanded that she share his robes at night, she would be handed from brave to brave, to be sexually abused by the whole male population of the tribe. Such had not been the case. That fate, at least, she had been spared. Eventually she learned the reason. She was now considered such a pariah that she was taboo to the braves. And if one were to dare break the taboo, he would be punished severely if caught.

However, she was spared nothing else. Or so it seemed to Sarah. She knew now how fortunate she was to have spent the one winter in the wilderness with Sean. It had toughened her. If she had been forced to undergo the abuse of the past few months prior to the winter with Sean, she would never have managed to survive.

She was always hungry, fed only scraps after the others in the chief's tepee had eaten. She wore a deer-skin dress until it became so tattered she could almost have shed it like a snake's skin, then was given another worn, cast-off garment. When she had been good enough, by their standards, Sarah was allowed to sleep inside the tepee, but she had never been given a buffalo robe, much less a bed; always she had to curl up on the ground to sleep. In the beginning, the hardest thing of all that she had to endure was their refusal to allow her to wash. Every time the tribe had camped near a stream, Sarah had hurried in, clothes and all to wash herself. Each time, with calculated cruelty, they had let her dabble just for a moment in the water, then jerked the leash taut, hauling her out.

Sarah finally figured out a way to thwart this particular cruelty. She gave up all attempts at cleanliness. She did not wash, not even when the opportunity was offered. She became filthy, smoke-blackened, and stinking. So rank did she become, that she noticed that even some Pawnees detoured around her.

It was a victory of sorts, at least in her own mind. Recalling her raging at Sean about keeping himself clean, Sarah had to laugh at herself, laughter that threatened to get out of control.

Sean, if you could only see me now! Of course, he never would; she need have no concern about that. Sarah had long since given up any hope of Sean coming to her rescue. However, she clung stubbornly to the hope that she would be able to do it herself, a hope that grew more forlorn with every passing day.

One chill afternoon, a Pawnee brave rode into camp in a high state of excitement, seeking out Chief White Buffalo. By now Sarah could understand enough Pawnee to catch the drift of what the brave was saying. He had been sent out on a scouting expedition and had discovered a small herd of buffalo a full sun's ride distant.

Their last buffalo hunt had been three weeks past, and they had slaughtered many buffalo, enough to make pemmican to last them through the winter. Yet White Buffalo gravely agreed with the excited braves—a last buffalo feast would be fitting before the snows came, driving the buffalo south. He had already decided that they would winter here; there was water, and the small niche of the valley where the camp was situated snuggled up against high bluffs to the north, giving them protection against the howling north wind. So they would not strike camp for this hunt. White Buffalo decreed that all the braves, except for a few left behind to guard the village, would go. The women would remain at the camp. Ponies would be taken, with travois hooked to them. The buffalo the braves killed would be lashed to the travois and brought back to the village for the women to skin and butcher. They prepared to leave at once, so they would arrive at the hunting grounds with the sun, make their kills, and return before the next night.

It was Sarah's private opinion that the thrill of the hunt was what drew the braves, more than any desire for a feast; and that was the reason the women were being left behind in this instance. Yet it would be pleasant to be rid of the braves for a night and a day, even though Sarah knew that in all probability the women would take advantage of their absence to torment her. Somewhat to her surprise, they left her alone the rest of the afternoon and evening, allowing her to perform the onerous chores in peace. Sarah supposed they were growing bored with tormenting her.

Without White Buffalo's glowering presence, the tepee seemed almost peaceful that night. Sarah was so accustomed to the three wives either tormenting or completely ignoring her that she was scarcely aware of their being there. She waited until they had served themselves from the pot of buffalo stew, meat chunks mixed with spicy herbs, then helped herself to what little was left. Afterward, she curled up to sleep. One end of the leash around her neck was always wrapped around the arm of one of the wives, so if she so much as stirred in the night the woman would be alerted.

Sarah was awakened with such suddenness that she would have screamed but for the hand clamped around her mouth. The fire had died, and the tepee was pitch black and cold. In her fright Sarah started to thrash, then went limp as the merest whisper sounded in her ear, "It's me, colleen. It's Sean. Quiet now, very quiet."

Sarah's mind reeled at the very impossibility of it. She lay inert, scarcely breathing, her heart thudding so loudly it sounded like a drum in her ears. It hardly seemed possible that the Indian women couldn't hear it. Sean took his hand away from her mouth. She felt him fumbling at the rawhide cord around her neck. Sarah wanted to warn him that the other end was held by one of the women, but before she could think of a way, she could feel a knife sawing gently at the rawhide.

Then Sean gripped her shoulder reassuringly. He nudged her, indicating that she should follow him. She turned over on her stomach, and side by side they crawled to the rear of the tepee. There, Sean pushed aside the buffalo hides and she realized that he had slit the hides to make his entry.

Once outside, they crawled on for a few yards, then Sean tapped her on the shoulder, a signal to stand up.

Her wits about her now, Sarah said in a whisper, "Thank God for you, Sean!"

He pulled her to him, and for a brief moment, Sarah felt his lean body against hers, and the warm pressure of his lips on her mouth. At that moment, she could not remember anything that had given her more pleasure and comfort.

"Now, lass," he whispered fiercely. "Let's see about getting out of here with our skins!"

There was a moon tonight, Sarah knew, but it was hidden behind the clouds, and she could see very little. Sean seemed to have the eyes of a cat. His hand gripping her wrist, he led her along. All of a sudden, a dog barked, once, twice, shrilly, and then the others joined in.

Sean gave her a hard shove. "Straight ahead, Sarah. The horses are south, about a hundred yards from the village."

He hung back a little as Sarah began to hurry, stumbling in the dark.

They were just at the edge of the village, when a bloodcurdling yell erupted from behind her, and Sarah heard a grunt from Sean.

She whirled, taking a few steps back. At first all she could see was what looked like a tall, humpbacked figure swaying back and forth. In a moment she realized that an Indian brave had jumped astride Sean's back. Sean was desperately trying to dislodge him, but the brave had his legs wrapped around Sean's chest. One hand was buried in Sean's hair, the other brandishing a tomahawk. Now Sean gave a mighty heave and threw the Indian over his head. The brave landed on the ground, rolled over once, and was on his feet in a weaving crouch, the tomahawk swishing back and forth.

In a rush Sean closed, grappling with the brave. In that moment the moon popped out from behind scudding clouds, and moonlight glinted off Sean's knife blade as it made a downward arch. Sarah knew that they had only seconds before other braves would come boiling out of the tepees.

A yowl of agony came from the Pawnee, and he collapsed slowly to the ground. Sean pulled his knife free and ran toward Sarah. Behind him she saw braves hurrying from tepees, some fitting arrows to their bows. The sudden emergence of the moon had illuminated the scene brightly.

"Sean, look out!" she shouted, just as he seemed to stumble. He staggered a few steps forward, back arched at an odd angle. Then he righted himself and came on, seizing her hand.

"You damned, contrary-headed wench, why didn't you hurry on to the horses, like I told you to?"

Even as he talked, he was tugging her along. They were both at a dead run now. Sarah heard arrows whistling about them.

And then, capriciously, the moon slid behind a cloud, and the night went dark again.

"Thanks be to the saints!" Sean said with rasping breath. His grip on her wrist tightened, slowing her. "The horses should be about— Ah, there they are!"

He gripped Sarah under the armpits, started to hoist her onto a horse, and grunted something under his breath, setting her back down.

"Sean," Sarah said in alarm, "what is it? What's wrong?"

"Nothing, darlin'. What could be wrong? Everything's right as rain, now that I've found you again." He took a fresh grip on her, at the waist this time. "Now, up you go!" He helped her into the saddle.

He swung up onto the other horse. "We'll ride slow now, let the horses pick their way. This area is infested with prairie dog holes. If one of the horses steps into a hole and breaks a leg, we're done for. They're disorganized back there, and it'll be a while before they start after us. And if we were to start off at a gallop, they could put an ear to the ground and track our progress. It'll be daylight in about two hours. Then we can set a harder pace."

With Sean in the lead, they set off in a southerly direction. After a little Sean said, "I've been lurking out here, watching the village for three days, waiting for my chance. Where did the chief and his braves ride away to yesterday afternoon?"

"They went after buffalo."

"Many braves left behind?"

"Not more than seven or eight."

"That's to our advantage, I'm after thinking. Probably send about four after us, the others holding back to guard the camp and pass the word to the chief when he returns. The ones after us will leave a broad trail. When the chief comes back with the main group, *that's* when we'll have to worry. He'll be after us in full cry. But hopefully, we'll have a long lead on them by then. If necessary, I can probably deal with those immediately behind us."

"Sean, how on earth did you find me? I had long since given up on you."

"It's a long story, lass, and better told when we have more time." She heard his soft laughter. "But giving up— No, it never crossed my mind."

"Sean, before we ride farther, could you get this rawhide from around my neck? It pains me."

"Of course, Sarah. Pull your horse near."

Sarah kneed her mount alongside his. Sean felt for the rawhide noose, then carefully inserted the tip of his knife under it. She endured the discomfort without complaint as he sawed at it. It took a long time, but suddenly the pressure was gone. Sarah breathed a sigh of relief.

Sean said, "You're probably going to have a red mark around your neck for weeks."

"That, I can put up with. Now, I feel that I'm finally free!"

"To keep you free, we'd better ride on."

They rode in silence now. Occasionally, Sean would hold out a hand and catch the reins of Sarah's mount, pulling the horses to a halt, then listening intently. Sarah was half-asleep in the saddle and paid little attention.

As dawn began to lighten the sky to the east, Sarah roused a little, glancing over at Sean. He was riding slumped forward in the saddle, swaying with the motion of his horse. When it was fully light, Sarah said, "Sean?"

He sat up with a jerk, glancing over at her with unfocused eyes. Then he recognized her and smiled. The smile seemed forced, but Sarah thought little of it, knowing he must be dreadfully weary.

He looked around. "Daylight, is it?"

He slid from the horse and kneeled on the ground, his ear placed against it. Sarah also got down, stretching. She walked around his horse to where he was kneeling just as he said, "I hear no sound of hoofbeats."

He started to get up, lurched, and had to catch at the stirrup. He slowly pulled himself erect, in the doing turning his back to her.

Sarah gasped, hand going to her mouth. There was the tufted tip of an arrow protruding from his back, embedded in the shoulder muscle.

"Sean, my God! In your back! There's . . ."

He turned a pale, sweating face to her. He tried to smile and failed, face contorting in a grimace of pain. "I know, Sarah. I caught an arrow back in the camp."

She made a motion toward him and stopped. "Why didn't you tell me?"

"We had to get away first. Besides, what good would it have done to tell you?" He managed a smile now. "I saw no need to alarm you, lass."

"But what are we going to do?"

"We're going to ride a little farther until we find a

ravine or some place where we can hole up for a little."

"Sean, can you ride like that?"

"I've managed so far, haven't I?"

"But what about the arrow?"

"When we find a place where we can defend ourselves, if it become necessary, we'll build a small fire, and you're going to cut it out of my back."

Sarah felt the color drain from her face. "Dear God, Sean, I can't do that!"

"You're going to have to do it, Mistress Moody." His face settled into grim lines. "It's either that, or I'm a dead man!"

Chapter Twenty-two

They rode for almost two hours, with Sean, gray-faced and sweating heavily, clinging to the front of the saddle. At last they came to a spot that suited him—a sudden dip in the prairie, like a small indentation in some cosmic table. It was deep enough to conceal both them and the horses, with spring of fresh water to one side. There was a small greening of grass around the edges of the spring, affording the horses some graze. On the north rim of the cup, facing the direction from which the Pawnee would approach, were several large semi-flat boulders.

"Sort of like a fort," Sean said thickly, when he had inspected it. "We couldn't find a better spot."

Sarah had to help him down off the horse, and she found, to her dismay, that his skin was clammy and cold to the touch.

He sank to the ground, leaning on his right shoulder against a rock. He motioned weakly. "Take care of the horses first, Sarah. In my packs you'll find a bottle of rum, a sharp knife, and flint and steel to make a fire. You'll need them all, I'm thinking."

Sarah bundled him up in one of his sleeping robes, then gathered wood for a fire.

"Not too big a fire, lass. We don't want too much smoke. It might be spotted by the red sculpins out there."

"Maybe they haven't followed us," she said hopefully. "We should have seen some sign of them by now."

"They're out there, you can wager on it," he said soberly. "My sneaking you out from under their noses is an insult to their pride. They won't give up all that easy."

When the fire was going, Sarah heated a pan of water. Rooting through one of Sean's packs, she found a bar of soap, a mere sliver. She uttered a cry of delight. Quickly she washed her face and hands. She longed to wash her whole body, but that would have to wait.

Watching her, Sean said gently. "I'm after thinking they gave you a rough time, eh, colleen?"

"It wasn't a pleasant time, but I've survived."

"Aye, you have that. You are a survivor, Mistress Moody. I was depending on that quality about you. Most women would not have endured this long. Or they would have killed themselves."

Sarah looked at him, those violet eyes bleak. "That thought entered my mind many times."

"But you didn't do it. You never would." He stirred and groaned. "You'd better hand me the rum bottle, let me suck on it a little. I'm thinking it's not going to be pleasant when you cut the arrow out."

"Sean, I'm not sure I can do it!"

"You can do it, darlin'. Anyway, you have no choice. Either you cut it out or you'll be burying me out here."

She fetched the rum bottle, and Sean took several deep drags on it, while she followed his instructions and heated the knife blade, turning it several times in the flames. She helped him remove the top of his buckskins and the shirt underneath.

"Here, pour rum around the wound."

Sarah splashed rum around the arrow, washing away the blood, then returned the bottle to Sean. He lay on his right side, taking sips from the bottle.

"I don't think it's buried too deep. Now don't be squeamish, just follow the arrow shaft with the point of the knife until you hit the arrowhead. Then gouge it out. If I scream, yell, or carry on, close your ears to it, lass. It has to be done."

Sarah's stomach knotted with tension. She concentrated all her attention on the task, ignoring the blood that began to flow, and continued to probe for the arrowhead. Sean did not cry out, not so much as a whisper came from him, yet she could feel his back muscles tense as she went deeper and deeper. Suddenly the point of the knife struck something hard. Trying to make the knife blade an extension of her hand, Sarah began to pry, with her free hand tugging gently at the arrow shaft.

She felt the arrowhead move. Sean grunted sharply, then went limp, slumping over, face down. He had fainted, thank God! Sarah hurried now, taking advantage of his unconscious state. In another few minutes she had pulled the arrowhead free. It left an ugly, gaping wound in his back. She wet a cloth in hot water and washed the wound as best she could. After a moment's hesitation, she picked up the rum bottle and poured the liquor directly into the wound. The fumes of the rum and the stench of blood caused her empty stomach to spasm.

Sean's eyelids flickered. She touched his cheek, noticing that his dear face was thin and wan-looking.

His ordeal must have been nearly as great as her own, Sarah thought. She felt a surge of guilt and love.

His eyes opened. He blinked at her for a moment, eyes as vacant as a blind man's. Then he smiled painfully. "Did you get it out?"

"I got it out." She nudged the bloody arrow on the ground with her toe. Even though the day was chilly, Sarah found that she was perspiring heavily. She wiped her brow.

"That's my good lass." His voice was weak. "Now, one more chore to do. Heat the knife blade again, red-hot this time."

She stared at him in bewilderment. "What for?"

"You have to cauterize the wound."

Sarah shook her head. "I don't understand."

"You use the hot knife blade to scorch the flesh around the wound."

Sarah swallowed the bile rising in her throat. Well, she had managed the other; she would manage this.

Seeing her expression, he said relentlessly, "It has to be done. Hopefully, it will stop any infection, if it's not already too late for that." He smiled more easily. "I'll probably swoon again and won't feel much."

Through the red haze of pain, Sean watched Sarah set her chin and turn to the small fire with the knife. His admiration for her was strong. She was a rare woman, this lass.

Sarah came back with the knife blade rosy red. She bent over him, and Sean felt the pain, the most excruciating he had ever experienced. He bit down hard on his lip to keep from screaming, and then he welcomed blessed unconsciousness again.

The stench of Sean's sizzling flesh as she laid the knife blade against the edges of the wound made

Sarah ill. She gritted her teeth and doggedly continued. Soon, she was done, all the exposed flesh seared. At least it had stopped the bleeding.

She dropped the knife and lurched a few feet away, where she fell to her knees and retched again and again. Finally she leaned back against one of the boulders and closed her eyes.

She heard Sean call weakly, "Sarah?"

She was on her feet at once, hurrying to kneel beside him. "Is the pain terrible, Sean?"

"Aye, it hurts, but I can endure. It will be better soon, I'm sure. In my packs you'll find two extra clean shirts. Tear one into strips so you can bind up the wound, wrapping the strips around my chest. The Indians use leaves or cobwebs to bind a wound. But the leaves are all dead and brown, and no cobwebs do I see, so we have to make do with what we have."

Sarah found the shirts and ripped one, making a pad of one piece to fold over the wound. She bound the other strips tightly around his chest. Then she helped him to shrug into the upper part of the buckskins again.

"You should try to sleep a while, Sean."

"Yes, I will. But do not let me sleep too long. We should ride again as soon as I'm feeling a little better. And you keep watch now, colleen. If you spot those redskins, wake me at once. I'm sorry, Sarah." He patted her hand and squeezed. "I know you must be weary to the bone, but if I'm to ride, I must rest."

"I'll be all right," she said quietly. "In the last few months, I've learned to do without much sleep."

She helped make him as comfortable as possible and watched until he was asleep. Some color had come back into his face, and the sight encouraged her. She found a place on the rim of the small valley and sat where she could look north. Once or twice, she caught herself dozing off, coming awake with a start. Each time she swept the horizon with her gaze. Sean had been wise to select this spot. As long as it was daylight, there was no chance the Indians could sneak up on them unobserved.

Two hours later, she saw a small dust cloud to the north. She squinted. In a little while she could make out three, no, four horses coming toward them. They were moving slowly, still a distance away. Even as she watched, Sarah saw one Indian leap down from his pony and scrutinize the ground. Then he remounted, and they came on, a little faster now.

Sarah scrambled down the slope and gently shook Sean. In an urgent voice she said, "Sean? Wake up!"

He opened bleary eyes, blinked at her once, then came fully alert. "They're coming?"

She nodded. "Four of them."

"How far?"

"It's hard for me to judge. I'd hazard two miles."

"All right, lass," he said briskly. "We'll be ready for them."

He got to his feet, wincing with pain. But aside from that, he gave no sign of his injury. "Fetch Katie and my powder horn and bullet pouch. Also, get the two pistols from my packs. Bring them all up to me." He was already moving up the slope in a crouch.

Sarah hurried to do his bidding. When she made it up the rim where Sean crouched between the rocks, he was looking at the approaching Indians. He took the long rifle, quickly primed and loaded it. Then he did the same with the pistols and placed them side by side on the ground by his right hand.

"I'm going to wait, Sarah, until they are within pistol range, since I can get off only one shot with Katie. Then I'll use the pistols, while you reload the rifle. Think you can do that?"

"I've watched you enough times. Yes, I can do it."

"That's my good lass." There was something of his old devil-may-care rakishness in the grin he gave her. "Hopefully, the red sculpins will come riding up pretty much unsuspecting." He settled down, grimacing as he did so. "I'm after thinking it's fortunate we are that I took the blasted arrow in the left shoulder."

Sarah knew he had to be in much pain, yet he was smiling as he made a small hollow for himself.

Sean was hurting; every tiny movement sent waves of pain through him. He was in the best position he could manage, the barrel of the rifle resting on the ground, the butt against his right shoulder. He had tried to bring his left hand up to brace the rifle barrel as he normally would, but the pain was too much to bear. He didn't know how accurate he would be in this position, yet he thought it best not to pass his doubts on to Sarah. He concentrated all of his attention on the approaching Indians. They had slowed somewhat now, about a hundred yards away, and were fanning out, as if sniffing something wrong, but still they came on. Sean lined his rifle up with the one on the far right, who was hanging back slightly.

Sarah watched the Pawnees come closer and closer with growing apprehension. They loomed large and larger in her vision, until they seemed almost close enough to touch. Why didn't Sean fire?

The Indians came on, and it was all Sarah could do not to give way to panic and run. Then, the rifle cracked, and she saw an Indian on the far right catapult backward off his horse. Quick as light, Sean thrust the rifle at her and snatched up the pistols. Sarah went about reloading the rifle. Her fingers seemed to move with a mind of their own, and she was amazed at how quickly she had it ready to fire again. Dimly, she had been aware of both pistols being discharged, one right after the other.

She thrust the rifle at Sean. "Here!"

"I don't need it now. Fortune favored me." He was smiling. "Look!"

Sarah glanced through the crack between the rocks. Three of the ponies, empty of riders, were milling about. The fourth Pawnee had wheeled his pony and was riding hard back the way he had come. Then she saw three still figures on the ground. With a gasp she said. "You killed all three?"

"One thing I'm good at, colleen." He chuckled. "I've been handling weapons of one kind or another since age fifteen or thereabouts."

"The other one— Will he come back?"

"Not alone. He'll wait for the main tribe to catch up. But he'll be there, never fear, always on our arses, leaving a broad trail for the others to follow."

"But why won't he, why won't *they*, give up?"

"They're contrary stubborn, like a certain wench I know. No, Sarah, I doubt they'll give up so easy. My snatching you from under their noses, now three of their braves dead— It'll be too much of a blow to the chief's pride. If it gets bruited about, especially that he just gave up, he'll be the laughingstock of every tribe on the prairie. And now we'd better be on our way."

"Now?" she said in dismay. "Sean, you're in no condition to ride!"

"No condition or not, I'm riding. This place is fine for holding off three or four Pawnee, but not a whole damned tribe. We have to put as much distance behind us as possible and hope that your Chief White Buffalo is delayed."

He got to his feet with grunting effort. His face was gray, and he was sweating heavily. She reached out to touch his forehead. "Sean, you're afire with fever!"

He motioned brusquely. "No more talk, Mistress Moody. Let's ride!"

Sarah had to help him saddle the horses, and then she had to assist him into the saddle. He tried to sit upright and groaned aloud with pain. He said, "There's a rawhide rope in one of my packs. Get it, Sarah, and tie me into the saddle."

A look at his determined face, and Sarah knew that it was useless to argue. She found the rawhide and lashed him to the saddle.

Just before they rode out, Sean glanced to the north. Clouds were moving in, low and coming fast, stretching from east to west. "I smell snow in those clouds. If we're fortunate, a storm will catch us before nightfall and cover our tracks."

As they rode out of the hollow, Sarah looked back. In the far distance she saw a horse and rider. As they began to move, so did he.

Sean said, "The sculpin's there, is he?"

"Yes, you're right. He's following us."

"We-ell, we're safe from him. He won't dare tackle us on his own. He'll wait for reinforcements."

The lone Pawnee stayed behind them, far back,

25

never approaching close, but always keeping them in sight.

Two hours later the afternoon had grown dark, the clouds lowering, with thick, gray-black bellies, and Sean's prediction came true. The first snowflakes began to fall, and the temperature dropped steadily. Sarah draped one of Sean's buffalo robes around his shoulders, and the other around her own.

She rode always close to him now, as he drifted in and out of delirium. She listened as he mumbled, "Sarah lass, I'm coming. I'll find you. I'll never give up." Then he threw back his head and shouted to the heavens, "Sarah? By the saints, where are you?"

Tears flooded her eyes. She touched his arm, and said, "I'm here, Sean. Right here."

He looked around, eyes clearing. "Sarah? Ah, Sarah love. I was having a bad dream. In the dream I had wandered the prairie until I had a long gray beard, and never could I find you." He became more alert. "The Pawnee? He still back there?"

She looked back. The snow was falling heavily now, already several inches covering the ground, and she could see only a few yards behind them.

"I don't know, Sean," she said helplessly. "I can't see!"

"That's fine, lass." He groped for her hand. "If we cannot see him, then he can't see us. And if he stays too far back, the snow will cover our tracks. Keep a sharp eye out. If you see him, warn me."

"But the storm is getting worse, Sean! We'll get lost! And how can we make camp tonight?"

"There's a cave to the south. I stumbled across it on my way up here and stayed there during a rainstorm. I even left a supply of firewood there. It's dry and snug as our old dugout, darlin'." His grin was a rictus of pain. "We can wait out the storm there. There's even room for the animals. With the snow covering our tracks, the Pawnee will never find us. Snow here in November usually melts in a day or so, then we can continue on."

"How'll we ever find this cave in this weather?"

"With this." From his pocket Sean took a small compass. He fiddled with it for a few minutes, peering closely at it in the gathering darkness. "Here, here's the bearing, Sarah." He showed it to her. "You tote it with you and keep us on that course if we stray. With this fever raging in me, I'm after thinking I won't always be rational. Just before we reach the cave, there's a stream we have to cross and a giant cottonwood on the east bank. The cave's in a bluff not thirty yards distant from the tree. When we reach that point, try to rouse me."

They rode on, Sean drifting in and out of unconsciousness. Sarah held the reins of his horse in one hand, and she let the horses set their own pace. It was full dark now, so dark that even the falling snow looked black. She had to hold the compass inches before her eyes to read it and often had to correct their course. They rode for what seemed hours to Sarah, and she was drooping with weariness. Fortunately, the cold did not intensify, but Sarah knew that it would become colder before long, and they could easily freeze, even on the horses.

Abruptly, she became aware that the horses had stopped. She drummed her heels against her mount's sides, but he stubbornly refused to budge. Leaning forward, she realized that she couldn't see the horse's head. She heard a strange, yet familiar sound. She puzzled over it for a moment before she realized what it meant. The horses were drinking water!

"Sean," she cried, "we're here, I think! This must be the stream you mentioned!" When he made no response, she reached out to touch him. His head lolled loosely on his shoulders, and he mumbled incoherently.

Now what was she going to do? Sarah looked both ways, but could see only a few feet in the driving snow. Where was the big cottonwood he had mentioned?

Sarah was afraid to wander far from the horses. Blundering about in the snowy dark, she could be lost within yards. Finally she got down, carefully holding onto the reins. She let the horses drink their fill, before she led them across the shallow brook, ignoring the icy water soaking her feet. The reins to both animals held tightly in her grip, she followed the stream to her right. Within a few feet she ran almost head-on into a tree trunk. Squinting, she saw that it was indeed a huge cottonwood.

Sean had told her that the cave was situated in a bluff not thirty yards away. Sarah peered into the snow, fearful of leaving the stream and the cottonwood, since they were the only points of reference she had. It seemed to her that almost straight ahead, and a little to her right, was an area of darkness greater than that surrounding her.

Taking a deep breath, Sarah struck off in that direction. The horses went along readily enough; perhaps they sensed shelter not far away. The ground sloped up steeply the way she was going, and the snow was slippery underfoot. She slipped and fell on her face once, but never let loose of the reins. Then she ran into a clump of thick bushes. She felt along until she found a way around it, and suddenly the black maw of the cave entrance loomed before her.

The horses showed no reluctance to enter the cave. It was high enough for them to enter without trouble. It was dark as pitch inside, but since the entrance faced south, they were cut off from the wind and driving snow, and it at least *seemed* warmer.

Sarah let the reins drop to the ground and advanced cautiously, feeling ahead with one foot. In a moment she hit something. Kneeling, Sarah found it to be a pile of wood. She scraped together a small stack of sticks, then got Sean's flint and steel out of the packs. Her fingers were numb from the cold, and it took her a long time to strike a spark. Once, she dropped the flint and heard it roll away from her. In a panic, fearing she had lost it in the dark, Sarah felt around the ground inch by inch until she finally found it.

When she had a small blaze going, she stacked dry wood in a pyramid and watched until it caught. Then she went to tend Sean first. He roused a little as she untied him and was able to get off mostly by his own efforts. He stood swaying while Sarah gathered up both buffalo robes. She led him to the fire; he was shivering uncontrollably. The ground was sandy against one wall near the fire. Sarah hollowed it out a little with her foot, then spread one robe on the ground and eased Sean down onto it. She threw the second robe over him.

Sarah was very cold herself, her wet feet almost frozen. She endured the discomfort until she had removed the packs and the saddles from the horses, leading the animals to the very back of the cave. The cave was quite roomy, much more spacious than their dugout of last winter. Sarah snatched up a cooking pot and hurried outside. She made several trips, toting in enough snow to make a nice pile near the entrance. She filled the pot with snow and placed it on a pile of coals. When it had melted, she started a pot of tea, removing her moccasins while it brewed. She rubbed her feet briskly to restore circulation, then held them close to the fire. The cave heated surprisingly fast; it was already warm. Occasionally an icy gust of wind would come in through the entrance, but it was not enough to be a bother.

Sean groaned, thrashing about in his fevered slumber. Sarah went to him. With much effort she managed to remove his buckskins and shirt, then the makeshift bandage. The wound was bleeding again, and a foul odor came from it. She kneeled by him in despair. What was she to do? He badly needed medical attention, but they were hundreds of miles from the nearest doctor. With the storm raging outside, she couldn't look for herbs; she didn't know what herbs to look for anyway. She recalled Sean's mention of cobwebs. She searched along the walls of the cave and was able to gather a handful of cobwebs. She made a wad of them and placed it over the wound, then replaced the old bandage with a clean one, binding it up again.

Just as she finished, Sean said faintly, "Sarah?"

"Yes, love?"

He was looking at her, his eyes sane again. "Did we make the cave?"

"Yes, Sean, I found it. There's a fire going, see?" She raised his head enough so he could look. "And there's tea brewing. It should be warming for you."

She fetched a cup of the steaming tea and held his

head while he drank. He seemed to rally slightly, his voice stronger now. "The horses?"

"They're in here with us." She nodded toward the back of the cave.

"See what you've come to, lass? Remember the dugout, and my talk of taking the mules inside with us? You turned up that pretty nose and set yourself stubbornly against it."

She smiled slightly and smoothed the hair back from his hot forehead. "The circumstances are somewhat different."

"Aye, they are indeed. Sarah, one thing you'll have to do, should we be confined here for any length of time. You'll have to forage under the snow for grass and bring it in to feed the animals. Else they will starve. Some grass is still there, especially near the creek. That's how the buffalo survive, you know. Deep in winter snow, they use those great heads to shake the snow loose, forming a hole down to the grass. If things get bad enough, you may have to force them to eat tree bark. . . ."

Sarah sensed that he was rambling. His eyes had that glassy stare again. Suddenly he coughed wrackingly and cried out in pain.

She reached out to touch him. "Sean, are you all right?"

His eyes cleared. "I'll make out fine. I don't suppose any of the rum's left?"

"No, we used it all. But I made a poultice of cobwebs and put it on your back."

He smiled more easily. "That's my fine darlin'."

"There's some meat in your packs. It's a little tough and strong, but if I boiled it, it should make tasty, hot broth."

"I'm not hungry, but I suppose my belly needs something." He put his head back, suddenly exhausted. But even with his eyes closed, Sean was still aware, and he lay listening to Sarah's movements as she rummaged in the packs and came back to the fire. At last she came to him with a cup of hot broth, raising his head so he could drink. It tasted terrible, yet it filled his empty stomach, so he made no comment about the taste. He fell back again when he was finished. He said, "Put something under my head so I can watch you. I'm too damned weak to hold it up myself."

Sarah dragged a saddle over, cushioned it with a part of the buffalo robe he was lying on, then tucked the second one around him.

"Is that comfortable? Are you warm enough?" she asked anxiously.

"Comfortable as I can be, under the existing conditions," he replied with a wry grin.

He closed his eyes to slits, pretending sleep, but watching her all the while. It was a pleasure to observe her after all this time.

Chewing on a piece of tough meat from the pot, Sarah went about stacking more wood on the fire. Then she toted skillet after skillet from the fast-melting pile by the cave entrance and dumped it into another pot on the fire, until the pot was finally full. She looked over at him and said softly, "Sean?"

Sean made no response, sensing what was about to happen. His surmise was correct. Testing the water with her finger until it was hot enough to suit her, Sarah quickly divested herself of the filthy garments until she was naked. Sean felt his pulse quicken at the sight of her loveliness. Although she was gaunt now, her body was still breathtakingly beautiful. Using his sliver of soap and a scrap of his shirt for a washcloth, she washed herself all over, a small area at a time.

When she was finally done, she was clean and rosy from the heat of the fire, only her face and hands brown from long exposure to the sun. The rest of her body was pink and white, and Sean felt a strong arousal as he watched her slowly turn before the fire, letting the flames dry her.

Then, with another glance at him, she started toward the packs. Sean knew that she was about to put on his spare buckskins. He said in a thick voice, "No, darlin'. First, come here."

Startled, Sarah turned quickly. "I thought you were asleep!" A blush stained her cheeks. "And all the while you were watching me!"

"That I was, colleen, and a fetching sight it was," he drawled. "Come here." He threw the top robe off.

Sarah approached hesitantly. "Sean, do you think you should, in your condition?"

"My condition is grand, as you'll discover. It's been a long time, Sarah."

"I know, Sean," she said in a soft voice. She kneeled beside him, tenderly stroking his face. Then she stretched out beside him. "Sean, I don't feel— clean. Not after all that has happened. You can't know. . . ."

"I do know, and we'll not talk about it, ever," he said roughly. "To me, you are as sweet and pure as the day I first clapped eyes on you."

He turned on his right side, facing her, carefully concealing the sharp pain he felt. He kissed her. Sarah sighed softly and opened her mouth to him. His free hand caressed her short hair. "Your poor hair. Before, it was so black, so long, so lovely. That is the worst crime of all."

His hand moved down her flank, stroking. In a moment his passion grew urgent. He fumbled with his breeches.

"No, let me, Sean."

With infinite care she proceeded to undress him. When his manhood was exposed, she drew a deep breath. "Your condition is grand. Oh, yes!"

When he was undressed, he made an effort to rise, but Sarah gently pushed him back. "No, Sean. You lie still."

Sean made a token protest, but the pain every time he moved was considerable. He fell back. In a moment Sarah rose and tenderly and slowly fitted herself to him.

"Ahh, darlin', it has indeed been a long time," he said huskily.

Then all thought was washed away as a great tide of passion swept over him.

At first Sarah had only intended to serve his need, but despite herself, her own passion flowered. Only at the last moment did Sean move, his hips arching to meet hers, as they cleaved together in mutual ecstasy.

When she finally disengaged herself and lay again beside him, Sean stroked her hair. "Darlin', it's loving you I am. I think I have loved you from the first moment on that river bank out of New Orleans. If I had not found you, I think I might have died mourning you."

"Oh, love!" She raised her head to kiss him gently. She recalled all those times when she had been sure that Sean Flanagan could never love any woman. She had been wrong, and now her heart swelled with a

386

great tenderness for him. And then she saw the sheen of sweat on his face and realized that he was in delirium again and had not heard her.

Sarah lay beside him for a long time, her thoughts gray and bleak. She had a strong premonition of his death. He was very ill, there was no doubt of that, and there was little she could do to help him. This was the hardest of all to bear. After all that Sean had done for her, there was no way she could repay him in kind.

Sarah lay by his side until the fire died down, and she grew cold. Then she pulled the robe up over him and went to pile more wood on the fire.

Chapter Twenty-three

The snowstorm lasted for two nights and a full day. Sean grew steadily worse, drifting in and out of delirium, his lucid moments becoming fewer and fewer. His wound, each time Sarah substituted clean rags for the old, looked very bad, the stench offensive to her nostrils.

She felt so useless! There was nothing, nothing she could do for him. She kept herself busy, resting in snatches. As the stack of dry wood began to dwindle, she ventured out into the storm, searching for dead wood, carrying armload after armload back to the cave. She even broke branches off the trees along the stream. Since they were partially frozen, they snapped easily, with a sound like a pistol shot, and although green and wet, they burned when dumped onto the roaring fire. Also, heeding Sean's advice, Sarah took a skillet down to the banks of the stream and scooped away snow until she could get down to the earth and pluck handfuls of the grass, which she took back to feed the horses. Fortunately, it wasn't snowing hard enough to cover her tracks before she returned to the cave each time, so there was little danger of her getting lost in the storm.

On the second night in the cave, while Sarah was changing the rags on the wound, Sean spoke in a thick voice. Accustomed as she was to his ravings, Sarah paid little heed.

Then, in a clearer voice, he said, "It's bad, lass?"

With a start she looked into his eyes. They were clear and rational. Slowly, she nodded. "It's bad, Sean." In an agony of despair, she cried out, "I feel so bloody helpless!"

"Don't, darlin'." He groped for her hand and squeezed weakly. "Don't scourge yourself. There's naught you can do. Sometimes, an Indian will smear some poisonous plant on his arrows. Likely that is what happened in this instance."

"Maybe if I rode for help?"

He smiled. "Lass, lass," he chided. "There's no help for hundreds of miles. I'd be dead long before you could make it."

Sarah knew that he was right. If he didn't die from the infection, he would starve to death.

"But perhaps it would be best if you rode on anyway, soon as the snow stops falling. The more distance between you and the Pawnee, the better, although I'm after thinking they've given us up for dead now, in this storm."

"No!" she cried. "I'll never leave you!"

He smiled again, squeezed her hand, and then his hand fell limp, and the glaze of fever filmed his eyes.

On the morning of the second day, Sarah looked out and saw that the snow had stopped. The sun glittered off the snow, until it hurt her eyes.

She whirled around. "Sean, the snow has stopped!" She ran to him.

He mumbled, opening his eyes to stare up at her without comprehension. He said in a surprisingly strong voice, "I will gladly kill the blackest of villains,

Giles Brock, for what he did to Sarah! Some sweet day I will find him and kill him!" He slumped back, mumbling again.

She wet a cloth and gently washed his face. During the past two days a stubble of beard had sprouted on his face. She could not recall ever seeing Sean when he wasn't clean-shaven; not even during those long, cold days when they had been isolated in the dugout.

Weighed down with melancholy, Sarah got to her feet. Then determination filled her. Their meager supply of food was gone. They needed fresh meat, Sean especially. She recalled that rabbits had a way of coming out of their burrows following a fresh fall of snow, foraging for food.

She took Sean's pistols, made them ready to fire, and left the cave. Already the snow was mushy underfoot, and water dripped from the branches of the trees as the ice melted. The stream at the foot of the slope was running free within its snow-covered banks. Sarah reminded herself to bring the horses down to drink later in the day. She proceeded slowly, her gaze darting about, her vision adjusted somewhat to the glare of the snow.

About fifty yards from the cave entrance she saw a dart of movement ahead. A rabbit, his white coat making him almost invisible against the snow, was hopping toward the stream. Sarah slipped behind the trunk of an aspen, then peered around it, holding her breath. Unsuspecting, the rabbit was coming in her direction. Now it stopped, standing on its hind feet to nibble on a bush.

Sarah drew a deep breath, held it, and took careful aim with the pistol. She fired, the weapon jumping in her hand. The rabbit was knocked to the snow, rolling over twice. Sarah ran to it. It lay without moving, a hole near the heart, just where she had aimed. Any revulsion she might have felt was overcome by the thought of what juicy eating the plump rabbit would provide.

Picking it up by the hind legs, she hastened back to the cave. She rushed inside, skidding to a stop as her gaze went at once to Sean's robe. He wasn't there!

She caught a movement out of the corner of her eyes and looked around to see him kneeling a few feet away, clumsily trying to prime the long rifle.

Sarah ran to him. In a scolding voice, she said, "Sean! What on earth are you doing?"

Sean looked up at her dazedly. "I heard a shot."

"It was me!" She held up the rabbit. "I just killed our dinner!"

He slumped back to the ground, letting the rifle fall. His eyes clear, he smiled widely. "Ah, lass! 'Tis proud I am of you!"

She put the rabbit down and helped him back to his robe. He sank down with a sigh. "I'm weak as a babe."

"When I get some rabbit broth in you, your strength will come back." She smiled, trying to believe her own lie.

"You're right, colleen, I'm sure it will."

Sarah very quickly skinned and gutted the rabbit with Sean's knife. Then she cut off the hind legs and rinsed all the pieces in hot water. She piled wood on the fire until it was burning brightly and hurried down to the stream for a fresh pan of water, breaking off five green sticks from the cottonwood to take back with her.

In the cave she dropped the body of the rabbit into

a pan of water, adding a pinch of salt from Sean's meager supply, and set it on the fire to boil. Next, she made two X's with four of the green sticks, wedging the bases into the ground, spitting the hind legs of the rabbit in the fifth stick, as Sean had taught her, and hanging it over the flames. Last of all, she started a pot of tea. Most of Sean's supplies were running low, she thought with a smile, but there was still a bloody lot of tea left!

All the while Sean was in a stupor, sometimes muttering unintelligibly, at other times snoring strenuously.

Sarah kept a close watch on the meat, turning the spitted pieces frequently, so they would brown evenly, and using Sean's knife to break apart the carcass in the broth pot, carefully extracting the bones. Soon, the cave was redolent with cooking odors, so mouthwatering that Sarah's stomach rumbled outrageously.

When the rabbit in the stewing pot was well done, the meat so tenderly cooked it disintegrated into small pieces, she poured some of it into a cup and went to Sean.

She had some difficulty rousing him. At first he tried to push the cup away. Craftily, Sarah waved it under his nose.

Sean raised his head, sniffing. "We-ell, that does smell good," he said doubtfully.

"It *is* good, and it'll be good for you. Now drink it, Sean Flanagan!"

She helped prop him up a little against the saddle. He had to sit lopsidedly, favoring the left shoulder. But he did drink greedily of the broth, and Sarah picked the meat pieces out and fed them to him with her fingers. He even accepted a second cup.

The broth and meat brought some color to his cheeks and a lift to his spirits, and Sean thought, Could it be I'm going to make it, after all? Then he knew he was lying to himself.

His gaze was drawn to the rabbit on the spit, browned evenly now. He insisted, "Now you eat. The hunter must be hungry, too."

Sarah eagerly plucked the rabbit pieces from the spit and ate them, almost burning her mouth in her haste. Never had anything tasted so marvelous!

Sean watched her with love. He felt the fever sweep over him again. He was alternately hot and cold, shivering. He tried to hide it from her. He fought back the delirium. He said, "That stream down there eventually wanders into the Missouri, Sarah. All you have to do is follow it, then follow the Missouri south and east when it turns. It will in time take you to St. Louis."

Sarah, just finished with the rabbit and licking the grease from her fingers, glanced at him sharply. "What *are* you talking about, Sean?"

Ignoring her, he continued, "When you get to St. Louis, go at once to Jacques Fortier. I have a great deal of money on deposit with Jacques. It's all yours, Sarah. Just before I left, I told him that it was to belong to you, if you came back and I didn't."

Frightened, she ran to kneel beside him. "Sean, don't talk such nonsense! We'll make it out together!"

"No, lass." His smile was melancholy as he took her hand. "We have never lied to each other. I will never leave this cave. I shall die here. If you weren't such a stubborn wench, you'd not wait around for that to happen, but would leave now, get as far as possible before another storm hits."

"Sean, please. I can't bear to hear you talk this way." Head bowed, she was weeping silently. "You don't know how much you mean to me."

"I know, darlin', I know more than you think," he said gently. "The other night, I said I loved you, didn't I? I vaguely recall spouting something like that."

Dumbly, she nodded.

"I thought as much. And I do, I always have. I love you more than life itself." He sighed. "But I know that Jeb Hawkins has captured your heart."

Her head came up. "He didn't even bother to come after me!"

Sean looked puzzled. "But how could he have? He didn't know you were even in St. Louis."

Having been so incautious as to tell him that much, Sarah told him of meeting Jeb at the landing in St. Louis and of spending some time with him. At first she intended to be completely honest and tell of the time she spent in Jeb's cabin and her promise to return to him, but the look of pain in Sean's eyes stopped her. "So, you see," Sarah concluded, "he did know I was in St. Louis, yet he didn't come looking for me."

"But how could he know where to look, Sarah?"

"You did, and you found me!"

He sighed. "I was very fortunate. It was only by chance that I stumbled across the fact of the death of the coach driver, and that Brock and Pommet brought you to the stables. A stable hand overheard the sculpins talking about selling you to an Indian tribe. As for the rest . . ." He shrugged, something of the old, lazy, self-mocking grin on his face. "It was a combination of the luck of the Irish and sheer, dogged persistence."

"And I will always be grateful to you, love." Tears still standing in her eyes, she kissed him.

"And I, Mistress Moody, am simply grateful for having met you, for having known you." He sank back with a weary sigh, not letting go of her hand.

"You sleep now. Rest, Sean," she said briskly. "No more talk of dying. You have survived worse wounds. You've told me of being wounded many times before in battle."

Yes, but never under such conditions as this, Sean thought to himself. Still with his hand in hers, he drifted into a fevered sleep.

Sarah dried her tears and went about tidying up. She took the horses down to the stream and let them drink their fill, then staked them out to graze in an area near the branch where some grass remained. The snow was melting fast now.

Still apprehensive about the Pawnee, Sarah struggled up to the top of the bluff above the cave and looked north. The terrain was a little broken, but she could see for miles in the clear air. Nothing moved. She finally concluded that they had nothing to fear now. The chief of the Pawnee had either given up the chase or decided that they had perished in the storm.

Returning to the cave, she checked on Sean. He was deep in delirium. Nothing he said made sense, and he didn't even rouse when she changed the bandage. The wound was very bad, and she finally faced the truth. Sean Flanagan was dying.

Deep in depression, she wandered outside and

stood looking south both in longing and trepidation. Could she make all those miles on her own? What perils confronted her in all that desolation? Loneliness, she suspected, could be her worst enemy.

At sundown, she let the horses drink again and led them back into the cave. She heated up a cup of the remaining broth, but she couldn't get Sean to drink it. She drank some herself, fed wood to the fire, and sat, her thoughts sluggish, staring across the flames at Sean.

Once he struggled to sit up, crying out, "Sarah?"

She hastened to him, kneeling to take his hand. "I'm here, love, right here."

He stared at her face hungrily, reaching out a hand with a great effort to touch her shorn hair. "It'll grow out again, lass. In time your hair will be as long and beautiful as ever."

"Yes, Sean, I know," she whispered, holding back tears.

His hand fell of its own weight, and his eyes closed.

Sarah made a bed for herself by the fire, heaped more wood on it, and snuggled down, facing the warmth of the flames. Since she had slept little the night before, she fell into a deep sleep.

It was after daylight when she awoke. The fire had died, and the cave was cold, but Sarah felt more rested than she had in a long time. She sat up, stretching luxuriously. Remembering, she glanced over at Sean. He was still under the robe. Before checking on him, she stoked up the fire again, then went around to drop to her knees beside him.

"Sean? It's morning."

He didn't stir, and his face looked strange and pale. She knew before she reached out to touch his cheek and found it cold as ice. Sean was dead. He had died sometime during the night, while she slept. She pulled the robe up over his face and ran from the cave. Down by the stream, she leaned against the cottonwood, grinding her face into the rough bark and wept until there were no more tears left in her. Finally she straightened up resolutely and marched back to the cave.

She buried Sean on the slope halfway between the cave entrance and the stream. The ground was soft from the melted snow, and she was able to scoop out a shallow grave with the skillet. It took her a long time, but she didn't slacken her efforts until she judged it was deep enough to keep out marauding animals.

Then she returned to the cave to perform the most awful chore of her life. Using the bottom buffalo robe, she pulled Sean's body out of the cave and down to the grave. She started to roll him into the robe, then hesitated.

Words came into her mind, so vividly that for a moment she imagined Sean speaking to her in that wry voice. "Don't be a nitwit, colleen. I'm after thinking you will have more need of the robe than I will."

It was true, she would have need of it. She also thought of burying the long rifle, his Katie, with him. But that would also be a foolish, sentimental gesture. She would need the rifle as well.

Sarah had to turn her face aside as she pushed dirt into the shallow grave, only turning back when she could no longer see his face. Finished, she stood for a moment, groping for something to say. Never a very religious person, she could think of no fitting prayer.

Finally she whispered, "Good-bye, Sean. Good-bye, love."

She went back to the cave for the last time. It was now into the afternoon, and she knew that the wise thing to do would be to stay the night in the cave and get an early start in the morning, but she simply could not face a night alone, not after all the nights spent there with Sean.

She saddled one horse and lashed the packs onto the other one, leaving the second saddle in the cave. It would only be an unnecessary load. When she had to change horses, she would also change saddles. Sean's spare buckskins that she had been wearing were much too large, but they would serve the purpose. Now, from a distance, she would look like a man, and Sarah had no intention of letting anyone get close enough to tell otherwise. She had seen enough to know what could happen to a lone woman in this country, and she had no intention of being easy prey again.

She rode out, the long rifle propped across the saddle in front of her and the pistols handy in the saddlebags. The second horse she led. She rode away resolutely, without once looking back.

The weather remained clear and reasonably warm. The snow had all melted now, except for a few patches lingering on in shady spots. Occasionally, Sarah would glance back, looking for the Pawnees or for low clouds on the horizon heralding an approaching storm.

She faithfully followed the meandering stream. Just before sundown, she spotted a doe grazing ahead. She slid off the horse and moved forward quietly until she came to a small tree. Two branches formed a crook just at shoulder height. The grazing doe, about thirty yards distant, had failed to notice her. Sarah rested the rifle in the crook of the branches, as she had seen Sean do, and fired. She forgot about the recoil, and the heavy rifle knocked her sprawling. Scrambling to her feet, she ran forward. She couldn't see the doe and thought despairingly that she had missed.

Then Sarah saw the animal, lying still in the grass. She gave a whoop, smiling for the first time since she began her journey. She picked up the rifle from where it had fallen and gave it a fond pat. "Good for you, Katie."

She started, glancing around to see if she'd been overheard, talking aloud to a rifle.

Before going back to skin and butcher the deer, she tied off the horses, then primed and reloaded the rifle, which she took along with her. She attacked the deer with no hesitation whatsoever, using the knife easily.

It's strange, she thought sardonically, how the drive to survive overcomes most, if not all, compunctions.

Thanks to Sean's teachings last winter and the summer's experience with buffalo kills, Sarah did a creditable job of butchering the doe. It was dark by the time she had finished. She found a small, sheltered nook in the river bank for a camp and enough dry driftwood to make a nice fire. She ate well and afterward sat by the fire physically, at least, content.

Then she did something that she was to do often during the coming dreary weeks on the prairie, something that she later credited with saving her sanity. She talked aloud to Sean, as if he sat cross-legged across the fire from her.

"I'll wager you never thought I could kill, gut,

400

skin, and butcher a doe, did you, Sean Flanagan? But I did, you see, and I'll make it out. I won't fail your faith in me, love, I swear!"

Rolled up in the buffalo robes, Sarah went to sleep with tears drying on her cheeks, and Katie by her side.

The weather remained stable for longer than Sarah had any right to expect. The nights were very cold, but the days were warm when the sun climbed high. Once, she rode through a thunderstorm, and one night it rained hard. But no snow fell, and the ground and the stream had yet to freeze, although most mornings Sarah found some ice edging the water. With the continued mild weather, she had no trouble with food. The prairie teemed with small game, and her marksmanship steadily improved. She knew full well that the shot with which she had killed the deer had been a matter of blind luck, since immediately afterward she missed with the rifle more often than not. But by the end of the second week of travel, she had become an acceptable marksman.

Twice, she saw people at a distance. The first time it was a half-dozen Indians. Before they approached too close, she slid down off the horse and fired the rifle in their direction, quickly reloading. They didn't approach closer, but followed along parallel to her for about an hour, then turned and galloped away. The second time, it was two men in buckskins. At the sight of her, one man waved an arm and hailed her. They were still some distance away. Although she knew they were white, probably fur trappers, Sarah wanted nothing to do with them and certainly did not want them to learn she was female. Again, she got down and fired a shot in their direction. They drew their horses up, milling about for a moment in consternation. Then one shook a fist at her, and they wheeled their mounts and rode off.

Late in the afternoon, two weeks after Sean's death, Sarah saw low clouds scurrying in from the north. Realizing that she was confronted with a blizzard, she sought shelter. All she could find was a small rise in the gully on the north side of the stream and a large cottonwood growing at a slant. Tethering the horses to the tree, she gathered what firewood she could find. By the time she had a fire going, the day had grown very dark, although it was only the middle of the afternoon, and the wind was very cold, increasing in velocity.

She was fortunate to have killed game that morning, so there was food on hand. When the full force of the blizzard struck, day seemingly turned into night. The snowfall formed a thick, gray curtain, and the wind, cutting as a knife blade, seemed to come at her from every direction at once.

Sarah huddled in her robes before the fire. Despite the cold, she finally went to sleep in a sitting position. She awoke shivering with cold. The fire had gone out, covered over by snow. Her efforts to get it going again were futile. Finally she had to give up, her fingers so numb with cold she could no longer hold the flint and steel. She was fearful she might lose them in the snow, and they were as precious as life itself.

In the end she stood between the horses, throwing the robes across their backs and leaning on one with her arms across the animal's back. She slept that way, on her feet, in snatches, for what seemed an eternity. Once, in her sleep, she slumped to the ground. She struggled partly awake. It seemed so warm down there, and she wanted desperately to sink back into sleep, but a small part of her mind snarled a warning. She knew she was close to the point of freezing.

Stepping away from the horses, Sarah ran in place, pumping her arms and legs for a long time, until she was weary enough to drop. Snuggling again between the horses, she tied one of the reins so tightly around one wrist that every time she started to slump to the ground, the pain snapped her awake.

There was no way to tell time; there was no difference between night and day, and Sarah didn't even dare venture to the packs for a bite to eat. Later, she estimated that the blizzard had lasted for two days. When the snow finally stopped falling, it was daylight, yet Sarah had no idea of the time, since the sky was still obscured by clouds. It was iron cold, and the snow was deep, drifts higher than her head at every place there had been an obstruction against the driving wind. Sarah realized that this snow would not melt so quickly; it probably would not melt until spring.

Doggedly, she went about clearing snow off the ground so she could start a fire. The wood was wet, and she had to resort to using some of the pitifully few rags she had, as a starter. Finally she got a blaze going and piled on the wet wood. It sizzled and popped, but it gradually caught fire as it dried out. The leaping flames melted the snow for several feet around.

Sarah started a pot of tea. To get water for it, she broke a hole in the thick layer of ice on the creek. While the tea brewed, she led the horses down to the hole in the ice and let them drink. She recalled Sean telling her that horses would eat the bark of certain trees, if they did not have access to grass. She had no idea which trees, so she went about stripping handfuls of bark from different trees along the creek and made a pile of the bark by the fire. The horses nuzzled at it, looked at her with eyes that seemed accusing, but they did find some pieces they would eat.

Sarah drank two cups of scalding tea, the first hot liquid she had had in her stomach since the storm hit. The meat in the packs was frozen solid. She heated a pan of water and dropped in the frozen chunks, waiting impatiently for the lengthy time it took to cook, then she drank the broth and ate the meat pieces greedily. Sarah hadn't realized she was so weak from hunger. She felt her strength flowing back at once.

The urge to pack up and ride on was strong in her. The blizzard had frightened Sarah more than she realized. She yearned to ride and ride, to put this terrible, killing prairie behind her, but common sense prevailed. She would postpone leaving until morning. A good night's rest was imperative. She forced herself away from the comfort of the fire and scoured the area for all the wood she could find. By that time it had grown quite dark, and she knew that her decision had been wise. Night would have fallen before she had gotten very far.

Wrapping herself in the robes, she went to sleep. Apparently her experience with the blizzard had honed whatever survival instinct she possessed, for each time the fire died down and the cold crept around her, Sarah roused long enough to stoke up the fire again.

The dazzle of the morning sun awoke her a final

time. She got up, tossed the last of the wood onto the fire, brewed tea and heated up the remainder of last night's broth. As this heated, Sarah saddled the horse she intended to ride, then she hastily gulped the tea and broth and put everything into the packs.

She found the going very slow. The horses had to labor, picking their way. The snow was so deep in places that the animals sank to their bellies, and Sarah had to dismount and help them out of the drifts. Snow was everywhere, piled in huge drifts. It was better along the stream, but even there she sometimes had to break the ice and lead the horses along in the water to avoid great drifts of snow against the bank.

At the end of the day, she had made very little progress and was weary to the bone. In late afternoon she began keeping watch ahead and was able to kill another rabbit for her supper.

This set the pattern for the days to follow. Dreary day after dreary day, she rode along the wandering stream. As she had suspected, the snow did not melt this time. The weather continued to be very cold, and a hard crust formed on the snow; she had to be watchful that the animals didn't break through the treacherous spots.

Only once did another blizzard strike, brief but fierce, layering the ground with several more inches of snow. The experience of the first blizzard had taught Sarah what she should and should not do, and during this one, she slept not at all, remaining awake, feeding the fire she had started and keeping it going until the storm was over.

As the days passed, Sarah lost all track of time. She changed mounts frequently, for the horses were becoming gaunt and worn, with very little food to sustain them. Fortunately they were fine horses, strong and young.

One day, at least a month after she began her trek, Sarah noticed without much interest that the banks alongside the stream were steepening, and the ground seemed to be sloping down. Then, at midday, she rode out of a cut and saw the wide sweep of a river, into which the stream emptied.

The Missouri!

She slumped in the saddle in dismay. The river was frozen solid. It had been her fervent hope that once she reached the Missouri, she could hail a flatboat on down to St. Louis. But no water craft could navigate this frozen river. There would be no traffic on the Missouri until the spring thaw.

In that moment, Sarah was as close to admitting defeat as she had been since being taken aboard the *North Star* on the London docks. She knew it was several hundred miles yet to St. Louis; just how many she had no idea, but she knew it meant many weeks, even months, of weary riding, and the worst of winter was yet to come. There just seeemed no way that she could survive the hardships of the long journey on her own.

How much time passed she didn't know, but her horse grew impatient and joggled her, tossing his head. Sarah broke out of her apathy with a start. She straightened up, pushing all thought of defeat from her mind.

"Sean love, you told me I could make it," she said aloud. "And I will, I bloody well will! Some way or another, I'll make it!"

Spring came early that year to St. Louis. It had

been a severe winter; even parts of the Mississippi had frozen, and river traffic had been slowed considerably. Many river boats were tied up at the landing for weeks at a time. Now, in the middle of March, the ice was breaking up, and the Mississippi was stirring sluggishly to life.

In his trading post, Jacques Fortier was busy. Trappers and fur traders had began trickling in with their winter's catch, and Jacques was readying some shipments for downriver. He was hunched over the counter, working on his account books, humming under his breath, happy that trade would soon be brisk.

Suddenly he sensed a presence. He had heard no sound, but a strange feeling passed over him, and his glance came up. Coming toward him was a small, slender man in worn and tattered buckskins— No, it was a woman! *Mon Dieu!* A woman in man's clothing. His first thought was that she was Indian, but her skin was too pale. She was very thin, almost emaciated.

"Monsieur Fortier?" she said, in a voice that sounded rusty from long disuse. "Do you remember me? Sarah Moody?"

"Sarah Moody?" He gaped as at an apparition. Then his stunned brain began to function again. He slapped his forehead. "*Mon Dieu!* Mademoiselle Sarah Moody! What has transpired with you? Sean . . ." He looked eagerly past her. "Where is the Irishman?"

"Sean Flanagan is dead, sir," she said. "He died back on the Platte, from an arrow in his back."

"Sean is dead? *Mon Dieu,* this is most distressing news!" Then he gaped at her again. "All that distance— You came all that way on your own, Mademoiselle?"

"In a way. You might say Sean was with me, but yes, I made it on my own," she said steadily. "There were times, many times, when I thought I would not. But here I am." She smiled for the first time.

"So you are, so you are," he said heartily. He started around the counter. "You must be starving. And you have need of clothes. . . ."

"Monsieur Fortier." She motioned him back. "It is my understanding that Sean left funds on deposit here for me."

"He did. That was the last thing the unfortunate man said to me." Fortier spoke with dramatic mournfulness. "If he did not return, but Sarah Moody does, it all goes to her."

"And the trunk of clothes I purchased last spring— You still have that?"

"Indeed I do, Mademoiselle. It is in my storeroom. Sean brought it back on that last day."

"Then if you would fetch me a carriage, please, sir, in which to transport myself and the trunk to the Foster House. . . ."

Jacques Fortier stared at her with mingled astonishment and amusement, as this woman, as filthy and tattered as any Indian woman six months in a dugout, seemed to undergo a metamorphosis almost before his very eyes, turning into a lady, a lady of quality.

"And advance me a sum of money from Sean's funds."

Hiding a smile, Fortier murmured, "You may rest assured, Mademoiselle. At once." He made a small bow.

Sarah Moody colored, then smiled sheepishly. "I am sorry, Monsieur Fortier. It's just that I have been through hell and . . ."

She swayed and would have fallen if Fortier hadn't moved quickly to catch her. "And I, Mademoiselle, tender my apologies for mocking you." He raised his voice. "Marie!"

Sarah caught at his sleeve. "Outside are Sean's horses, his packs, pistols, and rifle. Will you buy them for whatever they are worth?"

"*Naturellement,* Mademoiselle Moody. Trust me."

"Wait— Not the rifle. Not Katie. That I intend to keep. Never to use, but I refuse to part with it."

Marie Fortier came bustling in. Fortier said, *"Mon cheri,* will you see to Mademoiselle Moody? She is faint from hunger. Perhaps a tot of French brandy and some of the good soup you have simmering? Meanwhile, I shall fetch her a carriage."

As Fortier started out, Sarah said quickly, "Are there many keelboats docked at the landing?"

Fortier looked at her quizzically. "A great many, Mademoiselle. The winter has been hard, and many boats have wintered here. But now that the thaw is upon us, they are preparing to leave or have already done so."

Sarah started to ask about Jeb Hawkins, then changed her mind. She would come to that later.

In her room at the Foster House, Sarah lingered long in her bath, reveling in the hot water and all the soap she could use.

Dulcie Foster had raised her eyebrows when Sarah, once again in tattered buckskins, had presented herself at the door. The big woman sniffed disapprov-

27

ingly; more, Sarah suspected, from the man's attire than the condition of the buckskins. But she grudgingly rented Sarah a room and had her loutish son lug water up.

Sarah's thoughts were occupied as she bathed. She was of two minds about seeking out Jeb. She longed to see him. Yet Sean's death, although months back, still weighed heavily on her spirit. She knew it would seem silly should she voice it to anyone, but the idea of going now to Jeb, at least immediately, struck her as somehow being unfaithful to Sean's memory.

And Jeb himself— Would he greet her with delight or chilly displeasure? She had not returned that morning to the landing, as she had promised. Would he believe her explanation, or even listen to her? And with that, an irrational anger awoke in Sarah. What right did he have to scorn her? *He* had not come searching for her, paying with his life. It had been Sean Flanagan who had loved her enough to come after her at the risk of his life, not Jeb Hawkins!

Even if Jeb listened to her explanation and believed it, what would his reaction be? The degradation, the sexual abuse, she had undergone—Sean had understood. But would Jeb? Jeb Hawkins was a man possessed of a moral code almost Puritan in its rigidity. He had broken that code with her on board the *North Star,* and Sarah was perceptive enough to realize that he had suffered pangs of guilt. Perhaps he even felt guilty about that hour of dalliance on board his keelboat.

Well, to bloody hell with Jeb Hawkins and his moral code!

Angrily, she got out of the tub and dried herself.

Clean and warm for the first time in an eternity,

Sarah felt a lassitude creep over her. She stretched out across the soft bed and went to sleep, with only the comforter over her. She slept for two hours and awoke refreshed, her mind made up as to what she would do. She had to at least speak with Jeb. She owed him that much; she owed *herself* that much.

She creamed and scented her body—spare and gaunt now from deprivation, showing the delicate bone structure, almost a stranger to her after the long months spent covered by primitive garments. Her skin responded to the creams and oils, becoming sleek and rosy. Her face had remained remarkably unaffected by the rough weather and lack of care. It was only the hands that now showed what she had been through; only time would heal the marks that heavy work had put upon them.

Her hair, grown out now to a fair length, Sarah arranged in curls atop her head. Looking at her serious-eyed face in the glass, Sarah could almost see the girl she had been on that night she had walked down Chick Lane in London town.

Leaving the Foster House, Sarah strolled along until she saw an empty carriage. She hailed it and told the driver to take her to the river landing.

As the carriage wheeled down the incline onto the busy landing, Sarah's resolve faltered. She ordered the driver to stop at the bottom of the slope. Paying him, she got out and walked along slowly. The landing was so busy, with boats loading, ladies and gentlemen of every station in life darting about, that Sarah went virtually unnoticed in the throng.

And there, up ahead, were Jeb's two keelboats, freshly painted. Sarah's pulse quickened, and she began to walk faster, afire with anticipation, all her reservations swept away at the sight of Jeb.

He was standing at the bow of one keelboat, directing loading operations, that red beard like a flag of command. Smoke billowed up from the cigar between his fingers. Still some distance away, Sarah hurried faster.

A woman came out of the cabin behind Jeb and stopped at his side. She was dressed in the latest fashion; full-bodied and young, with long hair the color of cornsilk. And she was beautiful.

She placed a hand on Jeb's arm, smiling fondly up at him. Jeb turned his attention to her. He put his own hand on hers. Then he placed his arm around her shoulders, laughing down into her upturned face.

Sarah's steps faltered, and she came to a stop, staring with a wildly beating heart. Her spirits plummeted. Clearly, they were on familiar terms. They were lovers! This knowledge drove into Sarah's heart like a splinter of ice. They could even be man and wife.

Sarah stood for a moment longer, sunk into the depths of despair, knowing he had found another love.

With dragging footsteps, she turned away and started back toward the hill, walking rapidly now, afraid Jeb would see her.

It was evident that he was loading his keelboats in preparation for departure. He would be gone on the morrow. Then, she would return to the landing and arrange passage for herself on another keelboat.

PART FOUR

The Promise

Chapter Twenty-four

Jeb Hawkins had learned to love the Mississippi—old Mrs. Sippi, as Cap Clayborne had called the river.

Nearing the middle of his third year, with his keel-boats plying the river to New Orleans and back, Jeb knew her twists and turns by heart. He supposed his knowing the river so intimately was the reason he loved the life he was leading. A man could spend his entire life captaining a ship on the high seas and never know it all.

Early on, an old riverman had told him: "She's tricky, a tricky bitch, this old river. But just like a rambunctious bitch-woman, she can be conquered, should a man take the time and trouble to learn her ways. You've got to be as knowing of her as your own bedroom. Know where every sandbar is by heart. Most river boat men are afeared to venture down her at night. You see, son, clear starlight throws such heavy shadows that, if you ain't knowing, you would run away from every bunch of timber on the bank, talking the black shadow it throws for the river bank. You can't see a snag at night, o'course, but if you know where it is aforehand, you can steer around it. Pitch-black nights, now that's a different thing entire. All shores look like straight lines then, but you'll know better, if you have the shape of her in your head. That's what you have to do, son, have the shape of her in your noggin!"

This Jeb proceeded to do, until he did indeed know the river, every inch of it. In a way he had to relearn the Mississippi again on every trip, since it changed constantly—a sandbar disappearing, a new one showing up at a different spot, and at flood time the channel itself changed, shifting slightly. Jeb was thankful that he had a retentive memory. Now he could navigate the river at night, the shape of the shore, every sandbar and snag, burned into his brain as clear as a picture. This was also a great aid toward his success and prosperity. Most river boat men *were* frightened to navigate old Mrs. Sippi at night, and Jeb could therefore make faster trips with his keelboats than the others.

He was prosperous now, beyond anything he had dreamed of in the beginning. The loss of the *North Star* and his captain's status was nothing more than a sour memory.

In addition, Jeb had found, to his amusement, that he had mellowed somewhat. His prosperity accounted for a part of that, naturally. But much of it he attributed to the camaraderie between keelboat captain and crew. No longer was there a great distance between Jeb and his men, as there had been during his days as a ship's master. He delighted in their crude humor, their rough and ready ways, and their willingness to work hard and long for him. Jeb had no trouble finding all the men he needed nowadays. The good wages he paid, the fine condition in which he kept his keelboats, the good food the men were served, his many innovations that made work on his keelboats easier on the crew—all of this was common knowledge along the river, and men were eager to be taken on as members of his crew. Jeb did not roister with them in The Swamp in New Orleans or Natchez-Under-the-Hill. But he did drink with them, and he entered into their roughhousing with gusto. He was proud of the fact that he could outfight any man in his crew; his ability to do this earned him even more respect from the men.

Jeb still operated only two keelboats, but Cap's old one had been replaced by a new, larger one. Aside from hauling all the cargo his boats could handle, he now had a thriving passenger business. The newer keelboat had more luxurious accommodations; he had even added a dining room. Ezra Boggs was still with him. Jeb had been dubious at first about putting Ezra in charge of the galley, but the man rose to the occasion and ran the galley with flair and authority. The dining room had a reputation for serving excellent food. A number of people looked upon a trip up and down the river on his passenger keelboat as a pleasure cruise and repeated the trip once or twice a year.

In addition, Jeb's keelboats had a record for safe passage. Giles Brock's crew of pirates still plagued the river traffic and made the trip perilous for most boats. He was considered a scourge now. However, he had never been able to successfully bring off an attack on Jeb's boats. He had tried; once or twice a year he and his villainous crew made the attempt, but they were driven off every time. Jeb was pleased with his safety record; he had not lost a single life, neither crewmen nor passengers, to Brock's pirates, since that black day when Brock and his men had murdered Cap Clayborne.

This reputation for safe passage was one reason women ventured to travel on his passenger boat alone. There was another reason, Jeb was soon to realize. Although not a vain man, he recognized that he had a certain attraction for women. At first he had spurned their advances, but being a virile man and viewing with distaste the idea of cavorting with whores in places like The Swamp, he eventually let down his reserve. Nowadays, more often than not, women shared his cabin during the lengthy trips, and Jeb pleasured himself with them.

One woman, a blonde-haired beauty named Hester Valance, journeyed with him two or three times a year. She was a widow of thirty, with a good deal of wealth left to her by her dead husband, at present residing in New Orleans. Hester made no demands on him, other than sexually. She was a lovely woman, a delightful companion, with a lively sense of humor, and was robust in bed.

His openly sharing his cabin with Hester, Jeb supposed, was a fairly accurate measure of the change in him. He made no effort to hide it from the crew or the other passengers. In times past, he would not have dreamed of such flagrant behavior. Certainly never on board the *North Star*. Except for the one regrettable episode with Sarah Moody.

He still thought of Sarah from time to time, with longing and some pain. In the beginning he had asked everywhere for word of her and Sean Flanagan, but not a whisper did he hear. They could both have dropped off the face of the earth. Yet it *had* been two years now, two busy, fruitful years, since that last dalliance with Sarah on the keelboat. At first Jeb had been hurt and bitter toward her. Time had mellowed those feelings as well. After all, Sarah Moody had received bad treatment at his hands, so he had small cause to blame her if she had chosen this Irish fellow over him.

It was in the spring of the second year following Sarah's disappearance that Jeb docked his two keelboats at the St. Louis landing. Hester Valance was with him. It had been an uneventful and certainly pleasurable voyage up from New Orleans.

As he stood in the bow of his passenger keelboat, supervising the unloading of cargo and smoking a cigar, Jeb noticed a mule coming down the road from town. As the mule approached, Jeb saw a lad of about twelve on the animal's back. To Jeb's surprise, the youth drew the mule to a halt opposite the bow of the keelboat.

"Be you Captain Hawkins, sir?"

"I be, lad, yes, I be," Jeb said, grinning.

"Word had reached Monsieur Fortier of your arrival," the youth said. "He sent me to inquire if you would be so kind as to call on him at your convenience. 'Tis a business matter, sir."

"Monsieur Fortier? Oh, *Jacques* Fortier!" Jeb's interest perked up. "What matter of business does he have to transact with me, lad?"

"That I know not, sir. He just sent me to see if you would come."

Jeb thought for a moment. Jacques Fortier undoubtedly bought and shipped more furs than any other merchant in St. Louis. He had never done business with Fortier, and since Jeb had all the business he could handle anyway, he had not sought Fortier's favor; he had never even made the merchant's acquaintance. Yet, what harm would it do to talk to the man? It would give him an excuse to get into town and escape the tedium of supervising the unloading of cargo, which Tim, now a grown man, actually did anyway. He said, "All right, tell Monsieur Fortier that I will call on him. And lad, on your way back into the village, would you hail an empty carriage and send it down to the landing for me?"

"That I will, Captain Hawkins." The lad executed a clumsy salute and loped away on the mule.

Jeb called Tim to him. "I'm going into town, Tim. See that the unloading goes smoothly, if you please."

"I'll see to it, Captain." Although Tim had attained nearly his full growth now and was in every way a man, Jeb had not been able to stop the youth from addressing him as captain and had finally given up.

Ten minutes later, a carriage came clattering down to the landing. Jeb got in and directed the driver to take him to Fortier's establishment.

Jeb found the rotund little Frenchman sunk in gloom. Although he had never met the man, Jeb had heard that Fortier was always cheerful and bouncy with good humor.

After mutual introductions, Fortier burst out, "I just received word this morning that Thad Turner's keelboat was ambushed down the river a ways. He was loaded with trade goods for me. Now the goods are all gone, Thad is dead, his keelboat stolen, and it is all the doing of that devil's spawn, Giles Brock! *Mon Dieu!* That *merde* must be done away with!"

"He will be, when enough people become outraged enough," Jeb said. "The trouble is, no one seems sure who has the authority to do anything. The Spanish do not care, the French have no real authority. And the Americans— Well, they haven't been hurt enough yet by Brock's depredations, and they have no legal authority on the river anyway. Every river boat man has to protect his own."

"But you, Captain Hawkins. I have heard of you having skirmishes with this villain, but you have yet to lose a cargo to him. Why is that?"

"I am always prepared for him. I hire fighting men and train them much as would the master of a battleship. They're too much for his gang of cutthroats to handle."

"That is why I wished to see you." Fortier sighed. "Thad Turner had been handling my shipments for years. He was *mon ami,* my friend. Now that he is dead, I must turn to someone else." Fortier spread plump hands in a shrug. "And who but to you, Captain Hawkins?"

Jeb suppressed a surge of excitement. To gain for himself Fortier's shipping business on an exclusive basis would be a plum.

Maintaining a disinterested expression, he said carefully, "I appreciate that, sir, but I *do* have other commitments."

"I am willing to pay higher shipping rates," Fortier said eagerly. "It will be worth it to me to guarantee safe passage for my furs."

"Such a guarantee I cannot give you. But I do have an idea, something I have been mulling over. It will strengthen the defense of my boats immeasurably." Jeb's face became grim. "If Giles Brock dares attack me again, he will sorely rue the day."

"That is exactly the sort of assurance I need," Fortier exclaimed. He was animated now, the death of his friend forgotten. He was once more the shrewd businessman. "Will you handle my shipments? I assure you that I will have enough furs for New Orleans, and trade goods coming back to my store to pay you well."

Jeb made a show of further hesitation, then nodded. "All right, Monsieur Fortier, we have a bargain."

They shook hands, and Fortier became brisk as they went into details. However, from time to time the Frenchman would pause to soundly curse Giles Brock. Jeb, scarcely listening, suddenly straightened up at something the man said. A prickle went down his spine.

He said harshly, "What did you just say, Fortier?"

Fortier glanced up from the papers spread on the counter before him, his face blank. "Pardon?"

"Something about a woman." Jeb gestured impatiently. "And Giles Brock."

"Oh." Fortier's face cleared. "The blackguard seized a white woman right here on the streets of St. Louis and sold her as a slave to a tribe of Pawnee."

"Her name! The woman's name, man!" Jeb's tone was urgent.

"Sarah Moody, Mademoiselle Sarah Moody."

"By the Lord Jehovah! That filthy, rotten scum!" Jeb's hands clenched into fists, anger racing through him. "What happened to her, do you know?"

"*Naturellement*. She came into my store—oh, one year back now. *Mon Dieu!* Looking like an apparition, she did." Fortier slapped his cheeks.

"She is all right then?"

"As far as my knowledge goes, she is. I have not seen the lady since."

"There was a man, Sean Flanagan. What of him?"

"Ah, poor Sean." Fortier assumed a mournful expression. "He is dead, dead of an Indian arrow. He went after Mademoiselle Moody, tracking her across the prairie for months on end. He finally managed her rescue and paid for it with his life. Did you know Sean Flanagan?"

"No, but I know the woman. I know Sarah Moody. Lord God, that poor woman has suffered a sorry fate since I brought her to these shores. I am thankful she has survived once again."

Fortier's eyes widened. "You brought her here?"

"Never mind that." Jeb leaned forward, hands gripping the edge of the counter until the knuckles were white. "Where is Sarah now? Do you know?"

"Only what she told me." Fortier elevated his eyebrows. "She mentioned New Orleans. That has been some time, you must understand, so I do not know . . ."

Giles Brock and Rhys Pommet were having everything their own way. Brock's band of river pirates now numbered thirty or so, the number fluctuating from time to time, but the number was large enough to overpower almost any river boat they attacked. Brock had recently captured two keelboats he kept for his own; one had belonged to Thad Turner. Brock ravaged the river, and the rich plunder kept his men happy. They could enter most of the river towns without fear of capture and roister to their heart's desire. The number of rivermen they had slaughtered mounted with every foray.

Once a tavern wench, sitting in Brock's lap, asked coyly, "How many river boat men have you killed now, Giles?"

Brock laughed loudly, a drunken roar. "Who bothers to count, wench?"

He had become somewhat of a dandy, wearing fine breeches, ruffled white shirts, which he threw away after wearing once, and expensive boots. Even into battle he wore the fine garments, standing out vividly amid the roughly dressed men of his bloody crew.

Pommet warned him. "You going into battle dressed like that, Giles— Some day you'll sorely regret it. You might as well wear a red flag, you stand out so from the rest of us."

"Let them see me, let them. I *want* them to know that it's Giles Brock clawing at their arses before they die!" Brock was beginning to believe himself invincible. He had long since lost any compunction he ever had about killing. He went into the sneak attacks on the river boats with gusto, thirsting with blood lust. He was like a wild man, shooting until his weapons were empty, then slashing with a saber at close range.

Rhys Pommet still killed with the same passionless efficiency of old. Once, after the bloody slaughter of a river boat crew, he remarked to Brock, "Giles, you spook me a little these days. You get such a wild, almost crazy look about you. Even the men are afeared of you."

"So they should be, so they should be! I'm their leader, and they better by God fear me! I want every man along this river to be fearing Giles Brock."

One thing stuck in Brock's craw. His failure to best Jeb Hawkins in battle gnawed at his soul like a cancer. Over the past two years, he had tried every ploy he knew to capture Hawkins' boats, which were always heavily laden with booty, and kill Hawkins in the bargain. But always he failed. The sneak attacks he had tried while Hawkins' boats were being towed upriver by mules never succeeded because the crafty devil had out scouts, who warned Hawkins well in advance of their approach. And nowadays Hawkins, unlike other keelboat operators, traveled the Mississippi at night while going south with the current, so he was seldom vulnerable to attack from land. How Hawkins managed this Brock had yet to figure out. In the beginning he and his crew had followed along the river bank. Brock had been positive that Hawkins would run aground at night and be at his mercy. Never once had this happened. The man *must* be a devil, to be able to see like a cat in the dark.

Brock was far from giving up. He had devised a new scheme, one he was certain would succeed. That was the reason for the two keelboats. He intended to move boldly out into the river, masquerading as an honest keelboat operator, with fake cargo on board both boats. Then he would, seemingly by accident, come close enough to Hawkins' boats for his men to open fire. To all appearances, the men on deck would be hard working keelboat men, the remainder of the band hidden in the cabins until the moment of attack.

Brock had received word that Jeb Hawkins was docked in St. Louis and would soon be departing downriver with a cargo of furs. On this late spring day, Brock had his two keelboats hidden in Cottonwood Creek, a location he used so frequently nowadays that he had established a headquarters of a sort along the creek, with two crude log structures. One was long and low, quarters for the men, and the other, fitted up more comfortably, was Brock's own. He had a man in St. Louis with two fast horses. The instant this man knew when Hawkins was to depart, he was to ride day and night to Cottonwood Creek and give Brock notice of Hawkins' imminent arrival.

Brock knew the men were getting edgy. They had laid up for over two weeks now, waiting for the word to go into action. They spent their time drinking and gambling. An indication of the growing restlessness was the frequent quarrels that broke out between them almost daily, usually over a card game. Brock let them fight it out, calculating it would tend to calm them down. Only once did he have anything to say. One quarrel had resulted in a man being shot to death.

When informed of this, he came roaring out of his cabin and stormed into the long house. "Now heed this, you river scum! If you feel the need to fight one another, that's grand with me. But not with killing weapons. No more killings! We're going to need all the men we've got when we go after Jeb Hawkins. So, the next man who kills another is going to be shot down by me! Is that clear enough for you bastards?"

"It's all this idle time, Mister Brock," one man whined. "We got nothing to do."

"You'll be busy soon enough," Brock snarled, "once Hawkins comes kiting down the river."

"It's all right for ye to talk," another muttered. "Ye've got a wench to tumble. We'uns would like some, too. We've had whores in here afore. . . ."

"It's different this time, damn your eyes! I don't want to have a gaggle of females left behind when we get the word. As for me, I'm your leader. I do as I damn well please, and no sass from any of you! Now is that clear? If not . . ." He drew a pistol from his belt. "If any of you has any more bellyaching, speak up!"

They all fell silent, drawing back from Brock in fright, knowing that he wouldn't hesitate to kill any man daring to open his mouth.

Brock did have a woman with him, a tavern wench he had taken away with him from his last visit to The Swamp—a young and comely girl, if somewhat uneducated and crude. But she was a lusty wench in bed, giving Brock all he could handle. She was willing to go at it day and night if he had been up to it.

Brock was tumbling her on the floor of his cabin the afternoon his man came riding back from St. Louis. Such had been their urgency that they hadn't taken time to use the crude bed against one wall. Brock had just rolled off her, heaving great gasps of air, when a knock sounded on the door.

He raised his head to growl, "What is it? Damnation, can't a man have some time of his own?"

"It's Rhys, Giles. Jethro is back from St. Louis with news."

Alert, Brock sat up. "I'll be out in a minute."

He threw on his clothes in a great hurry. The wench was asleep, a wanton sprawl of arms and legs. He'd have to send her back to New Orleans before they embarked on their venture. She knew nothing of what was about to take place, and he didn't want her to know. Most times, he not only did not care who knew about his forays against the river boats but wanted everybody to know. This time, he had a suspicion there would be somewhat of a hue and cry raised when it was learned that he had captured Hawkins' boats and killed the man. Jeb Hawkins was one of the most respected and popular men on the river, a fact that galled Brock to the core.

Dressed, he went outside the cabin. Pommet was

waiting for him. He motioned toward the long cabin. "Jethro's over there."

Together, they strode across to the other cabin. All the men were gathered, excitedly milling around Jethro Pardee, a small, scrawny man with a toothless, evil grin. He flashed that grin now at the sight of Brock. "He's left St. Louis, Mister Brock. Jeb Hawkins is on his way down the river!"

"How far behind you?"

"I left the night before, when I learned he was departing the next morning. I rode like the wind to get here. . . ."

"How far behind, damn you?"

"I'd guage two days, a day and a half," Jethro Pardee said hastily.

"All right." Brock faced the men, hands on hips. He raised his voice. "Now you river rats needn't grumble about idle hands any longer. Get ready to board the keelboats. You'll have all the action you can handle soon, as well as your pockets lined with plunder. We'll stand ready to stick our snouts out onto the river. I'll send a man to stand watch on the bluff. He'll spot Master Jeb Hawkins in time to warn us of his approach!"

Jeb kept men on watch around the clock on both boats, with orders to warn him the instant they saw anything even remotely suspicious. Some sixth sense had been nagging at him—somewhere along the river Giles Brock was going to mount an attack. Except for one thing, Jeb hoped he would. He was ready for him, more than ready.

But since learning of Sarah's possible whereabouts, Jeb had been anxious to reach New Orleans and search for her, impatient with any delays. He had been in a state of ever-changing moods since leaving St. Louis, buoyed in spirits one minute at the news of her, then plunged into gloom the next by the knowledge that she had made no effort to get in touch with him. Why hadn't she? Had she been so saddened by this Sean Flanagan's death that she wanted no truck with him? Was she still mourning the fellow?

Because of his changing moods, Jeb wasn't very good company for Hester, and he realized it.

With her usual good humor, Hester complained very little. She made her only actual complaint while they were having a noon hour meal in his cabin several days out of St. Louis. "Something is bothering you, my dear. You've been stalking about with a face like a storm cloud, and when I try to talk to you, I get about as much response as I would from one of your mules. Would you care to share it with me? Or is it too personal?"

"I'm sorry, madam," Jeb said apologetically. "It *is* personal, true." And then he decided to tell her, if she cared to listen. It had been bottled up inside him too long. He directed a candid gaze at her. "We have no bonds on one another, we have agreed on that. We have our fun, but it is not permanent. We agreed to those terms, did we not?"

For just a moment her laughing brown eyes became grave, and a shadow of pain darkened them. Or was he imagining it?

Then she was smiling again. She reached across the small table to lightly touch his hand. "You are right, Jeb Hawkins. Although I do like you, and we do enjoy each other, what woman in her right senses would want to share you with a mistress?"

"A mistress?" Jeb gave her a startled look.

Hester laughed merrily. "Why, this old river." She gestured with a toss of her head. "The Mississippi is your mistress, Jeb."

"Oh, that." He grinned. "Perhaps, in a sense." He finished off the wine they'd shared with the food and fired a cigar from the candle on the table. "Now I'll tell you about Sarah Moody."

Hester listened, absorbed, with her elbows propped on the table, her chin resting on her hands.

When he was finished, she clapped her hands softly. "Heavens, what a romantic story!"

He looked at her, searching for sarcasm. If any was intended, it didn't show.

Now she sobered. "But sad, too. Of course, you'll find her. You must! And then it will end happily for you."

"I'm not so sure, Hester. I am no longer sure of her feelings toward me."

"You blame yourself, don't you, for the trials the poor woman has suffered," Hester said, her gaze intent on his face.

He shrugged. "In a way. There is no denying that her troubles began when I brought her here."

"I think you know little of women, Jeb Hawkins. If she loves you, and I am convinced she does, she has long since forgiven you."

He slapped the table with his hand. "Then why didn't she make contact with me when she returned? By the Lord Jehovah, she knows that I ply the river. It would have been easy enough for her to get word to me!"

"As to that, I know not. Perhaps she thought it would be unseemly of her to pursue you. You say she is a lady. . . ."

At that moment there was a rap on the door. "Cap Hawkins?" It was the voice of Ezra Boggs.

Jeb strode to the door and threw it wide. "Yes, Ezra?"

"Two keelboats just came sneaking into the river, out of Cottonwood Creek," Boggs said excitedly. "Looks almighty suspicious."

It was rumored along the river that Cottonwood Creek was where Giles Brock and his pirates rendezvoused between raids. Jeb felt his blood begin to race. "I'll be right up, Ezra. Meanwhile, wave the other keelboat in close, alongside us."

Boggs grinned delightedly. "They're in for a surprise, eh, Cap?"

"If it's who I think it is, he is indeed," Jeb said grimly. "Now hurry along."

Boggs hastened down the corridor. Jeb turned back into the cabin. "You stay in here, Hester. It'll be safer here."

"Jeb, I want to watch!" she said, her eyes shining.

"You will stay in the cabin, madam, as will all the other ladies on board!"

From his desk Jeb took a cigar and lit it, then grabbed two pistols, which he stuck into his belt, and ran out of the cabin. Outside, his glance went to the other keelboat first. Tim, in charge of the second boat, was at the steering oar, and men were manning the oars in the bow, maneuvering the boat alongside. Jeb nodded in approval. Then he looked north. Two small keelboats were indeed moving down on them, men at the oars on both. The boats looked innocent

431

enough, with only a normal-size crew in sight, yet Jeb was well aware that the long cabins could be full of pirates. And the covered bundles both on deck and the tops of the cabins could well be false cargo.

Under most circumstances, Jeb would simply put all his men at the oars and the poles. They were so brawny, so well-trained, they could usually draw away from any pursuing boat with ease. Of course, if the two boats behind them were empty of cargo, it would be more difficult to do, since Jeb's boats were heavily laden. He was still confident that he could outrun them, but he had no intention of doing so, if this was Giles Brock and his bloody crew. Despite his haste to get to New Orleans, Jeb was prepared and eager for the confrontation. If the plan he had in mind worked, the river would be free of Giles Brock at long last.

His other keelboat was near enough now for Jeb to call softly across the water, "Tim? What do you think?"

"It's Giles Brock, Captain." Tim nodded. "See the man at the sweep oar on the boat to the right? See how he is dressed? Like a peacock. Could only be Giles Brock, sir!"

"Good enough, Tim. You know what to do."

Both Tim and the man handling the steering oar on the passenger boat had orders to maintain as straight a course as possible. Jeb strode to the bow. He propped his foot on a canvas-covered, cylinder-shaped object and smoked his cigar coolly. He had already given detailed instructions on how it was to be handled—they would wait until the boats charging down on them were just beyond pistol range.

As the pursuing boats drew closer, Jeb gestured

silently to two men standing behind him. He stood back and watched as they whipped the canvas off the cannon on which Jeb had been resting his foot. It was a four-pounder, held fast by chains fastened to each side of the boat. Otherwise, the backlash would send the cannon careening along the deck, destroying everything in its path. When Jeb had had the idea of arming the boats with cannon, he had trained the men long and hard in how to operate them.

As the two men began to ram the powder home, Jeb glanced across at his other boat. Two men there were similarly engaged. Jeb looked again at the keel-boats behind them. Since his own were moving only as fast as the current would carry them, Brock's boats were closing fast.

In a calm voice, Jeb said, "Ready?"

"She's ready to fire, Jeb," said one of the men.

"Fine. Be ready to reload faster than ever before. One ball might not do it, but I think two balls landing on their decks will sink both their vessels."

In that moment Jeb saw men pouring out of the cabins of the other boats, armed to the teeth with pistols and rifles. As the men with the rifles dropped to their knees to aim, Jeb chopped his hand down in a signal, then lit the short cannon fuse with his cigar.

Pistols and rifles cracked from the pursuing boats, but the range was still too great, and there were no direct hits.

Then the two cannons roared almost simultaneously. Jeb stepped to one side and forward, out of the cloud of smoke. With a grunt of satisfaction he saw they had made direct hits on both boats, the cannonballs striking just forward of the cabins, piercing the decks, and, he was sure, going on through the bottom planking as well.

The cannons firing had caused great consternation among the pirates. Men were yelling and milling about in confusion. Already some had leaped overboard.

"Ready to fire!"

Again Jeb applied the burning end of his cigar to the fuse. Once more both cannons thundered. This time, the cannonballs smashed into the cabins of the trailing keelboats.

Acting on prior orders from Jeb, his men lined up at the bows with pistols and rifles and swept a deadly stream of fire across the decks of the pirate boats. Men were mowed down like rows of grain. Such was the total confusion and terror across the way that not another shot was fired in their direction.

As his men reloaded for a second fusillade, Jeb noted with satisfaction that both of Brock's boats were already sinking. With two holes in each, they would sink even faster. The pirates were scrambling to leap into the river. Such had been their confidence in the success of their sneak attack that they had not even towed skiffs along. As least Jeb could see none.

Jeb shouted at the top of his voice, "Hold your fire, men! They're done for. No need to waste powder and ball."

A cheer went up from the crew. The decks across the way were empty now, except for the dead or dying, and the keelboats were up to the cabins in water. Even as Jeb watched, one was sucked under by the current.

He stepped to the edge of the boat and shouted

across, "Tim, did you see what happened to Giles Brock?"

"No, Captain. What with all the smoke and confusion, I took my eyes off him for a moment. When I looked again, he was gone."

Jeb hoped, with a savagery unlike him, that Giles Brock had died. He deserved it for all the rivermen he had had killed and for all the suffering he had caused Sarah. But whatever had happened to Brock personally, his gang of bloody pirates was finished. More than half of them had been killed, Jeb was certain, and the others would scatter, no longer trusting Brock's leadership, not after he had led them into such a massacre. No longer would Giles Brock be the scourge of the river!

Now that the firing had stopped, passengers were emerging from their cabins, crowding out on deck.

Jeb said reassuringly, "It's all right, ladies and gentlemen. The battle is over. Nothing to fear now." He shouted across the way, "Drop back to your regular position, Tim, and let's get under way!"

In a few minutes the second keelboat had fallen in behind about thirty yards, and they were under way again.

Now they could proceed with all speed to New Orleans. And I will have good news to convey to Sarah, Jeb thought; should I find her. Giles Brock had paid dearly for the indignities he had inflicted on her.

When the first cannonball came whistling toward them, plowing through the decking, Brock's first reaction had been that of stunned disbelief. A cannon mounted on a keelboat? Such a thing was unheard of!

On the heels of that disbelief came a gut-wrenching

435

fear, a fear such as he had never experienced. They had no chance against two cannon. And the odds were heavy that he would die within the next few minutes.

The impact of the second round of cannonballs brought back a measure of sanity. He began to shout and rant, trying to rally the men. They were milling about in confusion and panic, and paid him not the slightest heed. Then came the fusillade of heavy pistol and rifle fire. Brock glanced across to where Rhys Pommet was manning the steering oar on the other boat. He was just in time to see Pommet take a direct hit from a rifle ball. He tumbled backward into the river, limp as a rag doll.

Brock's terror returned full force. He stared down at the roiling brown water, feeling the old panic. He had always been terrified of water and was an awkward swimmer. Then he felt the keelboat tilt, and one look told him that it was sinking rapidly.

Closing his eyes and holding his nose between thumb and forefinger, he went feet first into the water. He sank like a stone. He began struggling toward the surface. Finally he popped up, gulping for air. Both boats were gone, the water was littered with debris, and others of his crew were swimming for the shore. Brock saw an oar floating toward him. He grabbed it, and using it to buoy him somewhat, he started toward the river bank. It seemed miles distant.

When his feet finally struck bottom, he staggered forward until he was out of the water and collapsed face down on the sand. He lay there for a long time, until he regained a measure of his strength and was able to roll over and sit up. The oar had floated ashore with him. He saw one of his crew members coming toward him, water dripping from his clothing. Brock tried to think of the man's name. All he could remember was Walt.

Using the oar, Brock levered himself to his feet. He tried to dredge up a smile of encouragement. "Well, it looks like we came a cropper this time. But next time will be different, my word on it. Next time we'll . . ."

"Next time!" The man bared his teeth like a cornered animal. "There'll be no next time, you bastard! Not for me, not for most of the men. You know why? 'Cause most of 'em are dead out there in the river. And whose fault is that? Yours, Mister Clever-by-Half Brock! Even Rhys is dead and gone!"

"Now wait," Brock said, hating himself for the wheedling note in his voice. "How could I know that Hawkins would have cannon on his boats?"

Walt sneered. "You always telling us you know it all, telling us you the one who made us feared and respected, and got the booty for us. Well, no more! After today, no riverman will follow you or take orders from you! So good-bye, Mister Brock. I'm getting my arse out of here to some place where it's safe!"

The man's words infuriated Brock, but he knew they were all too true. He had known that from the moment they were shot out of the river. With Pommet, his good right hand, gone, and his crew deserting him, he was finished. Black fury at Jeb Hawkins rose in his throat, almost choking him. As Walt started to walk away, Brock swung the oar in a blind rage. It smashed into the man's skull with a sickening sound. Walt staggered several feet along the river bank and landed on his face, dead before he struck the ground.

"I'm the leader, you scum. No man of mine talks back to me like that," Brock muttered. "And that goes for the rest of you. No man of mine stands up to me!"

He glanced around, blinking stupidly when he saw that he stood alone on the sandy bank, his words echoing in the empty air.

With a great effort, Brock got his rage back under some semblance of control. When his head was clear again, he realized that he had been on the brink of madness. Not that it wasn't enough to drive any sane man crazy. Once again, Jeb Hawkins had stripped him of everything. First, he had burned the *North Star* out from under him. Now, just when he was becoming king of the river, his keelboats had been blasted out of the water, his crew fleeing in terror. All Jeb Hawkins' doing!

Even if it meant his own death, Brock was determined that Hawkins would pay for this.

He took a moment to assess his situation. Fortunately, he had come ashore near the mouth of Cottonwood Creek. If he hurried, he could get back to the camp before any of the others. There were horses at camp, and a supply of pistols and powder and balls. It was possible that some of his cowardly crew would hasten back long enough to steal everything worth taking.

Brock began to hurry. If he was to reach New Orleans before Hawkins unloaded and started back upriver again, he would need at least two horses. And pistols, of course pistols!

Once he had found Hawkins in New Orleans, he would stalk the man until the chance presented itself and shoot him in the back. This time he would make sure that Jeb Hawkins was dead!

Chapter Twenty-five

With the great influx of river boat men into New Orleans, a need arose for places for them to roister while their boats were docked. The need was soon filled. Not one but two areas eventually became popular. Front Street, near where the boats docked, was lined with drinking establishments, their back rooms given over to gambling. A spot even more popular, out back of the town proper, soon became known as The Swamp. The Swamp comprised an area of several blocks, crowded with saloons, gambling dens, and bordellos, all housed in shacks, built of rough cypress planks or lumber from broken-up flatboats. The Swamp was the more popular of the two, since it was completely lawless—no law officer dared venture into the district. Front Street was policed to some extent.

Although no license was required to operate a gambling establishment, all gambling was at first confined to these particular areas, and persons of gentility dared not enter them, not without risk to life and limb.

The first establishment offering gambling for the gentry was opened a few blocks south of Front Street. It was a two-story structure, known simply as Katie's Casino. It not only offered gambling, but magnificent cuisine as well. Riffraff were not only discouraged, but physically kept out of the establishment by a brawny, six-foot-six Cajun, named Jean, who guarded the entrance zealously. For these reasons, Katie's Casino attracted not only the male gentry of New Orleans, but it was also a place they could bring their wives or mistresses, dine at their leisure, and gamble afterward.

The interior of the building was tastefully and luxuriously furnished. Draperies of the finest velvet framed the windows and could be closed to shut out the gaze of the curious. Excellent paintings adorned the walls, which were papered with the finest French wallpaper.

Unlike the Front Street saloons, where the noise could rattle a man's brains, Katie's Casino was quiet. Usually, the only sounds were the relatively quiet murmur of gentlemanly conversation, the rattle of dice in the cups, and the clicking of the roulette wheel. A handsome, young musician in residence played the pianoforte in the parlor, or salon, where meals were served in the evenings, and where the gentlemen could gather to talk before proceeding to the gaming tables.

There was no bar, as such, but waiters circulated through the main room and salon taking orders for drinks. The most popular games in the main casino were faro, roulette, and *vingt-et-un*. There were also several smaller rooms for members of the gentry who thought it unseemly to be seen gambling in public. In these rooms, men played baccarat, ecarta, or whatever games suited their fancy.

Only a select few knew that the name of the beautifully gowned lady with long, lustrous black hair and violet eyes was Sarah Moody. In fact, many addressed her familiarly as Katie, and Sarah never bothered to correct them.

When she had arrived in New Orleans two years before, Sarah soon discovered that, while gambling was common among the river boat men, there was no place where refined gentlemen and ladies could indulge their desire for gambling.

She set about correcting that lack. With the money Sean had left to her, she bought the large, two-story, wooden house near Front Street and renovated it, sparing no expense. She then hired a staff to operate the tables, insisting on strict honesty. Since Sean had taught her a great deal about gambling, Sarah was knowledgeable enough to watch a new man and tell if he tried to cheat the patrons or steal from her. Since there was no establishment such as hers within a great distance of New Orleans, she had to teach most of the employees herself. She also hired a French chef, stranded in New Orleans, to supervise the kitchen.

Sarah did not advertise. It wasn't necessary, since the reputation of her casino spread by word of mouth until the establishment was flourishing within a very short time. Now, she often had to turn away people. Instinctively she realized that if she allowed too great a number of people in to gamble or dine, the noise level would rise correspondingly, eventually destroying the genteel atmosphere she sought.

When Sarah first opened Katie's Casino, she was courted vigorously by the young bloods. She spurned one and all. Also, in the beginning she had nightly handled one of the roulette tables herself, sensing that it would be an added drawing card. Now she made only one token appearance in the casino, taking over the roulette table for the last round of play a few minutes before midnight. This became her trademark, and eventually the crowd, males predominant, was largest just before midnight. Katie's Casino opened at seven in the evening, and all play stopped at the stroke of midnight.

It was not too long after Sarah opened the establishment that some of the more pious New Orleanians raised a cry of outrage and tried to get the government to close down the casino. But since the governor of New Orleans himself was an avid gamester, they received no support from that individual. He was delighted that such a genteel place was available to him. As a token of appeasement to those outraged New Orleanians, Sarah did not open on Sundays.

As much as Sarah enjoyed her prosperity and success, she enjoyed those free Sundays more, especially since Randolph Colter had entered her life six months back. Sarah had purchased an open carriage and a team of two beautiful horses. On Sundays she and Rand would ride out of the stench of the city and into the countryside with a picnic hamper, spending most of the day under a moss-laden cypress.

During the rest of the week, Sarah rarely went out of the house. She had living quarters upstairs, using money lavishly to furnish and decorate the rooms. She would never become accustomed to the filth on the streets of New Orleans. People threw their garbage out into the streets, and pigs ranged along the gutters, feeding off the garbage. And the streets were not safe for a woman alone. It wasn't unusual for a drunken river boat man, wandering up from Front

Street or The Swamp, to accost a woman even in daylight.

Rand Colter was a tall, handsome man of thirty-some years, with wavy brown hair and sardonic black eyes. He had a somewhat debauched look, which only added to the dashing, debonair air about him. Sarah knew very little of his past, except that he was well-educated and came from an old Virginia family. She was confident that he had been involved in some sort of scandal in Virginia and had been exiled to New Orleans. He told Sarah later that he had been drunk for a month the night he wandered into her place. Ordinarily Jean, the hulking doorman, would not allow an intoxicated man inside, but Rand had been dressed in a gentleman's fine clothes and was obviously of the gentry, so Jean had permitted him to enter.

Even drunk, Rand had won heavily at cards that night, and he became a regular patron over the next few weeks. With Sarah, he was always charming, courteous, and did not press his suit as did the other young bucks. Although he was always well into his cups, he never made trouble.

Probably nothing would ever have happened between them if one young man hadn't become particularly obnoxious with Sarah. She had often seen the young man, a son of one of the town's wealthiest families by the name of Kirby Grant, in the casino. He was continually pushing himself on her, arrogantly confident of his charms with the ladies, but Sarah had always managed to get rid of him.

On this particular night, when Sarah came down for her midnight appearance, Kirby Grant cornered her against one wall. He had been drinking, his handsome face flushed. "Why do you continue to avoid me, madam? You treat me as if I had the pox."

"I treat you no differently than I do other men, sir," she said coolly.

"Think you're the high and mighty fine lady, do you?" He sneered. "The operator of a gambling house . . ."

Sarah said quietly, "This is a refined place, sir, where ladies and gentlemen may dine or gamble, as they wish."

"You know what I think? In my opinion a woman who runs a gambling house is no better than the madam of a bordello! Mayhap you should be over in The Swamp with others of your kind!"

Sarah's open hand lashed out without warning, striking him across the cheek.

Kirby Grant touched his rapidly reddening cheek, his face showing disbelief. Then his green eyes slitted with fury, and he seized her by the arm, shaking her.

"Is this drunken lout being a nuisance, madam?" a languid voice drawled.

Sarah looked around to see Randolph Colter standing near. She gasped out, "Yes, he is!"

"Then I suggest, sir, that you unhand her immediately," Rand Colter said, a thread of steel in his voice. He held a pair of gloves in his hands.

"What affair is this of yours?" Kirby Grant blustered, but he did let go of Sarah's arm.

"It's the affair of any gentleman when a drunken lout places a rough hand on a lady."

"A gentleman! I know of you. You're a gambler and a drunkard." Kirby Grant sneered. "As for this woman . . ." He gestured at Sarah. "She's nothing more than a tart!"

Fast as light, Rand flicked his gloves across Kirby Grant's face.

Grant went pale with rage. "You will pay with your life for that, sir!"

"You're calling me out, is that it?" Rand said quietly. "Shall we meet under the dueling oaks at dawn on the morrow then?"

Kirby Grant backed a step, suddenly sober. He licked his lips and flicked a glance at Sarah. Then he motioned grandly. " 'Tis not worth my taking a life, not even yours, Colter."

"That is most kind of you, sir," Rand said dryly. As Kirby Grant started to turn away, Rand added in that steely voice, "But I must warn you, sir. If you so much as speak to this lady again, I shall call *you* out!"

Kirby Grant threw him a murderous glare, then wheeled and stalked out.

Sarah drew a shuddering breath. "Thank God, it went no further! I would hate to see men dueling over me. But I must thank you, sir, for coming to my rescue. He was becoming rather—difficult."

"It was my pleasure, madam." He bowed slightly. "I am Randolph Colter."

"Yes, I know who you are. I make it a point to learn at least the names of my guests. I am Sarah Moody."

"Ah!" His black eyes glinted with amusement. "So it is not Katie then. I thought the name ill became you, madam. But why then the name of your house?"

Sarah smiled. "The reason for that must remain my secret." She looked at him curiously. "Tell me— Would you really have put your life at stake for a woman whose name you didn't even know?"

He shrugged negligently. "I would have, yes. My life means little to me."

"That is indeed a curious attitude." She made a sudden decision. "Would you share a midnight supper with me in my rooms, Mr. Colter?"

He stared at her in surprise. Then he smiled charmingly. "It would be my pleasure, madam."

Sarah was already regretting her impulsive invitation. She was nervous about being alone in her quarters with a man. It would be the first time any man, other than her employees, had been there. When the young bloods of New Orleans began trying to pay court to her, Sarah had rebuffed them because she wanted nothing to do with a man, any man. She had suffered too much at the hands of men. But of late some of her reserve had melted, and the healthy needs of her body had begun to plague her. She still thought of Jeb Hawkins often, yet she knew it was a waste of time. He had found another woman, and it was unlikely she would ever see him again. Sarah had little hope that he would ever venture inside a gambling establishment such as hers.

She soon found that her fears about inviting Rand for supper were unnecessary. He was the perfect gentleman. He was charming, witty, and kept her laughing through most of the meal and a glass of brandy afterward. Strangely enough, he reminded her a little of Sean. Not that he resembled Sean physically, but he had something of the same wry, self-depreciating humor. He had little of Sean's kind nature, however. She sensed a cruel streak in Rand, a feeling that she later found to be true.

Rand talked of many things, but never of his

origins. The only time he was short with her was when she inquired as to where he had come from.

"I'm from the state of Virginia, madam," he said curtly and would not discuss it further.

He made no overtures toward her that first night. They did not become lovers until after she employed him to manage the casino, several weeks later.

Business had recently increased so greatly that it was really becoming more than she could handle properly. She began thinking about employing Rand after that first supper in her quarters. She invited him twice more during the following weeks and was intrigued when he did not make any attempt to make love to her. And perhaps even a little piqued, she thought wryly.

There was a change in him, however, and one she approved of heartily. Although he still gambled heavily, usually winning, he slackened off on his drinking. During their suppers together, he arrived sober and drank little more than a glass or two of wine and an after-dinner brandy.

She invited him a fourth time. In this instance, while they waited for their supper to be served, she said, "I've noticed a change in you, Rand. You're not drinking so much. What is the reason for that? Not that I don't approve," she added hastily.

He looked startled, then smiled sardonically. "You are correct, madam. And I really can't give you a reasonable explanation. It just seemed— Well, I seem to have less cause to drink. And of course," he said gallantly, "it is not fitting to sup with a lady of your quality while besotted."

Sarah felt her color rise. "Thank you for the compliment, sir. But to be truthful, I wasn't fishing for a compliment. I have a good reason for asking."

"And what might that be, Sarah?"

"I need— Well, I need someone to manage my place. It's simply too much for me to manage on my own now."

"And you're offering this position to *me?*" He stared at her in open astonishment. "An outcast, a profligate, a drunkard, a gamester, some even say an out and out blackguard? You have taken leave of your senses, madam!"

"All those things matter not to me." Sarah waved his objections away. "I have watched you carefully, Rand Colter, and it is my belief you would do a fine job. Besides...." She laughed suddenly. "It might even save me money. The way you have of winning, you could in the end bankrupt me!" She looked at him steadily. "Will you accept the task, Rand?"

Rand scrubbed a hand down across his face. "Me, Randolph Colter, in charge of a gambling house! If they learn of that in Virginia!" He threw back his head and laughed loud and long. He sobered abruptly. "If it is your wish, madam."

"It is my wish, and I will pay you . . ."

"My compensation is not of any great consequence. We can settle the practical matters later." He became thoughtful. "You have a nice business here. You must have put much thought and care into it. I do have one suggestion, if I may?"

"If you accept the job, I am open to any suggestions."

"Your clientele is becoming too unwieldy, Sarah. Why should you not make it a private club, open to members only? I realize you manage well in keeping out the river riffraff. But if only members, carefully selected of course, were to dine and gamble here, I think it would become even more lucrative. There is something about a private club that appeals to the gentry. That way, they are always assured of associating with only their peers."

Sarah smiled and clapped her hands. "That's a grand idea, Rand!"

"And one other suggestion . . ." He hesitated. "I do not know why you selected Katie's as a name, but it lacks the touch of class necessary. If you'll forgive me, it has the sound of a bordello." He grimaced. "I would suggest some other name. . . ."

"No!" she said vehemently. "That I will *not* change. And my reasons are my own. Any other suggestions from you I am willing to listen to. But I will never change the name."

His features hardened for a moment, taking on a cruel cast. Then his full mouth curved in amusement. "Did anyone ever tell you, Sarah Moody, that you are a stubborn wench?"

"Someone has, yes," she said gravely. "Someone very special to me."

Rand Colter took over the management of Sarah's gambling house, and as she had been certain it would, the transition went smoothly. Rand stopped drinking almost entirely. Dressed in dove-colored breeches, a ruffled white shirt, a brocade waistcoat, and polished black boots, he made a charming host for the casino. He had an instinct for knowing when trouble was brewing. When a loser was on the verge of becoming a nuisance, or some male guest threatened to become obstreperous from too much

449

drink, Rand moved in smoothly and eased the troublemaker out, usually without giving offense. With the implementation of his Members Only suggestion, the number of patrons remained about the same, but Rand carefully weeded out the less affluent ones, and the club members taking their places had the wealth to weather heavy gambling losses.

One evening, two weeks after Rand took over the management, Sarah, before she supervised the last spin at the roulette table, invited him again to have a midnight supper in her quarters.

It was on this night that they became lovers, which had been Sarah's intention when extending the invitation.

Rand was a virile lover, not as polished and tender as Sean, but he gave Sarah intense pleasure. There was indeed, she discovered, a strong streak of cruelty in him, a driving, brutal force that would not be denied. Not that he hurt her in any way, but she was certain that if a woman flirted with Rand up to a certain point, then refused to submit to his desires, he could be cruel and hurting, and not above taking such a woman by force.

After it was over, Sarah said in a small voice, "I suppose you think I'm a wanton hussy, inviting you here for only one purpose."

"Not at all, my dear." Even in the dark, she sensed that his face wore that mocking grin. "You are my employer, and I would not dream of forcing my attentions on you. I was waiting for you to make the initial advance."

"But confident that I would!" she said tartly.

He laughed. "But of course, my dear. Of course!"

It was soon after that that they began riding out of the city on Sundays. On this particular Sunday in May, the weather was beautiful; it was not yet late enough in the year for the sultry, steaming summer heat. While Rand drove the team expertly, Sarah rode with her head back, breathing deeply of the fresh, flower-scented air.

Her thoughts were on Rand. Not with any particular fondness, for there were times when she was repelled by his coldness, his small cruelties, and occasional outright brutality.

That side of him had been starkly revealed earlier in the week. A waiter, a black man, had dropped a tray of champagne glasses, spilling the wine on several guests, right in the thick of the heavy play at the roulette table during Sarah's traditional last spin. A man too far in his cups had deliberately stuck out a foot, tripping the waiter. It was only by chance that Sarah had observed this.

Rand had said nothing at the time, but when the guests were all gone, the casino doors locked, he had sought out the waiter. Sarah, suspecting what might happen, had been hovering nearby.

In a cold rage, Rand had stepped up to the waiter and slapped him across the face. "That is for dropping the tray, nigger! If you do it again, you no longer work here, and I will horsewhip you in the bargain!"

"That's enough, Rand," Sarah had said, stepping in.

"What was that, madam?" Rand had whipped around. Even in a savage rage, Rand was in full control of himself, his face like a mask of stone.

"You are my manager, but I will tolerate no abuse of the employees. Is that understood?"

"Understood, madam," Rand had said icily. "By your leave, madam." Turning on his heel, he had left without another word. They had not shared an intimate moment since.

Sarah hadn't even been sure they would have their regular Sunday outing, until Rand drove up in the carriage at the usual time.

He had handed her into the carriage, apparently his old, charming, well-mannered self. The remarks they had exchanged during the ride had not touched upon the episode with the waiter.

Sarah was beginning to realize that she was having doubts about their personal relationship. In the first ardor of her newly aroused sensuality, she had plunged into pleasure, with no thought of anything else but to sate the long-starved needs of her body.

Now it occurred to her that she had subconsciously been thinking all week of a way to end it between them. Strangely enough, she doubted Rand would care much one way or another, although it would probably be a blow to his male pride if *she* made the first move to end it. Sarah was certain that he had other women from time to time. It was unlikely that such a charmer, with his sensual, amoral nature, would not respond to the advances of any beautiful woman. Rand was still an enigma to her and probably would always remain so. Yet she did wish him to continue as her manager. He was very good at it, and his assuming the task had removed a great load from her shoulders.

They were out of the city now. In a moment Rand turned the carriage east, toward the river, following a narrow, rutted lane. Sarah knew that he was heading for their favorite picnic spot. It was located on a grassy knoll, with the Mississippi flowing past within view.

Rand drew the carriage up beneath a huge cypress, dripping with moss. He got out and came around to give Sarah a hand down. He carried a blanket to spread for her underneath the cypress, then went to unhitch the horses and stake them out to graze. While he was doing that, Sarah arranged herself against the cypress trunk and gazed out on the wide sweep of river, quite muddy now and riding high from the spring thaw in the north.

As Sarah watched, she saw two keelboats making their way down the river, one following the other about thirty yards apart. Something stirred in her heart. Could they possibly be Jeb's boats? The distance was too great for her to be positive. But if it was Jeb, what did it matter?

"I've bloody well got to forget him! I saw that clearly for myself in St. Louis!"

"Forget who, my dear?" said Rand's amused voice.

She glanced up with a start, not realizing she had spoken aloud. She made a small gesture. "Nothing of importance. Just someone in my past I keep telling myself to forget."

"A man, of course." He sprawled on the blanket on his side, facing her with his chin propped on one hand.

"Why should you think that?" she retorted.

"What else would come into the mind of a lovely lady like yourself but the memory of a man?" Idly he smoothed her skirt down, his long, supple fingers holding her leg. Sarah suppressed a shiver. Even if

453

she was becoming disenchanted with Rand Colter, he still had the power to arouse her with a touch.

"Speaking of your past, dear Sarah," he went on, "you are something of a lady of mystery. You have told me little of yourself before you came to New Orleans. Only that you are London-born. Yet you have been in this country for three years. Many things must have happened to you in all that time."

She wondered how this urbane, cultured man would react to the telling of the things that had happened to her. She said coolly, "Speaking of that, Mr. Colter, I know nothing of you."

"Oh, it's a dark and bloody tale, most depressing. I am sure a lady such as yourself would swoon away at the telling."

Sarah sensed that he was laughing at her, and she was sure that anything he told her would be a falsehood anyway. She shrugged and said dourly, "You may keep your dark past a secret. It's all the same to me."

"Is it now?" he murmured.

His hand had crept up under her skirt, the tips of his fingers stroking her bare flesh. He leaned toward her, his full mouth descending on hers. It crossed her mind to deny him this time, yet his stroking fingers and the kiss set her blood to racing, and she sank back with a sigh.

Soon, he had her dress pushed up, and then was kneeling between her spread thighs. . . .

This time he was rough with her, his thrustings pounding her hard against the ground. Sarah cried out in protest and began to struggle. Grinning widely, he seized her by the shoulders and pinned her to the earth. He was rough, hurting, and showed no concern at all for her own rising passion. Under his continued assault, that flare of passion dwindled and died, and she suffered through the rest of it, lying inert beneath him, her face turned away.

When Rand had shuddered out his lust and rolled away to lie panting beside her, Sarah said caustically, "That was little more than rape, Rand."

It was a moment before he answered. "Perhaps it was. Should I add that to my long list of sins?"

"Was this a punishment for my chastisement of you the other evening?"

He gave a grunt of astonishment. "You are very perceptive, Sarah Moody, and continue to amaze me. Perhaps you are correct. Should I apologize, madam?"

"Apologies are not necessary." All the while Sarah had made no move to sit up and pull her dress down. Now she did. "Yet I must tell you this— What just happened brings to an end any intimate relationship between us."

"I suspected as much." Rand also sat up. "Does that mean that I am no longer in your employ?"

"Not at all," she said calmly. "I fail to see what one has to do with the other. You are a more than competent manager, and I am certain that, with your charm, you will have no difficulty at all in finding a new bed companion."

"You are a marvel, Sarah Moody!" He shouted laughter. "Indeed you are!" He arranged his clothing and got to his feet. "I will hitch up the team and return you to the village."

"Not before we have our picnic. I find that I am hungry. Will you fetch the hamper of food, Rand?"

He laughed again, staring down at her. Sarah remained perfectly composed. Shaking his head, Rand went to fetch the picnic hamper.

As they ate the cold chicken and shared the bottle of wine, Sarah chatted casually about the casino, talking of some new plans she had in mind. At first Rand was reserved, but shortly he seemed to adjust to their new relationship and entered into the conversation easily. They sat talking well into the afternoon.

Finally, Sarah hid a yawn behind her hand. "I'm drowsy. I think I'll nap for a little."

Rand made his last remark about what had happened earlier. "You're not afraid I'll try to rape you again, madam?"

"I believe, sir, that you would not find it so easy the second time. Should you ever try to force yourself on me again, you will regret it. That, I promise you!"

Rand said nothing. There was a slight smile on his lips and an admiring glint in his eyes. Then, with a nod, he got up and strolled down toward the river. Sarah stretched out on the blanket and went to sleep. She slept for well over an hour. When she awoke, she found Rand leaning against the cypress trunk, looking off into the distance. There was a somber, withdrawn air about him.

Sarah said, "Shall we start back now?"

He nodded. "I'll hitch up the team."

Sarah folded the blanket and carried it and the picnic hamper to the carriage. She climbed in without waiting for him to lend a hand. The ride back to New Orleans was conducted mainly in silence. Sarah sensed that Rand was not in a talkative mood, and she respected his silence.

Her own thoughts were gloomy. Was she doomed to be disappointed in every man she met? It was not that she had loved Rand Colter or even felt affection for him. But it seemed that all the men she came into contact with hurt her in some way or another, with the exception of Sean, of course. She sighed and dismissed it from her thoughts. She could manage without a man.

They were coming into town now. Rand uttered an exclamation and pointed. "There's a fire!"

Sarah sat up, staring in alarm at the billowing clouds of smoke. "It looks near my place! Dear God, I hope not!" New Orleanians lived in terror of fire, she had learned. The whole town had been leveled by flames a number of times in the past.

Rand whipped up the horses, and they went racing down the street. In a few minutes the carriage went around a corner, almost on two wheels, and Sarah leaned forward, straining to see.

She breathed a sigh of relief. "It's not mine, thank God!"

The building on fire was three doors down from hers. As they drew nearer, Sarah saw that a bucket brigade had been formed leading down to the river. But the building was too far gone; they would never save it.

At least with the bucket brigade formed, they would be able to keep the fire from spreading, so Katie's Casino was safe—this time.

30

Chapter Twenty-six

The minute the last of his cargo was unloaded, Jeb started his search for Sarah. Since he had no idea of how long the search might take, he dismissed the crew for a week. They deserved a rest and some relaxation after the battle with Brock's gang of pirates. Unlike most river boat owners, Jeb had no fears that they would not return at the end of the week. They would sample the delights of Front Street and The Swamp, and might still be drunk when they came back to the boats, but Jeb was confident they would show up. They valued their jobs too much to risk losing them.

He had no hint of where to look for Sarah. He began with the ladies shops and stores, asking the shopkeepers if they had a customer named Sarah Moody. He was greeted with puzzled shrugs. No one he talked to had ever heard of her. As the days passed, he even began stopping strangers on the street and asking his question. For four days he trudged the streets of New Orleans without success, returning each night weary of limb and body to his cabin on the keelboat.

Tim and Ezra Boggs were staying on the boats, keeping watch. Each night Tim asked eagerly, "Any word of Mistress Moody, Captain?"

"Not a single word, lad," Jeb said in his growing discouragement.

He was almost convinced that either Fortier had been mistaken about Sarah's destination, or she had come and gone. But even if she had been in New Orleans for only a short time, it seemed to him that *someone* must have struck up an acquaintance with her.

On the fifth, equally discouraging day, he found Hester Valance waiting for him when he returned to the keelboat. His spirits lightened at the sight of her. After he had told her of Sarah, Hester had been withdrawn, and they had not shared the cabin bed again. If he could not find Sarah, at least there was always Hester. However, he soon found that was not her purpose here.

He started to escort her to his cabin, calling to Ezra Boggs, "Ezra, prepare us a good supper."

"No, Jeb." Hester placed a hand on his arm. "That is not the reason I'm here. I think I have good news for you. But perhaps we should go into your cabin while we talk."

Inside the cabin, the door closed, he turned to her eagerly. "What news, Hester? You mean news of Sarah?"

"I believe so, but I am not sure. Last evening, I was invited to supper by a gentleman, at a place called Katie's Casino. It's a gambling house, but they also serve delicious suppers."

"Yes, I know. I have passed it almost every day, but since I had no reason to enter, I . . ." He broke off, bewildered. "But Hester, I fail to see what that has to do with Sarah!"

"Well . . ." She hesitated, her face grave. "The

place belongs to a woman. She appears in the casino only at the last play of the roulette wheel just before midnight closing. I did not learn her name, but from the description you gave of your Sarah Moody— Well, I have a strong feeling this woman is she."

Jeb was shaking his head. "No, no, it can't be! Sarah operating a gambling house? She wouldn't do that, not Sarah. She is too much a lady."

Hester studied him with amusement. "I fail to see what being a lady has to do with it. New Orleans, as well as most of the towns along the Mississippi provide gambling. Nobody looks askance on a woman in that profession. Now if she was operating a bordello, it might be a different matter. It strikes me, Jeb Hawkins, that that Puritan streak of yours is nagging you again."

"But where would she get the funds? She came to this country without a shilling!"

"That, I do not know." Hester shrugged. "Perhaps some . . ." She stopped abruptly.

"Some man, is that what you're thinking?" he said sharply. "Some man has provided the funds?"

"It's possible, I suppose. But why should that concern you? You told me you were going to look for her. This woman may be Sarah Moody, she may not. It's up to you to decide whether you wish to find out."

He turned away to stare out the cabin's one porthole. He took a cigar from his pocket and put it in his mouth. Then anger rose in him. Facing around, he said, "I cannot accept it, Hester. I don't believe you!"

"That, Jeb Hawkins, is your problem." Now he saw that she was growing angry. "I came here to help you.

461

But if you can only call me a liar, if that is all the gratitude I am to receive . . ." Weeping, she ran from the cabin.

"Hester, wait! I didn't mean to call you . . ." He took two short steps after her, then stopped. For the first time it occurred to him that Hester was in love with him, and almost anything he said to her now would be wrong.

With a sigh he turned back inside. He lit the cigar and went up on deck. He stood long at the bow of the boat, smoking and staring out at the town. He could hear the sounds of revelry coming from Front Street. Jeb never frequented the places there, but he had been inside a couple, looking for his men, and knew what went on in them. If the woman Hester had seen was Sarah, would her place be like those along Front Street?

With that thought, Jeb knew that he halfway believed Hester and that he was going to meet this woman. He had no choice. Throwing the cigar butt into the water, he went to his cabin to wash and put on clean clothes.

A half-hour later he was knocking on the door of Katie's Casino. From the outside it was unpretentious enough, looking more like a residence than a gambling house. Certainly he could hear no sounds of revelry from inside.

He knocked again, impatiently. The door swung open in his face, just enough to let a giant of a man step outside. "What for you knock, man?"

Jeb stared at him, angered by the man's arrogant manner. "I want to go inside."

"Jean not know you, man. This private place. Only

462

members allowed inside. No strangers. Mistress give orders."

Jeb was seething. He couldn't recall ever being so furious. The frustrations of the past week, the possibility that Sarah might be inside, and now to be denied entry by this great dullard! For a dangerous moment he was on the edge of trying to fight his way inside the place.

He took a steadying breath and said evenly, "Suppose you send word in to your mistress that Jeb Hawkins wishes an audience with her?"

The big man looked at him in disdain. "Mistress may not like."

"Damnation, man!" Jeb exploded. "Just take the message to her, will you?"

The giant considered for a moment, then nodded. "You wait here, man."

He went back inside, slamming the door in Jeb's face. Still angry, Jeb paced back and forth at the foot of the short steps. But in a surprisingly short time, Jean was back. More cordial now, he said, "Mistress will see you. Please to follow me."

Jeb trailed the man inside the building. There was a small entryway, curtained off from the main room. Jeb was astonished when he went down two steps into the casino. It was one large room, lit brilliantly by candle chandeliers, and there were at least a hundred people at the gaming tables. Yet it was an orderly, very quiet crowd. Jeb noticed several women among the group, but it was clear they were not doxies there to serve drinks and entertain the men; they were obviously ladies of quality, and they were gambling right along with the men. This was certainly no ordinary place. The people he saw were all of the gentry, stylishly dressed and coiffured, many of the women glittering with expensive jewelry.

Momentarily dazzled by such splendor, Jeb had slowed his step. Suddenly he noticed a handsome dandy of a man, with wavy brown hair and sardonic black eyes, standing off to one side, studying him with a dark scowl.

Then Jean, several steps ahead, stopped and called back, "Man, why you tarrying? Mistress waiting."

Jeb hastened to catch up to him and followed the big man into a curtained alcove, then up steep stairs against one wall. On the second floor, the giant started down the hall. But as their footsteps sounded on the wooden floor, a door was flung open, and Sarah came rushing out.

"Jeb!" She ran a few steps toward him, then stopped.

Jeb also came to a halt. It was Sarah right enough, but a Sarah he had never seen before. She had attained the full bloom of womanhood now and was so lovely that his breath caught in his throat. She had been dressed in fine clothes that afternoon on the landing in St. Louis, but now she wore a dress that had to have cost a tidy sum, and back then her figure had been gaunted by the winter in the wilderness. Now, she had filled out, her body ripe and voluptuous, her breasts mounded temptingly above the low bodice of her dress.

Jeb supposed he had been expecting to see a Sarah showing signs of a debauched life. Instead, she looked as fresh and innocent as the first time he had seen her. Despite the fact that he knew beyond a doubt that this was Sarah Moody, he said, "Sarah? Is it really you?"

Sarah's heart was pounding. Jeb was as handsome as ever, and just the sight of him was enough to send the blood rushing through her body. She laughed nervously. "Yes, Jeb, it's me." She turned to Jean. "You may go, Jean. Go out to the kitchen and tell them to prepare a supper for two and send it up to my rooms."

The big man ducked his head. "Yes, mistress."

Sarah stepped close to place her hand lightly on Jeb's arm. She was seized by a temptation to kiss him, yet there was a strange reserve about him that warned her off. "Come in, Jeb."

Jeb followed Sarah into her rooms. As she closed the door, he assumed that stance she remembered so well, feet planted wide apart, as though braced against the roll of the sea, his hands locked together behind his back. He slowly looked around the room, eyes widening at the fine furnishings.

Finally his eyes came to rest on her. His expression was unreadable. "You have done very well for yourself, Sarah."

"Yes, fortune has been good to me." She laughed, and again it was a nervous sound. "Surely you would not begrudge me, after all the travails I have been through?"

"It all depends on . . ." He bit the words off, taking a cigar from his pocket.

Sarah hurried to fetch a candle. As he bent his head to light the cigar, she wanted to reach out and stroke his hair. After all this time, when she had given up any thought of ever seeing him again, he had come to her! Sarah knew she was acting like a silly schoolgirl, but she couldn't seem to help herself.

She said brightly, "Would you like a brandy, Jeb?"

He blew smoke, his gaze intent on her. He shook his head. "Not just now. Sarah, I learned you were in St. Louis a year back, at the same time my boats were docked there. Why didn't you come and let me know you were there? I thought that you and this Flanagan fellow had gone away together, for good."

Happy as she was to see Jeb, Sarah found herself reacting angrily to his slightly accusing tone. She said tightly, "Sean Flanagan is dead."

"I know. Fortier told me. I'm sorry about that. . . ."

"And you know why he is dead, Jeb? Giles Brock sold me as a slave to the Pawnee. Sean tracked me down. For almost a year he looked for me. When he did find me, in rescuing me, he took an arrow in the back and died out there on the prairie. And you, who only an hour before I was taken had told me you loved me, you did not search for me at all!"

"Sarah, be reasonable." He gestured. "I had no idea such a thing had happened to you. I simply thought you had decided in favor of Flanagan and gone off with him. If I had known of your fate, I would have searched to the ends of the earth for you."

Sarah looked into his face for a long time. Finally she sighed and gave a slight shrug. "Well, it's all behind me now."

"Not so. You still have not answered my question. Why didn't you seek me out in St. Louis?"

"I did. I came down to the landing. . . ."

He said sharply, "I didn't see you! Why didn't you make your presence known to me?"

"But I saw *you*," she said just as sharply. "I saw you with a woman, a yellow-haired woman. It was

466

clear she was very close to you, and you looked quite happy with her."

Jeb looked puzzled for a long moment. Then he smiled, shrugging. "Oh, that was just Hester. Hester Valance."

"*Just* Hester? What is she then, your doxie?"

He made an angry sound. "Hester is not a doxie. She is every inch a lady."

"But you were bedding her, weren't you? Probably still are."

"Sarah, what does that matter?" Then he nodded. "To be honest, yes. After all, was I expected to remain celibate all this time?"

"I didn't know what I expected. But you certainly couldn't have expected me to stride boldly up to you, while standing there with another woman on your arm. Suppose she had been your wife? I had no way of knowing. It would have been embarrassing for both of us." She became angry and made her voice jeering. "Jebadiah Hawkins, the lordly ship's master, with the strictest morals, taking a woman into his bed without wedding her! I thought you only did that to women captured off the streets of London, and then you take them by force."

"Sarah, I have tried to make amends for that. And what right have you to assume such a righteous attitude? Did you not share your bed with this Irish fellow?"

"Yes, I did!" She clenched her fists, furious now. "Not only Sean, who was at least a gentleman about it, but Giles Brock and Rhys Pommet both used me cruelly, and then sold me to a Pawnee chief as his wife, who took me by force night after night. Does that not disgust you, Jeb Hawkins?"

"No, it does not disgust me, Sarah. You are not to be blamed for that," he said slowly. "It moves me to pity. . . ." He reached out a hand to her.

Sarah slapped his hand away, eyes flashing. "I do not want your damned pity! All I ever wanted from you was love, not your bloody pity!"

"I didn't mean it in that manner. . . ." His voice hardened. "It would seem that this life here has coarsened you. Never before have I heard you employ such foul language."

"Foul language! 'Tis nothing to what *I* have heard." She laughed bitterly. "And—this life, as you call it, has not hardened me, not in the way you mean."

"Speaking of your gambling house, how did you get the funds to start it? It must have cost a great deal."

"It did, yes. It strikes me it's none of your affair where I got the funds, but I will tell you. It came from Sean Flanagan. Sean left word with Jacques Fortier that if he died, all his worldly goods would come to me. Those worldly goods were considerable. I shall always be grateful to him."

"Indeed I should think you would be. But that is of no matter. I am pleased by your good fortune. However, why should you invest it in such a place as this?"

"And why should I not, pray?"

"This is not the proper place for a lady such as yourself to be operating."

"You mean, because gambling is a sin?"

"Well— Yes." He shifted his feet uncomfortably. The Bible speaks against it."

"Does it indeed? Strange, is it not, that every river

town has gambling of some form or another. Do not your boatmen gamble?"

"Of course they do! They also frequent bordellos. That is not what I'm talking about. It is just that a woman, a lady especially, should not be the mistress of a place such as this!"

"What does the Bible suggest that a woman alone, in a strange country, and after being used most foully, should do to earn a livelihood? How would you suggest that I should have invested Sean's money?"

"A dressmaking shop, perhaps. . . ."

"Dressmaking shop!" Sarah laughed in derision. "New Orleans is the most sophisticated town along the Mississippi, yet do you have any conception of just how many ladies have their garments made in shops? A mere handful. I would have starved long since. Of course . . ." Furious beyond reason now, purposely taunting him, she said, "Of course, there is another profession I could have taken up. You mentioned it a moment ago, I believe. It was the reason Brock's hirelings seized me in London. I was to serve as a doxie for King George's Redcoats and would probably have done so had not Brock seized the *North Star*. God knows I have had enough experience these three years past. In fact, not too long back, a besotted patron said he thought that a profession befitting me. Do you think that, Jeb? If I had used Sean's funds to open a bordello, would you then have felt more at ease visiting me?"

Jeb's face flushed a dark red. He lashed out, striking her across the cheek. Sarah reeled back a few steps, her eyes hard and bright.

"The Sarah Moody I once knew would never have

said something like that," Jeb said in a grating voice. "You *have* changed."

"Of course I've changed, you bloody idiot! Can't you realize that?" Her eyes were wild, her voice savage. "But that still doesn't mean that I'm a woman of sin, a strumpet, as you seem to regard me!"

She made a fetching sight—her color high, eyes flashing. Into his memory flooded the vision of loveliness he had seen that afternoon on the keelboat, Sarah naked and in bed with him. The vivid memory inflamed his senses, and he felt blood engorge his manhood. It pushed him beyond caution, beyond any thought of decorum.

"If I do so regard you, madam, then so you must be! Shall we see?"

He moved toward her. The sight of his burning eyes, his sensual mouth curling in passion, sent Sarah backing away from him. She was a little frightened and still angry, yet she could not deny that her own senses were stirred. A languor stole over her, and she felt a warm heaviness in her body. However, she was determined that he would not have her, not this way, not in brutal, unloving lust.

Jeb hooked strong fingers in her low bodice and roughly ripped it all the way down the front. Her breasts fell free, white and full and lovely, the nipples like budding roses.

Breathing heavily, Jeb seized the torn edges of her gown and ripped it from her. Except for shoes, stockings, and garters, she stood fully exposed to his gaze. In a thick voice, he said, "Where is your boudoir, Mistress Moody?"

Sarah felt herself trembling, but stood her ground. "Jeb! I will not submit to you in this manner!"

"By the Lord Jehovah, you will, madam! You have stood here taunting me, playing the wanton, until I am beyond listening to your pleas for mercy!"

"I'm not pleading, damn you! I'm . . ."

Without another word, he swept her up in his arms and strode into the other room, where he dropped her unceremoniously onto the four-poster bed. Sarah attempted to rise, but Jeb pushed her back roughly. "Do not provoke me further, Sarah!"

Abruptly, she stopped struggling, lying quiet and still.

Jeb eyed her suspiciously for a moment, then stood back to remove his clothes.

Sarah said in a dull voice, "Why should I bother to fight you for my honor? You took care of any honor I might have had on board the *North Star*. And since then others have soiled me even more. You took me by force then. Why should a second time trouble me? If you name me for a strumpet because I have managed to survive travails that most women would have quailed away from, then have your way with me. And damn you forever after!"

Jeb stopped his undressing and stared at her with a stunned expression.

"Go ahead, Jeb Hawkins! Rape me! Why should you hesitate now? Is it because of the luxury of my surroundings? You seem to think that I raised myself to this station by whoring my way, so do not let that stop you."

There was a look of utter shock on his face now. "Dear God, what am I doing?" he said in a stricken whisper. He already had one leg out of his breeches. Quickly he stepped back into them and straightened his disarranged clothing.

"My apologies, madam," he said stiffly. "I will respect your wishes, and you need not concern yourself about me ever again. You will see me no more."

Jeb turned on his heel and left the room without looking back. He passed through the outer door and into the hall. As he turned toward the stairs, he saw the handsome dandy he'd glimpsed downstairs rushing toward him. The man was carrying a pistol and was moving so rapidly he was barely able to stop before colliding with Jeb.

In an icy voice, the dandy asked, "What is going on up here? I thought I heard screaming. Is Sarah . . ."

In a tone equally cold, Jeb said, "Be at ease, fellow. Your Mistress Moody has come to no harm, I assure you."

"How do I know that? You just back up into her rooms until I learn for myself."

He started to bring the pistol up. The rage that had been boiling in Jeb the last hour, erupted. He took one swift step and brought the edge of his work-toughened hand down across the dandy's wrist. The pistol clattered to the floor. Jeb did not stop with that. He clubbed the man across the face with his fist, knocking him sprawling against the wall. Without sparing him another glance, Jeb strode on. He moved more cautiously now, having no idea what he might be confronted with downstairs.

Yet, once down the stairs and through the curtain into the main casino, he found nothing amiss. Play at the tables was continuing without interruption. He strode on, pushing aside the curtains into the entryway. The hulking giant called Jean was not there. Jeb pushed open the door and went outside.

After Jeb stormed out, Sarah sat for several minutes on the bed. She was still coldly angry, and yet, strangely, she also felt humiliated by the way he had left her. And his last words echoed in her mind: "You will see me no more."

A sense of loss crept over her. She had never been torn by such conflicting emotions: anger at the growing contempt in Jeb's manner as they had talked, and now this feeling of a great loss. There was no use lying to herself. Despite his open contempt for her and the near-rape, she loved him; she would always love him. It was illogical. Why should she love a man who had treated her so?

She laughed suddenly. There was seldom any logic to love; she should know that by now. What reason had she ever given Sean to love her?

Well, to bloody hell with Jeb Hawkins! Love him or not, she could manage well enough without him. She had done so in the past and would do so again. Time would take care of Jeb Hawkins, as it did all things, covering over the hurt until it was just a memory, painful perhaps, but something she could live with.

Getting out of bed, she threw a dressing gown around her, went through the sitting room, and out into the hall. There, she found Rand sitting slumped against the wall. He raised his head and gave her a dazed look. There was a bleeding cut on his cheek.

"Rand, what on earth happened to you?" She reached down a hand to help him up.

Rand shook his head and smiled wryly, wincing with pain. "I am not sure, Sarah. I thought I heard you screaming. I came hurrying up and met some bearded madman just coming out of your rooms. I

31

held a pistol on him. He knocked the pistol out of my hand, then sent me crashing to the floor. He hit me hard enough to stun an ox!"

So Jeb hadn't been all that calm and collected, Sarah thought; or he wouldn't have vented his ire on Rand! But just as quickly as that small thrill of triumph excited her, it passed, for Jeb was gone from her life for good.

She said, "You're not badly hurt, Rand?"

"Oh, no, I will survive. With a sore face and an aching skull, but I will survive, madam. I have suffered worse."

"Then go downstairs and close up the casino for the evening."

"Sarah, whatever are you saying?" He stared at her in dismay. "It's only ten o'clock!"

"At this moment, I have no concern for the time. Just go down and turn everybody out, the help as well. I want everybody out as soon as possible."

"Sarah, you can't do this! You've never done this before, and they're expecting you down for the last play. You'll offend them, and many may not come back."

"I don't care! I want everybody out, so I can be alone."

"Including me, Sarah?" he asked softly.

"Including you!" Then she relented her harsh manner. "I'm sorry, Rand. I don't mean to sound so harsh. But I've had a bad experience, and I need to be alone. Please?"

"If that is your wish, madam. This experience you speak of— Would you care to tell me of it? This bearded fellow, did he do something to offend you? If he did, I will seek him out and challenge him!"

"No, Rand. That is exactly what I do not want. I'll be all right on the morrow. I'll put it all behind me."

Rand stared at her curiously, opened his mouth to speak, then changed his mind. "Good night then, madam. Sleep well."

Sarah restrained a bitter laugh. It was doubtful she would sleep well this night, or for several to come!

At the head of the stairs Rand stepped aside for Jean, who was carrying two trays of food.

Sarah started to tell him to take the trays back to the kitchen. But there was no need to cause more gossip than necessary among the employees. Rand she could trust to be close-mouthed, but if it became bruited about that the mistress had a gentleman in her rooms, and he had left without remaining for supper, she would be the subject of secretive laughter.

She held the door open for Jean, and he placed the covered trays on the table. Sarah said, "That will be all, Jean. For reasons I will not explain, we are closing early tonight. You may go home now."

Jean simply nodded, his broad face showing no more expression than usual. Sarah closed the door after him, then went straight to the liquor cabinet and poured a generous dollop of brandy. She drank it, welcoming the warmth in her belly and the easing of tension that soon followed.

Her anger had cooled now, yet she was weighed with disappointment over Jeb's churlish behavior. It had never once entered her mind that he would disapprove so much of her running a gambling establishment, although, given his Puritan conscience, she should have anticipated such a reaction.

Pouring more brandy, Sarah paced the sitting room, warming the brandy glass between her hands, taking a sip from time to time. She had been sure she had put Jeb Hawkins out of her mind for good, yet his appearance tonight had stirred her passions anew. Even during the height of their quarrel, while he flailed at her with his tongue, even when she lay naked on the bed tensed against his expected assault—her treacherous body had wanted him. She closed her eyes, remembering that hour of tumultuous, overwhelming passion on board his keelboat. Sarah knew she would never experience that much passion for any other man, and would never be able to respond with all her body and soul to love again. Although she had thoroughly enjoyed those times she had shared Sean's buffalo robes, it had not been the same as with Jeb. So, if not with Sean Flanagan, who had loved her, who then?

Sarah realized that she would have to reconcile herself to these facts, bitter though they might be.

She stumbled suddenly, almost falling over the divan. She had drunk too much brandy and had not eaten since midday.

Putting aside the brandy glass, she uncovered one of the trays and took a few bites of a chicken leg. Then, in a sudden burst of emotion, she flung the chicken leg from her, unheeding that it struck the wall and fell to the floor. The tears that she had choked back all evening came now in a flood. She sank down on the divan and wept, tears of grief and loss and pain.

Chapter Twenty-seven

For the first time in his life Jeb Hawkins was drinking in a waterfront tavern. Not just drinking, but well on his way to getting drunk. He had turned into the first place he'd come to on Front Street, a crude wooden structure with a hand-lettered sign hanging crookedly over the front—Scarface Jack's.

The man behind the bar—a wooden, splintered plank resting on barrels, with a sailcloth curtain tacked across the front—was aptly named. At some time past he had been in a saber fight, and a terrible scar began at the hairline over his left eye, which was covered by a black eye patch, and extended down to his jawbone. He was one of the most villainous-looking men Jeb had ever seen. The place was packed to the walls. Jeb hadn't bothered to check and see if any of his own men were there. In his present mood, he didn't care if they saw him drinking. With shouting, laughter, and drunken singing, the noise level was such that Jeb had to lean across the plank bar and shout in Scarface Jack's ear, "A bottle of brandy."

"Got no brandy, mate. Too fine a drink for the likes of them that come in here. Ale I got, and rum aplenty. That don't suit your fancy, you'll have to go some other place than mine."

"A bottle of rum, then."

Scarface Jack reached under the plank bar and

brought up a bottle of dark rum. He plunked it down and didn't let go of the neck of the bottle until Jeb had dumped enough coins on the plank to satisfy him.

Jeb asked, "How about a glass?"

"A glass, is it? Now ain't you the fine gentleman!" The man laughed coarsely. "You want a glass, go some place else. No glasses here. I do that, mate, these river rats'll be wanting them washed next!"

There were no tables in the long room, only more planks on barrels. Even the seats were halved-out barrels with planks across them. Men sat elbow to elbow drinking. Jeb finally found a place for himself at the far end of one plank in the back. He sat down, fired a cigar from the sputtering candle, then took a stiff drink. He shuddered, making a face. The rum had a horrible taste.

"Grand rum, ain't it?" the man next to him said.

Jeb ignored the friendly overture, deliberately turning his face away. The man snarled an oath and turned to the man on his right. Jeb took another strong pull, feeling the raw liquor grab at his guts.

Drawing on the cigar to dull the taste of the rum, Jeb finally turned his thoughts to Sarah. How could she stoop so low as to operate a gambling house? How could the refined lady's maid he'd first seen on board the *North Star* have fallen so far? He well knew that females, without husband or kin, had a rough time of it in this frontier country, but surely she could have found a more decent means of earning her living!

He remembered what she and Jacques Fortier had told him of those long months of Indian slavery and the sexual abuse by Brock and Pommet. . . .

He smashed a fist hard on the plank. By the Lord Jehovah, he had forgotten to tell Sarah that Brock and Pommet had at long last paid for their crimes against her and against humanity. She would have been pleased by that bit of news. Sarah Moody was a proud, independent and, yes, stubborn woman. She liked to make her own way and was rightly proud of her ability to survive hardship and adversity. And to be abused by villains such as Brock and Pommet and not be able to avenge herself on them must be very frustrating.

Jeb paused with the rum bottle halfway to his mouth. To survive, yes, Sarah had that ability. How many women would have managed to survive what she had these past three years and still retain their pride and dignity, and become even more beautiful for it?

That, of course, was what she had been trying to explain to him tonight.

What had he done in return? He had acted like an overfastidious female lifting her skirts to tiptoe around a steaming pile of ordure; he had ranted on like some Bible-thumping fanatic; and then he had been on the verge of raping her! God, what she must think of him! Only a few days back, he had been congratulating himself on the manner in which he had adapted to the ways of this new country and, in the doing, had managed to survive, which was nothing more than Sarah had done. Her trials had been much more trying than his.

Jeb looked deep inside himself, searching his soul, and was sickened by what he saw. His behavior toward Sarah was inexcusable, he realized that now. He loved Sarah, loved her desperately. Seeing her tonight had brought that fact painfully home to him, even in his childish fit of anger. There would never be another woman that he could love with the same passion as Sarah.

He sat up, his mind racing. Was it too late to make amends? Could she find it in her heart to forgive him? Could they put that bitter exchange of mutual recriminations behind them and start afresh? Sarah had been glad to see him. Now that his anger had dissipated, Jeb knew that. Her dear face had lit up with love at the sight of him.

Even if it was too late, Jeb knew that he had to make the effort. If he did not, he would never be able to forgive himself. He pushed the half-empty rum bottle over to the man who had spoken to him earlier.

"Here, friend. Drink hearty," he said, grinning foolishly. The man looked at him with mouth agape.

Jeb got to his feet and staggered slightly, catching at the plank for support. He was intoxicated. Unaccustomed to drinking that much so quickly, the rum had taken a hold on him. Shaking his head to clear it, Jeb oriented himself, spied the entrance, and made for it, trying to walk straight. Hopefully, the fresh air would clear away the rum fumes.

At another plank table near the front, a man had been watching Jeb from the moment Hawkins had entered Scarface Jack's. Giles Brock had been sitting there for some little time, hunched over a tankard of ale, all he could afford, his mood black as sin.

He had reached the pirate camp too late. Others had been there before him and had taken all the horses, pistols, balls, and powder. Even what clothes Brock had left in his cabin were gone. The fine clothes he had worn on the keelboat were torn and had shrunk from immersion in the river. Scavenging like a hungry rat, he had been able to find only a few scraps of food.

Finally, out of desperation, Brock perched on a tree branch extending out over the trail wandering down to New Orleans. With a short length of wood in his hands, he perched there until a lone rider passed beneath the tree. Brock killed him with one blow from the chunk of wood, then dragged him off the trail into the bushes and stripped him of his clothing. The dead man's clothes were the rough, serviceable garments of the river boat men and were too large for Brock. But they covered his body, and Brock now had a pistol, with powder and ball pouch, a bundle of food, and, most important of all, the horse.

With only one horse it took Brock much longer than he had anticipated to ride to New Orleans. He had just arrived in the city this very night and had stopped in this riverfront tavern to rest and gnaw on a chunk of bread and drink a tankard of ale, paid for by the coins he had found in his victim's pockets. The dead man's greatcoat, which Brock now wore, concealed the pistol stuck in his belt.

Sure that Jeb Hawkins had already unloaded his cargo and headed back upriver, Brock had been sunk in gloom when he glanced up and saw Hawkins stride into the tavern. Brock's first fear was of being recognized. He ducked his head and pulled the dirty cap down over his forehead. What with a week's growth of beard and the rough clothing, and Hawkins undoubtedly believing him dead, perhaps fortune would favor him. As Hawkins stopped at the plank bar, Brock stole a look from under the cap, watching as Hawkins ordered a bottle of rum and made his way to the back without a single look around.

It struck him that Hawkins was acting strangely; his face wore a dark scowl of anger. Brock did not bother to question his good fortune at finding the keelboat captain still in New Orleans. The murderous rage that had burned in him for over a week renewed itself with the sight of his nemesis, and he took great pleasure in trying to scheme the best way to ambush Hawkins. Since Hawkins seemed to be drinking the rum at a great rate, perhaps he would become besotted and make everything easy. From time to time, Brock stole a glance down the room and was fortunate to be looking at Hawkins when the man stood up suddenly, staggering with drink, then started toward the front. For a panic-stricken moment, Brock was positive that Hawkins was coming straight for him, that he had been recognized. But Hawkins walked right past and on outside.

Brock waited for a full minute, then stood up and sidled out. The only lights in the street outside came from the open doors of the taverns, and the street was mostly pockets of darkness. Brock looked north first. When he didn't see his man, Brock feared that he had waited too long. Then he looked south down the street just in time to see Hawkins striding past a lighted doorway, about fifty yards distant. Brock slunk after him, hurrying past the splashes of light from the doorways and keeping as much to the dark spots as possible.

He didn't want to shoot Hawkins here. With so many taverns about, the shot might be heard. But soon, they were out of the tavern section, and the street grew darker. Brock drew the pistol from his belt, stopped long enough to put in powder and ball, then hurried to catch up, the pistol held cocked in his hand. Moving as quietly as possible, he began gaining on Hawkins. Not once had the man looked around.

Something about Hawkins' behavior puzzled Brock. Where was he going? There seemed to be a determined purpose about him. Did he have quarters on some street along here and was headed for bed? That did not strike Brock as likely. He knew that Hawkins had a fine cabin on his passenger keelboat, and rumor had it that he always slept there. Of course, he could be visiting some wench.

That must be it!

Grinning to himself with glee, Brock dropped back a little. Now that would be the best time to kill Master Hawkins—in bed with a wench, his breeches down. Brock laughed, covering his mouth with one hand to stifle the sound. He decided to wait a little longer and see if his hunch was correct.

Suddenly Jeb Hawkins turned in before a large, two-story house, mounting the short steps. Brock slipped behind a concealing tree. The house was dark, except for a dim candle flicker showing through a crack in the curtains in an upstairs room.

He could hear Hawkins pounding on the door. Once he shouted something, something Brock couldn't quite make out. Brock was dismayed now, certain that he had missed his best chance. He hadn't expected such a fine house as this. Even if Hawkins had wenching in mind, there was sure to be more than one person inside a house this size. It was too big a risk to take—to sneak up and shoot Hawkins in the back now. Brock muttered an oath under his breath; he would have to wait until Hawkins was finished with his business here and came outside again.

Now Brock saw a light moving downstairs, approaching the front door. Once again, Hawkins shouted something and pounded on the door.

The door swung open, and a woman stood framed in the doorway, a candle held near her face.

Brock literally staggered from shock. It couldn't be! It was not possible!

Yet it was. Without a doubt the woman in the doorway was Sarah Moody!

By all the devils in hell, was he never to be rid of this pair?

Brock leaned weakly against the tree trunk and watched Sarah Moody and Jeb Hawkins go inside, the door closing after them.

When Sarah heard the pounding on the door, she had been sitting on the divan for what seemed hours, staring at nothing, thinking of nothing. Her head ached from the emotional upset and all the brandy she had drunk. On first hearing the pounding, she thought it was an extension of the throbbing in her head. Then, when she finally identified the sound, she sat for several minutes, debating whether or not to answer the door.

The pounding continued, and then she heard a voice shouting. Thinking that something might be amiss, she picked up the candle, drew the dressing gown around her, and went downstairs.

It wasn't until she was in the entryway that she recognized the voice as Jeb's. A thrill of happiness went through her. Then she forced herself to be calm and said coldly, "What do you want, Jeb Hawkins? I thought we'd said it all?"

"Sarah—I wouldn't blame you for not seeing me." Even through the thick door, Sarah could hear the note of pleading in his voice. "But please let me in. I need to talk to you. I swear by the Lord Jehovah that no bitter words will come from me!"

Sarah hesitated only a moment, then threw back the bolt and stepped into the doorway, the candle held by her face. "Can you give me one reason why I should talk to you again, sir?"

"Because I love you, Sarah. And I want to plead for your forgiveness, if you can find it in your heart," he said wretchedly.

Already she felt herself softening inside. Still keeping her voice cold, Sarah said, "Very well. I will talk to you. But forgiveness will come hard."

She stood back for him to enter and wrinkled her nose at the rum fumes coming from him. "You're drunk, Jeb!"

"Not drunk, Sarah. Not now. I was on my way to getting drunk when sanity finally returned to me."

Sarah slammed and bolted the door. As she turned back, Jeb took her hand.

"Sarah, I was wrong. I acted like the lowest cad. . . ."

"Not here. We had better talk upstairs."

Holding the candle high, she led the way upstairs. But she was careful to leave the door to the sitting room standing wide.

She faced him determinedly. "Now, sir, what reason could you have for this sudden change of heart?"

. Jeb took a deep breath, then said quietly, "Because

I realized a number of things. You *have* changed, Sarah, I will not deny that, just as you did not. You have managed to survive the Lord knows what and come through a better woman for it. When I was in here earlier, I reverted to being Captain Jeb Hawkins of the *North Star*. In those days, I would have laughed if someone told me I would some day become captain of a lowly keelboat, and I would not have believed it if I also had been told of the things I had to do to get where I am. Tonight, with you, I was the old Jeb Hawkins, and I even tried to take you by force as I did then. But I know now that I am *not* that Jeb Hawkins, not any longer. What has happened to you, what has happened to me, these past three years has made us what we are right *now*, and that is the important thing. So. . . ." His face reflected both misery and yearning. "Can you forget those terrible things I said? Can you forgive me?"

Sarah looked at him steadily, her heart hammering. An almost forgotten hope returned, causing her to feel a bittersweet pain. She said, "And that is all?"

"Except for one thing, the most important of all. I love you, Sarah. I love you with everything there is in me to love."

"Oh, Jeb darling. Of course I forgive you! And I love you, you don't know now much!"

She ran into his arms. Jeb held her gently, smoothing her hair, making crooning sounds of love, while she clung to him, as if in fear that they would be torn apart again.

After a moment, Sarah raised her head from his shoulder. Her face was wet with tears, yet her voice was sharp as she said, "But that does not mean that I will become your slave, as do many women to their men. I have had enough of that. I will be my own woman!"

Jeb laughed, the old rumbling laughter. "I wouldn't expect anything else of you, darling Sarah. I want no slavey, but a woman of independence. And that, you most certainly are."

His laughter died, and he kissed her. Sarah's response was immediate and fierce. She clung to him, fingers digging into his back. Still locked together, they moved toward the bedroom. There, Sarah stood back. She said breathlessly, "Since we are about to finish what you started, I need not dress," and shrugged out of the dressing gown, letting it fall around her feet.

Jeb sucked in his breath, his hungry gaze raking over her. Sarah stood proudly; she could feel his eyes on her almost like the touch of his hands.

Sarah crossed to the bed. Jeb quickly undressed and went to her. They made slow, tender, yet ardent love, until the urgency of their bodies demanded that they become one. Then it was a swift and almost savage mating, their long-denied love for each other consummated at last. As he took her, Jeb murmured endearments. Sarah, swept up by mindless passion, heard only the murmur of his voice, yet she had no need to understand the words. Their meaning was clear.

As the maelstrom of their passion reached a mutual peak, Sarah rose to meet him, clinging desperately and crying out, "Dear Jeb, darling Jeb! I love you!"

Giles Brock stood under the tree in a dazed state for a long time, not moving, scarcely thinking. Then, slowly, an idea sprouted in his mind. As it grew and grew, he grinned from ear to ear.

487

Fire, that was the answer! Roast them both alive in the flames of hell. It would be their just desserts. Burn them to a cinder, yes, burn them to a cinder. Then never again would he be plagued by Master Jeb Hawkins and Mistress Sarah Moody!

Now to put the plan into action. First, he would need the means to put the torch to the building. He began to run toward the house, greatcoat flapping around his ankles. He veered down the side. The kitchen, yes, the kitchen. Here in this hot climate the kitchen was always in a separate building, so the cooking fires would not heat up the main house.

He rounded the corner, and there it was, a small structure set back a few yards. The door was open, and Brock could even see a faint glow of flames from inside.

With no thought of caution he ran inside and toward the huge fireplace. A small figure by the fire started up from a doze. A black boy, no doubt left here all night to keep the fire stoked up for the morning.

The boy cried out in fright, "Who are you, sar? I has orders not to let anybody . . ."

In a single, swift motion, Brock drew the pistol from his waist and slashed the boy alongside the head. He crumpled in a heap on the stone hearth. Brock stood over him for a moment, lips drawn back in a silent snarl. When the boy made no further sound or movement, Brock looked wildly around the room, seeking something he could use to accomplish his purpose. For once, fate was with him. Propped in one corner was an unlit torch, a long stick with a pitch-soaked cloth wrapped around one end. Snatching it up, Brock stuck it into the flames. When it caught fire, he ran out of the kitchen, trying to muffle the laughter which threatened to engulf him.

At the corner of the main house, he bent down, holding the torch to the wooden foundation until the beams caught fire. He no longer could contain his laughter. It swelled out of him; a wild hooting that he did not recognize as coming from his own mouth. He hurried to the next corner, and the next. . . .

Beside Jeb, Sarah stirred from a light slumber and opened her eyes. Instantly she recalled the events of the past hour and felt across the bed. Yes, Jeb was there. It had not been a dream. A small sigh of contentment escaped her. She felt surrounded, protected by happiness.

A sound from below broke through her pleasant reverie. Sarah was certain she had heard someone calling her name. Raising herself up on one elbow, she touched Jeb's arm.

"Jeb?"

He awoke with a start. "Yes, love, what is it?"

"I heard something downstairs. There— There it is again! Did you hear it?"

Jeb coughed and rubbed at his eyes. "I heard something, yes. I'd better see what it is."

He rolled off the bed and began throwing on his clothes by the light of the guttering candle in the sitting room. Sarah got out of bed after him, picking up her dressing gown from the floor.

Jeb leaned over and gently kissed her cheek. "Sarah, you'd better stay up here while I look. It could be some ruffian from Front Street ransacking your house."

"No, I'm going with you!"

"Well, I was warned." He laughed. "A woman of independence."

"But I think whoever it is is calling my name, darling."

With Jeb carrying a lighted candle, they hurried out into the hall. At the top of the stairs, he slowed, sniffing. "Do you smell smoke?"

Before she could answer, a weak voice called from below, "Mistress Moody?"

"That's Eli, the kitchen boy!" Sarah said, hurrying down the stairs.

They found the kitchen boy where he had fallen trying to make it up the stairs. The side of his face was bloody. Sarah knelt beside him. "Eli, what happened to you?"

"Mistress . . ." His eyes opened. "A man—A madman, he busts into the kitchen and hits me with his pistol. Now he outside, setting fire to the house!"

As if to verify his words, a current of air carried the acrid smell of burning wood and cloth to Sarah's nostrils. "Oh, dear God!" she cried.

"We have to get out of here," Jeb said. "This place will go up fast! Sarah, stay close to me." Jeb scooped Eli up in his arms and headed for the front door. He called back, "Come along, Sarah!"

Sarah started after him, then stopped. All her valuables—jewelry, money, letters of credit—were in a small strongbox upstairs. If the house burned, and the strongbox with it, she would be destitute. She hesitated in indecision. Already the house was filling with smoke, and she could see flames leaping outside the windows.

She called after Jeb, but he was already out the door with Eli. Surely she would have time.

Sarah turned and started back up the stairs. She realized her mistake before she was halfway up. The stairwell was acting as a chimney, and it was filling rapidly with thick smoke. Blindly, Sarah felt her way along the wall, choking and coughing. She knew now that she would never make it upstairs and down again. Panic spread through her body, cold and numbing, freezing her in her tracks. With a great effort of will, she forced herself to move. Turning, she stumbled over the hem of her dressing gown and fell headlong. She heard the dull sound that her head made as it struck the wall, and then the smoke overcame her, pressing her back, back, until unconsciousness claimed her.

Outside, Jeb placed Eli on the ground and started to turn to reassure Sarah. In that instant, he saw Giles Brock standing at some distance from the house, a flaming torch in his hand. The man's face bore an idiot smile as he stared fixedly at the flames. He was wearing a large greatcoat that hung loosely about his ankles, giving him an odd appearance that was greatly at variance with the elegant killer that Jeb had glimpsed at the steering oar on the attacking keelboat. Quickly, Jeb strode toward the man, all else driven from his mind.

Brock didn't move as Jeb approached, and finally they stood face to face. "So we finally meet again, Mister Mate," Jeb said harshly. "I thought the score was settled with you, yet you live to bring more evil down upon us."

Brock stared at him out of mad eyes. "Hawkins? Master Hawkins?" The man drew back. "Can't be you. Burned you to a cinder, I did." He moaned, taking another step backward. "You devil out of hell, you've come back to haunt me!"

"No, Mister Brock, I am not dead. I am very much alive, as you will see." Jeb clenched his hands into fists, advancing on the man.

Brock backed yet another step, his face reflecting horror and disbelief. Then, without warning, he swung the flaming torch at Jeb's head. Jeb managed to duck just enough for the torch to whistle over his head. With Brock still slightly off-balance, Jeb closed with him. He seized the wrist of the arm holding the torch and gave it a vicious twist. Brock grunted, and the torch flew out of his hand.

Jeb hit him then, hit him on the side of the head with all his strength. Brock staggered, arms windmilling in an effort to regain his balance, and Jeb hit him again. He felt a knuckle crack.

This last blow knocked Brock sprawling on his back. As Jeb moved forward with deadly purpose, he saw his former shipmate clawing at his belt. A pistol appeared in his hand. Jeb heard it being cocked and saw it coming up to bear on him.

He left his feet in a flying leap. As he came down sprawled on top of Brock, Jeb struck downward at the hand holding the weapon. There was the muffled sound of a shot, just as Jeb's full weight landed on Brock.

Jeb lay still for a moment, wondering dimly why he felt no pain. How could Brock have missed him at such close range? Then he was aware that the man under him was lying very still. Jeb raised up, looking down. Brock's eyes were open and vacant, but vacant in death this time, not madness. Jeb saw the reason why. At the very last second his fist must have deflected the pistol just enough so that the ball struck Brock instead. There was a red spot over Brock's heart.

Jeb got to his feet. He felt disoriented, slightly dazed. After all this time, it was hard to believe that the villainous career of Giles Brock had ended so suddenly, so easily. Oddly enough, Jeb did not feel the triumph he had expected. At one time Brock had been a fair seaman. It was too bad that his evil nature had come to rule him. But Sarah would be . . .

With a start, Jeb glanced around. He noticed with surprise that a bucket brigade had already formed, a number of people strung out in a ragged line down to the river. It was a futile endeavor, however. The flames were already climbing toward the second story. The front door, made of stouter wood, stood framed by flames. But soon that, too, would catch.

But where was Sarah? Jeb remembered then that in his haste to get Eli out of the house, he hadn't spared a glance back to see if Sarah was behind him.

Dear God, the idiot woman must still be inside that inferno!

Jeb whirled about and shucked the greatcoat off the dead Brock. He grabbed a bucket of water out of the hands of one man and doused the greatcoat with it.

Throwing the wet coat over his head and shoulders, Jeb started in a run for the front door of the burning house. He bounded up the steps and kicked the door wide. The house was filled with smoke, as dense as any fog he had ever encountered at sea and far more painful to the throat and lungs.

He shouted, "Sarah? Where are you?"

Hearing no response, he felt his way along the wall. The curtains at the alcove by the foot of the stairs were aflame. Jeb ripped them free and flung them back into the room. He called Sarah's name again, a cold dread rising from the pit of his stomach. Was he going to lose her again?

His foot struck the bottom step of the stairs, and he heard a soft moan above him. He started up the stairs on his hands and knees. On the fourth step up, his groping fingers encountered a body. It had to be Sarah. He prayed to Jehovah that she was still alive.

Jeb picked her up as gently as possible, but in so doing he had to discard Brock's greatcoat. As he started out with Sarah in his arms, the flames seemed to reach for them. It was like trying to pass through the flames of hell.

Confused by the lack of visibility, Jeb lost his bearings and wasn't sure where the front door was located. Then he felt a current of air and followed it into the entryway and outside into blessed fresh air. Breathing in great gasps, he managed to stagger from the burning building. As he started to put Sarah down, Jeb lost his balance and fell to his knees.

The jolt cause Sarah to moan again. Her eyes fluttered open, and she stared at him for a moment without recognition. Finally her eyes cleared, and she smiled wanly. "I remember falling, striking my head." She turned her face toward the house, now completely aflame. "You saved me," she said. It was not a question.

Jeb nodded.

"I'm always causing you trouble, aren't I, darling?" She looked stricken. "Your beard, it's singed." She reached out a hand to touch his beard.

"It'll grow back, I'm sure." His strength returning

now, he said grimly, "It was Giles Brock, Sarah. He set fire to your house."

She struggled to rise, her voice growing stronger. "That evil man! Will I, will *we,* never be free of him?"

"He will bother you no more, Sarah. Giles Brock is dead. . . ."

They were interrupted by a great roar and the sounds of splintering wood. Sarah watched in distress as the house collapsed in on itself, the second story falling into the flames. Now it was nothing but a mass of flaming wood.

"My sympathies, Sarah," said a weary voice.

For a moment Sarah almost didn't recognize Rand Colter. His fine clothes were water-and-mud stained, his face and hands black with soot.

"Thank you, Rand. And thank you for trying to help put it out."

"All a wasted effort, as you can see. But we had to try."

Sarah said, "I won't be able to reopen the casino, Rand. I'm sorry. What will you do?"

"I will manage." He shrugged. "Don't concern yourself for my sake, Sarah. Somehow I always manage to overcome life's adversities." His glance settled on Jeb.

Sarah introduced the two men. Jeb stood up, and they warily shook hands. Jeb said, "You're the man I knocked down. My apologies, sir."

Smiling slightly, Rand touched his jaw. "Apologies accepted, Mr. Hawkins. You do have a powerful potency in your fists, sir." He bowed his head at Sarah. "Good-bye, Mistress Moody. Despite the loss of your casino, I believe that you have found what you have truly wanted all along."

"Good-bye, Rand," she said softly.

As Rand walked away, Jeb turned to Sarah. "Now, you foolish woman, what in the name of Jehovah were you doing still in that house? I thought you were right behind me."

"All I have in the world, Jeb, besides the house, was upstairs in a small strongbox." She looked sadly at the ruined building. "Now it's all gone, everything. I'm right back where I started!"

"Not quite, love. . . ."

"Look at me!" She plucked at the smoke-blackened dressing gown. "This is the only garment I have left in the world! Just like the day I was taken aboard your ship."

"That we can take care of when the shops open on the morrow. Darling Sarah . . ." He dropped to one knee and took her hand. "I love you, you know that. There's a place for you, a place where you belong, in my cabin aboard the keelboat."

She peered at him suspiciously. "Are you asking me to wed you, Jeb Hawkins?"

He looked astonished. "Of course! What else did you think? It's a good life, Sarah, life on the river. You'll come to love it, as I have."

"Well, I suppose I shall have to, won't I, seeing that I have nowhere else to go?"

Jeb leaned toward her, and Sarah threw her arms around his neck. They kissed, ignoring the stares of those few people left, standing ready with buckets of water to keep the fire from spreading.

The kiss was long and ardent. Finally Jeb broke

their embrace and helped Sarah up. "Shall we go, love?"

"We might as well. There's nothing left here for me. But one thing, Jeb Hawkins . . ." She frowned at him. "We'll be wed soon?"

Laughing, he took her arm. "In the morning. The minute we can find a minister to do the honors. My solemn promise on that, love!"

They started off into the night. A short distance away, Sarah stopped and looked back, a long, lingering look. Then she faced about resolutely, took his arm, and did not look back again as they went along the narrow street leading down to the river and the keelboat.

PREVIEW

LOVE,
FOREVER
MORE

by

Patricia Matthews

*(The following pages are excerpts edited from
the first chapter of this new novel scheduled
for publication in December, 1977.)*

Serena Foster sat drowsing on the seat of the covered wagon. Eyes closed, she was peripherally aware of the heat of the blazing desert sun through the material of the poke bonnet, which her mother made her wear to protect her hair.

The steady clop-clop of the mules' hooves, and the rocking of the wagon—to which she had, after four long months, become adjusted—all contributed to the almost hypnotic inducement to sleep. Serena felt bone tired. Tired of the weary months of travel, after tearing the roots of nineteen years from her home soil back in Illinois, tired of the heat and the dust that even now permeated her hair and clothing, and stung her nostrils.

They had left Independence, Missouri, in mid-May of this year 1863, as a part of a wagon train bound for Oregon, and had stayed with the train through the terrible haul over the Rockies and across the salt flats. Once across the salt flats, the Foster wagon had branched off—destination Virginia City, in the territory of Nevada. They were now on the last leg of their arduous journey, crossing the Forty-Mile Desert, hopefully only a few days from Virginia City.

Suddenly, the wagon rocked as the mules shied, and a hoarse shout broke the near stillness. Serena's eyes flew open, as she turned in the direction from which the shout had come. Toward their wagon, across the scorched earth, a figure came stumbling toward them. It appeared to be a man, on foot.

Serena removed her bonnet, shaking out long, heavy hair the color of corn silk. At nineteen, she was just reaching the ripeness of womanhood; a medium-sized girl with fine features and large, luminous gray eyes.

The mules slumped in the harness, heads down, and the three people waited with some apprehension as the approaching figure stumbled closer.

* * *

Serena looked at the shambling figure, and frowned at her father. "Daddy, the poor man can hardly walk. He has no weapon that I can see." She started to get down from the wagon seat.

Hiram gestured sharply. "No, daughter. Stay where you

are. If he's a lost pilgrim, and needs succor, I will provide it."

With a resigned sigh, Serena remained on the wagon seat. She loved her parents, but sometimes they were annoyingly over-protective. If they had their way, they'd keep her a child forever, shielded from all contact with, and knowledge of, the world. She knew they were thinking only of her welfare, but if she was always to be protected, always shielded, how could she ever taste the tang and flavor of life, the life she longed for? Their way, life might be safe, but it had a dull, flat taste, about as exciting as unsalted soup. Sometimes of late, Serena found herself wanting to do something wild, something daring. What, she was not sure, but she wanted to do *something*.

The stranger was quite close now. Serena could see her father relax, reassured by the stranger's appearance. The man was tall and broad-shouldered, twenty-two or thereabouts. He wore Wellington boots, and a black, broadcloth suit, now covered with dust like ash fallen from a prairie fire. His hair was black and long under the broad brim of his hat, and his wide-cheeked face wore a dark stubble of beard.

*　　*　　*

". . . and he pulled a gun on me, took my horse, and rode off into the night. He left me a canteen of water and some food, and pointed out where the wagon trail was. He said I'd come across a wagon sooner or later." Clendenning's voice was bitter. "Jeremiah warned me not to get involved in the devil's game, but I was too headstrong to heed. Now look at what condition I'm in!"

"I wouldn't fret about it. In this rough country, it's happened to more experienced men than you. Who's Jeremiah?"

"My father."

Clendenning sank back, as if the telling of it had exhausted him. As he lay quietly, Serena studied his face. It was a strong face, and she suspected that if he survived the trials he would undoubtedly face out here, he would be able soon to hold his own.

Suddenly conscious of his nearness, she felt an odd mixture of excitement and apprehension. Due to her

501

parents' protectiveness, Serena knew little of the opposite sex, and could not remember being so close to a man, other than her father. She felt a strong curiosity concerning everything about this young stranger.

* * *

Serena made her way through the twisted willows until she was well out of sight of the camp. The desert sand ran down to the water's edge, and the water was brackish, smelling faintly of sulphur. But it would serve her purpose. Although she knew her mother would disapprove, Serena undressed down to the skin, shaking the dust out of her dress and petticoats before laying them on a nearby bush.

Back at the campfire, Clendenning began to salivate at the cooking odors. His shrunken stomach rebelled, and began to cramp. Hastily he got to his feet. "Excuse me, folks. I'll be back shortly."

Mercy Foster glanced up from her cooking with a worried frown. "You suppose it's right, Hiram, for him to go off, with Serena out there alone?"

"You concern yourself too much, Mercy." Hiram squeezed her shoulder. "After all, this young man is a preacher's son. Besides . . ." He indulged himself in a rare flash of humor. "In his condition, I very much doubt he could offer Serena any harm."

At that moment Serena had no thought of any harm to herself. She was floating in the heavy water, busily soaping and scrubbing, humming to herself. It was sheer luxury. Not since she had left home had she been able to so indulge herself. On the wagon trip, water had been too scanty to use for washing, and her mother would never let her go bathing in the rivers they camped beside.

It was full dark when she finally emerged, clean and refreshed, from the water. She began to hurry now, drying herself briskly with the rough towels, and then getting into her clothes. Supper should soon be ready, and if she knew her folks, they would be worrying about her.

Just as she pulled her dress over her head, Serena heard the sudden thunder of hooves, and stood still to listen. It sounded like several horses, and they were heading for the wagon. She gathered up the towels, and hurried toward the campfire. She had taken only a few steps, when she was frozen in her tracks by the sound of gunfire. A terrible coldness clawed with icy fingers at her stomach, and then panic sent her running, fighting through the thicket of willows.

Now she could see the campfire, and several horses milling about. Without any thought of danger to herself, Serena plunged ahead. Just before she was about to burst through the willows into the clearing, she was seized around the waist from behind, and thrown to the ground. She opened her mouth to scream, but a hand was clamped around her lips, and she choked back the sound.

A voice whispered in her ear, "Quiet now. It's me, Clendenning. Don't make a sound, or they'll know we're here."

Serena ceased struggling. From where she lay on the ground, she could see the wagon and the campfire clearly. But where were her parents? And she was puzzled by the activity and the appearance of the half-dozen mounted men, who all wore handkerchiefs over the lower half of their faces. They had tied ropes to the wheels of the wagon on one side, and as she watched, the ropes were tossed over the canvas top. Two men on horseback took the ends of the ropes, hooked them around their saddle horns, and sent their horses plunging forward. The ropes tightened, and the wagon slowly began to tilt as the horses strained against the ropes. Then, with a rumbling crash and a cloud of dust, the wagon fell onto its side.

The flames of the campfire flared up at the rush of air from the wagon's falling, and Serena's gaze was drawn to two still figures on the ground. Her mother and father!

Serena moaned deep in her throat, and began to struggle against Clendenning's hold.

"No, Serena, no!" he whispered fiercely. "I think they're dead, and I'm sorry as can be. But if we rush out there, those men, whoever they are, will kill us, too. We have nothing with which to defend ourselves."

The mounted men milled about for a few more moments, then one fired his pistol into the air, motioned with it, and they rode off into the night.

Clendenning waited until the sound of hoofbeats had died away, then let Serena go. She was up at once and running. When she reached the clearing, Serena dropped to her knees beside her parents where they lay in the dust. Hiram Foster was half across his wife, as though he had tried to throw himself between her and the gunfire. They were both dead; each had been shot several times.

At the sound of Clendenning's footsteps, Serena looked up at him with streaming eyes. "But why? Why on earth would someone do this? We have nothing to steal!"

Clendenning shook his head. "I don't know, Serena. It seems such a senseless thing."

Serena, sobbing brokenheartedly now, reached out to touch her mother's face tenderly. The whole thing had happened with such violent suddenness that her mind was numb with shock and disbelieving horror . . .

The tragic and sudden death of her parents casts Serena adrift in a frightening, wild new world. After an unplanned night of intimacy with young Clendenning she awakens to realize she is really alone for the first time. The couple manage to make their way to Virginia City where, after an argument, they go their separate ways. Serena is fascinated —and aghast—by the brawling, lusty town . . . especially by a dashing gambling man, Darrel Quick. Her life soon becomes a series of breathtaking adventures that take her to San Francisco, the exotic excesses of the Barbary Coast, the mysterious enclaves of Chinatown, and the inner circles of Nob Hill society. Somehow, this lovely over-protected girl from Missouri is able to survive amidst the madness of these times, the pursuit of men lusting for her body, and the ugly suspicion of murder! But Serena wants more than survival. Now she must prove her innocence by finding a murderer—and the one man who can be her love, forever more . . .